*"We are not men—we are T'ings; we are not beasts—
we are T'ings. You made us T'ings!"*
~ Bela Lugosi as Beast-Man to Dr. Moreau, vivisectionist,

Todd Browning's *The Island of Lost Souls* (1932)

T'ings

Gregory Wolos

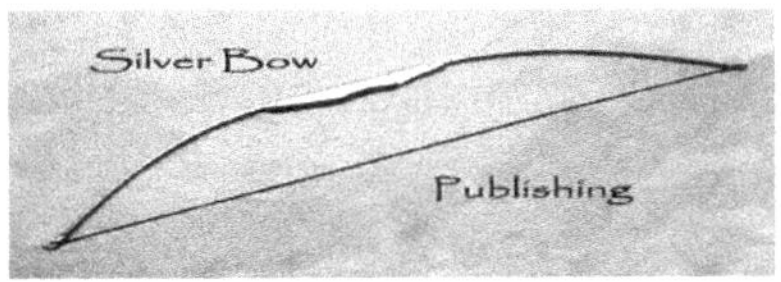

720 – Sixth Street, Unit # 5
New Westminster, BC
V3C 3C5   CANADA

Title: T'ings
Author: Gregory Wolos
Publisher: Silver Bow Publishing
Cover Art: "Sun Dance" painting by Candice James
Layout/Design/Editing: Candice James

ISBN: 978-1-77403-297-8 paperback
ISBN: 978-1-77403-298-5 e- book
© Silver Bow Publishing 2024

Library and Archives Canada Cataloguing in Publication

Title: T'ings / Gregory Wolos.
Other titles: Things
Names: Wolos, Gregory J., author.
Identifiers: Canadiana (print) 20240327713 | Canadiana (ebook) 20240327764 | ISBN 9781774032978
   (softcover) | ISBN 9781774032985 (Kindle)
Subjects: LCGFT: Novels.
Classification: LCC PS3573.0528 T56 2024 | DDC 813/.54—dc23

For Noah Kucij

Contents

Part I—The Walchuks

Part II—The Kleins

Part III— No More to Rise Forever /

Part I
The Walchuks

Chapter 1—Premiere

December 9, 1991

Their limo stopped. The raindrops on the windows glittered like diamonds from the light cast by the theatre marquis. Raymond Walchuk battled a sinking stomach over what might be considered a bad omen. Really, the foul weather was no more than meteorological probability. February was Los Angeles' wettest month, and the day's rainfall had been chill and steady. Not ideal premiere weather. Not the prime ambience for his tenth film—his first big budget family blockbuster— to be making its debut.

A pair of young men, tuxedoed under their yellow rain slickers, yanked open the limo door, and, in spite of the umbrellas they held and the gleam of their smiles, there was no escaping the fact that the Walchuk party was about to become wet and miserable. Raymond worried about the temperature control in the theatre. Would the air conditioners chill the audience to their bones? Would they heat the place to a rainforest humidity? Three occupied the limo's back seats— Raymond sat between Bronwyn O'Savage, the young production assistant he was escorting, and Carl, his nearly seven-year-old son, whose tuxedo sleeves were so long they covered his hands and whose black curls had been plastered over his forehead by an excess of gel and rainwater. Bronwyn, closest to the open door, hesitated like a paratrooper about to launch herself out of a plane. The rain chattered on the pavement, and she collapsed back onto Raymond's lap. He felt her shiver through the sheer, sleeveless gown she'd no doubt spent hours choosing for the occasion.

"Congratulations, Mr. Walchuk!" one of the umbrella-bearing young men shouted over Bronwyn, as if from the wind-swept deck of a foundering ship. "Quite a day for it—*Kong's Daughter*—amazing!"

And then they were outside. Raymond leaned from under what felt like a canopy of a hundred umbrellas, searching for the title of his movie on the marquis, hoping to frame an indelible memory, but though he saw the words, the lasting image would be the pelting rain, as taut as the strings of a harp over the glowing background. He thought of the original King Kong movie, the scene where the giant ape had been brought for display to a Broadway theatre, halfway around the world from the beast's island home, and how the sweep of searchlights celebrated the event in the New York cityscape of the early 1930's. Raymond took a deep breath. It was December 9, 1991, almost sixty years since the original King Kong had debuted at this very theater.

There'd be puddles in the sidewalk handprints of Hollywood icons all along the sidewalk, but this wasn't the time for sightseeing. Something tugged on the tail of Raymond's tux jacket, and he thought, though he'd already walked a few dozen paces, that somehow it had got slammed in the limo door. But the tugger was his boy Carl, who was trying to get his father's attention.

"My feet are wet," the boy whined, and then his father felt it, too, the squelch of the carpet, which was saturated to a deep crimson.

"Mine too," Raymond said, flashing a "what-can-you-do about-it?" grin. Carl grimaced back. The boy's eyelashes sparkled with raindrops. He lifted the stuffed ape he was carrying up to his chin.

"Kika doesn't mind," the boy said. "She doesn't mind the water—she's brave, remember? *'We never saw her sink—she was swimming. Maybe she'll make it to another island—maybe all the way to America!'"* Carl was quoting the last line of *Kong's Daughter*, spoken by one of the film's human protagonists (who Raymond presumed were already drying off inside the theatre) after the heroic giant gorilla disappeared into the sea following the cataclysm that destroys Kong's Island.

Raymond glanced at Bronwyn, who splashed along stoically beside him, and for a second her youth surprised him. Out of a habit born from ten years of marriage, he'd expected his companion to be his recent ex-wife Christine, Carl's mother. "Ten movies, and this is my first premiere," he said.

"Nobody fusses over grade-B slashers," Bronwyn replied, the curt comment reinforcing her similarity to Christine. Bronwyn had also been poking her head out from under the umbrella, and the money she'd probably spent on her hair in preparation for this event had definitely been wasted. She was looking not at the marquis, but from side to side. "No paparazzi. Everything's been shifted inside." With a brisk gesture that also reminded Raymond of Christine, Bronwyn stabbed an arm back toward Carl, who twisted away, protecting his Kika doll.

"Your hand," Bronwyn said. "I don't want your monkey. Hold my hand and get up here. The photographers will be waiting inside, and you should be up here with your father. I'll drop back out of sight once we get in the door. 'Father and child.' That's what everyone will want to see."

A surprise flash of light burst from behind the umbrella bearers, and Raymond flinched, thinking lightning. But it was a lone photographer, hooded like the grim reaper, who'd braved the rain, intent on catching the director and his party at their soggiest. Raymond forced himself to chuckle, reminded again of the original *King Kong*: "*Stop the cameras, he thinks you're hurting the girl!*" the promoter Carl Denham warned the photographers as the chained monster raged at the flashbulbs exploding around him in the packed theatre. "*Aah—let the big monkey roar!*" a reporter sneered, and the lights bombarded Kong like anti-aircraft flak—right up until the gorilla ripped off his chains as if they were made of paper, smashed his way out of the theater, and destroyed half of Manhattan.

Bronwyn was right—the lobby of Grauman's Chinese Theatre was crammed with soaked photographers, and, in spite of the air conditioning, the space was practically as steamy as a rainforest. They surrounded the movie's sleekly gowned and tuxedoed human stars, who saw Carl and waved over the heads of their entourages, the paparazzi, and the rest of the attendees as they took turns posing beside a ten foot tall cardboard cutout of golden Kika— still only half the height her computer animated incarnation commanded in Raymond's film. On either side of the cutout were tables covered with Kika dolls identical to Carl's.

"Dammit," Bronwyn swore through teeth clenched in a smile. "All those ape dolls—there's supposed to be somebody handing them out to kids. Where are the kids? This is a *family* film. Who was responsible for inviting children? Not me." Raymond could barely hear the lament, and his response, "We'll just have to hope the adults are young at heart," came back to him as if his head was underwater. Had the rain clogged his ears? They surged back and forth with the seething crowd. Raymond felt faint—he'd forgotten to hydrate. *Water, water, everywhere . . .* he thought.

"Water—" he whispered into Bronwyn's ear, surprised by the twinkle of the earring he was close enough to nibble. Didn't Christine have earrings like it? "Do you see any bottles?" Her scent of damp perfume reminded him of the one and only time they'd had sex, the evening after the wrap-party on Kiriwina, the Papua New Guinea island where most of *Kong's Daughter*'s live action exteriors had been filmed.

Bronwyn lifted herself onto the toes of water-stained high-heels, gazed around the jammed lobby, and shook her head.

"Nope," she said, frowning, "Somebody dropped that ball, too." Then she broke suddenly into another artificial grin, and Raymond turned to see a tidal wave of photographers rushing toward them. Bronwyn pushed Carl, who Raymond had nearly lost track of, toward his father. "Lift him up," she ventriloquized between clamped teeth. She leaned closer. "Parent-child, remember? The theme? Why the studio fought for PG without the '13'. Family film? He's not too big to lift—he looks young. He's short for his age." Raymond wrapped his arms around his giggling, glassy-eyed son and hoisted him high. The child wrapped one arm around his father's neck and with the other held his golden Kika aloft in a triumphant salute as the cameras flashed away.

The crowd drained slowly from the lobby into the theater and Raymond, Carl, and Bronwyn were seated up front in the row behind the movie's cast. From the stage, a young celebrity whose name Raymond didn't catch introduced the actors, who stood to acknowledge the applause. Carl bounced excitedly on one side of his father, craning his neck to get a look at the crowd behind them. Too late, Raymond realized he should have taken the boy to the restroom before the film started, a detail the boy's mother would not have neglected. Bronwyn, also checking out the crowd, was definitely not thinking motherly thoughts.

And then he heard his name, *Raymond Walchuk*—and he rose, so fast he nearly blacked out, to applause that reminded him of the rain outside, how it fell in sheets, and the thought of sheets of any kind forced a nervy yawn out of him. He snatched the Kika doll his son shook and waved it as if it was an award. In spite of the theater's vastness, he was breathless and unsteady. He reached for the back of his seat but his hand squeezed Bronwyn's shoulder instead. She leaned into Raymond's side, buttressing him through the audience's acknowledgement. Their applause splashed on and on, and Raymond thought again of the handprints outside the theatre, confused them with footprints and wondered if they'd be washed away. As he sagged back into his seat, he remembered his thirst and realized with dismay he'd be waterless for hours. He found himself staring at Bronwyn's white shoulder and the bright red finger prints left by his grip.

The house lights were cut, and the darkness dropped on Raymond like a thick curtain. The abrupt silence was so overwhelming he wondered if he'd gone deaf, and thought about snapping his fingers next to his ear to test. Carl held fast to his father's wrist as Raymond clutched his armrest. Brief melodies accompanied the opening montage of production companies that suddenly lit the screen. He wasn't deaf after all! The huge, glowing screen frosted Bronwyn's expressionless profile. She didn't offer an encouraging glance. He wouldn't have expected one from Christine either. His ex-wife hated the kind of movies with which he'd begun his career—the slashers and horror films from which *Kong's Daughter* could be seen as either a departure or an evolution. Raymond had a formula for those—they always began with a grisly death. He tried to remember the opening of the film he was about to see but drew a blank.

"The energy—is the energy good? I don't feel any energy," he whispered to Bronwyn, who shushed him without looking his way. He turned to Carl, who, scooched back in his seat and sucking on a lollipop, was staring saucer-eyed at the screen. Who'd given him the candy? With a throb of panic, Raymond worried that the film they were about to see—what movie was it?—would open with gore so shocking his son would be traumatized for life, and Christine would never forgive him. Then the screen filled with an aerial view of a sparkling ocean, and Raymond remembered where he was and why he was there: *Kong's Daughter*.

The sapphire blue water glittered endlessly in silence. Raymond felt like he was flying, saw that he and everyone else in the audience was being transported high above the ocean at great speed. Gradually, the angle of the shot tilted toward the horizon. A dot appeared: an island. BA-BOOM! A startling drumbeat broke the silence and shook the theatre impressively. A few gasps from the audience. *I made this*, Carl thought. The island's rim of sandy beaches gave way to impenetrable jungle. A mountain rose in the distance, its shadowed heights eye level with whatever was approaching. At the mountain's apex stood a rock formation that slowly resolved into a skull. BA-BOOM! Far below, a lush jungle slid by. BA-BOOM! The drum beat slowly and steadily. The jungle opened to a marshy delta at the foot of the mountain, glimpsed a moment before the point of view swept upward. Dead ahead loomed the mouth of the giant skull shape forming the mountain's crest.

The mouth of the skull was a cave, and inside something was moving. When a golden ape lumbered into view, the audience released a gust of satisfaction. The solitary gorilla squatted on the stony ground, surrounded by a rubble of bones. BA-BOOM! The ape looked up from the bones, directly into the camera, and even Raymond, who had seen the shot a thousand times, caught his breath. The look in those honey-colored eyes—how had the CGI geniuses put it there? The shot closed in on those eyes until they filled the screen, and in them could be seen the creature's youth. And her loneliness. And hopefulness. And playfulness. A lingering gaze into those eyes revealed a being not only fearless and powerful, but also gentle and kind. And, undeniably, they were the eyes of a female. At least, that's what Raymond had wanted his audience to see. He saw it—did they?

A shadow fell, and in the black mirrors of the huge pupils a shape resolved—the pterodactyl that had delivered the audience across the ocean, over the island, to the peak of the golden ape's mountain. Abruptly, the point of view changed—the audience was no longer looking *into* the giant ape's eyes, but *out* of them, directly at the huge, hovering monster. Its wings flapped like sails, a thirty foot span, and it's pincer jaws snapped open and shut as if it had something nasty to say, but couldn't quite get the words out. The point of view dipped—the ape was crouching—a fur-backed hand opened and closed on the three-horned skull of a triceratops and lifted it from ground. The pulse of the drum sped up: BA-BOOM, BA-BOOM, BA-BOOM.

Raymond released something between a gulp and a yawn and shut his eyes. He knew, of course, what was coming—the point of view would shift again, and the audience would see the battle between the ape and the flying monster. The drumbeat intensified. Carl's grip on Raymond's arm tightened. Too much for a child? Instead of the action on the screen, Raymond visualized the *Kong's Daughter* storyboard—panel by panel the sketches unfurled. He heard his son laugh. Okay, then—that meant the ape had caught a wing of the pterodactyl and was spinning it in the air. There it was, pictured on the storyboard. The drumbeats stopped. Darkness encroached on the boundaries of the sketch. Raymond yawned, deeply this time. A smothering calmness absorbed him, and then he was in the air again, but not with the pterodactyl.

He is deep in a dream that is more than a dream: he's drifted two years into the past, and he sits, not in a theatre, but in a small airplane, fighting airsickness, his Moleskine notebook in his hand. The growling engine is deafening. Carl sits beside him. The boy's been asleep for most of the five hour flight from Port Moresby, Papua New Guinea. In this dream that is more than a dream they are descending onto Kiriwina Island for the first time. It's 1989, and there's a movie to be made.

* * *

June 24, 1989

Raymond dated his latest entry in his Moleskine and snapped it shut. He always closed his eyes at landings, and now he waited for the first bump of contact to melt into a gentle roll before he allowed himself a look around. Palm trees fringed the strip of the landing field left over from the second World War. The family legend was that his father helped build this strip out of crushed coral, and his dad's stories about his year on the island contributed to Raymond's choice of the remote place as a possible site for his project. But where were the nearly naked island girls decked in flowers, the muscled drummers, the torch jugglers pictured on the brochure he'd left back at the Port Moresby hotel?

When the pilot cut the engine, the silence woke little Carl, who blinked in confusion. They'd taxied a few hundred feet up to a jeep painted school bus yellow, and Raymond had a vision of the morning pick-up in front of the house on his boy's first day of kindergarten, just one year past: the bus doors folded open, Carl stepped up with a shrug of his Snoopy knapsack, then remembered to look back at Raymond and his mom. His parents stood shoulder to shoulder on the front stoop, waving, and Carl nodded back at them. The memory froze, then disappeared in a haze of white light—the same effect Raymond used in his slasher films the moment before a slaying. *"Cleansing the palate,"* he called it. The divorce was still fresh—he felt the absence of Christine's touch. This excursion with Carl to Kiriwina Island to scout out a setting for his Kong film was Raymond's first trip as a joint-custodial parent.

With Raymond and his son safely unloaded, the pilot smiled through the open window of his cockpit and guaranteed that he'd be back in a week. The plane peeled down the runway, lifted, and veered over the palms into a cloudless sky. Carl's shoulder felt like the nub of a baby bird's wing under Raymond's hand as father guided son toward the yellow jeep. The driver, a skinny young Islander, tossed their bags into the space behind the back seats.

"Welcome back, Walchuk clan," he said. His accent hinted at Australian. "Pah-pui."

"Pah-pui," Raymond replied, bowing to what he took for an island greeting.

"*I'm* Pah-pui Frederico," the young man clarified. "Call me P. P." He tickled Carl with a quick finger, and the boy doubled over with a giggle-snort, then squinted up for his father's approval. Raymond winked but lifted a brow at the driver.

"We've never been here before. Why '*Welcome back.*'?"

"Your blood's been here, right?" The band of the headphones the young man pushed off his ears settled in his 'fro.

"'Blood'?"

Pah-pui waved Raymond into the jeep, hoisted Carl in beside his dad and climbed behind the wheel in front of them. "Wouldn't be a lot of Walchuks listed in the Kiriwina phone book, if there was such a thing." He caught Raymond's eye in the rearview. "But your father would be."

"Oh—yes." The jeep growled to a start, and they jolted toward the trees. Raymond had to shout over the engine's roar. "My father built this strip during the war. He loved this place. He thought it was the most blessed spot on earth. He said he found our family's luck on this island. But you're not old enough to remember my father. That was almost fifty years ago."

P. P. didn't answer. He'd tugged his headphones back over his ears, and was bouncing in his seat, either to music or on account of the rutted road. They lurched into a rainforest, where, somehow, the odor of rot settled Raymond's stomach and revived his appetite. He and Carl hadn't eaten since before leaving Port Moresby. There were crackers and water bottles in their luggage. If their lodge was a long way off, they would have some food. Raymond measured P. P.'s head bobs, hesitant to startle him with a shoulder tap. Each time the driver rocked forward, he exposed the printing on the back of his T-shirt: "*Boston Red Sox, 1986 World Champions.*"

The road split a swamp, and they drove through oozing stretches mottled by patches of sunlight that broke through the canopy of trees. "Pew!" Carl pinched his nose. Remembering that he'd flown to this isolated locale to plan a movie, Raymond considered angles and framed shots. He imagined mud-caked Islanders and terrified Western adventurers splashing in retreat from gigantic monsters: dinosaurs, and, of course, the huge ape: *The Son of Kong*! His intuition appeared to be on target—Kiriwina Island seemed to be the perfect setting for Raymond's re-envisioning of that undervalued 1933 sequel. True there was no mountain—but there weren't really any giant creatures either. The studio had guaranteed him an unlimited CGI budget—at least far more than the shoestring he was used to filming with. He'd have his mountain—and his fantastical creatures—without even needing to start from a molehill.

His gaze lingered on the back of P. P.'s T-shirt. It was wrong. Boston hadn't won the World Series back in '86. Three years ago, the victors had been the Mets—there'd been that big error, the grounder through what's-his-name's legs, and New York wound up winning in seven games.

The jeep braked, and Raymond threw one arm across Carl's chest and braced himself on P. P.'s back with the other, his palm flat on the false declaration of Boston's victory. The driver turned. Tattoos of snakes wriggled down his neck.

"You're here to make a movie, right?"

"What? Yes—I'm scouting locations."

"We studied your movies. In Port Moresby. I was in college for hotel management. They only had one non-business elective—American Film Studies. Our professor showed us all of your films. *Only* your movies, in fact. The course was like a Raymond Walchuk festival. We became connoisseurs of the slasher genre *a la* Walchuk. But you must have something special in mind for us Kiriwinans. I've been wondering about it since we got your reservation at the lodge. Something big time. A huge monster, right? You're smart. Do your filming here and you'll save the studio a bunch of money. Certainly would help out our economy, though I guess that remains to be seen. We've got other issues."

So much information so fast—Raymond's low budget thrillers were the subject of a film class? P. P.'s Papua New Guinea professor was either a renegade needle in the haystack of critical appreciation or was playing a private joke on his students. Or was P. P. pulling Raymond's leg, and there was no such class at all?

"What are your 'other issues'?"

"Problems in the magic department," P. P. said, blinking eyes so dark they seemed pupil-less. He patted his Walkman. "Did you bring batteries with you? Been without music for two weeks. Double-A?

"Daddy?" Carl yanked on Raymond's arm, but his father was pre-occupied with a dawning realization—championship T-shirts were made up for *both* teams. How else would the merchandise be ready to hand out the instant a big game ended? Every triumph spawned an "anti-verse" of victorious losers, and these mislabeled shirts clothed the populations of third world countries. Raymond and Carl had become guests in loser paradise.

"Daddy—" Carl was still trying to get Raymond's attention. The child pointed at something in the swamp.

"Right you are, little man," P. P. said. "This is tour stop number one. That's a Japanese Zero. Been there since your grandfather's war." The fuselage of the half-sunken plane lay in the muck like a sleeping crocodile. "Maybe you could use this shot as a tribute to the Japanese and Godzilla," he said to Raymond

"Kong, actually. We're checking out your island for *The Son of Kong.*"

"Right. Knew that. About time somebody re-made it. A junior classic—get it? Kong's the eighth wonder of the world, so his kid's got to be the ninth. A blockbuster!"

"That's the hope. I've got batteries, by the way. I'll give them to you when we get to the lodge. How long?"

"Twenty minutes. Where's the missus?"

Christine? Raymond had forgotten that he'd included her in the reservation. When he booked the trip, the divorce hadn't seemed like a *fate accompli*. He'd fantasized a reconciliation on the tropical island. Then he'd found out about Klaus—the German chess champion who was his ex-wife's new lover; they'd be together in Cleveland while Raymond and Carl were in the tropics. Christine would be promoting her magazine at the gaming convention sponsoring the tournament Klaus was expected to win. Christine had given Raymond a note when he'd picked up his son for their trip. "Ray and Carl," it read, "Value the experience! You're sure to have a lovely time—Christine/Mom." She must have written it quickly—"lovely time" looked like "lonely time."

They rumbled on through the stinking swamp. Every Thanksgiving dinner Raymond's dad would remind the family of his love for Kiriwina. The senior Walchuk had been lucky—he hadn't had to spend the war scorching the enemy out of Pacific Island caves with a flame thrower. But the pilot of the Zero must have had a family—what did they talk about around the table on Japanese holidays?

"Cleveland," Raymond said. "The missus is in Cleveland."

"Cleveland. That's where they're building the Rock and Roll Hall of Fame." His eyes still forward, P. P. flipped a thumbs-up.

"Really?" Somebody ten thousand miles from civilization knew this about Cleveland, but Raymond didn't?

The vehicle stopped. P. P. carried Raymond and Carl's luggage to their cabin, advertised as a "rustic bungalow" by the proprietors of the Kiriwina Lodge. There were half a dozen of these bungalows at the edge of the village. One served as the lodge office. Raymond and Carl's cabin had a thatched roof, a dirt floor, bamboo walls, two cots, a chemical toilet behind a curtain, and a wash basin beneath a small mirror. Every movement disturbed mosquito netting, which hung like cobwebs from one of Raymond's horror movies. "Got rats the size of puppies," P. P. warned, "but the snakes get most of them. Get your garbage into the cans behind your cabin right away, and make sure you put the lid on tight. That's rule number one."

"I bet the snakes here are bigger than Elvis," Carl said.

P. P. laughed. "Nobody's bigger than Elvis."

"He means the pet snake he used to have back home," Raymond said.

P. P. laughed again. "Sure," he said. "Snakes are super pets. *Swallow*, right, Mr. Walchuk? One of my favorites."

P. P. handed Raymond a copy of the Lodge brochure, along with a typed insert—*Your Stay on the Island of Love*. "I wrote this up myself. Tells you a little bit about us."

***

A half hour later, Raymond lay on one of the cots, glancing absently at P. P.'s insert. Carl stood at the cabin's open doorway, which opened onto a path that passed through the twenty-odd huts of the village and led down to the beach. The huts of the villagers were about half the size of the lodge cabin. According to what Raymond had just read, much of Island life involved the cultivation, accumulation, and consumption of yams. Down at the beach a dozen black canoes marked the yellow sand like exclamation points, and beyond them an indigo sea stretched to the horizon under a milky sky.

"I don't see any kids, Carl said. "Are they in the houses?"

"Maybe everyone's off collecting yams," Raymond guessed. P. P.'s insert credited the research of Georgiano Frederico "a famous Italian anthropologist who visited the island thirty years ago and became intimate with the islanders and their customs." Wasn't P. P.'s last name Frederico? The pamphlet mentioned one custom they'd already learned from their host: eating was a private act on Kiriwina Island. They'd secluded themselves in their cabin for their first island meal of mashed yams, fried mud crabs, and Coke. It had been Carl's job to dispose of their trash in the garbage cans. "No rats or snakes," he'd announced upon his return.

"See those canoes down by the beach?" Raymond asked his son. "It says here that they've got special carvings we should take a look at. According to this, 'the traditional designs worked into the prows of the boats take years to complete and depict family and community history, tribal customs, and the secrets of Kiriwinan magic.'" He looked up from the pamphlet at Carl. "'Magic!' Your grandfather told me about the canoes and the magic."

"Daddy—"

"Hold it a second." Raymond's attention had been caught by the title of the next section of P. P.'s pamphlet: *The Erotic Sex Games of Island Children*. He reread the first paragraph twice, certain at first that he'd misunderstood. What it described were acts of "sexual foreplay enjoyed by children younger than eight." Western visitors, the pamphlet said, "often find such pre-mating rituals among children disturbing and refer ironically to Kiriwina as 'The Island of Love.'" A knot formed in Raymond's gut—he looked at Carl. Raymond's father hadn't mentioned anything about "pre-mating rituals" in the long monologues in which he'd extolled the virtues of Kiriwina Island. Something to ask P. P. about—how would a Hollywood film set, and all the attention that attracted, deal with such island "rituals." And what about Carl—what would he see? How would Raymond explain it? Would there have to be a "birds and bees" moment?

"Someone's coming, Daddy. A kid."

Raymond slid the pamphlet under his pillow and joined Carl at the bungalow entrance. He started to place his hand on the boy's shoulder but, struck unexpectedly by the late afternoon sun, he instead lifted it to shield his eyes.

Their visitor wasn't a child—it was a legless man, hunching his way over the path to their cabin, using his arms as fulcrums to swing his trunk forward, over and over, with the mechanized rhythm of a toy. He appeared to be very old. He had thick shoulders. Tattoos purpled his parchment skin, and silver hair sprouted from under his red, white, and blue scarf. A strip of rubber tire under his abbreviated torso was held in place by hemp suspenders. A permanent grin creased his face, and his eyelids drooped. The legless visitor planted himself before them, stuck out a hand as broad as a catcher's mitt, and burst into a high pitched chatter. Carl, who stood eye level with the half man, retreated behind his father.

"Hello?" Raymond tried, without stemming the old man's rant, which spilled from him like a prayer. P. P., toting a plastic bucket full of gray water, materialized from out of nowhere and silenced the visitor with a clap on his tatooed shoulder.

"Grandpa says, 'Welcome back, Mr. Frederico.'"

"I thought *you* were Mr. Frederico," Raymond said.

"Didn't you read the pamphlet?"

"Most—not all of it yet."

"It's a little complicated. Grandpa here is my wife's grandfather, and Giorgiano Frederico—the anthropologist who studied Kiriwina—is *her* father. Me, I married into the name. Bottom line is, Giorgiano Frederico, who left the island before his daughter was born, is Grandpa's son-in-law."

Raymond mulled over the explanation. "And Grandpa here thinks *I'm* Giorgiano Frederico?"

P. P. smiled. The old man in the doorway, locked upright on his knotted arms, blocked the view of the village, beach, and sea. "He lets himself think you're every white man. We don't get that many visitors— whatever the essence of a white man is, that's you—pearls on the same necklace—past, present, and future."

"But right now he really believes I'm Frederico the anthropologist? His son-in-law?"

"Yes sir. Georgiano's avatar, anyway. And you're also interchangeable with your own father and the soldiers he was here with during the war. It's not a sign of disrespect. The old ones remember the names like charms: Johnson. Warren. Barnes. Walchuk." P. P. paused, reflecting. "*Like* charms, but not magical. Maybe Grandpa's confused enough to be willing to tell you about the real magic—did you read about our magic?"

"I didn't get to the details."

"The spells are part of Island tradition. For centuries one generation has 'sold' the magic to the next. It was ritual. But now Grandpa's generation is on strike—they won't sell the young people on the Island the old secrets. They won't take anything that's offered—not shells, not yams, electric razors or Walkmen. Today's Kiriwinans are not deserving, they say. Too modern—the old ones don't trust anyone under thirty, you know what I mean? They're committing cultural suicide. In protest. Remember I mentioned a magic issue? That's it." P.

P. set down his pail, which sloshed dirty water over his sneakers. "Grandpa only gave my wife—his own granddaughter—half the beauty spell. She's good enough looking without it, but she doesn't *feel* beautiful. It's psychological, you know? You'll meet her tonight at our welcoming celebration. Torches and dancing, the whole thing. And your little guy can play with my girls. Twins, just about his age."

Raymond remembered the mention of "pre-mating rituals" and frowned. P. P. mistook his expression, thinking he was looking at Grandpa, who'd been standing as still as a stone gargoyle during the conversation.

"Sharks," P. P. stage-whispered. "That's the story, anyway. Before my time. Hey—when I was in that film class, Grandpa's 'condition' gave me an idea for a screenplay. My final project—I got a B+. I'll let you have it free, because you're making your Kong movie here, right? You're Island family, whether you're a Frederico or a Walchuk. I call my movie *Stumpy*. It's about a half-man who's a crazy murderer. My best effect is to let the camera linger on a sleeping victim's face while the audience listens to Stumpy grunt and drag himself closer and closer. I figured out how to shoot it cheap, too, without computer animation: when we show Stumpy, we'd get a regular actor and bury him up to the waist. Then we change the sets and lights and props around him."

"Sounds promising," Raymond said, not sure if P. P. was serious.

"I don't know—maybe in Hollywood there are enough real half-people, so we wouldn't have to bury anybody. Veterans from your Vietnam War." P. P. grinned. "Original idea, right?"

"*Freaks*," Raymond said. "Didn't you study it in film class? One of my influences."

"*Freaks*?"

"1932. The director Todd Browning's *Dracula* was such a huge success the studio gave him carte blanche for his next horror film. So he used real circus freaks, including a half-man. Nobody would touch Browning after that, not a single studio. But now the film's a classic. I'm surprised your professor didn't show it instead of my stuff."

P. P. smiled stiffly. The sparkle left his eyes. He stooped and picked up his bucket. Raymond felt bad for puncturing his host's balloon. "But your Stumpy idea isn't exactly like *Freaks*. It's part of a great tradition. More like you're paying homage."

"You and the boy should take naps," P. P. said quietly. "Keep out of the heat of the day—save your energy for tonight's party." His gaze dropped to his Keds. "There's a lot to learn—Come on!" he barked at Grandpa, adding a few curt syllables Raymond didn't understand.

There was so much Raymond's father never told about Kiriwina Island. For dozens of Thanksgivings, the senior Walchuk, full of Thanksgiving turkey, mashed potatoes, stuffing, and three or four beers, had rhapsodized as if he were composing lyrics to a Broadway tune about the glorious sunsets and tropical breezes and his amazing luck at being stationed there during the war in the Pacific. And though his father had hinted about magic, he'd said nothing about fighter planes or half-men or the "erotic love games" of children. Had he simply been oblivious? Maybe, like the elders of Kiriwina, he'd deemed young Raymond unworthy of the Island's secrets.

When closed up, the cabin was surprisingly dark and cool. Carl slept. Something trapped in the mosquito net fluttered noisily while Raymond drifted into an uneasy slumber. He dreamed of Stumpy—he heard the metronymic wheeze and drag of P. P.'s creation. Dream-Stumpy wore a ship captain's hat. He owned a gentle Saint Bernard dog that licked his master's twisted features. Man and dog lived in a tool shed among rusted farm implements. A sickly band of orphaned children visited him daily. In the darkest corner of the tool shed, what was that? Two orphans—doing what? Kissing? *What?*

Raymond woke with a sweat-dampened shirt. How seriously should he be taking P. P. Frederico? The young man might be the P. T. Barnum of Papua New Guinea, and Raymond might be the sucker he'd been waiting for. What had P. P. actually delivered so far besides a sideshow featuring a rusted fighter plane, a half man, some supposed magical spells, and saucy rumors of juvenile eroticism? What wouldn't he say to keep Raymond's interest in the island piqued? A major film production would mean a lot of yams.

Raymond sat up. Where *was* Carl? Nowhere in the dark room— not on his cot or behind the curtain that hid the toilet. He stumbled to the cabin door and yanked it open, squinting. How far could the boy have wandered? It wasn't like Carl to go off exploring on his own. On set visits he always hung near his father. Raymond pictured Christine's features, twisted in accusation. *What were you doing? Sleeping?* What had P. P. said about the Island's threats? Snakes? What else? Before they'd left for Kiriwina, Raymond had pointed out their destination to his son on a map of the world.

"It's just a hand's-breadth away from home," he'd demonstrated, his thumb on Papua New Guinea and his pinky on southern California. He'd said that to make his son feel less uneasy about the distance they'd be traveling. But maybe that had been a mistake—maybe he should have emphasized caution.

When Raymond stepped out of his cabin, the pink and orange sky over the ocean dazzled him like a tropical drink. An amber sun dappled a purple sea, and the dwellings and trees facing west glowed red. Without warning, P. P. popped up beside him like a genie from a lantern. And standing beside the young Islander was—*Christine?* Raymond gasped, lost his balance, saw stars. Thoughts of magic twisted around his guilt and worry. He fixed his gaze between the couple, down the beach.

"I'm looking for Carl," he mumbled. "He can't be far. Where should we look first?"

"Whoa, buddy—you okay?" Raymond felt a hand—P. P.'s?—on his shoulder.

"Mr. Walchuk?" A female voice, but lacking the tone— the accusation— Raymond expected. "Mr. Walchuk, I'm Bronwyn O'Savage. From the studio? They sent me to help you out. I'm your assistant. Didn't they tell you? Are you okay?"

"Probably our eating customs got you off base. Maybe jet lag," P. P. said. "You want to sit down, boss?"

Raymond blinked at the woman. Not Christine. Not Christine at all, though she might have been his ex's much younger sister. Sunglasses covered her eyes, but her hair was longer and lighter. Why did he think "sister"? As if his ex-wife was his only reference point for all women. Raymond gathered himself, assuming a mask of confidence. It was necessary to look like a boss.

"I'm okay—I just woke up—a little dazed. And you're right, I'm hungry. Nice to meet you—" He shook the young woman's hand, hardly feeling it, remembering instead the giant mitt of P. P.'s grandfather-in-law, a hand he'd never touched. He cursed himself for his posturing. Shouldn't he be screaming for help to find his missing son? Still, he played it cool.

"Bronwyn,' you said?"

"Bronwyn O'Savage. Sent here by the studio. To help with details. Keep a record."

"She got the next-to-next-to-next-to last cabin," P. P. said. "We're never full up."

Raymond grunted a laugh. He nodded at P. P. and Bronwyn. An assistant? Didn't the studio trust his judgment? He craned his neck, stood on tip-toes and looked down the empty path between the village huts.

"Listen, you didn't happen to see Carl poking around somewhere, did you? He must have decided to do some exploring on his own while I was napping. It's not like him to wander off."

P. P. laughed and patted Raymond on the shoulder. "No worries, boss. My girls came and got him—the twins. While you were napping. He must have gotten all the sleep he needed on the plane trip over here. No telling where they could be. Playing something, I guess, probably down by the beach. Maybe they're showing him the yam fields. Children belong with children, right?"

"Sure," Raymond said. A wave of relief swept over him, but his calm was short-lived. Children with children. *The island of love.* Damn. Did P. P. invent that stuff about children and sex games just for his pamphlet? But why—what purpose would such a story have? Such a phenomenon certainly wouldn't make Kiriwina more attractive to tourists. Raymond scanned the shoreline. "Did you say they might be at the beach? Carl doesn't know how to swim."

"He'll learn someday." P. P. smiled.

"I mean he shouldn't go in the water unsupervised."

"Nobody's going in the water. Land is safe. No telling what's in the water. Look what happened to Grandpa."

Bronwyn lifted her sunglasses, settling them in her blond hair. Her brow furrowed. "Who's Grandpa? What happened to him?" From her tone, Raymond could tell she was accumulating information, doing her job. Site assessment. Her eyes were brown. Christine's were gray.

P. P. winked. "Should we tell her, Mr. Walchuk? Or should we save it for a surprise? He paused. "Grandpa's got a pretty noticeable handicap. Bottom half of him got eaten by a shark. See those old guys down by the canoes? You probably can't tell from here, but he's the one who looks like he's sitting down."

Bronwyn turned and stared down the beach. "I can't really see," she said. "Was he really attacked by a shark?"

P. P. shrugged. "That's the story. I wasn't there. Long time ago. Why don't you two go down and say hello? You can meet the other elders, Mr. Walchuk. Who knows who they'll think you are. And Lord knows what they'll make of you, Ms. O'Savage. Probably accuse each other of giving out their magic spells. I bet you'll run into the kids along the way."

"Magic spells?" Bronwyn's skeptical look swung between P. P. and Raymond.

"You haven't had a chance to look over the pamphlet that explains our Island curiosities," P. P. said. "I've got to clean your toilet, Mr. Walchuk. Why don't you fill Ms. O'Savage in on the state of things here in Kiriwina. And then tonight we party. A real wing-ding. Give you an idea of what kind of atmosphere we can conjure up here on the island. Truly cinematic." P.P had placed his hand over his heart, as if making a promise, then disappeared into Raymond's cabin. Raymond stood awkwardly next to Bronwyn.

"You're worried about your boy, aren't you?" she asked. "Go look for him. I still have to unpack. I'll read up on the island lore. Magic?" She wagged her head doubtingly. "Why don't we meet up in an hour—we can discuss your thoughts about the feasibility of this place, then come up with an action plan. The studio has some budgetary concerns regarding—well, we'll talk about those later. My cabin's next to yours." She held out her hand, a down-to-business gesture, Raymond shook it, and the young woman was gone.

Should he have filled her in on the island information she wouldn't find in P.P's pamphlet—the generational conflict, for example—how might that affect the work atmosphere on the island? He blushed—what would she think when she read about the Island of Love and what that meant regarding children?

Raymond, gazing down at the beach, remembered his lakeside honeymoon with Christine, more than a decade past. She'd lost her wedding ring in the sand, and he'd found it. It had seemed like a miracle then. What time was it now in Cleveland, Ohio? Was she dressing for dinner? Maybe Klaus had already won the chess tournament, and the couple would be celebrating. Maybe she smiled at her new love in the mirror as she tilted her head to insert a diamond earring, her thoughts ten thousand miles from Raymond and her son. Raymond frowned. Where *was* Carl?

P. P. poked his head out of the cabin door. "Hey— since *Son of Kong* has already been done, how are we going to make our version better?"

Our version? "Special effects. We're better at faking than they were in 1933. And some better subplots. Involve more children. The idea is to make it a family film."

"I've got a ton of ideas," P. P. said. "We've got to get a little ape doll on the market. The original was white, wasn't it? What color is your baby going to be? I say you got to go mixed—something bronze-ish—coppery-gold, sleek as a trophy. And one more thing—" P. P. folded his arms over his chest and cocked his head. "It's almost the 90's, man. Who said it had to be 'Son'? Why don't we make this *Kong's Daughter*? You can call the little doll Kika."

* * *

Still no sign of Carl. Raymond walked toward the fire where the old men had gathered. The outrigger canoes behind them were much larger than they looked from back up at the doorway of his cabin. He couldn't organize his thoughts—Christine, Bronwyn O'Savage, half-men—and now Kika? Baby Kong as a girl? Why not? What would the studio say? How much authority did this young Bronwyn have? She couldn't have been more than twenty-five.

"Mr. Walchuk—"

Raymond spun to find a compact island woman smiling up at him. Her eyes were so shockingly blue he couldn't hold them, and his gaze slipped back and forth to the little girls flanking her. All three wore pink flowers and flaunted long skirts that looked like they were made from the kind of cheap plastic grass used to line Easter baskets.

"I loved, just loved, *Slitter*, Mr. Walchuk," the woman said in a tinkling voice. "The way the murdering man with the big scar sighs, 'Wee-wee-wee, all the way home' every time after he kills someone, it gives me chills." The woman hugged herself, and the little girls mimicked her, rocking on their bare feet. Raymond nodded, speechless. The young woman bit her lip and raised an eyebrow. "Didn't P. P. tell you we met in film class?"

Of course— Pah-pui's wife— Georgiano Frederico's daughter— that would explain the blue eyes.

"Pah-pui's not from the island, did you know that? He's a Port Moresby boy. Port Moresby is supposed to be the third least livable city in the world. Pah-pui said it should be first-worst. Then maybe people would have heard of it. Growing up there is survival of the fittest." She leaned toward Raymond as if to share a secret, then tipped forward.

"Oops—" She caught herself with the wooden crutch she pulled from behind her. Through her flimsy skirt, Raymond saw a thigh-high plaster cast covered with writing and pictures. P.P's wife shimmied to disguise the stumble, and her girls swished their skirts. "I didn't finish my degree," she said. "The kids came, you know?"

"There he is!" one of the little girls squealed.

"Catch him!" her twin shouted, and the children flew past Raymond, their feet kicking up bursts of yellow sand. He caught a glimpse of Carl, who'd been approaching from the beach. The boy saw the girls and cut behind the nearest hut.

"'The Island of Love,'" Pah-pui's wife murmured. Raymond started to call out, but his son's name caught in his throat. Seconds later, the girls dragged Carl back into view, each clinging to an arm. He allowed himself to be led up to the conversing adults. He wore an expression Raymond didn't recognize, something between a smile and frown. Was there panic in his eyes?

"I thought I saw you with Mom before," he said. "But that was just some other lady, wasn't it?" The girls were tugging him back and forth between them.

"Ms. O'Savage," Raymond said. "The studio sent her. She's here to help figure out stuff about the movie."

* * *

The sky and ocean were merging in the dusk, erasing the horizon. Raymond watched Carl run with the girls along the sand toward the water, P. P.'s wife limping behind. Grandpa and the other elders surrounded a beachside fire burning inside a circle of stones, and Raymond joined them. Some of the men sat cross-legged in the sand while others squatted on top of plastic milk crates. Legless Grandpa had propped himself like a chess piece against a canoe. He wagged his head and warbled something the others nodded to vigorously. When Grandpa paused, all eyes jumped to Raymond. Who had they decided he was? What should he try to look like?

"Help!" Up the beach Carl had been frolicking with Pah-pui's daughters, and now he was flat on his back. One of the girls straddled his chest. The other twin pulled at his shorts. Did he really want help? It sounded like he was laughing. The girl sitting on him bent and kissed his forehead, then began bucking.

"Hey Carl," Raymond called, "you okay?"

His son ignored him. He shook off the smooching girl, got to his feet, and, shorts sagging to his knees, waddled bare-assed into the water. "It's warm!" he shouted back to the twins, who splashed in after him. Carl tugged up his pants and lifted his arms in "touchdown" surrender. His figure was a silhouette in the waning light. The girls caught up and wrapped themselves around him, and Carl turned his head toward the fire where Raymond sat—he could sense the boy trying to pick him out. P. P.'s wife stood at the water's edge, careful to keep her plaster cast dry.

The flames at Raymond's feet cast a fluttering light over the prow of the canoe Grandpa leaned on. The carvings covering it were inscrutable and provocative, the curves and bodies of almost-things reminiscent of the sculptures decorating a gothic cathedral. Raymond's flesh goose-bumped as if he heard the groaning chords of an organ fugue. Grandpa's eyes glittered. Did he and the other old men actually confuse the filmmaker with an anthropologist who'd left the island decades ago? Raymond stared into the center of the crackling fire. His companions were certain their world was coming to an end. No more magic. He'd ask to rent their canoes for his movie.

"*Riot of Blood*—wasn't that your first?" When P. P. appeared beside Raymond, dark veils dropped over the faces of the elders. "In class we discussed your choice of the word 'riot' for the title. Kurosawa uses "throne" because he's remaking *Macbeth*. Your choice is so much more inspired—the ambiguity! Is it violence with comic overtones—or comedy with violent undertones? Can you have it both ways? 'Walchuk's choice of "riot" shows the touch of a genius,' our professor said."

P. P. was a master of flattery. What *was* this island? Raymond imagined his father winking at him from the embers of the little fire. "My good fortune on Kiriwina," he'd said, "is your legacy." Another image in the fire: a young Islander frog-kicking through the sea. Viewed from beneath, he might have been flying. Then a shark-shaped shadow passed like a pair of scissors, slicing the swimmer in two, the half with the arms and head still stroking, the lower half absorbed by the shadow.

It grew darker. Raymond squinted at the children playing in the surf. Too dark for swimming, wasn't it? Were sharks nocturnal? The three silhouettes were no longer linked. Two little girl figures stood waist-deep in the shallows. One dark head was barely visible a hundred yards from shore. P. P.'s wife was waving her crutch.

"Hey—" Raymond shouted. He lifted an arm, hoping his son would signal back. Carl's feet surely touched bottom. Raymond couldn't feel his own legs. Was it the distance or the darkness that sucked the boy from view with each passing swell? While Raymond gaped, the old men, without a word, abandoned the fire, surrounded a canoe, and pushed it into the sea. Four took paddling positions, and Grandpa perched himself in the prow. The outrigger cut through the black water, away from Raymond and toward Carl, white splashes exploding with each paddle dip. Grandpa, one hand locked in the prow's carvings, posed motionlessly, like the figurehead on an old ship. Raymond had lost sight of Carl, but the paddlers must be nearing him. Suddenly, Grandpa teetered forward, reached down with his free hand, and *deus ex-machina*-cally plucked Raymond's son from the sea, settling the coughing boy on the bottom of the canoe. Magic? Luck?

Raymond staggered across the sand and into the foaming surf to greet the returning heroes. Grandpa leaned out from the canoe to deliver the dripping boy. Shivering, Carl hugged his father so tightly Raymond could barely sigh his "thank you" to the elders. Back on dry land, the little girls clung to their mother. From inland came the sound of drums, announcing the onset of the evening's celebration.

***

Raymond had slept—dreamed—through the entire premiere of *Kong's Daughter*. The drums he shuddered awake to were not the drums of Kiriwina Island from two years past. As he blinked into focus, he found himself gazing straight up at what looked like a frozen explosion—as if he was staring upward through the cone of a volcano. It took him a moment to recognize the theatre's elaborate chandelier. This was *now*, the end of 1991, and this was *his* movie: *Kong's Daughter*, he repeated to himself. His focus descended to the screen and the rolling credits—names, roles, and jobs in simple white font on a black background. The drum beat penetrating his chest synced up with his heart—unless it was the other way around, and the throb of his heart controlled the drums—*was* the drums. So he'd been asleep all the way through the movie's climax—the cataclysm that destroyed Kong's Island, the eruption of Skull Mountain, secretly volcanic—who knew? The orphaned children and their adult charges had been saved by the mighty Kika. Raymond hadn't heard the final line, the one Carl had quoted. The words, predictive of a sequel, were shouted by the heroine to a weeping child in the safety of a helicopter—*"We never saw Kika sink—she was swimming. Maybe she'll make it to another island— maybe all the way to America!"*

Raymond's arms were pinned down, the right by Carl, who had squirmed out of his seat and was half in his father's lap, the left by Bronwyn, her own pale arm wrapped over his like a slender python. He buried his face in his son's curls, still damp from—not the sea. The rain—hadn't it been raining? Raymond sighed, relieved, at exactly what he wasn't sure. Carl tugged away, looked at his father with wet eyes.

"That was great, Dad! It was so good—and I recognized all the island parts!"

Bronwyn squeezed Raymond's wrist. She was nodding, radiant. "They loved it," she mouthed. She got to her feet, her hand on his shoulder. She said something he couldn't hear. Something about going to look for P. P.? The theatre was filled with a rumbling, buoyant hubbub that became apparent after the credits ended, the drums stilled, and the house lights brightened further. "Interviews—meet me in the lobby," Bronwyn exclaimed over the din and stepped into an aisle, bowing to familiar, well-wishing faces crowding over to congratulate the director and cast.

"Dad—Dad!" Carl pulled at his father's sleeve, and Raymond, feeling hollow and not eager to face the adult world waiting to crush him with compliments, gave his full attention to his son. The boy's face was inches from his—his lips were purple, which made his skin look even whiter than usual. His breath smelled like the grape lollipop he'd been sucking while Raymond dreamed of Kiriwina.

"I know it was a movie," Carl whispered, "and I know there wasn't really any Skull Mountain on Kiriwina. But—the island's really okay, isn't it? It didn't sink?"

Raymond tried to ignore the crowd gathering in the aisle, pressing toward his seat. Each time someone called his name he flinched. He turned his back to shield his private conversation.

"Shh—" a voice said. "Let him have a moment with his son."

Carl licked his ghoulish lips with a purple tongue. He batted his eyelids. His Kika doll was pinned under his elbow by its neck. The ape grinned at Raymond incongruously.

"Of course the island's okay," Raymond assured, unable to keep from glancing at the faces behind his son. More than okay. Kiriwina had been a blessing—magic, luck, a continuation of a family legacy. Who could think it otherwise?

"It's just that—when everything sank into the sea in the movie, I kept waiting for the canoe, and Grandpa, and it doesn't show up, and I felt like—" Carl's voice was barely audible. "Like I was going down."

Raymond pulled the boy close, crushing the monkey between them. He couldn't tell whether or not Carl was about to cry. "It's okay," he said. "You're safe."

"And the girls. I'm worried about the girls. I worry about them a lot."

"The girls? The twins? They're okay, too." When Carl pulled his head back, Raymond wondered if those awful lips had stained his shirt. Bronwyn would have a fit. Carl's eyes were slits.

"Are you sure?" the boy croaked.

Chapter 2— Old Yeller

Raymond and Carl watched the end of *Old Yeller*. The old film still made Raymond cry, and he dabbed at his eyes, too choked up to talk to his son. Carl lay belly down on the sofa as the credits rolled and music played. His feet were close enough for his father to grab, and Raymond suppressed an urge to reach over and tickle their soles. Crushed under Carl's chest was his Kika doll. At age ten, he was too old for stuffed animals, but on his weekend visits to his father's Carl and his trusty Kika were inseparable. The rest of the week the doll waited on his bed as stoically as a ventriloquist's dummy. Carl's Kika was not alone—an army of pristine, plastic-wrapped little apes were scattered everywhere around the house. They spilled out of closets, crowded kitchen counters, and peeked out of half open cartons shoved into corners. "A lifetime supply of gifts," Raymond called them, "sure to be collector's items. And," he said to Carl, "they keep me company during the week while you're at your mother's."

"The plastic wrap makes them look like spacemen," Carl once noted, "or deep sea divers without air hoses." After that observation, whenever Raymond looked at the wrapped gorillas, they seemed to be struggling for breath.

Carl's weekend visits usually ended with a video because Raymond saw it as his responsibility to refine the boy's film education. The boy had been no more than five when he'd attended his first film session with his father. "It's like Halloween!" Carl said as he watched his father's crew lay out a murder victim and an armload of severed limbs around the set. With all the scaffolding and lights and cameras, even a kindergartner couldn't confuse a movie set with the real world. When Carl saw a Pepsi-swigging ghoul chatting up a gaffer a second before Raymond yelled, "Action!" how could the child take it seriously when the same ghoul whacked a rubber torso with a hatchet and kicked a mannequin arm down a pretend gutter, all the while whistling Wagner's "Flying Dutchman"?

But the completed versions of Raymond's bread and butter slashers were something else entirely, obviously inappropriate for a little boy who only dimly suspected that his father was a Dr. Frankenstein who could breathe life into artifice. In Raymond's hands rubber became flesh, ketchup transubstantiated into blood, and a fake alley became the altar of unspeakable horrors. The only film of his father's Carl had seen was the family-oriented *Kong's Daughter*, and even that experience had left him confused over the boundary between reality and fantasy.

So for his son's weekend film sessions, Raymond kept to the classics. Only once had he misjudged the suitability of a movie: just last month Carl had begged to watch *Freaks*, the old horror film he'd heard his father call "inspirational."

"You said there's a real half-man in it, like Grandpa from Kiriwina," Carl begged.

"It might be a little too disturbing," Raymond warned. "There are a lot of other scary-looking people in it." But Carl had persisted, and Raymond, understanding that he might be pushing the boy's limits, plugged in the video cassette. The half-man didn't trouble Carl. Neither did the real pinheads or the armless, legless man they called "the Worm." When the boy saw these "freaks," he winced and uttered an "Ew," but kept watching, transfixed. It was the chicken-woman that had traumatized him.

The chicken-woman—the silly, fake-looking thing revealed at the film's conclusion. Supposedly, the tribe of freaks had created the clucking monstrosity, somehow carving and stitching her out of the beautiful-but-evil bareback rider who had violated their trust. When Carl saw the human-faced ball of feathers, he'd burst into tears. Raymond at first had trouble taking his son's fright seriously. He couldn't remember the last time he'd seen the boy cry.

"But she's so ridiculous. She couldn't happen—not like the real freaks, and they didn't bother you."

"She started out so beautiful, then they changed her," Carl sobbed. He slept next to his father that night, and the next day Carl soothed his son with a Disney cartoon marathon. Raymond thought the chicken-woman episode was over and done with when he delivered Carl back to Christine at the end of the weekend, but his ex-wife's call came after midnight.

"He's crying into his pillow, Raymond. He's afraid of the shadows in his room. How can you do this? Are you trying to sabotage your relationship with him? Don't you want to see him? Or is it my relationship with him you're trying to sabotage—mine and Klaus's? Is that it?"

Caught off guard at that late hour, Raymond argued that sometimes films touch viewers in unexpected ways, and that being frightened could be considered cathartic. "Kafka wrote that a work of fiction should be like 'an ice-ax to break up the frozen sea inside us,'" he argued, remembering the time he'd brought Carl home with a rubber ax fixed in his head, a gift from the make-up staff. "Movies can do that, too."

"He's just a little boy, Raymond. He doesn't need any axes, yours or Kafka's. Right now your son is weeping in Klaus's arms. Klaus is singing him old German lullabies. That's where we're at now—German lullabies. Are you trying to pull our son into your perverted little world?"

"I don't make those kinds of movies anymore. I'm the king of family films now." Raymond sighed. He would keep the peace. "But you're right. I misjudged. I'm sorry." He agreed to exclude horror films from the weekend film sessions. There was nothing to be gained from antagonizing Christine, and he didn't want to undermine Klaus, though the chess master was often out of the country for weeks at a time.

"I'll be more careful," Raymond told his ex. "But if you saw this chicken-woman that scared him, you'd wonder . . ."

"Be a father, Raymond," Christine snapped. "Your son has his own inner life. It's not all about you."

And so father and son came to the end of *Old Yeller*, and it was Raymond who was crying. As soon as he sniffed away a final tear, he'd direct Carl to load up his backpack so the boy would be ready for his mom's pick-up. Memory shots of the romping yeller-dog played behind the credits. How did Carl stay dry-eyed? Old Yeller, mischievous, courageous—and when his young master had to shoot the dog when it turned rabid, the act was a beautiful thing—solitary, generous, necessary, and heroic. Like George shooting Lennie in *Of Mice and Men*. Raymond would look for a copy of the book for Carl. Killing Old Yeller was a rite of passage. Interesting how many "rites" had to do with issues of life and death. And pets. Raymond considered Elvis, the cornsnake that ultimately failed its audition as a Walchuk family pet. He'd bought the thing for Carl on a whim, stopping at a pet store on his way home from the Mexican desert where he'd been shooting scenes for *Swallow*, his horror film about an oversized anaconda that terrorizes a group of teenage campers after gobbling up the residents of a Mexican village. Raymond had carried the pencil-sized baby snake into his home inside the aquarium the pet store clerk had promised would be a "perfect environment."

"He's all yours," Raymond had told little Carl, who stood on tip-toe to gaze at the tiny snake sunning itself under a heat lamp on a patch of astro-turf. "What are you going to name him?" Raymond peeked at Christine, who was chopping vegetables on the granite counter. She'd barely met his eye since he'd entered the house after two weeks' absence. Too late he wondered if maybe he should have bought her something, too.

"How about 'Elvis'?" Carl piped. He tapped on the glass. The snake, lying in the shape of an S, didn't move.

"That's not bad," Raymond said, "but you don't have to go with the first thing that comes to your mind. Think about it a little. A pet is something you have to take seriously."

Christine stopped chopping. "There's nothing wrong with 'Elvis,'" she said, frowning.

"Sure," Raymond said. "Anything you want, buddy. Hey, you know what it eats? Pinkies." Raymond shook a small plastic bag. His wife had resumed her dinner preparations, and he watched the flash of her knife.

"What are pinkies?" Carl asked.

"Frozen baby mice. The size of the eraser on the end of a pencil." Raymond watched Christine pause mid-chop. Her shoulders lifted and sank, but she didn't look up. "Want to see?"

"Sure!" Carl yipped, and his father opened the bag, inside of which was a frosted over ziploc pouch.

"I can't see them," Carl said.

"We'll take one out later and feed him." Raymond closed he bag. 'Elvis' we're going with, right? The pet store guy said you dunk a pinky in a cup of water to soften it."

"And where are you planning on storing your 'pinkies'?" Christine's hands were on her hips, and she squinted skeptically at her husband.

"Where else?" Raymond said. "The freezer. Don't worry, I'll make sure we don't mix them up with our food. We'll label a Tupperware container with a skull and crossbones. I don't know, though. They're probably delicious." He tousled Carl's hair. "Probably taste like jelly beans."

"Yuch!" Carl squeaked. He pressed his face against the tank, fogging the glass with his breath.

"Well, don't get too attached," Christine said. "This is going to be a trial run. We'll see how it goes. Maybe learning how to care for something will teach you responsibility." When Christine turned to Raymond, she was smiling so hard her lips had lost their color. Was she talking about the snake or their marriage?

"That's right," he said. "Elvis will be a father-son project. Something we can do together.

"I love Elvis," Carl sighed.

Months passed, and Elvis grew. Raymond returned from another longer than usual absence—he'd been back to Mexico, filming zombie mutant attacks. His wife barely glanced up from her desk to welcome him.

"Carl has something to tell you about your sinewy friend," she said, meaning the snake, and probably "sinuous" instead of "sinewy," but Raymond congratulated himself on not correcting her. He found Carl in his bedroom, staring through the terrarium glass at his snake, which was now almost a yard long.

"We keep running out of pinkies," Carl said. "Elvis eats six at a time now. They don't have enough at the pet store. He needs to eat something bigger. He needs full-sized mice. They sell them live just for feeding things."

"I have to tell your mother we need to keep live mice?"

Carl shook his head. He held up a thin paperback book: *Know Your Cornsnake*. "It says pet snakes can be injured by live mice. The mice fight back, and they scratch the snake's skin, and it causes an infection."

Raymond pictured a string of blood-pearls laced across Elvis's snout. "You can read that book?" he asked. What grade was his boy in? Kindergarten? First?

"Some of the words. Mommy read it to me. She says you and I have some figuring out to do."

The solution, it turned out, was frozen adult mice—but few pet stores stocked them. It took a dozen phone calls to locate a supply at Exotic Birds and Reptiles, a pet store almost two hours away, where father and son drove and purchased a bag of fifty frozen mice, bred hairless for lab experiments—enough for a year of Elvis feedings. On the ride home, Carl lifted the clear plastic bag of mice and shook it. The little bodies shifted like eggrolls.

"It's heavy," he said, and stuck the bag on the floor between his feet.

At home, father and son needed a larger Tupperware container than the one they'd used for pinkies. After drawing on the required skull and crossbones warning, Raymond wedged it in the freezer behind a box of heat-and-serve lasagna.

"It takes up a lot of space," Carl whispered, worried about what his mother might think.

"Well, let's tread lightly," Raymond said.

But a few hours later, a call came from the bathroom.

"Dad—Dad, I need help."

When Raymond joined Carl, his son was standing in front of the bathroom sink, his hand on a butter knife sunk half an inch deep into an icy brick.

"I'm having trouble with the new mice," the boy said. "They're all stuck together." He pried the knife sideways until it curved like a leaping fish. Raymond studied the frozen block. He could make out a few compressed ears, the faint outlines of a half dozen pairs of legs, but couldn't define an individual body. The cause of the problem was immediately apparent: during the drive back from the pet store, the bag of little bodies had been pushed up against the car heater at Carl's feet, which had defrosted them. In the Walchuk family freezer the thawed mice had fused into a single giant mouse-block— fifty naked carcasses welded seamlessly together.

Raymond moved his son to the side and grasped the knife. He applied pressure at different angles, but nothing happened. A blue cup half full of lukewarm water for defrosting waited under the toothbrush holder. Raymond gave another useless tug, then paused to think.

"It's like *The Sword in the Stone*," Carl said, and Raymond grunted. He shut the bathroom door and looked into the mirror.

"What?" Carl asked his father's reflection. Raymond contemplated his son's face: Christine's lips without the disdainful twist; Raymond's eyes, though calmer; the nose—Raymond's arc, his mother's nostrils. From which of their ancestors had the boy inherited his dark curls? And what about the inner depths the toothpaste-flecked mirror didn't reveal? But the scene— Raymond's and Carl's heads side by side—could be a Norman Rockwell painting. Someone who saw only their faces might assume that father and son were building a birdhouse together or carving a racecar for a Cub Scout Pinewood Derby. Maybe they'd think Raymond was passing down a family hobby, something as delicately masculine as inserting a ship through the neck of a bottle. Raymond watched his features compress as he forced the knife into the block of mouse.

"It's really stuck." Carl's voice bounced off the tiled walls.

"Shh—" A mouse-shaped shadow began to emerge at the blade's entry point. Like a figure embedded in a glacier. A fissure cut across its torso. "Let me do this alone," Raymond said. "Go distract your mother—she doesn't need to know what's going on in here." Their eyes met in the mirror. The boy's lashes fluttered, and he left the bathroom.

And that's how the feeding of Elvis went. For weeks Raymond prepared the snake's meals, the task having shifted from a PG rating to an R for excessive gore. Raymond was never able to carve a single intact body from the mouse-block. During meal-prep, chips and chunks of mouse littered the sink counter. Only as the bits defrosted did they reassume their shapes as legs, heads and half-haunches. Then they bled. Raymond set each morsel on a paper towel. The wound ends sparkled like scarlet lips under the fluorescent bathroom lights, and the bloodstains bloomed like rose bouquets. The largest chunks were dunked in the cup of warm water—the crimson trails swirling from them reminded Raymond of dissolving tablets of Easter egg dye. Sometimes he pretended that the limbs belonged to a race of tiny people slaughtered in a Lilliputian genocide. Once his thoughts drifted to a question Christine had asked him years back, when they were falling in love. He'd told her about the plot of a movie he wanted to make someday, a twisted version of O. Henry's "Gift of the Magi." In Raymond's movie the couple in love was so poor that they resorted to cutting off their own body parts as gifts to exchange with their beloved: a toe for a thumb, an arm for a foot, and so on, year after year—until only their hearts were left.

"What would you cut off for me?" Christine asked.

"Anything," Raymond had answered. "Everything." He'd believed that he could suffer any physical pain or loss in the name of love.

After the mouse parts softened, Raymond hurried into Carl's room and dumped them into Elvis's tank. The snake usually struck instantly, but occasionally a head or leg was left to shrivel under the heat lamp until Raymond plucked it out a few days later.

A phone call from Carl's teacher: he'd been teasing a classmate, harassing her with threats about a dead mouse. Please talk to your son and call the girl's parents, the teacher asked. Better to nip misunderstandings in the bud.

"I told Molly I was going to bring her a mouse sandwich, Carl shrugged, "on toast. It was just a joke."

Christine made the call. The girl's parents were understanding—probably more so than Christine, who frowned at Carl and Raymond after hanging up the phone. "Your snake," she said, "is causing problems."

***

Raymond lay in bed, fading in and out of troubling dreams. He saw himself shivering on a ledge of Mount Everest. He pulled his cold feet from Christine, who slept beside him, worried that he'd wake her and her scorn. On a cliff above him, a boulder leaned insecurely. This egg-shaped rock was composed of the frozen bodies of countless mice, their outlines webbing its surface.

"Humpty-Dumpty sat on a wall," a disembodied voice whispered. Hours before, after Carl had been put to bed and Christine was watching television, Raymond had been chiseling out mouse bits for Elvis, when he'd gagged and nearly vomited while wiping up blood from the sink. He'd looked at the mouse egg—it was the size of a softball. How many more feedings would it yield? What would the Walchuk boys do when they'd chipped off the last bit of mouse? Did Carl even like his snake? Except for teasing little girls about "mouse sandwiches," the kid never mentioned his pet. In fact, the snake's terrarium had been moved into Carl's closet because the brightness of the heat lamp kept the kid from sleeping. Being holed up in a closet was no life for anything, not even a snake.

Raymond slid out of bed and shrugged into his robe. He peered down at his soundly sleeping wife, thought of the leftover mouse parts in Elvis's tank, and shuddered. In the dark, how did he even know he was looking at Christine? It could have been anybody. He padded into the kitchen and switched on the light, squinting against its harshness. He opened the freezer and took out the Tupperware container with the skull and crossbones. Moments later, he stood in his backyard. The grass was soft under his slippers and the air was thick and warm. Raymond looked at the stars, then tossed the mouse egg over his neighbor's stockade fence. If snakes knew happiness, wouldn't Elvis prefer life back in a pet store, where he could spend his day eyeing tanks full of rodents and cages full of colorful birds?

***

Old Yeller. Raymond studied Carl, still lying on his stomach on the couch. His eyes were closed, though he was awake. He was lifting one leg part way up and letting it fall, over and over, in a way that reminded Raymond of someone chopping wood. What was the kid thinking? About the movie? Maybe a technical point Raymond could address? Since the *Freaks* incident, Raymond had tried to do a better job reading his son's emotions, but instead of becoming more sensitive, had he become merely hesitant? Maybe Carl was anxious to return home—to Christine and Klaus's house. Raymond wondered what his son's night-time routine was there.

"Time to get a move on, Son of Kong," he said after the movie's theme music ended and the screen blinked to an empty blue.

"Okay, Papa Kong." Carl hoisted himself onto the sofa and looked at his father. "Dad—I want to be an actor."

It took Raymond a moment to process the statement. Acting? That would be logical given Raymond's career and the kid's exposure to film-making. And *Old Yeller*—an old film, pure sentiment, about a boy becoming a man—of course seeing a movie like that might trigger a declaration like the one Carl had just made. But maybe it wasn't acting Carl was interested in—maybe he just wanted to identify with the movie's young hero. Maybe all he wanted was a companion. A dog. Something other than a snake, which demanded much, but returned so little—a snake could never be man's best friend.

"Acting—we'll have to talk about that. You know, I've been thinking that you should talk to your mom and Klaus about getting a dog. Dogs are almost human. Or maybe I could get one, and it would be yours, too. We could share it." Raymond surprised himself with his second suggestion. He could almost feel a little pup tugging at its leash as he walked it down his street.

"No, Dad. You're away too much. And Klaus is too allergic to keep a dog at our house. Really allergic. He's always worried about getting a sinus infection right before a big match. Like, he'll be sitting over the chessboard, and his nose will drip. Right on the pawn, one time." Carl grinned and mimicked his stepfather: "'The king and queen or the brave knights—no, they are too noble for snot.'" The imitation was spot-on, but it pained Raymond to hear how completely his son's stepfather had become integrated into the boy's life. Carl continued his imitation, furrowing his brow to achieve Klaus's default expression.

"'The bishop—ach, he would have me excommunicated if I snotted on him! But the lowly pawn—it is his lot in life to bathe in the fluids of my nose.'" Carl's face relaxed, and he became a child again. "What's 'excommunicate'?"

"It means to get thrown out of the church."

"You mean like for talking too much in class?"

"Sort of—" Did Carl treat his mom and Klaus to imitations of Raymond? "—But no, not really. Not just thrown out of any one specific building. It means you're not supposed to be part of that religion anymore. It doesn't recognize you."

"Who doesn't recognize you?"

"I don't know. The powers that be."

"What powers? God?"

"I suppose so," Raymond shrugged. "You get the God Boot, capital G, capital B. No heaven for you. Get your rear in gear, little Kong. Your momma will here in a minute."

"What about acting?"

"We'll talk to your mother. I'm sure she'll have lots to say on the subject. She has very strong feelings about the art of film making."

"But what do *you* think?" Carl stared at Raymond with an unfamiliar face—his features seemed sharper, less boyish. Was his son growing up before his eyes, or was the boy *imitating* maturation?

"I think I have to think about it."

The digital clock under the TV read 6:15, which meant the ever-punctual Christine would arrive shortly. While Carl fetched his bag, Raymond switched on the television, and a doll-faced newscaster appeared. Her porcelain cuteness lacked gravitas, and her voice was shrill. She'd never progress beyond weekend substitute anchor for a local station. Had she reached the height of her ambitions, or did she hope for more? Raymond searched the anchor's face for a hint of melancholy.

"A developing tragedy," she began, and Raymond muted her with a touch of his thumb. Carl wanted to act. Raymond knew a host of casting agents, and auditions would be a snap to arrange. Bronwyn O'Savage had recently left her studio job and joined a casting agency that specialized in children, hadn't she? And there were plenty of parts Raymond himself could invent for his son. The boy could play a victim's child or little brother. Raymond visualized his kid dashing down a dark alley—he could become trapped, somehow, and come face to face with the film's villain. Raymond reflected—how would he rescue the boy? His thoughts darkened—he had a vision of the surf at Kiriwina Island, of standing paralyzed, knee deep in the water, as an ancient half-man lowered his nearly drowned son into his arms.

He felt Carl standing behind his chair. His breath tickled Raymond's bald spot—the silver-dollar sized circle of pale flesh he'd discovered when he watched himself in HBO's "Making of *Kong's Daughter*." The Kewpie-doll-faced anchor had disappeared from the screen, which now displayed a pair of photographs, school pictures of a boy and a girl around Carl's age. The children looked alike. Maybe twins: they shared the same gap between large front teeth, the same lank hair and protruding ears, and the same pale eyes, the girl's slightly crossed behind her glasses.

Cut to a shot of a woman standing on a porch, supporting herself on its iron rail. Paint flaked from the door behind her. Reporters pushed microphones in her face. Neighbors hung in the background—an older woman with a purple head wrap, a boy straddling a bicycle. But then the shot narrowed to the face of the woman on the porch—of course she was related to the two children, the twins in the photographs. She squinted behind glasses similar to her daughter's. Her nostrils dilated and her cheeks quivered as her big teeth clamped on her lower lip. Her ear poked through her thin hair.

Something very bad must have happened. As in Raymond's slasher films, the clues all pointed toward a tragedy: an accident, a kidnapping, a murder. Carl didn't need to see any of this. It wasn't a movie under production: it was the ugly side of life. He'd promised Christine to keep such horrors away from their son.

"I was listening to the news while you were packing up," Raymond said without looking at his son. "Very sad. A couple of kids lost their dog. Nobody can find it." Raymond's throat tightened around his lie. "It's been missing for days."

Carl didn't speak. Had he believed the dog story? When Raymond finally turned to look at him, he froze. His son's face mirrored the features of the mother on the news: the boy wore a grimace that exaggerated the size of his teeth; his nose was red and his nostril's flared; a pale ear stuck out of his suddenly flattened curls. His half-shut eyes were oddly colorless. The doorbell rang. Christine had arrived to claim her child, but neither Raymond nor Carl moved. The boy's eyes filled with tears, and Raymond was lightheaded with fear and pride— the boy was acting, wasn't he?

Chapter 3: Pinocchio—New Hampshire, 1993

The iconic author ushered Raymond and Carl to his writing bunker, a healthy walk from the main house. At its wooden door, which he unlocked with a brass key on a short leather strap, he pointed to a nearby bench that overlooked a lush, New Hampshire valley. The two men and the boy squinted against the morning sun. "Would you wait for us, please," the writer asked Raymond. "I'd like to speak to your boy alone."

"Of course," Raymond said, and the old man laid his hand on Carl's shoulder and guided the child into the squat building. The wide-eyed gaze his son tossed back as the door shut clutched at Raymond's heart. But there couldn't be danger—Raymond hadn't sent the boy into locked seclusion with just anyone. This was Salinger. And Salinger was interested in Raymond's screenplay based on the short story "Teddy."

Raymond had been careful to submit the screenplay through the writer's agent—at all costs he'd wanted to avoid the appearance of intruding on the great man's privacy. And his boldness had borne fruit. He'd been summoned to the New Hampshire residence for a nine AM meeting. Father and son had flown into Boston on the redeye, slept in a hotel near the airport, and had risen before dawn for the long drive through the New England countryside in their rented car.

Raymond had brought the boy along for luck and company. The kid was a budding actor, and Raymond had a hunch the author would be a sucker for Carl's deep, dark eyes and black curls. The boy's fragile sturdiness—or was it his sturdy fragility— would certainly attract Salinger's attention.

The Walchuks had rehearsed their meeting en route, as they dipped over hills and rounded curves through pines and scrub oaks.

"We'll get it into the conversation that you're an actor," Raymond told Carl. "We'll plant that seed. Tell him you 'grew yourself' if he asks your age. That comes straight from his story. It's in my screenplay. Then we'll make sure to steer the conversation to my directing experience."

"I don't want him to think I'm a phony," Carl had yawned. Raymond had given the boy the story and script to read, and while Raymond thought his son a little young to understand everything in them, he trusted the boy's intuition. "I can tell he likes children," Carl said.

The first words Salinger had spoken as he shook Raymond's hand on the front porch of his home were directed at Carl. There'd been a sheen to the moment, *sans* the sentimentality. The writer had guessed why the ten-year-old was there.

"So, you think you can be my Teddy?" he'd asked the boy while holding fast to his father's hand. "Follow me out back."

* * *

Raymond checked his watch and squirmed on the bench. A large, broad-winged bird, maybe an eagle, circled over the valley beneath him, oaks and pines descending toward an invisible river. It was only a matter of time before the bird zeroed in on some unsuspecting thing scurrying through the wildflowers. Was anyone or anything watching *him* with such intensity, Raymond wondered, then smirked. That sniper's-eye view—that was the old Raymond, wasn't it, the one famous for the paranoia of horror films? Hadn't he broken that mold with *Kong's Daughter*? A monster film, sure, but tender-hearted also. And lucrative enough to give him the freedom to branch out— prove he had a sensitive, intellectual side. Raymond peeked at the sun, then lowered his gaze to Salinger's bunker. It was about fifteen feet square, without windows on either of its visible sides. If he hadn't been told to wait on the bench, he would have walked its perimeter. What could the old man and his boy be talking about?

The circling raptor was gone. While Raymond's thoughts wandered, it must have streaked from the sky and snatched the life out of some rodent. He remembered Elvis, the pet snake that hadn't worked out, and the frozen egg composed of fused naked mouse bodies. Hadn't the egg, in a dream, teetered on a Humpty Dumpty wall? There'd been a tumble, the giant egg had cracked open—and—was this really the origin story?—Kika, Kong's daughter, had sat in the bottom half of the shell like a toddler in a bath tub. But it must have been a baby boy ape in the egg dream—baby Kong hadn't become a girl until P. P. Frederico suggested the idea on Raymond's very first day on Kiriwina Island.

The bunker door finally opened, and Carl appeared, followed by the author. Sunlight rinsed the color from the scene. The exit of old man and boy had the look of an important event captured by chance on 8mm film—the kind of overexposed historical clip often seen of dignitaries descending from an aircraft or of a passing motorcade or of famous children dashing from ocean waves. Carl frowned in the bright sun. Salinger seemed more crooked than he'd been when he'd greeted the Walchuks on his porch. His leathery face was impossible to read. Raymond stood and waited beside the bench.

"This is some boy you've got here," Salinger said. "The two of you will transform 'Teddy' into a remarkable film. Thank you. I promised the boy a bowl of ice cream." He looked down at Carl, then up at Raymond. "Unless your father thinks it's early for sweets."

***

Raymond quizzed his son in a whisper while the author was busy in the kitchen.
"What was it like in there? What did he say? What did you do?"
"It was dark except for two lamps," Carl said. "One standing up behind an armchair, the other on his desk next to one of those old-fashioned typewriters. He told me to sit in the big chair, and he rolled his desk chair around to talk to me. There were stacks of paper on the desk and on a table, and against the walls were those old-fashioned metal file cabinets. Tall ones. Three or four. There were stacks of paper on those, too. The place smelled like old newspapers and dirty socks."
Raymond nodded, surprised to find himself trembling.
"Would you like a glass of iced tea?" the author called.
"Please," Raymond shouted. "If it's not any trouble." There was no response.
"Did you give him the line about growing yourself?" Raymond asked, but Carl lifted a brow because Salinger was back. He handed the boy a blue bowl of vanilla ice cream and perched on the edge of a chair across from father and son. He seemed to have forgotten his offer of tea.
"I loved the first *Son of Kong*, the old one," he said. His eyes reminded Raymond of those gag glasses that blinked when the wearer nodded his head. "I wasn't much older than the boy here when I saw it. It was more poignant than *King Kong*—that was more just about a big ape causing trouble. And I have to say, Mr. Walchuk, your remake of the sequel captured its innocent charm—yet you produced something unique and beautiful. That's why I invited you here. I don't

see many movies, but yours is a jewel. I felt like a child again watching it. Where, may I ask, was it filmed? The landscape is stunning."

"Kiriwina Island," Raymond said after clearing his dry throat. "It's a stone's throw from Papua New Guinea. My father was stationed there during the war—World War II."

The author scowled. Or was he smiling? He craned his vulture neck, then braced himself on the armrests of his chair and pushed himself to his feet, stretching to his full height before sinking back into himself. "It was a delight meeting you both," he said. "Maybe we'll see each other again. But, please, let's communicate from now on through my agent." He waved, like royalty. "I grant full permission for you to move ahead with the 'Teddy' project." He winked at Carl. "And you'll be wonderful, Pinocchio. You can put your bowl in the sink when you're done with your ice cream. Don't gobble, or you'll get one of those headaches. Now if you two will excuse me, I've got some work to do. Let yourselves out." He shuffled past them and through the back door. Raymond and Carl watched him make his way down the path back to his bunker.

* * *

"'Pinocchio?'" Raymond asked a few minutes later. It wasn't quite noon, but they were already in the car for their drive back to Logan Airport. "What was that about?"

Carl slouched against the passenger door. "He said that most people were wooden puppets, but I had what it took to become 'a real boy.' He said it was a tribute to you. He said he knows a thing or two about good parents. The ice cream was chewy, Dad. I don't think ice cream's supposed to be chewy."

"Probably old," Raymond said. "So—did you talk about the screenplay? Did he get specific about the things he liked?"

The boy shook his head. "No. We sat down, and he kind of gave me a quiz. He pulled a sheet of paper from the top of one of the piles and handed it to me. He asked, 'What do you see there, boy?'"

"What was it? A story?"

"I just glanced at it. There was a title: 'Edna's Daughter,' or something."

"'Esme's'? 'Esme's Daughter?'"

"Ed-nay?"

49

"*ESS*-may." Raymond thought of his own blockbuster—had the great author also chosen to write a sequel about a daughter? Dare Raymond think his own film had inspired a sequel to a classic short story?

"Something like that. Do you know who he reminded me of? Remember when we watched *Plan 9 from Outer Space*? You told me that half way through making it Bela Lugosi died. He was playing some kind of weird space vampire, right? So Ed Wood got his dentist to play the part. The dentist kept his arm up to hide his face behind his cape. That's who Mr. Salinger reminded me of—the dentist-vampire. The whole time we were with him I felt like he was hiding his face."

"So what did you do? Did you read the title back to him? You didn't say 'Edna,' did you?"

"My stomach hurts. No, I didn't read anything. I turned the paper over and looked at the blank side. Then I tore it up. In half, then in quarters, then in eighths. I dropped the pieces on the floor."

Raymond lifted his foot from the accelerator. "You did what?" He turned to Carl, who had closed his eyes, his cheek against the window glass. He was rubbing his belly as the car coasted along the country road. He lifted a shoulder. "I ripped it up. Mr. Salinger stared at me and kind of tilted his head. 'You need to tear up one sheet a day,' I said, 'from all of these.' I waved around his room at the stacks of paper. 'And don't start writing anything new until you're through ripping up every single sheet.' He was quiet for a minute. Then he asked, 'Just one page a day?' I told him one would be a full day's work if he did it right. 'Think of how many days you've got until you're done,' I told him. There were piles and piles. It'll take him a really long time."

For a moment Raymond couldn't see—he'd had dreams where he was driving and suddenly went blind and could feel himself swerving through the dark toward the edge of a cliff. But he was wide awake now, and he blinked, and, thank God, there was the road. He fixed his attention on the double yellow line, and his foot found the gas pedal. "And then?" he asked.

"And then he called me Pinocchio, and, like I said, told me I had the rare chance to be a real boy. I forgot to tell you that—he said 'rare chance.' Dad, is there a place to pull over? I think I have to throw up."

Chapter 4—Friday

The feature article of the Sunday New York Times "Arts" section stung Christine like a slap: "A Family Affair: an interview with *Teddy* director Raymond Walchuk and star/son Carl."

She resisted the urge to read it and tossed the newspaper aside. What could she learn that she didn't already know? Her ex Raymond had ingratiated himself with the reclusive Salinger and dragged their son into the limelight. Before *Teddy*, Carl's on-screen resume included only a dash down a dark alley in one of Raymond's friend's horror films—P. P. Frederico's first film after following his mentor from that Pacific island. Christine had helped the boy land one gig—a photo for the cover of a board game, *Jabber-Babble*— "where superfluous verbiage could spell your doom." She gave the game's manufacturer an advertising discount in her magazine in exchange for the job. The "J" of "Jabber-Babble" hid Carl's mouth, and they'd dyed his hair blond, but his eyes sparkled amid the happy faces of his box cover family. The laughing *faux*-mom rested her hand on Carl's shoulder.

Christine had been in Finland at a chess tournament with her second husband Klaus when *Teddy* premiered, and she still hadn't seen the film. But she couldn't avoid the posters: Carl as the title character stood alone against a pale background—was he on the deck of a fogged-in ocean liner? He wore baggy shorts, and an over-sized T-shirt drooped from his shoulders. Her son's curls had been straightened, and an ethereal gleam lit his eyes. She couldn't see herself in those eyes; they were undeniably Raymond's.

She might be the primary custodial parent, but the promotional schedule for *Teddy* had kept Carl away from Christine and Karl's home for a month. The boy belonged to Raymond. "Son of Kong," her ex-husband called their child, and Carl called his father "Papa Kong." No room for a "Mama Kong" among all these giant apes. More than one critic of Raymond's megahit *Kong's Daughter* had pointed out the absence of a maternal presence in the film. Who had actually given birth to the colossal baby? Christine thought of the *Jabber-Babble* box cover and tried unsuccessfully to picture her own face smiling next to her son instead of the fake mother's. In their worst pre-divorce quarrels, Raymond had accused her of being "devoid of an imagination."

Christine rose for more coffee and stopped at her new computer. Tomorrow she'd be meeting with representatives of a tech company to discuss the possibility of shifting her magazine *MindGames* to the internet. "Online journals are the future," they'd insisted. "Game players tend to embrace new technologies." That made sense—and stepping into the future required an imagination, didn't it? She sat at the computer and turned it on, and it glowed with life. She had a message. She cupped the mouse, slid the cursor up the screen, and clicked. The sender was "Raymond." The subject was "stuff."

Christine smirked and shook her head. She'd left off reading the paper to escape her ex-husband, but here he was. What was "stuff"? Carl was getting more acting offers, she knew, mostly for silly movies meant to capitalize on his sudden fame. The advice from her son's agent, Bronwyn O'Savage, another of Raymond's connections, had been "strike while the iron is hot—it's rare for child performers to sustain a career beyond a few years." But Raymond had resisted the quick money. "Carl is special," he'd argued. "He's no Disney-boy. He's got depth." *Depth*—her ex's new mantra. After a career built on monster movies, it was hard to believe an indie like *Teddy* was more than a one shot deal. And what if the boy got busy? What if father and son were working on different films? Wouldn't Carl require an on-set parent chaperone? If Raymond couldn't be with their son, what would be expected of her? *MindGames* was her baby and was on the cusp of a huge transformation. When had she agreed to sacrifice her own career for a child's? Christine clicked on the message. It was from Carl, who was apparently using his father's account.

hello-hello, mom!
sorry for no capital letters and bad punctuation and bad spelling. dad says that's how email should be. it's supposed to be FAST—capital letters are for EMPHASIS. we're in Frisco (dad calls it). last stop on the tour. saw the bridge, rode a trolley, ate lobster (watched dad eat lobster, actually. it looked like he was eating a pet. remember Elvis?) people recognize me here. i get called teddy on the street its confusing sometimes, but a hot good feeling pushes into my head and body when it happens and i like that.

dad says we'll be home in to days. how's Klaus? is he winning in Zurich? chess news is hard to find on the rode. i'm losing my game—nobody to play with. there's a movie—

A movie. Christine's face flushed. Here came the requests. She scrolled down.

it's about Jesus when he was my age. i think it would be interesting, but it would mean no school after xmas for a couple of months or so. dad says i'll have a teacher. it's in FRENCH. i would have to speak FRENCH! dad says they would teach me how to say the words. i might FEEL them, but i might not KNOW what they mean. sounds weird but i think i understand. it's by jen-pol something who dad says is famous he says we'll all have to sit down and have a BIG POW-WOW about it. maybe klaus will be in france for a big match or something. maybe you'll want to take a vacation.

And there was the expected imposition. A vacation? Who had time for a vacation?

nobody knows about those years (about jesus when he was my age). their sort of missing. dad says i should read the bible. it's funny not using capitals—punctuation is harder to not use it makes me feel like im talking while im falling asleep and language is disappearing
got to go
see you in soon
LOVE AND KISSES CARL

A blank screen. Cursor blinking. Christine was lost in thought. When they were first married, Raymond had tried to explain a world he claimed lay just beyond her reach. This world was in books she *had* to read and in movies she *had* to see. The hint of this world had drawn her to Raymond when they were in college—had lit him up in her eyes, as if he was an advertisement for what the future of adults was all about. But it was a place she'd never caught a glimpse of, and as her husband began a career making silly horror films, it was somewhere she no longer cared to visit. And it wasn't at all for adults.

But Raymond persisted. He'd snort with merriment over the Sunday comics, lean across the sofa, and stick them under her chin. Her eyes darted from panel to panel. What did Raymond want her to see? What signaled irony, and why was it valuable? What was its point? Christine believed in her own intelligence. She'd graduated with honors, and Raymond hadn't. But how did things add up to funny?

Long ago, on their honeymoon in the mountains, Christine's new wedding band had slipped from her finger on the lake's beach. Before she'd noticed it was missing, Raymond had stooped and plucked it from the sand just a few feet from the water's edge. How had he caught the tiny glint?

"It was in a footprint," he said, and blew the sand off the ring. He held the band out to her, pinched between his thumb and forefinger, as if it was a clover, and he wanted his new wife to count its leaves. His gesture seemed to re-enact their wedding ceremony.

"It must have slipped off," he said. "Maybe we should have it re-sized."

Christine yanked her hand away, as if to slow things down, to give herself, this time, a moment to think it over. Raymond reached over, took her wrist, and slipped the ring back on her finger.

"A footprint," Raymond repeated. "Like the one Robinson Crusoe found when he discovered he wasn't alone on his island. Then he met Friday." Carl kissed Christine's forehead, which she offered with a bow. She was looking at sand when she felt his lips. "I'll call you 'Friday,'" he said, "even though today is Wednesday."

Had there been a choice? Of course she must have still loved him then. But she didn't like nicknames, didn't really understand where this one had come from, and "Friday" never stuck.

Christine nudged the mouse, and the screen brightened. *LOVE AND KISSES CARL*: the message read like it was being shouted. She guided the cursor past *reply* to *save*. She clicked, and the words from her newly famous son whisked away. She'd think of an appropriate response eventually. Coffee—wasn't that why she'd risen from the Sunday papers? She'd fill her mug, settle back on the couch, read, and wait for Klaus's call from Switzerland. After, she'd review the galleys of *MindGames'* next issue and make notes for the morning meeting with the tech people. And groceries: she'd type and print a list on this new computer. She'd make a template she could use week after week. For some reason, she thought of Bronwyn O'Savage, who reminded her of a younger version of herself. They were in the same Pilates class, and the instructor occasionally mixed up their names. Carl's agent was clear-sighted and organized. Her agency specialized in child performers, but Bronwyn was not the motherly type. She was all business, and she kept her children neatly compartmentalized—by age, by ethnicity, by handicap—but "handicap" was no longer the word. What was it, "challenged"? Organized by challenges.

Life, like most seemingly complex equations, could and should be simplified. Christine poured coffee into the mug Carl had given her for Mother's Day. "WORLD'S BEST MOM" was printed across it in caps. And if simplicity wasn't truth, she concluded, why value it?

Chapter 5—The Dry Boys—Paris, 1995

In Jean-Paul's film Carl played a juvenile Christ, and the young Jesus's Parisian tenement overlooked a black-topped schoolyard where adolescent Buddha and Mohammed played soccer without him every afternoon. But the tenement, the black-topped schoolyard, the soccer playing existed only in the filmmaker's imagination; in reality, the cast and crew were squeezed into a hotel suite. The furniture had been pushed against the walls to accommodate lights, cameras, and sound equipment. Two cameras focused on Carl as he sat on a metal radiator cover and gazed out the eighth-floor window, supposedly at the other holy boys playing soccer—"football," Jean-Paul called it. Carl strained to emote over what he didn't see—he stared at the late afternoon traffic clogging the rain-slicked avenue.

"You must look mournful, Carl," Jean-Paul insisted. "Mournful, but exultant. Your isolation is both your burden and your triumph. I don't see it in your eyes. Do you see it in his eyes, anyone?"

No one answered, not any of the film crew, or even Carl's father, who sat in a corner making notes in a paperback copy of *Crime and Punishment*. Giggles trickled from the adjoining room, Jean-Paul's bedroom, where Ernest and Philippe—Mohammed and Buddha—played games while they waited for their scenes to be shot. It had been raining for a week.

"When the rain stops, we will do the football," Jean-Paul told the two teenagers each morning before shutting them in the bedroom. "Now, you are the dry boys." Which was a joke, although Jean-Paul never smiled, because the working title of the film was *Les Garcons Seches*—"The Dry Boys." Carl didn't know whether or not Jesus was considered one of the dry boys. He didn't speak French, and the title's translation hadn't been explained to him. Now it would be awkward to ask.

Everyone involved in the film was lodged on the eighth floor of the hotel. After ten days, Carl had seen nothing of Paris. Not a single frame had been shot outside of Jean-Paul's suite. Meals were brought in. At night Carl returned to the room he shared with his father and watched French television—soccer, plotless movies, and incomprehensible interview shows—while Raymond pored over his Dostoevsky novel and jotted down ideas on a yellow legal pad.

"I don't get what Jean-Paul's doing," Carl complained one evening after another unsuccessful round of filming. On the television two scruffy intellectuals droned on and on, their voices hoarse from cigarette smoke Carl swore leaked from the TV and filled their hotel room. "I don't know what he wants."

Raymond marked his page and blinked at his son. "It's because you don't understand French," he said. "Jean-Paul should be tutoring you instead of having you memorize everything phonetically. He *tells* you what to feel, and there's a disconnect between the sounds coming out of your mouth and what's in your head."

"He says that's how prayers work. But to me it's just blah-blah-blah," Carl said. "And it's not just that I don't understand the language. It's the movie. I don't get it. Shouldn't I at least *get* it? Am I one of the "dry boys"? And why is whatever that means a secret?"

Raymond shrugged. "We all work differently. I like everything scripted with a storyboard: a beginning, middle, and an end. No improvisations. That's why I've always finished projects under budget, even a blockbuster like *Kong's Daughter*. That's how we did *Teddy*, remember? If I hadn't given Mr. Salinger a detailed screenplay right off, he'd never have approved it. But Jean-Paul seems to work more spontaneously."

"He calls Mr. Salinger 'the old Jew.'"

"I'm not sure Salinger's Jewish. Maybe half. The French are pretty anti-Semitic. Mr. Salinger fought in World War II, like your grandpa, but here in Europe instead of in the Pacific. A lot of the French were happy but resentful when they were liberated. People get that way when they're saved." Raymond smiled. "You're little Jesus, you should know all about saving. Some of the French hated Jews as much as the Nazis did. I would have thought somebody of Jean-Paul's generation would be over that. Sometimes there's a lingering cultural ethos, I guess. There—that's the history lesson you were supposed to get— when we filmed *Teddy*, you were required to have a tutor. But this is France. I'll have to do. Oo-lah-lah."

"Oo-lah-lah," Carl sighed. "Mrs. Abernathy smelled like cabbage dipped in vanilla perfume. She made me read Jane Austen and Dickens."

"Elizabeth Bennett and Emma and Oliver Twist and Fagin and Pip—getting to know them would be good for any kid. You're right about Jean-Paul, though. I'm not sure he's handling us right. We're something of a sensation, you know. The papers here are writing about us. *Kong's*

Daughter was huge in France, and *Teddy* got critical attention, just like back home. I've heard that paparazzi disguised as hotel staff have been trying to sneak up to our floor. They're calling this hotel the Bastille. Like we're in prison. We're due for a storming. That's the French Revolution."

"I know—'liberty, equality, fraternity.' I knew that."

"They're camped down in the lobby. Photographers want a shot of you. That's what they should be making a movie about: *Waiting for Teddy*."

Carl felt pressure behind his eyes, as if his head was swelling. He'd grown accustomed to public attention on his promotional tours for *Teddy* back in the U.S., and he wished he had the freedom to experience his international fame first hand. It might make the dreary filmmaking easier to take. "We need to revolt, Dad."

"Yeah—I think maybe our friend Jean-Paul is jealous."

"Of me?"

"Of both of us. We're huge. But the truth is he doesn't have the budget to use too many locations. And it's cheaper to keep you under wraps—no bodyguards required for his little Christ. He's saving time and money."

"Saving time? We shoot the same thing every day—me looking out the window. We never leave his hotel suite. And he's never satisfied. He's got to pay for the hotel, right? And we just sit around."

"He calls it 'interiorizing.' You're supposed to be an introspective Savior. In some ways his film is getting smaller and smaller." Raymond rubbed his chin. "Maybe it doesn't matter that you don't know the language. Maybe it's better." He made a note on his pad.

Carl picked up a ceramic ashtray from the end table beside his chair. Enameled flower petals decorated its rim. Its bowl was stained ash-gray. "I don't like not knowing what I'm saying."

"Nobody knows what anybody's saying in France. Like those guys—" Raymond nodded toward the men on TV. One rubbed his tired eyes with the heels of his hands while the other gestured with his cigarette. They seemed to be reciting separate monologues.

"Ernest and Philippe speak perfect French," Carl said.

"They *are* French." Raymond laughed. "And your Mohammed is a blond and your Buddha's a freckled redhead. And both are blue-eyed Aryans. I can't figure out if Jean-Paul's making some kind of ironic comment with his casting, or if he simply didn't try very hard. Maybe not trying is his ironic comment. Both kids are famous from French television, as I understand it. And Buddha was also in a vampire movie. They've got national box office appeal. But you're the star. Don't you talk to them? They speak English."

Carl spun the ashtray on the table, then squashed it under his palm. "They're not nice to me. They stick together, and I think they make jokes about me in French." The trip to Paris had been nasty and claustrophobic, not the "once in a lifetime" experience he'd been promised. It wouldn't have been difficult to let himself cry. He dropped his gaze to the ashtray. He felt his father's eyes gnawing at his face.

"How about we order room service?" Raymond asked. "*Carte blanche*—anything you want. See—that's how you learn French. Those kids are overcome with envy. It's their national emotion. American stars like you shine the brightest, everyone knows that. Christ, you know what I feel like doing? I feel like smoking. Let's smoke. Everybody here smokes. Let's get French. There's no such thing as being underage. Just don't tell your mother. Maybe the secret to speaking French is in the smoke." Raymond picked up the telephone and covered the mouthpiece. "How about cigarettes and ice cream? French vanilla. And something to drink. Orange soda? It'll be an international sugar-shock festival. We'll turn off the TV and I'll describe the characters in *Crime and Punishment*. You think French is tough, wait until you hear these names. Try Raskolnikov—try Svidrigaylov. I'll tell you about the screenplay I'm working up, then you'll tell me about *Great Expectations*. That's the one with Pip and the crazy lady in the wedding dress, right? You know what? Tomorrow I'll demand that you and I be allowed to sneak out into the streets for some sightseeing after you're done shooting. Maybe Jean-Paul will set us free if we go incognito."

"You're watching the other boys play football," Jean-Paul explained. The lights were rigged behind Carl to capture the side of his face, the gray world through the window, and his reflection in the glass. "Now say your line. It's your thoughts. There will be a close up of your lips later. Speak."

"*Zhu-zhu, zhu-zhu-zhu, zhu-zhu.*" Carl spat the words out as if they were cherry pits. Smoking with his dad the previous evening hadn't helped him grasp the language. His mouth and eyes were dry, and he felt feverish. He hadn't slept—he'd imagined black birds, hundreds, filling his room. They were still and silent, but he'd felt their collective mass. And the smoking had turned his ice cream into flavorless lumps, reminding him of the past-prime ice cream of Salinger's that had made him sick. Back before he was famous. Carl's stomach ached as he listened to the French director's instructions, which sounded like menu choices in a foreign restaurant.

"*Coupe*! Enough for now," Jean-Paul growled, and when Carl turned away from the window he caught a blinding glare before the lights were extinguished. "Go play with the other boys," the director said.

Carl would rather have kept sitting at the window. It was quiet now in Jean-Paul's bedroom where the "dry boys" waited, but an hour earlier there'd been loud laughter, and Jean-Paul had pounded on the door shouting "*See-lans*!" Carl imagined his co-stars, red-faced and cross-eyed on the other side, holding their breath and their titters. He was certain the boys had cracked the door open to watch him work. When he stood for the first time in hours, the bare skin on the back of his thighs stuck to the radiator cover. He slunk toward the bedroom where the dry boys hid.

The pair lay on Jean-Paul's king-sized bed, a deck of playing cards scattered between them. They greeted Carl with puckered smiles that looked like kisses and winked at him with pale blue eyes. Ernest-Mohammed batted long black lashes. When would it be their turn to act, Carl wondered. Were they only in the rain-delayed soccer scenes? Neither of them had an adult chaperone. Maybe their parents worked. Maybe they were orphans. Something had to explain why they were locked up all day in Jean-Paul's bedroom.

Carl cleared his throat. Maybe smoking one time had permanently roughened the voice one reviewer of *Teddy* had called "sweet as truth." The French boys sprawled in front of him probably smoked. While he'd been trapped at the window, Carl thought he'd felt his own body maturing—hair sprouting on his upper lip and chin and curlicuing under his arms and over his balls. But when he'd touched his face and snuck a quick hand up his shorts when he thought no one was looking, he was as smooth as ever. A vision of Kiriwina Island flashed before his eyes—of the twins on the beach, tugging at him, riding him, of the ocean, his kicking legs, saltwater filling his mouth and nose.

"*Ferme-la porte*—shut the door, *mon petit*," Philippe-Buddha rasped out of the corner of his mouth. "*Vite*- hurry up."

Carl bumped the door shut with his shoulder. "What's 'moo-ton,' he squeaked, hoping to deflect the teens' scrutiny with a question.

Jean-Paul had called him a '*moo-ton*' as he'd risen from his seat at the window.

"This," Philippe hissed. He poked the head of his penis out of his shorts. He flicked the plump nub with his finger, giggled, and tucked himself back. Carl averted his eyes. His cheeks burned.

Ernest ignored his partner. "'*Mouton* is sheep, Teedy," he said with mock sincerity, and flashed worried eyes. "Did someone call you a sheep? Jean-Paul said that?"

"Baa!" Philippe rolled onto his back. "Baa! That means you are a very bad actor."

Carl tried to grin. "He might have said something else. I'm not too good at French." What troubled Carl was that he'd *got* the holiness of Salinger's Teddy. But being Jean-Paul's Jesus left him feeling foolish.

"*Mouton*! Baa-baa-baa!" Philippe bleated at the ceiling, flapping his arms and legs as if he were making a snow angel in the sheets.

"Jean-Paul should have called you '*agneau*'—'lamb,'" Ernest said with false comfort. "Jesus was the lamb, right? *Mouton* is not such a nice thing to say. It means you're dumb." He smoothed back his platinum hair, sat up straight, and patted the edge of the bed. "Sit. Sit here by me, *mon petit*."'

Carl swayed forward, but his feet didn't move. He felt faint and wished his father were with him. True to the plan they'd hatched the previous evening, Raymond had announced to Jean-Paul before the morning shoot began that father and son would be leaving the hotel "to explore" after shooting ended for the day.

"You go yourself, right now. The boy is safe with us," Jean-Paul had insisted, shooing Raymond off with a backhand wave. "I think maybe you distract him."

Raymond had caught his son's eye and arched an eyebrow, seeking permission. "What do you say, buddy? I'd like to see some museums, and they might be closed later. What about it, Son of Kong— *Fil de Kong*. Can you handle some independence? Liberte, Egalite, Fraternite, right?"

Carl had bowed, thinking *No-no-no, please don't abandon me*. He'd frowned at his father. "Get me a postcard of the *Mona Lisa*, he said. "For Mom."

"Ah, *la Giaconda*," Jean-Paul had murmured, turning his back from the Walchuks to supervise his lighting crew.

"If I get to the Louvre." Raymond squeezed Carl's shoulder, pivoted, and left.

The eyes of the boys on the bed danced over Carl. It was silent out in the room where he'd been filming. His last line, what had it been—"*Zhu-zhu, zhu-zhu-zhu, zhu-zhu.*" Would Ernest and Philippe make fun of him if he asked for a translation? They were panting at him like dogs. Philippe sat up and crossed his legs in his nest of sheets and cards. He gripped his knees. A frightening Buddha. But the Buddha hadn't been the Buddha when he was a kid, had he? Had Mohammed been Mohammed? Carl was fairly sure that Jesus had always been Jesus.

"Teedy. Come over here, Teedy." Philippe wagged a finger at Carl. "Show me your teeties, Teedy." The redhead pinched his own nipples through his striped rugby shirt and wiggled his elbows. "*Teedy est une singe d'or,*" he screeched.

Carl wiped his nose with his shoulder.

"Philippe says you're a golden monkey," Ernest translated. "We liked your daddy's *Kong's Daughter*. We had Kika monkey dolls in France. But they were made cheap. They leaked their insides."

Philippe stuck out his lower lip, spread his arms and rocked from side to side. "*Maintenant, je suis un singe-mouton d'or, comme Teedy. Baa-eee-eee!*" he squealed.

"He says he's a golden monkey-sheep. Like you," Ernest said with a laugh. Carl hadn't pissed all day, but he was afraid these boys would somehow try to stop him before he got to the en suite bathroom. If he could get in its open door, he'd slam it shut and lock it and wouldn't come out until he heard his father's voice. If they ganged up on him out here in the bedroom, he'd wet himself. What would a monkey-sheep look like? He pictured a sheep with a simian, almost human face, and he nearly blacked out. A freak of nature! Like the chicken-woman from *Freaks*! If he were safe in the bathroom and looked in the mirror, would he see his face peering out of the filthy wool of an unsheared sheep? He scanned the bedroom, avoiding eye contact with Ernest and Philippe—maybe Jean-Paul had hidden a camera somewhere—maybe this was the climactic scene of his film. If he concentrated, could he make himself disappear? Could he will himself out of existence? But, even as he strained to shut them, his eyes opened wider.

"He sees a ghost," Philippe said. "He sees the ghost of Teedy."

As Teddy, Carl had felt transcendent—now, he felt empty, alone, and afraid.

"Teedy—" Ernest squinted at Carl. "Do you have a girlfriend?"

Carl shook his head.

"Did you ever kiss a girl?" Ernest asked. Behind him on the bed Philippe made smooching noises.

A cold shudder ran through Carl. "On the island," he murmured, "Kiriwina Island where my dad made *Kong's Daughter*, there were twins. Little girls. I was little, too. We—they touched me a lot. They kissed me, I think," Carl confessed, not sure if what he said was true or not, but desperate to deflect Ernest's interrogation.

"Island girls!" Ernest's pale eyes widened. He winked at Philippe. "Naked island girls, *comme* Gaugin, *n'est-ce pas?*"

"Gaugin?" Philippe grunted with a furrowing brow.

Ernest rolled his eyes at his companion. "*L'artiste*. Gaugin—he lived on Tahiti and painted naked girls."

Philippe shrugged.

"Mouton," Ernest muttered, shaking his head and turning back to Carl.

"Maybe you would like to be *my* girlfriend, Teedy?" Ernest patted the bed again and wagged his head for Carl to approach. "Or—I can be *your* girlfriend. Come here and I will give you a kiss." Philippe rocked back and forth in the middle of the bed, giggling deep in his throat.

Carl smelled something briny. Had he pissed himself? He looked at his crotch—his shorts appeared dry. Kiriwina Island. Could he tell these boys about how he nearly drowned, about how the old half man had lifted him from the sea? Would they find it an exciting story? Would it be enough to save him now?

Ernest rose from the bed and stepped up to Carl. The French teen stood nearly a head taller. His knee bumped Carl's thigh. "You're Jesus," Ernest whispered. "I'll taste you like a wafer, you see? The wafer is your body, yes? You pass yourself to me with your lips. Breathe like you're swimming. Do you like swimming?" He stooped slightly so that his head was level with Carl's. His breath smelled like peanut butter. Carl closed his eyes. He felt like he was melting.

His eyes popped open at the sudden pain—his chest. Ernest's lips were inches from his face, and the French boy was twisting Carl's nipples through his T-shirt as if they were dials on an old-fashioned radio. Carl shrieked and grabbed Ernest's wrists. They were thick and strong, and Ernest kept twisting.

A new voice boomed: "*Kwa-kwa-kwa?*" and Ernest's hands dropped. Someone had entered the room behind Carl's back. Ernest stepped away, his lips brushing Carl's ear. "Kiss-kiss," he whispered. Carl rubbed his burning nipples. Through his tears, he saw Philippe's freckles swimming on his face—he was nodding at something Ernest was saying to whoever stood behind him.

"Teedy asked us to teach him how to cry. It's a trick we use for sad scenes," Ernest explained over Carl's shoulder. Carl finally turned, wiping away his tears with his wrist. Two men stood in the doorway—Jean-Paul and another man with a froth of white hair and sunglasses. This strange looking man wore a trench coat, its shoulders darkened by rain. He spoke to Carl.

"You okay, kiddo?" The voice belonged to Carl's dad. The film crew had gathered behind him, admiring Raymond's disguise. When he took off his wig and sunglasses, Philippe snorted. "I'm incognito," Raymond said. "Nobody figured me out. No paparazzi, even when I took the glasses off in the Louvre. I got you that *Mona Lisa* postcard for your mother. You're sure you're okay?"

Carl nodded.

"Remind me to tell you about this artist I saw—Balthus," Raymond said.

"Balthus" Carl repeated. The name tasted like a bar of soap in his dry mouth.

"Ah, Balthasar Klossowski de Rola," Jean-Paul smiled, bending toward Carl to examine his tear-streaked face. "They are probably afraid of him in America. He steals innocence with the eyes of a voyeur. Some say he was mad."

"I get that." Raymond laid the hand holding his wig and glasses on Carl's shoulder and clapped the French director on the back with the other. "Those little girls in all his paintings, yes. Can we talk about those sometime, Jean-Paul?"

"*Oui*, later." Jean-Paul framed a headshot of Carl with his thumbs and forefingers. "*Mon enfant*," he whispered, "I think a good time to film would be right now. Come back to your window, *s'il vous plait.*"

Carl exhaled. When had he last taken a breath? He still had to pee, worse than ever. Sitting on the radiator cover would have been impossible if he didn't.

"Tomorrow we'll let you go out with Papa," Jean-Paul smiled. Without taking his eyes off Carl, he backed past Raymond out the bedroom door. "You'll go see the Eiffel Tower and Notre Dame. We'll make you into somebody else, too. Somebody nobody will know."

Chapter 6 "I'm a Bell"

There'd been nothing extraordinary about the way Bronwyn had found the right girl for Raymond's film. There were plenty of little girls in the files that matched his requirements, and she doubted that there'd be a need for an open call. As organized as Bronwyn was, it had really been her intuition—her knack for finding just the right child for a gig—that had led to her rapid rise to full partner in the Kidz, Limited Agency. In her first year after leaving the studio, she'd placed three in national commercials, two in sitcom pilots, and an unheard of four (playing siblings) in a major theatrical release. That she'd worked with a cast full of children on *Kong's Daughter* had opened the door for her career shift from production to casting, and she'd always be grateful to Raymond for his support. In fact, though his son Carl's starring role in *Teddy* had been a foregone conclusion, he'd allowed Bronwyn to take the credit—"a notch in your belt," he'd called it, and she'd been proud to see "Casting by Kidz, Limited, Bronwyn O'Savage," roll through the credits. The Oscar buzz for Carl's performance, though it never materialized in an actual nomination, had unquestionably burnished her reputation. Raymond and his ex-wife Christine, whom she knew peripherally from one of her exercise classes, had chosen not to follow her advice to hook their child into a Disney contract before he aged out of his cuteness, but the two parents had different reasons: Christine was not a fan of the industry, and Raymond felt both he and the boy had "evolved" toward parallel careers in "classy" independents.

And so Raymond's requirements for his *Svidrigaylov's Dream* project: "I need a little girl," he told Bronwyn over the phone. "Smallish, waifish, who'll look like she's six or seven." It was no secret, of course, that child performers usually were at least three to five years older than the roles they played. Usually, they were small for their age, which caused problems if they experienced growth spurts or changing voices during long filming stints. But Raymond Walchuk's request for a little girl came with a twist: "She has to *look* six or seven, but it has to be the kind of six or seven that's going on thirty."

"You mean precocious?" Bronwyn asked. Precocity had been *de riguer* for child characters in movies since the dawn of the silver screen.

"Not just your typical snotty kid with glasses and a big vocabulary. Not that at all, actually. I'll send you some material to look over that'll maybe give you an idea of what I need."

"Un-hunh. Any other special features? Ethnicity? Challenges?"

"She's Russian," Raymond said, adding without irony, "white Russian, I'd guess—we're talking about a novel published in the mid-nineteenth century. So, before the Russian Revolution. Nothing 'red' about it."

Bronwyn read back her notes, "'White Russian, six or seven going on thirty.' Anything else?" She sat back, tapping her lips with the end of her pen, blinking absently about the room. Her eyes swept over framed posters featuring agency stars: the red-headed freckle-face from the soup commercial, the wheelchair bound kid-rapper, the African twins pretending to play matching cellos in an insurance advertisement. Her gaze paused on Carl Walchuk—the *Teddy* poster. The boy's face hung in the center like a moon, his eyes coal black, his smile not quite a smile. She read the names at the bottom of the poster: Salinger, Walchuk, then Walchuk again. *I'm looking at your name, I'm looking at your boy*, she thought of telling Raymond, but that would have sounded too fanciful, almost romantic, and, though they'd become close during the filming of *Kong's Daughter*, though they'd even dated a few times and had been written up as a Hollywood couple, they'd only slept together once, after the wrap of *Kong's Daughter*, and she'd been too drunk to remember much about the episode. Bronwyn had resisted the pursuit of that kind of relationship, not so much because of the gap in their ages, but because of something she couldn't quite put her finger on. Something about Raymond's ambitions she'd never quite trusted. There were no posters of *Kong's Daughter* in her office or anywhere else in the agency. Kidz, Limited hadn't cast it, and though the big ape was a child, a "special," Kika wasn't real.

Bronwyn broke her stare-down with young Carl Walchuk's image, and her gaze slid off the *Teddy* poster. But all the children on her walls kept watching her. Like they seemed to every day. Waiting.

"It's a big role," Raymond said. "Central. A ton of screen time. But the character doesn't speak. She has a few—there are a few 'incarnations.'"

"'Six going on thirty,'" Bronwyn repeated.

"Exactly," Raymond said. "I'll send a messenger over with that background stuff. It should give you a pretty good idea of what I'm after."

* * *

The "stuff" came in a large manila envelope marked "Svidrigaylov's Dream" and consisted of an art book and a few pages photocopied from a novel—Dostoevsky's *Crime and Punishment*. Bronwyn spent little time considering either. The art book featured the work of someone she'd never heard of: a painter named Balthus. The painting on the cover was unsettling: an unsmiling woman sat on a chair, holding an unsmiling girl— naked from the waist down— across her lap as if the child was a guitar. In fact, "Guitar Lesson" was the painting's title. Bronwyn riffled through the pages of the art book, a knot growing in her stomach. If these prints were jokes, they weren't funny—so many unsmiling nude or partially clothed girls posing in awkward positions. Spread across chairs and beds, leaning on tables. In some of the pictures older men stood in the foreground or background wearing robes or long coats. But the eye was always drawn to the sexualized child. Bronwyn shuddered and flipped back to the introduction, looking for an explanation, a rationale, a thesis, and caught phrases like "disquieting narrative scenes" before settling on the editor's conclusion: "Skirting avant-garde movements such as Surrealism, he appropriated the techniques of such antecedents as Piero della Francesca and Gustave Courbet to depict the physical and psychic struggle of adolescence."

Bronwyn snapped the book shut and tossed it on her desk, then covered it with the envelope it had come in. *This is not real*, she thought, an assessment and a deflection. But the air around her desk seemed stained—both with an odor and a color that made her dizzy. She remembered a sheaf of photocopied images she'd received not so long ago from a television producer— pages of actual morgue photographs of unidentified female murder victims. Bronwyn had called the producer. "What do you want me to do with these?" she'd asked. She couldn't remember his exact reply, but the word "ambience" lingered. The crime lab investigation show that resulted had been a huge hit, though Bronwyn had no part in it—she'd handed off the request to an agency that dealt with adult cadavers.

Bronwyn sucked in her cheeks, bit down on the flesh, took a deep nasal breath. This is how shows were made. She didn't bother to look at the passage Raymond sent from *Crime and Punishment*. She'd save it for later. She'd tried and failed to read Dostoevsky's *Notes from Underground* when she was in college and had found the work impenetrable. She would find Raymond his girl: she worked in the entertainment industry, and procurement was her talent. There were plenty of children for any and all roles. Poor Raymond, she thought without sympathy. But she knew whoever she found for the role would consider it the break of a lifetime.

* * *

Bronwyn found Amabel Hadley's headshot in the slush pile of entries for the agency's annual contest. Not a contest, really: a winner would be announced, would make a few appearances around town at charitable events, and the agency would get some positive press. The hundreds of entrants, mostly girls, who entered and lost, would exaggerate their success over the years—as teenagers wouldn't they brag that they "nearly got picked" for a role in a Hollywood production? Bronwyn herself wasn't much more than a decade removed from such self- delusion. She'd wanted to be a dancer, but her breasts swelled too early, and to a disqualifying size. She'd begged for reduction surgery, and her mother had acquiesced, but after recovering from the surgery, her new slimmer self had somehow lost the thrill she'd always held for movement—she'd become irrecoverably awkward and graceless. *I have lost my balance*, she lamented, certain that her body would never be able to adapt to its sudden breastlessness. Had she seen her own "physical and psychic" adolescent failure in the awkward poses of the naked or nearly naked Balthus girls?

Amabel, whose age was given as ten, but was probably older, had been accompanied to Bronwyn's agency by a silver-haired woman who was asked to wait in the outer office while Bronwyn interviewed the child.

"She's my mother, not my grandmother," the child said, first off, after taking a seat across from smiling Bronwyn. The girl's voice was surprisingly husky, considering her small size. "I tell her to dye her hair, but she won't do it." The girl leaned forward on the desk and whispered confidentially, blinking green eyes opened wide with a confusing combination of sophistication and innocence. "They're really old, my parents. Why else would they name me something like Amabel? I believe I was a surprise."

"Amabel is a lovely name," Bronwyn said.

The little girl shrugged narrow shoulders. "'I'm a bell, you're a bell,' she sing-songed. "I get that a lot. And teachers who can't pronounce it the first day of class—'uh-MAH-bull,' one said once. My this-year's gym teacher." She sat back in her chair, looked around the room at the posters. "I'm good at school, except for gym. I have a very good memory. Shouldn't there be a poster for *Kong's Daughter* here? I mean, if this has something to do with a Raymond Walchuk movie? My mom said it did. I still have a Kika doll in my bedroom somewhere. In the closet, I think, buried under a lot of things I don't play with anymore." She stopped looking around the room caught and held Bronwyn's eyes with surprising directness. She seemed about to smile, but didn't. "*Oh-Savage*," she murmured mysteriously, as if testing the feel of Bronwyn's last name in her throat and on her lips. "Don't worry, though—if I meet Raymond Walchuk, I'll tell him I still sleep with my Kika doll every night." Amabel paused, closed her eyes, shook her shoulder length auburn hair. "I don't mind dying my hair. Or straightening it. I'll wear a wig or whatever you want."

Bronwyn considered the child before her. What did Raymond want? Six or seven going on thirty? The size was right, and the attitude. But what was it about the girls in the Balthus paintings he wanted to see? Bronwyn kept the book in the bottom drawer of her desk. Her plan was to have the agency photographer take pictures of the little girl in poses approximating the paintings—not as explicitly suggestive, of course—no nudity or hiked skirts—but just enough to capture the flavor. Bronwyn imagined contorting herself into some of those positions, which, though she'd found them difficult to look at, still sizzled in her mind's eye. Amabel yawned, batted her lashes over her big green eyes, and smiled. And Bronwyn had her epiphany, a hint of which must have been suggested the moment she'd picked up the little girl's head shot: it was all about the eyes. The eyes of the children in the Balthus paintings were gone—either mole-ishly closed or as dead as sharks— eyes without light, hope, life. The adolescent girls Balthus depicted in tortured poses were "AFTER"—that must have been why Raymond had sent the book. But the child he wanted for his film—for *Svidrigaylov's Dream* (she'd finally forced herself to wince her way through the photocopied pages describing a perverted Russian noble's nightmare)—was a child who would represent "BEFORE." And also "WHILE."

"You have very little experience," Bronwyn said.

"I was in my school's *Little Mermaid*. I was Aquata, one of Ariel's sisters. But I was an unofficial understudy for Ariel—I had all her lines memorized—I had everybody's lines and all the songs memorized. I just needed Ariel to get sick, but she didn't."

"No, that's perfect." Bronwyn nodded. She'd send Raymond a set of un-posed photographs of Amabel—candids. She'd take them herself. Bronwyn knew the director would have a hard time rejecting this girl. It would be up to him to put her in whatever positions he felt his film needed. *BEFORE. WHILE.* And Amabel, who was rocking slightly from side to side on her chair, probably singing a little song to herself, was about to begin the fairytale she believed was her dream.

Chapter 7—Svidrigaylov's Dream

"Let's make lemonade," the subject line of the group email from Carl's eighth grade teacher read, and Raymond almost deleted it. Something to do, no doubt, with refreshments for the *Alice in Wonderland* adaptation the boy was in. Then Raymond saw the name Mad Hatter highlighted in the message. The kid playing the part had come down with mono, and they'd decided to have a parent take over the role: *"Let's make the most out of an opportunity for family involvement—let's make lemonade out of our lemon. Any interested parent should reply ASAP."*

Why wouldn't Raymond assume the invitation was meant specifically for him? No other parent had directed a dozen films. *Kong's Daughter*, his re-envisioning of the 1933 sequel to *King Kong*, was still a holiday rental favorite, a near cult classic and the all-time number three grossing "requel." Plus, his boy Carl was Alice's White Rabbit, and Raymond had already directed him: of course everyone knew that J. D. Salinger himself had hand-picked father and son to bring his short story "Teddy" to the screen.

"I'm yours to squeeze," Raymond typed, sticking to the lemonade idea. He signed *"Raymond Walchuk"* and hit SEND.

***

Carl had told his father about the *Alice* show a month earlier when Raymond had picked him up for the weekend.

"I'm the White Rabbit, PK," he said after he slid into the car and tossed his backpack behind him. "We're doing a kind of Hip Hop version. *Alice in Shizzel-land.* I auditioned, and I'm in. Pizza Hut?"

"Of course." Raymond didn't show his surprise about the role—Carl had quit acting for a year, taking a break to have "a normal middle school experience." Truthfully, the demand for the boy had dried up. His last film, French, surreal, and under-publicized, had been a critical and box office flop. Raymond had worried that the experience with those nasty French boys had squelched some of Carl's spirit. Plus, the kid had shed some of his cuteness as he transitioned from childhood to adolescence. He had a fine-haired smudge of a mustache—shouldn't Klaus be teaching him to shave? Or was that still a father's responsibility? And then there were the complications regarding Raymond's career. But it was good to see Carl wetting his thespian toes again.

"Hip Hop?" Raymond said. "Why not? So—what about Alice? What's she look like? A little hotty? Does she drive men wild? Have you fallen in love yet?"

"PK—Dad—" Raymond could almost smell the heat of his son's blush. "This isn't *Lolita*." Raymond's attempt at a contrite frown was really a proud grin. How many ninth-graders would be familiar with such a title? "Dad, when you talk like that about young girls," Carl continued, "I mean, don't you get it? What if somebody heard you? Wasn't that what the lawsuit was all about?"

Raymond sniffed. "That was settled. If they didn't get the gist of the movie, they shouldn't have signed on in the first place." By "they" Raymond meant everyone who'd been involved with *Svidrigaylov's Dream*, from the studio executives who'd pulled the plug on the project midstream to the Hadley family—Amabel, the young actress at the center of the controversy, and her ancient parents who were too old to "get" anything.

"There was a restraining order—" Carl said.

"Which was a total over-reaction to the negative publicity. Which created more negative publicity—the damn thing snowballed. It fed it on itself. Like a snake swallowing its own tail—an ouroboros, right? *Crime and Punishment* is a classic, dammit."

"But you weren't doing the novel, PK."

"One chapter. A key chapter—a character study. That doesn't mean *I'm* the character, does it? Am I still on trial? You want my speech on artistic freedom again? Christ, *you're* doing *Alice in Shizzel-land*, for god's sake."

"You called a child 'my little hooker,' Carl said. "In a national interview."

"Oh, Jesus. I was complimenting her acting. That's what she was playing—a six year old hooker is what Svidrigaylov dreams her into. And Amabel was nearly twelve, not six. She was just short. Svidrigaylov dreams about finding an innocent, starving waif, and he feeds her and puts her to bed, and while he's congratulating himself for his charitable impulse, the little girl turns into a whore. It was a *dream*." And had there ever been eyes like Amabel's? "The film was supposed to explore his psychological state. So save me the criticism. No censorship between true *mensches*, right?" Raymond expected some leeway from his son—

familiarity and forgiveness were his due as the weekend parent. But Carl was pushing back harder than usual. Adolescent rebellion? Not exactly—the boy sounded more like a little parent than a tweenager.

"Svidrigaylov is a pervert, Dad. They couldn't let you finish making that movie. You crossed more than one line. You said, 'He's thinking fucky-fucky' to a little girl. Loud enough for everyone on set to hear."

But that's what was in Svid's mind—in what other way could Raymond have explained the scene? She had to be what Svidrigaylov thought he saw. "How else could I describe to her, what she was supposed to be? Jody Foster was a kid hooker in *Taxi Driver*, and nobody bitched at Scorcese. The Balthus paintings I was using as a motif—those little girls on laps, in beds, in chairs, everywhere—they're in every museum in the world. Lewis Carroll was as bad as Balthus and Svidrigaylov, Mister White Rabbit. And you know what some people say about Salinger."

Carl sighed. "This is making me uncomfortable, Dad. Nobody wants to know about Balthus's painting or Svidrigaylov's dream. No kid, anyway. Did Amabel have to *know* what she was supposed to be in order to do the scene? Couldn't you have gotten her to give the look you wanted without being so specific? You could have said you needed her to look like a sly fox or something. Not 'think fucky-fucky.'"

"'Sly fox.'" Raymond shook his head. "Somebody should make a Balthus movie," he muttered under his breath. He'd been having versions of this conversation with Carl for months. Once opened, the can of worms seemed unsealable. Raymond always ended up feeling slightly guilty—not about the ideas behind his failed Dostoevsky project, but about the impact the very public debacle might have had on his son.

"Are kids still talking about this Svid business at school?"

Carl didn't answer. Of course they were. The disaster that was *Svidrigaylov's Dream* had dominated the entertainment news for half a year. Free publicity for the supposedly-damaged kiddy-star. Amabel had settled with the studio for a tidy sum and secured a multi-million dollar deal with Disney for a series of fairy tale films. And she'd launched a personal clothing, line, "Scaredy Cat." The logo featured a come-hithery pair of green cat's eyes. Just a month ago Raymond had cut a picture out of a teen movie magazine that showed the girl, what, thirteen now? Fourteen? She was rouged, lipsticked, and mascara-ed, decked out in a slinky dress for a red carpet photo-shoot. She looked twice her age and twice as whorish as she would have if *Svidrigaylov's Dream* had made it to the screen. Raymond had stuck that magazine picture on his fridge. It proved a point about something. The picture had somehow disappeared, like Raymond's career. But Carl had a life of his own to live, and, whether what had happened to Raymond was right or wrong, a father's chief responsibility was to protect his child. It was that damned French film that started the trouble—Raymond should have been more attentive to Carl's discomfort during the production.

"Sorry for the mess," Raymond said. "But you're performing again—that's great. Tell me about the girl who's playing Alice. I didn't mean to go overboard."

Carl changed the subject. "Mom is in Atlanta negotiating something. I think she's selling *MindGames*. Klaus is home with me."

"She's selling her baby?"

"My multi-million dollar sibling. She was surprised I auditioned for a school show. Disappointed, maybe. I think she still wants me to be a scientist or something."

"And what about your Alice?"

"She's cool. She's in most of my classes. She's adopted. She was born in one of those poor countries in Africa."

"A black Hip Hop Alice. Good casting. Urban art. Black culture. How many African-American girls in your school?"

"A couple. She's got a good voice. And she's not African-American. She's African. And she's American. But that's not the same as African-American."

"Right. Of course. And her name is?" They'd arrived at Pizza Hut.

"Andrea. Andrea Convenience."

Raymond yanked the parking brake so hard that he and his son pitched forward. He knew that last name. A Convenience had once tried to murder him. *'Jerry Convenience'* — a silly name. Raymond told Carl about him and the murder plot while they ate. "In high school a few of us called him 'Seven' after the 7-11 marts. 'Convenience' stores, get it? He was a big guy who knew a lot about movies, which is why we were friends. He said his last name came from an 'immigrant forbearer' who picked it out of the dictionary because it resembled his old name."

"Why did he want to kill you?"

"Honor, I guess. I snubbed him and this other guy. Or talked trash behind their backs, I forget. Stole a girlfriend, maybe. It's funny—

you think you'd remember what almost got you killed." Raymond scratched his head. He took a bit of pizza, chewed, and swallowed. "The two of them took me for a ride. To the beach."

"You hate the water. We both do. It's your legacy."

"Right. Anyone with intelligence hates it. It's the opposite of land. Or air is, I guess, but water's not solid either, unless it's frozen, and that's something else. But those guys who wanted to kill me didn't know how I felt about the beach. Neither of them had talked to me in over a year, and we'd gone off to different colleges. Then Jerry called me out of the blue to go surfing, of all things. The pair of them looked more like morticians than surfers. Definitely indoor boys—all three of us."

"Why did you go?"

Raymond shrugged. "I didn't have anything else to do. I was curious. I thought maybe they forgot they hated me."

Carl shook his head. "People don't forget things that piss them off."

"Yeah," Raymond said. "I rode in the backseat of Jerry's station wagon, leaning on a purple surfboard that stuck out the hatch like a purple tongue. He must have gone out and bought one just for his plan. Nobody said a word for miles. It got uncomfortable. So I started mocking them."

Carl lifted an eyebrow. He opened his mouth to speak but decided against it.

Raymond noticed. "That's what friends do," he said. "Give and take. You and I do it."

"But I'm not trying to kill you."

Raymond smirked. "You're no mini-Oedipus, not yet anyway. But those guys, I didn't know what they had in mind. And I was good at mocking. 'Seven?' I said, 'you're way less than that. Not even six. Or three or two. You're not even zero. Ever diminishing nothingness. You're King Minus, and your touch creates a void. What you are,' I said, 'is Unfinite. Unfinity from this day hence.' And then I dubbed our other buddy, who was always kind of a curmudgeon, 'Unfunity,' so they'd be a matched pair.

"You said those things to your murderers?"

"Unfinity and Unfunity. Crazy. Let's call me brave. Retroactively."

"But you didn't know yet what they had in mind?"

"Nope. I only figured it out a few years ago. When you get older, you think about your life. And every once in a while you see something in the past you never realized was there. So I started thinking about the time those guys took me surfing, and everything jumped out at me. There was the surfboard—they intended to lure me into the water. And next to the surfboard there was a thick rope—and a burlap bag and a metal pipe. And I think there was an ax."

"An ax?"

"I'm pretty sure I remember an ax." While he described the scene for his son, Raymond pictured it: Jerry's white knuckles gripping the wheel, glances traded between his would-be assassins while they absorbed Raymond's insults. Then he envisioned a purple surfboard dipping and spinning over a dark wave, a rope strung with seaweed, a sinking burlap bag.

"This sounds familiar. It isn't in one of your old movies, is it? *Slasher II*, maybe?" After years of being "too young" to see Raymond's early films, Carl had recently immersed himself in his father's canon and, besides P. P. Frederico, was the closest thing Raymond had to a personal archivist.

"Nah—maybe I told you this before."

"No, I'd remember. What finally happened?"

"They killed me." Raymond smirked. "I'm a dead man. Your daddy's a ghost. Boo. All because of someone named Convenience, like your girlfriend." Raymond looked at the check the waitress had left and slapped his wallet on the table.

"She's not my girlfriend."

"Just a girl who's a friend, I get it. How does she spell her last name?"

"I'm not exactly sure. It starts with a K and ends with a 'wicz." It only sounds like Convenience. So, come on—what happened with your murder?"

"Oh—they chickened out, I guess. It got cloudy. Maybe it started to rain. They took me home, and I never saw them again. Anticlimactic, I suppose. But that doesn't change the blackness of their hearts."

Carl frowned. "And you can't remember why they wanted you dead."

Raymond chuckled. "Unfinity and Unfunity. That's pretty good, right?"

"And 'the blackness of their hearts." Carl shook his head.

Raymond again noticed his boy's mustache. The kid was becoming a man. Didn't Raymond owe him more than a story? "You know, if they don't murder you first, people will drift in and out of your life. You'll forget most of them. Others will leave footprints you can't wash away." Carl was silent. He studied his father's face with such intensity Raymond could almost feel the boy's gaze. "You're making those Teddy-eyes," Raymond said. "I haven't seen that look for a while. So—has Klaus talked to you about shaving?"

* * *

Raymond, ever hopeful of an offer to work, answered the phone call that interrupted the final round of *The Price is Right*. It was Ms. Klein, Carl's teacher and the director of *Alice in Shizzel-land*.

"This is about the play, Mr. Walchuk. You replied to the message regarding our need for a Mad Hatter. By the way, Carl is doing beautifully."

Beautifully? Did she mean his son's acting? She must have known that Carl was a professional—that he'd been famous. Or was the teacher suggesting that there was something else the boy had been struggling with and was in the process of overcoming? But—what about the Mad Hatter?

"The part is still open?" Raymond asked.

Ms. Klein hesitated. "Ye-ess." Auditions are tomorrow at 3:30. But we're not just looking for talent, Mr. Walchuk. We want to be sure the children are . . . *comfortable* with the parent that's chosen."

"I understand," Raymond said. "Nothing's guaranteed."

"Mr. Walchuk—you need to know, as someone experienced in dramatic presentations, that we're taking our production very seriously." Was she paying homage? Why wouldn't she?

"You mean you're preparing seriously," he said. "But the play's fun, isn't it? It's a little girl's fantasy. She's Alice, after all. Fun and Hip Hop. Fun in Shizzel-land."

"The theme of the show emerges through Alice's fantasy, yes. But some of the most dangerous human impulses could be said to begin with the fantastic. Our play deals with many challenging ideas. When it was originally performed on Broadway, one critic wrote it "kept a finger on the pulse of contemporary culture.' That's what it says in the play's production notes, prepared by the American Education

Council and sanctioned by the playwright herself. These notes inform us on the ways the play touches on important historical events."

"I thought *Alice in Wonderland* was mostly just a psychedelic dream," Raymond said. "Maybe a little about a child's loss of innocence. Sometimes a fantasy is just a fantasy. You're sure you're not overthinking this?"

"I haven't read *Alice in Wonderland*, Mr. Walchuk. We try to avoid an unbalanced curriculum here—too many dead white males dominated literary studies for far too long. *Alice in Shizzel-land* is more than just a fairy tale. It's won awards. It's *educational*. We've held bake sales for a year to pay for the production rights. This is an "all school" project: instruction in our classes is linked to the play's themes. English, History, even Math. No, I don't think we're 'over-thinking' anything. I assume you reviewed the Family Awareness Agreement Carl brought home. He returned it with your signature."

Raymond didn't recall signing any "Agreements." Had Carl forged his name? But he wouldn't throw his boy under the bus. "I skimmed it, sure."

"All right, then. You understand how we're approaching this. As I said, auditions for the part of Mad Hatter are at 3:30. Please be prompt."

***

Raymond lay back in his recliner, half-watching television, reviewing his career, waiting for phone calls. He was hungry and thought about popping a few burritos into the microwave, but the handle on his chair was broken, and to sit up he'd need the kind of strength he wasn't in the mood to exert. He pictured himself gripped in the giant hand of Kika, Kong's daughter—thought of the climactic scene where the great ape had held the sinking raft full of orphans aloft on the sinking molehill of Kong's Island while the sea raged around them: the ape knee deep, neck deep, then her head under. Only her arm stuck out of the water, her huge hand holding the raft full of screaming orphans aloft like it was the Statue of Liberty's torch. And finally the hero and heroine hook the raft with their helicopter, and Kika disappears below the waves. Maybe she's swimming to another island is the note of hope at the end of the film, leaving an opening for a sequel to the sequel. Raymond had circulated treatments, let it be known that he was ready and willing to return to projects less arty than his recent failure. A plastic-wrapped Kika doll sat on top of his television—maybe that's why his thoughts had drifted toward *Kong's Daughter.* Little golden gorillas surrounded him, his constant companions. Tonight, Kika's grin looked sinister. Raymond squirmed in his seat. Like just about every night, he wouldn't get up until he had to piss. He reached for his telephone and called Carl at his mother's.

"So what do you know—do I have any competition?"

"Dad, did you say something stupid to Ms. Klein? Today at rehearsal she kept looking at me, even when I wasn't on stage. In class, too."

"Some people are just star-struck. I thought you were used to that."

"No—it's not that. She looked worried about something."

"She and I just had a nice chat this morning, that's all. We talked about the play, and about what's going on in school. What're you reading in English now?"

"*The Diary of Ann Frank.*"

"Ms. Klein's pretty serious."

"I think she's going to become principal next year. Somebody said that."

"Wow. So—who else wants to be the Mad Hatter?"

"From what I hear, just Andrea's dad."

"That's the girl playing Alice? The Convenience girl? I'll kick her father's ass."

"It's not a fight, Dad."

"Of course not. Friendly competition." But the Convenience name, no matter how it was spelled, caused Raymond some concern. It was a bad omen, and, after ending the conversation with Carl, he rehashed the details of his near murder.

"Hey, PK!" Carl bounded up the hallway, rabbit ears flouncing. A slender girl skipped up from behind and slid to the boy's side in front of Raymond. Her braids were interwoven with colorful beads. She gazed up at Raymond with a closed-mouth grin that dimpled her cheeks. "This is Andrea," Carl said. "She's Alice."

"Well, Shizzel my dizzel!" Raymond offered his fist for a bump, which Andrea returned. Her lips parted, revealing elaborately wired braces. Was she tall for age, or was Carl short? His son was thirteen— no, fourteen— and still several inches shorter than his father. Would there be a growth spurt to accompany that shadow under his nose? Whiskers sprouted on the boy's chin, too. Or was that rabbit makeup?

Raymond was glad to see that Carl wore his ridiculous costume without any apparent embarrassment. Or fear—didn't the kid's furry jacket and leggings make him look a little like he was turning into a bunny? Had Carl gotten over his "Chicken-Woman" *Freak*-out? Raymond would try to remember to ask. He congratulated himself on being an attentive parent, and wondered if there was a percentage involved—how much should a father or mother be thinking about their child instead of themselves? Was it fifty-fifty? Could that be possible? Could you add the percentage from each parent to get closer to one hundred percent?

"This is Papa Kong," Carl said. Andrea closed her eyes and dipped a straight-backed bow, and Carl bowed beside her; they see-sawed, up and down, until they dissolved into giggles. Alice wore a pink T-shirt with a Scaredy Cat logo on the shoulder—Amabel Hadley's label. "This way," Carl waved, and Raymond followed the bounce of his son's pom-pom tail into the auditorium.

The play's set—a stylized cityscape—was more elaborate than Raymond had imagined for a middle school production. The storefronts, windows, and lampposts glowed luridly among threatening shadows. The effect was sophisticated—simultaneously open and claustrophobic—Shizzel-land as an idealized ghetto. Kids were scattered about the auditorium, a few in folding chairs with notebooks and texts, several on stage, adding details to the scenery. Overlapping yellow triangles being painted on a storefront window suggested a Star of David. In the aisle, a group of kids dressed in red baseball caps, baggy pants that clung to their hips, and gold chains, stomped and clapped in unison. A black heart was emblazoned on the caps and on the armbands worn by each dancer. Were they some kind of Ghetto Gestapo? Carl and Andrea dashed backstage to find Ms. Klein.

The instant the kids disappeared, a side door opened, and a thirty-something-ish woman with an untamable mass of dark hair entered the auditorium, followed by a man in a sports jacket and tie. When she saw Raymond standing alone in the center aisle, the woman glanced about, as if to account for all the lambs in her flock, then hurried forward with an extended hand.

"Mr. Walchuk? Dana Klein. And this is Mr. Konfeniwicz." As the man shook Raymond's hand, he corrected the teacher's pronunciation.

"Harry *Convenience*," he said.

"Call me Raymond." Harry was fair-haired and much slighter than the Convenience Raymond remembered. The man nodded and smiled, though his blue eyes glinted like polished cutlery.

"Daa-Deee!" Andrea, her grin an explosion of tinsel, hopped from the stage and threw her arms around Papa Harry.

"Puh-recious." Harry Convenience's voice was tired, as if he'd just left some dreary job he was having trouble forgetting. He hugged his daughter and kissed her forehead. Carl reappeared and gazed down from the stage. A large cardboard clock face swung from a chain at his waist. His oversized bunny feet reminded Carl of clown shoes. The mustache appeared darker, as if it had been penciled in.

"The kids are doing such an excellent job," Ms. Klein said. "And what do you think of our set?" She glanced at Raymond, he assumed his expert approval, then turned her attention to the group of Ghetto Stompers who'd gathered around the adults and glared at their director with folded arms.

"Ms. Klein—we need to work on this," a tall girl said.

"In a minute, kids, be patient." She held up a hand. "We'll start the Mad Hatter auditions shortly, gentlemen. I need to work with the dancers first, the numbers with Rabbit and Alice, so we'll have the fathers wait in a practice room." She looked at her wristwatch, then at Raymond and Harry Convenience. "You can rehearse your prepared recitations." Her eyes darted around the auditorium. "But for your song—I'm afraid the piano has been moved to the chorus room—the Cheshire Quartet needs extra work—so you'll have to sing *a cappella* when the time comes."

Both Ms. Klein and Harry Convenience stared at Raymond as if he'd asked a question. He hadn't, but a few big ones were on the tip of his tongue. Recitation? Song? Really? He couldn't admit to being so completely unprepared, but how had such a thing happened?

The tall ghetto dancer, shimmering with smiles and proud to exhibit her costume, escorted the men to an instrumental practice room not much larger than a closet. Inside were three folding chairs, a desk, and a few music stands.

"Good luck," the girl said with a wink, then twirled away with a choreographed step, shutting the door behind her. Raymond took a seat opposite Harry Convenience, who was studying him as if he were a lab specimen.

Raymond, attempting good fellowship, confessed. "Okay, so, the singing—I didn't know about that."

"I believe the requirement was mentioned in the original email," Harry Convenience said. "My wife read it, not me. I do what she tells me. I'm not really the theatrical type, but we like to stay involved in Andrea's life. You know what I mean."

Raymond nodded uncertainly. Did he mean because his daughter was African?

"Mr Walchuk, I'm a great admirer of one of your films."

"Oh. Thank you. Which one?"

"That *Kong's Daughter*. It had everything—adventure, great special effects, and most importantly, strong family values. It taught a good moral lesson." Harry Convenience's face burned bright red. "In fact," he continued, "that little baby Kong doll? That was the first present we gave to Andrea. Right in the airport when we met her for the first time in person. She was eight. She grabbed that doll and hugged it tight and wouldn't let go of it for days." He gave Raymond a disorienting smile-frown. "So I guess you could say you helped my little girl become an American. And a Convenience." He shook his head and looked around at the sound-proofing tiles covering the walls of their room. Was the man nervous about being alone with a show business personality? There was sheet music on one of the music stands, and Raymond remembered that he needed a song. What did he know all the words to? The "National Anthem"? "God Bless America"? Harry Convenience tapped his foot as if he was silently practicing his own song.

"Andrea made us watch that *Teddy* movie," he said. "Because your son is in it. I didn't see much in that one. Lots of talk. Nothing really happens. No moral center. Depressing, really. You boy was cute, though, when he was little."

Wait—this guy was criticizing Raymond's movie—and his son's present degree of cuteness?

"Frankly, I'm only here because you are, Mr. Walchuk." Raymond settled his ruffled feathers—he'd been right about Harry Convenience feeling awkward with someone famous—the man was a fan after all. Feeling an autograph request coming, Raymond patted his pants pocket for a pen and glanced at the desk for paper. He was about to ask who he should address the autograph to when Harry Convenience continued: "My wife and I talked it over. We decided you should be forgiven for all those horrible movies you made before *Kong's Daughter*. They're disgusting, but at least the Devil's work is punished in them—or so we're told. And we understand that you were beginning a career in a difficult industry and might be lured by easy profit. But—we also agree that we wouldn't be comfortable—" he paused so Harry could digest each word, "if you appeared in this play with our daughter. We spoke with many of the other parents, and they agreed, and well, I've been nominated, I guess you'd say. When Andrea told us you were auditioning, we couldn't take the risk there wouldn't be anybody else to pick. I'm here to give Ms. Klein another choice for the Mad Hatter. I'm the one the parents want."

"The parents?"

"Mr. Walchuk why are you here? Is it even legal for you to be around children? Have you registered yourself?"

"Excuse me? Registered?"

"Your status, sir."

Raymond was numb. "I have no status," he said.

"We're not naïve. We watch the news. We know all about that last . . . filth of yours. About your business with that little girl."

"You're talking about my movie?" Raymond asked. "*Svidridgaylov's Dream*?"

"Whatever." The worried father swatted at something invisible. "Some foreign name. Disgusting. And now you want to be here with our children. I saw the look you gave the little girl who brought us here."

Looked at whom? "It's not 'some foreign name.' It's my movie. It's got a name: *Svidrigaylov's Dream*. It's based on *Crime and Punishment* by Dostoevsky. The film explores the innate perversity of certain minds—even as they struggle intellectually to act with moral rectitude." Raymond's words echoed the statement his lawyer had prepared for a settlement meeting.

"Precisely. What kind of mind would choose to make something like that? And have a little girl perform in it? And dress her up, and insist that she act like a little—a little—"

"A little whore, Mr. Convenience. Is that what you're saying? God, man, it's only a movie. And it was never finished." Raymond shook his head. When was this going to be over? Did Carl have to deal with this every day? Raymond corrected himself: "I don't mean '*just* a movie.' What I did—do—is art. And the girl's parents knew what it was all about. They'd read the script."

"But the things you said—we've read them. You can't hide—" Harry Convenience's upper lip lifted with contempt.

"There's a little bit of Svidrigaylov in all of us, Mr. Convenience, whether we admit it or not."

The man nodded. "And that attitude is why we don't want you in *Alice*. When Ms. Klein contacted us about the situation—she's got a daughter of her own, you know—she suggested—" He broke off. Raymond blinked in disbelief. Ms. Klein had instigated Raymond's excommunication? So he'd been screwed from the start.

"Mr. Convenience," Raymond said, "Jerry. How is it that you let your daughter wear Scaredy Cat clothing? You know they're made by child laborers in third world sweat shops. Go fuck yourself, Jerry." *Third world*, Raymond thought. *Did you first worry about your daughter when you saw her weeping flies in a TV commercial?*

"My name is Harry, not Jerry."

"It's Jerry," Raymond said. "Jerry Convenience. Maybe Seven—Seven or Svid." Harry Convenience's eyes narrowed with angry confusion. His lips and nose joined in a snout. This man wanted to kill him, Raymond realized. "Unfinity," Raymond hissed. "You're less than nothing."

A double rap on the door, and the young dancer reentered. "Mr. Walchuk?" she asked. "Follow me."

"Ready." Raymond got to his feet, sliding a smile at Harry Convenience, who sat fuming. This child wasn't afraid of Raymond. Was it a crime to notice her prettiness? Wasn't something beautiful lost to the world if he didn't?

"Lead me to the slaughter," Raymond said.

***

Alone on stage, mindful of the Shizzel-land backdrop, Raymond steeled himself. He was here for his son. And for himself. Fifty-fifty. Ms. Klein's glasses glinted in the last row of the auditorium. "Recitation first, song next," she called. Kids sat in the front few rows, and Carl, with Andrea beside him, smiled from the wings. Harry Convenience's daughter gave Raymond a thumbs up. He cleared his throat.

"Here's a nursery rhyme I used to read to Carl:
There was a little girl,
And she had a little curl,
Right in the middle of her forehead.
And when she was good,
She was very, very good,
And when she was bad,
She was horrid."

Titters rose like moths. Raymond smirked and wagged a finger at no one in particular. "The lesson," he explained, "is to be careful about extremes." Was he being very, very bad? Then he remembered that he still didn't have a song, and a cold knot formed in his belly. Sweat trickled down his temples.

"Froggy," he heard Carl stage-whisper, and he looked at his son, who was nodding in the wings. "Froggy," the boy repeated with urgency, and Raymond had a memory, a flashback so intense it seemed he was reliving it.

In the memory, Carl was four, Christine and Raymond were still together, and the three of them had gone to sit with Raymond's mother at her nursing home. His mom was pretty much lost to dementia, but still tolerated her son's monthly hour of company and occasional pat on the wrist. She sat like a sphinx at a rec-room table in front of a blank television. Carl marched a pair of plastic tigers around and over his grandmother's arm, sing-songing the animals' conversation under his breath. Raymond and Christine watched the minute hand of the wall clock creep toward three o'clock, when they'd surrender the woman to her caretakers. Then another family had burst though the rec-room door, a rollicking band of sons and daughters and grandchildren and cousins. They followed the matriarch they wheeled in as if she were the grand marshal of a parade.

The Walchuks watched the group settle in—the new arrivals tossed smiles from their side of the room, sliced cake and passed it around on brightly colored paper plates, and chattered at the expressionless old woman they'd come to see.

"Sing us a song, Mom," a gravel-voiced woman said, and started one herself, clapping her hands: "Froggy went a courtin', and he did ride, um-hmm, um-hmm . . ."

Before she'd finished the verse, the whole mob had joined in, including the matriarch, who brought her fingertips together a beat behind, but sang on and on, delivering the "um-hmms" as if what little bit of life she had left in her depended on it. Raymond touched one of his mother's hands. He rubbed her knuckles in time to the tune.

On the drive home that afternoon, Raymond told Christine that when the time came for his family to visit him in a nursing home, "Froggy" was the song he wanted to sing. Right in the middle of the San Bernadino Freeway he blurted out the chorus, pounding on the steering wheel until Carl, and finally even Christine, sang along. When his wife asked, "Ray, are you crying?" he'd flipped on the windshield wipers, though it wasn't raining, and sang louder.

Raymond's decade old memory faded and he found himself standing center stage in the auditorium of Carl's middle school.

No other song besides "Froggy Went A Courtin'" would suit Raymond's *Alice in Shizzel-land* audition. As he belted out verse after verse, he pictured the representative of the deadly Convenience gang boiling in his soundproof cell. Raymond was fighting for his right to be the Mad Hatter, his son's Mad Hatter, a Mad Hatter all children could live with "comfortably." Was he a Pied Piper? A goat-footed balloon man? Maybe. But Raymond was certain his heart was right where it belonged. He filled the auditorium with his rendition of the wedding day trials and tribulations of Froggy, Miss Mousie, and Uncle Rat, and Carl and his classmates joined in, at least with the "um-hmms." Raymond sang about how the snake ate the cake and how the cat devoured the bride and her uncle. It amazed him that he could recall so many verses. And in the shadows, he was sure Ms. Klein was at the very least tapping her toe to Raymond's performance. Maybe she would lead the applause after his audience absorbed the final verse—it described the lily-white dove that swooped down from the heavens and gobbled up Froggy himself.

Part II
Jenna Klein

Chapter 8— Smooth

Jenna Klein expected the tattoo parlor to smell like seared flesh and hot tar, but it didn't. It smelled like hand sanitizer, and a little like nail polish remover— probably the ink. It didn't look like anything now because she had her eyes closed. Not everyone did lids. Almost nobody did lids. Laser, the proprietor of *Laser's Tattoos and Piercings* did lids, but Jenna had had to take two buses to get there. And she knew the minute she'd stepped onto the first bus outside her gated community that she'd forgotten her cell phone. She might as well have forgotten one of her senses. But since it had never, ever happened before, leaving her phone behind was a kind of message, wasn't it? Laser said nothing when Jenna told him she was eighteen, though she'd just turned fifteen last month.

"Stars of David," she said. "One on each eyelid." Twenty-five dollars per lid. Duct tape covered rips in the arms of the chair she'd settled into, as if customers had been tearing at them. "Won't you hit my eyeballs? I heard that you slide a spoon under." She shivered, imagining the spoon she'd plunged into her breakfast grapefruit cupping her naked eyeball, its handle pressed into her cheek, her lid stretched spoon-shaped.

"No spoon. I'm careful," Laser said. He was squat, but a big squat, like a giant dwarf. His neck was short, and his head was square. Before she shut her eyes, he'd been fiddling with his inking tool, checking its sharpness on stiff paper. The apparatus worked with a foot pedal, like her grandmother's sewing machine.

"Yeah," she said, "because you don't want me leaking out my vicious fluids." She imagined her cheeks wet with something like egg whites, like thick, sticky tears. "I wish I could watch."

"'Viscous,' not 'vicious.' Should I tape them down? It's hard to do that and tattoo them."

"You don't have to. What will it feel like?"

"Weird," he said. "You'll love it. Stars of David."

"Yeah. Yes," she said, and held her breath. Had Laser noticed her lack of eyelashes? That she had no eyebrows? Did he suspect that she hadn't any pubic hair? That under her hot pink wig her head was as smooth as a beach ball? Could he guess that she was devoted to the spunk and spirit of Amabel Hadley?

"I'm starting" Laser said.

"Okay."

"See you later," someone, a man, called. Jenna didn't remember seeing anyone in the parlor when she got there, and she nearly peeked. Whoever it was must have been in the back—there was a door, wasn't there?

"Later," Laser said. The front entrance jangled when it opened and shut.

There was a hum, and Jenna patted her thigh, but her phone wasn't there. Then her lid was alive with the crawling feet of bees. On Youtube she'd seen a man's face dripping with a live-bee mask. Through the tickling she felt the push and nip of Laser's tool: the first star was being formed. Soon there'd be a Star of David for each wink, double stars when she blinked. Amabel Hadley was Jewish and probably had a bat mitzvah. Jenna was Jewish, too; her divorced parents weren't religious, but she'd been to the bar and bat mitzvahs of relatives. She imagined Amabel Hadley's sweet voice filling the sanctuary as Amabel chanted her Torah portion. Those lucky enough to have been there must have died listening but been reborn as something better—flowers or butterflies. Or stars. Amabel had recorded two CDs, but guitars and synthesizers drowned out her lovely voice.

"Hummm—" Jenna buzzed along with the tattooing.

"Hurts?" The pressure of the tool's point lifted, and the bee dance stopped.

"Un-unh."

"Then shush. Shush unless it hurts."

"I thought you'd use a spoon."

"No spoon," Laser said. The hum resumed. Amabel Hadley was also smooth. Slick as a seal. *Alopecia universalis.* No hair at all—that's the *"universalis"* part—perfect, because it was total. Amabel's total baldness was one in 100,000 shots, which was a sign of her blessedness. The wigs only Jenna and maybe a chosen few knew she wore were made of natural hair, grown by young women hired to be suppliers. Amabel paid them with money from her Scaredy-Cat clothing empire and whatever she'd saved from her albums and the movies she used to make. They lived in a special house, these girls, but nobody knew where it was. Growing their hair long for Amabel was their sole occupation. They were like priestesses. Once their hair was shorn, they were never allowed to grow again; they'd shave themselves totally smooth, out of devotion to their employer. Then they'd move to the upper floors in the special house, which would be in a gated community much like Jenna's own, she imagined. Jenna wished she could give up her hair for Amabel's wigs, but she couldn't; she had alopecia, too. For real.

But Jenna's alopecia wasn't perfect like Amabel's. Jenna's was *"totalis,"* a funny word for "partial." Jenna's hair was patchy, and her mother had shaved her head and fitted her with her first wig before she was five. That first wig had been like a golden helmet, a grandmother's wig. Now Jenna chose her own wigs— shocking pink and purple— and did her shaving herself.

In all the world, only Jenna had guessed that it was Amabel Hadley's hidden alopecia, not her problems with drugs and alcohol, that had kept her out of movies since her late teens. The celebrity's addictions were a front—the truth had to be that she'd grown tired of hiding her baldness. Amabel's disease was probably the most closely guarded secret in show business. Jenna knew the power of this secret, because hairlessness changed the way you saw the world. You learned about hiding and intuiting.

Fifteen was paradise! Fifteen and smooth, and she'd have stars and stars every time she blinked. Jenna had an idea for a tattoo of a pair of baby lips about to take her nipple. Unlike the voluptuous Amabel Hadley, she was flat-chested. Jenna's mother and her Nana were also small-breasted women. But though a tattoo of a pair of baby lips about to take a nipple was a beautiful idea, how would you *do* it? Could you tattoo the indentation in the breast made by the baby's cheek? The tiny lips would be hovering in the air. How did you tattoo the air?

"Unh—"

"Sorry."

Jenna's eyes teared—not from pain, but for Amabel and her secret suffering. She hummed a tune along with the buzz of the tattooing machine, enunciating the lyrics in her head: "Little girl, little-little girl, my Sviddy-pretty kid, such a Sviddy-pretty kid." The words were the chorus to Amabel Hadley's only hit, "Sitting Pretty." Not really a hit, but they played it on the radio. Near the end of the song, spoken, but barely audible, you could hear Amabel sigh: *"I am the little girl of Svidrigaylov's dream."* Jenna might have ignored the line if she hadn't read the song lyrics that came with the CD. First she saw that even though the title of the song was "Sitting Pretty," it was spelled "Sviddy Pretty." Later she'd Google-searched "Svidrigaylov's Dream." It took a long time to find, because she'd had to guess at the spelling a million times. The google search stated:

1. *Svidrigaylov: a Russian noble in Dostoevsky's novel* Crime and Punishment*; Svidrigaylov's moral decay is illustrated by a nightmare in which he rescues an impoverished little girl who transforms into a prostitute before his eyes.*
2. Svidrigaylov's Dream*: a film begun by director Raymond Walchuk (see Kong's Daughter, Teddy); production was terminated over accusations that Walchuk was making "inappropriate sexual innuendoes" to twelve-year-old costar Amabel Hadley (see Switcheroo, Penny Starlight: Girl Astronaut, "Celebrity Rehab," Scaredy Cat Enterprises.) The subsequent scandal, settled out of court, effectively ended Walchuk's career and helped establish Hadley's.*

"First one's done. Need a break?"

"Un-unh." Jenna smelled blood now, faint, through the odors of sanitizer and ink.

"Okay. Keep 'em closed." Tickles and nips on her second lid—Jenna again reached for the phone she'd forgotten.

I am the little girl of Svidrigaylov's dream: that line, the beginning of history, was seared like a beautiful scar into Jenna's brain. Buried deep among thousands of Internet entries, Jenna found a photograph of Amabel Hadley at twelve dressed and made up as a dream prostitute. She'd looked like a sexy kindergartner. The brassy wig Amabel wore was identical to Jenna's childhood wig! (That wig had frightened her classmates. Why else had they avoided her?) The young Amabel's Scaredy Cat eyes, her lids, lashes, lips, cheeks and brows, all painted provocatively, had mesmerized Jenna. Poor Amabel! Had she been bald already? Or had the trauma of playing a prostitute while such a little girl, of suffering the director's inappropriate advances, shocked her system into rejecting her hair? Jenna had studied Amabel's subsequent films; she had poured over celebrity shot after celebrity shot. Everything was a wig, even—maybe especially—when the star's hair looked most natural. Jenna knew, swathed in borrowed hair, Amabel Hadley mourned her stolen childhood.

Late afternoon was the prickliest time for Jenna, and sitting in Laser's warm chair was nearly unbearable—so many hours after she'd risen at five AM to complete her first shaving. Before bed she would shave again, polish herself with creams, and luxuriate in the coolness of her sheets. By morning, dark, bristly islands would have re-surfaced.

There were other song lyrics—and Jenna knew that Amabel had hidden messages in them—messages that were a disguise, nonsense about "clubbin" and "parteez" and "lubbin' da boyz," each phrase like a band-aid strip covering a wound. Jenna peeled away the band-aids and translated the phrases into feelings: Amabel needed something to nurture. A baby would make up for the childhood she'd lost.

"Do you pluck out your eyelashes?"

Jenna didn't answer.

"Because some people can't grow them." Laser's monotone didn't harmonize with the buzz tracking across her lid. "Some people don't have hair anywhere," he said. Jenna tensed. There was something beneath Laser's words. She'd told him she was eighteen. She would have forged a document to prove it in order to get her stars. Did he suspect something about her or Amabel? A wave rose and fell inside Jenna and a blush warmed her cheeks. This morning she'd drawn her brows to match the arches over the green eyes of Amabel's Scaredy-Cat logo. (The tops were for tweens, and Jenna had grown too old for them—just old enough for the tattoos.) Boys would hurry home to their bedrooms after school, lock their doors, and dream of the stars and eyebrows she shared with Amabel.

"Your parents going to like them? They know you're here, right?" Laser asked while he worked. "They going to like you starry-eyed?"

"Mom will be surprised. What's not to love?" Her mother rolled her eyes at Jenna's pink and purple wigs, as if to say, "I was young once." Her father never seemed to notice anything about the way she looked on the weekends she actually saw him. The stars would be a declaration. The stars were a way to see and be seen, and with them she'd rise to the heavens with Amabel Hadley.

Before Amabel, Jenna had pulled clumps of hair from her Barbies and hid the dolls. After her epiphany about Amabel's perfect alopecia, she'd resurrected them, pulled out the rest of their hair, and moved the bald Barbies into her box of treasures. She could ask Laser: *Do you do invisible tattoos?*

Jenna felt a cool blot on the first tattooed lid. There was a whiff of antiseptic.

"That's a pad," Laser said. "To stop the bleeding. Almost done. Ready?"

"Un-hunh."

Jenna couldn't remember the interior of the tattoo parlor. The walls were draped with choices, weren't they? Strange shapes, symbols, and creatures. Elaborately lettered slogans meant to last a lifetime. She'd forgotten the shop's exterior, too, and its address. The address was in the phone that she'd noticed missing on the last of her bus connections through the deteriorating neighborhoods downtown. If she hadn't seen Laser's shop and pulled the cord to stop the bus, she'd have been totally lost. Even now she had no idea where she was, really. She might be deep in a forest, inside the witch's house with Hansel and Gretel, the house made of candy and cookies; she'd left nothing to mark her trail home. She saw footprints on midnight pavement shining under ultra-violet streetlamps. Above, countless six-pointed stars twinkled in a deep purple sky. She squirmed, and the buzz-tickle-nip stopped.

"Whoa!"

"Sorry," Jenna chirped. If she asked, would Laser tattoo a drop of milk, two drops, leaking from her nipple onto her breast—like milky tears? How much would that cost? But the drops of milk might look like blood. A moist weight compressed her second lid.

"Okay," Laser said. "Just sit for a couple of minutes."

"Done?"

"Done."

"I want to see."

"Wait."

Laser's voice was very close and far away at the same time. She smelled smoke. He was smoking while they waited. She wouldn't smoke, but she wasn't against it. Amabel Hadley smoked.

"Do you know Amabel Hadley?" she asked. "You know who she is, right?"

"The rehab queen?"

Jenna's felt her whole body frown, but then imagined a glow like the illuminated footprints she'd envisioned outside the tattoo parlor. She saw the meaning Laser hid beneath his words: *Amabel is beautiful!* What did he look like again—a face like a bull's?

"You're not really eighteen."

"Next month. Sorry I lied." Fifteen must be the legal age of something, she thought.

"You live a long way from here, right? You needed directions when you called." Smoke wafted into Jenna's face. Her eyelids stung under the pads. "You need a ride?"

"I guess. Can I see what I look like?"

"In a second. You live in the hills, right?"

"Way out. In a gated community. In a cul de sac." She knew so little about her own neighborhood. Gated. And surrounding hers were other gated communities. Maybe Amabel Hadley's girls, the hair suppliers, lived in one of them. Or maybe they lived on Jenna's block, safe behind the same gate that closed behind her each afternoon when the school bus dropped her off.

"I'll drive you. Let's get these off."

The pressure on her lids lifted and Jenna squinted. Laser turned off his work lamp. The parlor swam in shadows. She exercised her lids as if they were the drying wings of a new butterfly.

"Here." Laser handed her a mirror. The backs of his hands, his thick arms, even his neck were nearly black with arabesques, figures, and obscure lettering. But his face was as square and flat as if it had been squashed into a glass cube. A gold ring pierced his septum and hung over his upper lip. The hair he'd pulled back into a ponytail was threaded with silver. His eyes were small and black, and his teeth were very white, even though he smoked.

"Crazy wig," he said as Jenna stared at her new self. At first she couldn't see the change—the light was dim, and her lids retracted like a baby doll's. She winked, and there it was! A beautiful star, etched in thin lines of ink and blood. She switched eyes—the second star was as beautiful as the first. She fluttered her lashless lids, and the stars twinkled—perfectly under Amabel Hadley's Scaredy-Cat brows. She giggled and batted her stars at Laser, who nodded and flashed his teeth. He looked at her closely, admiring his work. He examined her so thoroughly, she felt him inside of her.

"Beautiful," he said.

Jenna remembered the bills folded in the pocket where her phone should have been and tugged them out. "Thanks," she said, and held the money toward Laser, half-expecting him to refuse it. But he didn't; the bills disappeared into his tattooed hand. He stepped back and took in all of her.

"Nice eyes. They go with the wig. It's getting dark. I'll take you home now."

"Okay. Thanks." Jenna stood for the first time in an hour. Figuring out the bus would have been a drag, though she could have shown off her stars to the other passengers. Her legs were weak. Laser took her arm. His touch was as gentle as the pressure of his tattooing tool—he handled her like she was one of those fancy Easter eggs.

"Amabel Hadley," he snorted and shook his head. "A life of bad choices."

Jenna was charmed by the meaning she was sure his words camouflaged.

"Wait," Laser said. His face closed in, his attention on her stars. "You're still bleeding. I've got to put the pads back on." Jenna suppressed an urge to wipe the oil glistening on his flat nose with a sterile towelette.

She waited, gripping the frame of the door she'd been led to, as Laser dabbed at each of her eyes. It stung. She smelled antibiotic ointment and tobacco on the fingers that swabbed her lids and laid fresh gauze over them. Tape stuck to her forehead and cheeks. She worried—silly, she knew, after tattooing— about the instant of pain when the tape would be stripped. And wouldn't her Amabel Hadley eyebrows be marred?

"I've got to lock up. Don't want to get robbed," Laser said, and left her, sightless, at the door that surely led through a back room to an alley where his car, probably a pickup truck, awaited. She heard the grating and clanging of metal—Laser was dragging the steel barriers across his shop front. The parlor felt empty and frigid. If she could see, her breath would be visible. She remembered there'd been someone in the shop when she'd arrived, someone who'd left after she closed her eyes. Just a voice. It was nice to think of Laser having a friend.

He was back. Jenna anticipated his touch; his cigarette breath warmed her face. She heard a deep sigh. If this had been a fairy tale, Laser would have been devoted to her service. She might have been a distressed damsel— she'd lost the royal infant the queen had placed in her care! Together, she and her protector had to find a child to replace the missing baby. They could look in one of the gated communities, where there were plenty of children. Jenna saw herself elevating a fresh, cooing infant before Queen Amabel Hadley. Even if Amabel guessed the child wasn't her own, nobody would mind. A child is a child. Behind Jenna, Laser would be kneeling with his square head bowed.

"Ready?" Laser asked, as if he knew what Jenna was imagining and was ready to begin the "once upon a time." She pawed the air. She was saving the fact of her smoothness as a gift for him. What would he say when she revealed it?

Chapter 9 – Dead White Male Body

Laser lay in bed with the mother of the girl he'd served nearly a year in prison for violating. All he'd done was tattoo the kid's eyelids per her request, though he'd been accused of more. After sentencing, he'd become a registered sex offender for "lewd or lascivious acts with a child under the age of sixteen." He'd been told she was eighteen. Nearly eighteen. The girl's mother stared at the tattoos on his chest.

"What's this hand?" She had eyes like her daughter's, but with long lashes that seemed fake—her kid, he'd found out the hard way, had alopecia, and hadn't any lashes at all.

"It's Mr. Antolini's."

Her eyes bucked to his. "Whose?"

"Antolini's. From a book. He's a guy who pats a confused boy on the head. That's hair under the fingers."

"Are they related? I think I read it. A memoir?"

"They're made-up characters. It's fiction. The guy just cares about the kid. Or whatever." Her eyes dropped back to the spot over his collar bone. Sometimes it was hard to see your own tattoos. It would not have been cool to tell her that her daughter inherited her eyes. Laser was not one for lingering looks.

One early spring, years ago when he was a teen, he'd driven to the beach; and at the shore he'd come upon a group of people, Hispanic, facing the water, some knee deep in the surf, some standing on the sand. Someone named Papi had slipped beneath the black waves. There'd been shouts of "Papi!" through cupped hands at a surface that was blank all the way out until it met the sky. Laser had stripped to his shorts and waded in up to his belly before the bone-numbing chill struck him, and he remembered that he was a weak swimmer. The undertow had pulled at his hips and thighs like a pair of giant hands. Shaking his head, he'd retreated to the packed sand, where he found himself facing a young woman.

The wind blew her dark hair straight at him, as though he lay on his back and she bent over him. Through her hair he could see her eyes, and they'd been full and empty at the same time. He'd run back to his car, shouting without looking back that he was going to get help, and he'd driven to a diner five miles down the highway. All he did was tell a waitress that she needed to call in an emergency, that someone was drowning.

People tried to hold your gaze either to look for your wounds or to show you theirs, Laser knew. The woman now reading his chest couldn't see the setting sun inked across his back. It had wriggling beams made up of words, one of which was "Papi."

"You've got a thing for hands—what about these?" Dana asked.

"Which?"

"These right here, the clasped ones." Her lips and the tip of her tongue marked a spot just below his nipple, and her hair bunched under his chin, black curls so cool they felt wet, like kelp, and smelled of expensive treatments. If Laser hadn't been propped up on his elbows, he might have run his fingers through those curls.

"From another book," he said. "Two guys on the deck of a whaling ship are kneading a tubful of spermaceti—smooth, soft stuff from a dead whale. They used to make perfume out of it. The guys were squeezing lumps out, and it felt so good they took each other's hand."

"Tastes fishy." Dana smacked her lips. "I know, a whale isn't a fish." She sat back on her heels and scanned Laser's body. "Whales are endangered." She wore only his denim shirt, unbuttoned. Her flesh, all he could see, was white and clean. "And it's a little gay, too."

"Brotherhood," he said. "The brotherhood of man."

"What are you, a test all over? Who's this?" She squinted close to read the name printed across his belly. "'S-V-I'—how do you even say it? Did you—or whoever did it— spell it wrong?"

"I did it. It's 'Svidrigaylov.' A character. He's Russian." He doubted if Dana could tell this was the newest of his tattoos, that he had done it in prison with a needle and homemade ink. He wouldn't tell her that her daughter had inspired it.

"That sounds familiar—kind of ominous. But Russian names all sound the same to me. 'SVIDRI-GAY-LOVE . . . SVIDRI-GUY-LOVE' . . . Really. Holding hands, patting heads . . ."

Laser thought the girl's mother should be smarter, or at least better educated. She was a school principal, after all. Most of what she'd asked about on his chest was from books he'd read in high school, the rest on his own, afterward. His body was kind of a test, though, and he couldn't really say she'd failed it, because none of the women he'd been with had offered more than a general "Cool!" or "I like that one," or "Those scare me," about his inkings. Just Willie Freeze, his first and only cellmate, had picked up the references, and in a heartbeat. *"Catcher in the Rye,"* he'd said about the patting hand, and *"Moby Dick"* about the clasped ones after Laser had given him the hint about the spermaceti squeezing. He'd watched Laser complete "SVIDRIGAYLOV" across his own stomach.

"You're lucky you're borderline, friend. If that girl you're in here for was as young as the girl that pimp Svidrigaylov turned into a hooker in his dream, you'd be screwed. And I don't mean screwed, I mean dead. Child molesters here, friend, they're screwed dead. This shit you've got inked all over you—you already have a dead white male body."

"Mmm." Laser had been finishing the second V. There was something satisfying about the jab of the pin, the blue-black ink—something where there'd been nothing on his belly.

"Damn—" Willie Freeze wagged his head. "Dos-toy-evsky. He should have been locked up just for *imagining* the crimes in his book." Then he got excited. "Hey, friend, you've got to ink my eyeballs. It can be done—I've heard about it, but never seen it. But I can imagine what I'd look like—yes! People would shiver whenever they saw me. I'd be king of the world! When people can't look you in the eye they'll believe whatever you tell them to hide the fact that they're afraid."

"Never did eyes, but I've seen it—you don't really want that."

"You *have* to tattoo my eyes, friend." Willie's voice and glare had been iron hard.

* * *

The mother of the girl he tattooed was playing with Laser's dick; it wasn't stiffening, but neither of them was ready for more sex yet. She was examining it the way she'd looked at his body art, like it was a curiosity, something that he had that she didn't.

Laser had tattooed Willie Freeze's eyes, turning the whites blue-black, and his cellmate had indeed been transformed into one fearsome mother-fucker: he looked like midnight had risen within him and would never leave. Willie had laughed like a demon when he'd seen himself in the mirror. Then, within an hour, he'd gotten knifed in the yard during a fight he'd started, and Laser had never seen or heard of him again. There was also a "Willie" in Laser's sunset.

* * *

Dana hated how she sounded. Like a coquette, like a little idiot, and here she was, forty, an educator, a professional. Forty-two. She'd taught literature, directed plays, and she had a finger on the pulse of what was politically correct and what wasn't. In general, she'd shown appropriate scorn for the influence of Dead White Males. Scorn was different from ignorance. But what did people sound like when they were having affairs? She had no script, but she was deeply, daringly involved in a scene with this man whose body was a museum—a library—of prompts. There was something about the strangely spelled name that made her uneasy—she'd heard it before, but arousal and insecurity clouded her memory. "If it's a Russian name, why didn't you use the Russian alphabet?" She was not a skilled teaser. Did everything she said have to come out stupid or inappropriate? Like a bubble urging its way up through hot mud, a memory connected to the Russian name took shape: years back, a man on stage, an old song about a frog. But then Laser spoke, and the bubble popped.

"I've inked in Cyrillic. But I don't read Russian."

They'd met when she'd rushed to his tattoo parlor, furious and frantic, insisting that Laser remove the Stars of David he'd tattooed on her daughter's eyelids. Thrusting the branded girl in front of her, she'd screamed at the thick man in the tattooing chair. He was reading a newspaper under his work lamp. "We're going to shut you down!" She'd been hoarse, intending to be as dangerous as she tried to appear.

That morning, Dana had found her daughter dressed and napping on top of her covers, as usual. The teen habitually rose at dawn to shave herself smooth from head to toe: the hair the alopecia didn't erase surfaced overnight in unsightly patches. Dana had started shaving the child in pre-school, but since the onset of puberty the girl had been doing it herself, night and morning, doubling up. With adolescence, her daughter had spurned the blond wig she'd worn since kindergarten in favor of a hot pink page boy. The new wig complemented a rich fantasy life that excluded Dana. But it had been a relief to roll her eyes at the excesses of a daughter who, if not exactly a normal teenager, at least overlapped with Dana's idea of one.

"Up, sleepy head, time for school," Dana had called. "Missed you last night." There'd been a late PTA meeting. Then she'd seen the stars, which the girl had fluttered drowsily at first, then defiantly as she realized why her mother was staring.

"Tattoos," she'd said, and Dana had shrieked. She'd looked up the address and raced with her daughter through commuter clogged downtown streets to *Laser's Tattoos and Piercings*.

The large man with the ring through his nose and the ponytail and the ink-stained arms lowered his paper, removed his glasses and nodded at them with a frowning grin, as if he'd expected them.

***

The minute he'd agreed to tattoo stars on the eyelids of the whip of a girl with the crazy pink wig and audacious, drawn-on brows, Laser had known there'd be trouble. But the kid had been right about the stars—she needed them. He'd tried to explain to the frenzied mother that he couldn't really help.

"It's a coincidence that my name is Laser. I don't do laser removal—I don't have the equipment. There are clinics that do that. Try *Tatt-off*. It's a chain—there's one in the mall near you."

"*Traitor!*" the sobbing girl had wailed, as if he were tearing out her heart.

Near you. That's the thing he shouldn't have said. He'd known not to say, *Laser removal might leave permanent scars*. He hadn't said, *People need irrational things sometimes, the stars look good, let her keep them*. He'd said *near you*, and it had come out that he had driven the girl home after tattooing her. Given the questionable safety of his neighborhood and the fact that she'd finally admitted to being a month shy of eighteen, a ride seemed the right thing to do. He wouldn't have guessed she was only fifteen.

After the half hour drive into the suburbs, he'd passed the entrance to her gated community before pulling over—when he saw the size of the houses and the lush lawns and the clean, broad, black streets on the other side of the gates, he'd decided to let her walk through them on her own. He had to admit, anybody checking them out in his pick up might have been curious about their story—a girl in a pink wig with white gauze taped over her eyes was not your everyday sighting. But her lids had bled a little, and Laser hadn't wanted to risk infection. Blind and oblivious, the girl had chattered about pop movie stars the whole way. Thank God she knew her own address—probably something she'd been forced to memorize in kindergarten. It was luck, and maybe a little instinct, that had led him to the neighborhood. She whimpered a little when he pulled off the tape holding down the gauze pads, but it couldn't have hurt more than the tattooing. Part of the sassy eyebrows she'd drawn on her forehead came off with the tape. He twisted his rearview mirror so she could admire herself. The bleeding had stopped. She closed one eye at a time, winking at herself, then at Laser. It was twilight, and she was smiling.

"I'm smooth, you know," she blurted. Then she yanked off her pink wig, revealing her completely hairless scalp. "Touch it," she said, and he'd patted her bald head. It was cool and dry. "I've got that alopecia disease," she said. "Don't worry, you won't get it from touching me. I've had it forever. But I get patchy, so I shave all over twice a day to stay smooth."

"Un-hunh." Laser was used to confessions. It took a long time to ink people, and maybe something about the permanence of what was happening to them made his customers spill their crimes, infidelities, and aspirations. Other people's secrets buzzed continually around his head. He was pretty good at keeping his judgments to himself. But it had been hard not to look at a girl when she wanted to show you she was smooth.

"It's itchy now, because the patches have started to grow in. I didn't tell you about the other tattoo I want— I want drops of milk coming from my tit, like there'd been a baby nursing, and someone pulled it away. But you can't let the drops look like blood. I want them right here—"

Before Laser could protest, she'd pulled up her t-shirt, and he'd turned his head away a second after he saw her place a finger two inches below a little nipple that looked like a boy's.

"You need to cover up," he'd ordered, staring hard into his side mirror back toward her neighborhood's gate because his eyes needed something else to look at besides this girl's nakedness. "I don't do breasts as a regular thing. Now cover up."

***

"*—the mall near you,*" he'd said. Only at the *Tatt-off* clinic in the mall, where her daughter wept with humiliation and pain at the stripping of her stars, had Dana wondered how the man responsible for disfiguring her child had known where they lived. The lasering left white lines on her daughter's lids, "which should fade, but no guarantees." In the SUV on the way home—there'd be no school for either mother or daughter—Jenna had nothing to say at first except "I hate you! And that bastard traitor— I should never have let him touch me! I want to go live with Daddy!" But Dana persisted with an interrogation, which finally yielded the story the teen repeated in court (where she'd hidden her baldness beneath the prim yellow wig of her childhood): "He covered my eyes and told me he wanted to give me a special tattoo, and he lifted my shirt and touched me where he said he'd put it." New, innocent eyebrows arched over her lightly scarred lids.

The girl had sat with her father at the trial, a man Dana thought the shadow of an ideal parent. He'd been less than the shadow of a husband, and had actually used the words "better prospects" when he'd moved out of the big house in the gated community. But he'd taken care of his fiduciary responsibilities to his ex-wife and child, and, with his golfing buddy attorney, kept a close eye on the criminal and civil proceedings. When he called Jenna "Pumpkin," she'd smirked and glanced at her mother.

A full year after the settlement of the civil suit and just weeks before Laser's release, Dana's daughter finally left home. While the girl stood at the front door, waiting among boxes and suitcases and rolled posters for her father, she'd confessed, "Except for the tattoos, Laser never touched me. All he did was give me a ride home. And I had sworn to him I was eighteen." Her nostrils dilated as if her lie had somehow been Dana's fault.

* * *

"Your legs are as pale as all of me," Dana said to Laser. "Can you tattoo me? Can you tattoo me now?" She was right about the whiteness of their bodies—all of hers, and his thick legs. Under the black hairs kinking from his thighs and shins and calves, his flesh was like a frog's belly. Except for some sun-freckling on her forearms and the brown thatch between her legs and the nipples so dark they were nearly black, she was as white as a satin sheet.

A second after asking for a tattoo, she blushed fiercely, the color spilling like soup from her cheeks down her neck to her chest. Laser had been easy enough to find. She'd learned in court that his real first name was Lazarus, and his address was a matter of public record. But she'd left her intended apology unspoken. What words could make up for the time he'd spent in prison and the livelihood he'd lost? All she'd said when he opened his door was, "She's gone to her father's," as if the tattoo artist had been waiting for her to deliver the news. Laser had invited her in and offered her seat in his tiny kitchen and a cup of tea while he finished tattooing something on a young man's bicep. His tattooing machine was about the only thing he hadn't lost. His apartment smelled of the ink and antiseptic of his art, his business conducted now without a license and by word of mouth.

While Laser bent over his work, inking with a steady hand, she'd found the hum of the machine soothing until she saw the muscle of the young man flinch. Getting tattooed had to hurt. Dana tried to picture her daughter in Laser's chair, but instead saw herself shaving the child's head. How she'd dreaded rising each morning, how she'd hated the dark, stubbly blotches that would surface on the little girl's scalp, despised the smell and the texture of the white cream she molded over them, and shuddered inside at the drag of the razor. But she'd tried to be a faithful and cheerful mother, humming a made-up tune like a lullaby, the only lyrics the refrain: "*Sooo*—smooth, *Sooo*—smooth." Surely she was owed *something* for her perseverance.

Now Dana's attention fixed again on Laser's tattoo of a hand patting a head. Who *was* Antolini? She felt herself on the edge of remembering. That very afternoon, a few hours earlier, minutes before she'd sent out the email canceling her faculty meeting so she could rush to her lover, Dana had touched the head of a boy who'd been banished from class for "bothering a girl." Seth was a hard child to like. He was overweight and smelled of baloney. She'd asked him to take a seat and tell her what happened.

"I just said her name," he whined.

"Whose name?"

"Jillian's.

"How did you say it?"

"JillianJillianJillianJillianJillianJillian—"

"Okay." Dana had smiled. "But why?"

Seth's gaze had sunk to the floor, and his lips pinched up under his nose.

"There are better ways to show someone you like them," Dana said. Standing, she'd moved to the boy. "Ways that aren't so silly. Try writing Jillian a poem. Or, if you want to keep things private, just for yourself, keep a journal." Then she'd placed her hand on top of the boy's head. A blessing. But the jelled texture of his hair reminded her of the glazed sugar crusting a pastry. After sending him back to class, she'd murmured, "LaserLaserLaserLaserLaser" while posting the cancelation of the faculty meeting.

***

This woman in his bed examining his tattoos, back now for the fourth—the fifth?—time, had small breasts like her daughter. He hadn't revealed the girl's specific tattoo request in his testimony—said nothing about the drops of mother's milk, stating only that the girl had asked for a tattoo on her chest.

"Your legs are as pale as all of me," her mother said. He expected her to ask why he hadn't tattooed his legs, and he had an answer ready. "Did you ever read Dante? The *Inferno*?" he'd begin, though he was already certain that she hadn't, despite the fact she'd taught English —"Well, at the very bottom of Hell, the worst offenders, those treacherous to loved ones, they're frozen for eternity in a lake of ice. The worst ones are up to their eyeballs. Me, I picture myself in ice up to my waist. My legs aren't available for inking." If she asked, that's what he would say, but she didn't.

Laser reached toward Dana and cupped one breast. It was warm, like a dove. On the back of his hand was the fierce head of a Chinese dragon, its scaled body twisting up his wrist, its stubby dog-legs clawed, its sharp, reptilian wings spread across his forearm.

"Mark me," he intoned in a too-deep voice. She wouldn't know he was doing the ghost of Hamlet's father. The ghost meant "Listen." He doubted she'd even seen any version of the play, even the Mel Gibson movie. But her clean skin suddenly goose-bumped, her eyebrows lifted and her lips pursed. On one of his back's wriggling sunbeams there was a pair of B's, followed by a second pair with a line through them: *To be or not to be*. He slid his hand down the woman's ribs to her hip. She was smiling—he liked the tiny lines that radiated from the corners of her eyes. Deeper creases framed her lips, and he liked those, too.

"Mark *you*?" Dana mimicked Laser's tone, a contralto the lowest she could dip. "What with? Where?" Meaning covered the man who touched her, but she felt blank. She waited. An answer didn't come, and she fell forward, her palms threatening to sear fresh prints among the symbols on his chest.

Chapter 10—Ghosts of Happiness

Stuckey propped himself on his elbow and studied the young woman sleeping beside him. He was making a mental picture—what he really wanted to do was take an actual picture with his iphone and save it forever. Sex after the third date! It wasn't so much that Jenna was his first—he'd exaggerated his sexual history so often and with such elaborate detail over the half dozen years since he'd graduated high school that he'd lost track of the truth. His own sex life, viewed through a haze of pot and beer, shimmered with images from Penthouse Forum letters and internet pornography. There had been a few other girls—but none like Jenna.

She was exotic. She was completely without hair! He didn't remember exactly the name of the disease that caused it, but she'd told him about it matter-of-factly on their very first date. They were in a diner, sharing a plate of French fries.

"I've only got little patches of hair." Her eyes were round and almost gold and popped out of her head, a little like a frog's, and Stuckey had looked close and seen she had no eyelashes and that her eyebrows weren't real. Most people didn't notice that frogs had beautiful eyes. "I shave the patches away and wear a wig. I shave wherever it's needed at least once a day. Twice, for special occasions." The way she'd smiled at Stuckey, lifting the corner of her mouth and dimpling one cheek, he felt like maybe he'd rated special occasion treatment.

Jenna had been the talk of the community college that nearly everybody from Stuckey's high school wound up at sooner or later—most, like him, just to take a course or two at night for something to do. It was a way to toss a pebble into the abyss of the future that sometimes opened up during lazy hours at whatever fast food restaurant or carpet warehouse or car wash they worked at. For Stuckey, it was the Walmart, where'd he been putting in hours for what seemed like half his life. Everybody at the community college knew everybody else. Jenna, nobody knew. She couldn't have been more than twenty, was pretty, but distant in the way that made guys afraid to approach her and girls say she was stuck up.

Rumors leaked out that there was no reason to challenge—that she was a rich kid from the bordering suburban school district who'd dropped out of a four-year-college for some mysterious reason—a crime or a scandal that nobody in Stuckey's circle had the energy to research. There was talk about an affair with a professor, a pregnancy, a baby, but nobody had any proof. Her hair was a different color every day—regular blond and brunette and black, but also pink and blue and purple. Some said so much dyeing would kill her roots. Others guessed she was wearing wigs.

In classes, though no one remembered her speaking, everyone, including the instructors, was a little uneasy in her presence. Then, one evening Stuckey had been sitting in a class he'd attended by mistake—he'd thought he was in room 201, Basic Business, and had joined a small group around a table. He was waiting for the instructor to stop talking about Shakespeare and get to the class material when it dawned on Stuckey he was in the wrong place, and he'd have to wait another hour for the break so he could sneak away unnoticed. He half-dozed, listened to the chatter, and when his eyes focused, he realized he was staring at the girl everybody talked about. She had blue hair that evening, and she smiled at him across the table. And when a break came, she'd followed him, touched his arm, and asked if he wanted to meet for coffee sometime.

"It's not catching, what I've got," she'd said in the diner, holding his gaze and dabbing at the mustard Stuckey had pointed to on the corner of her mouth. Her skin was so pale it was almost as blue as her wig. "You won't go bald yourself just because you're with me. If you start losing your hair, blame your genes." Then she'd told him he had eyes like Leonardo DiCaprio, which was why she'd asked him out, and he'd told her she had beautiful eyes, too, but he didn't say that they reminded him of a frog.

Now, two dates later, he was in bed with her, resisting the urge to slide his hand over the smooth slope of her scalp while she slept. Her head had been cool to his kisses. There'd been a bristly spot near her temple. Stuckey thought about his own five o'clock shadow and how his cheeks must have felt to Jenna's lips. The black wig squatting on his night table reminded him of a crow. There was a professional finish to Jenna's smoothness, as if she'd been sculpted from marble and polished. She was as hairless as any woman he'd seen in the magazines or on the porn sites. When his eyes swept down her curves, he looked for evidence of a pregnancy. What exactly would that be? Below her left nipple three drops were tattooed. At first Stuckey thought they were supposed to be drops of blood, and he imagined her nursing a baby vampire. But the drops looked more like tears. Jenna shifted, and Stuckey looked at her face to see if she was awake. Something showed through the purple coloring her eyelids—the faint outlines of six-pointed stars, one on each lid. Somehow these star-scars had escaped gossip. Stuckey wondered if she shadowed her lids and bugged her eyes to hide them. He settled back and tried to sleep, but he was too excited and nervous—the girl lying next to him made him feel like he was in a fairy tale.

Within weeks they'd moved in together, splitting the rent on a tiny bungalow on a side street paralleling a bluff that hung over the river. It would have been nice to have had a view of the water, but none of the windows faced it. Jenna Klein had some money saved up and didn't have to work right away to pay her share of the bills. She didn't sign up for any more classes, and Stuckey wasn't exactly sure how she killed time while he covered his shifts at Walmart, but he didn't pry. He didn't want to spoil the pleasant harmony he shared with his smooth girlfriend.

He didn't ask about the star tattoos or whether she'd ever been pregnant. She never mentioned family, and he didn't push that either. So she wouldn't feel pressured by the idea of relatives, he called his own parents, retired to a Florida trailer park, from work. And he stayed away from his sister, who lived in the next town, because he couldn't stand her husband. They had a toddler, though, Danny, who Stuckey liked and missed, even though they'd just confirmed that he had some kind of learning disability. For the most part, Stuckey and Jenna lived in the present, without history or plan.

Early on, Stuckey took Jenna shopping at his Walmart on his off day. He wanted his coworkers to see his pretty girlfriend, and he was proud when Harold, the store manager, nodded and winked from across Home Decorating. Jenna pulled a purple ski hat from a bin and tugged it on top of the day's wig, a platinum one. Stuckey sidled up beside her, and they'd looked at themselves together in the mirror. Jenna batted her lids. Green eye shadow covered the secret stars. Their reflection made a picture Stuckey couldn't figure out how to take without getting the phone in it.

"Do I look like Kate Winslet," Jenna Klein asked, blinking at herself, "from *Titanic*?"

"Sure," Stuckey, said although he hadn't seen the movie.

Now and then, when Stuckey got back home very late from his shift, he'd find Jenna undressed and asleep in their bed. He'd look at her hips, then between them, projecting the swell of pregnancy on the baby-smooth skin. A mystery.

After a while, Stuckey convinced himself that he and Jenna were building a future in their riverside bungalow. He quit classes at the community college and worked full time at Walmart, because they needed the money. He expected that any day now he might be promoted to assistant manager. They kept to themselves and stopped going out at night altogether. Staying home was fine with him—he kept the refrigerator stocked with beer, and one of his coworkers was a reliable source of weed. Jenna didn't drink or smoke, but they lived together compatibly. The only arguments they had were whether to watch a movie or his favorite reality TV shows. When he was tired or buzzed, Stuckey couldn't follow a plot. Jenna had DVRed the movie *Titanic* from HBO and watched it just about every night. As far as he knew, that was how she filled the time he was at work, too. Stuckey didn't complain, though, and even bought her the *Titanic* DVD with his employee discount. The movie was even cheaper because it was at least ten years old. It was on so often in the bungalow that before long he found himself mouthing dialogue from the film's first half. It flattered him that he reminded his girl of Leonardo DiCaprio, though maybe she only knew how to look at men was by comparing their features to the actor's. Because of his buzz, Stuckey always either fell asleep or slouched off to bed long before the movie ended.

Once, Stuckey got home from work and found Jenna watching television without her wig on. Usually bed was the only place she let herself be bald. Ritually, she'd shave and massage creams that smelled like dessert into her scalp before crawling between the sheets. When Stuckey walked in, Jenna glanced up and lifted a finger to her lips, then turned back to her show. Cool light from the TV flickered over her bare scalp. She looked like a beautiful alien.

When the power failed, Jenna and Stuckey were, as usual, watching *Titanic*— the ship hadn't hit the iceberg yet, and this particular night he'd abstained from weed and beer, determined to see the movie through to its end. Then everything went dark.

"Whoa," Stuckey whispered. He pawed for Jenna's hand. Her fingers were cold. "It's the wind," he said. Downed limbs from dead trees along the bluff frequently knocked out the electricity. With everything else silenced, they could hear the wind shushing through leaves and stirring branches that scratched against the cottage's aluminum siding. There was a hollow wump. "That's Dora's garbage can. She'll find it down the block tomorrow," Stuckey said.

"I'll get a candle," Jenna said, but she didn't move. Shadows of trees shook like cheerleaders' pom-poms at the window. It seemed like they'd slipped into some alternate version of their house, where light didn't exist. Jenna sang softly: *"Little girl, little-little girl, my Sviddy-pretty kid, such a Sviddy-pretty kid . . ."* Stuckey had heard her sing that snatch of a lyric before.

"What's that from?" Stuckey might not have asked if it hadn't been so dark and quiet.

"Just an old song," Jenna said. "Nobody ever heard of it."

Stuckey rubbed Jenna's fingernails with his thumb. They were unpolished and trimmed short. "Who sang it? What's a 'Sviddy-pretty'?"

Jenna sighed. She slipped her hand from Stuckey's and shucked her wig. She pushed it down between their thighs. To Stuckey it felt stiff, like a horse's tail. Jenna's head loomed like a planet. "Stuff I used to be into a long time ago. You know Amabel Hadley, right? I loved her movies when I was a kid. And, you know how everybody thinks they're a singer? She recorded a couple of CDs. Of course I bought them. She really can't sing. 'Sitting Pretty' is one of the only ones that got popular."

"You sang 'Sviddy-pretty.'"

"Un-hunh. You really had to be into Amabel to know about that. It's one of those hidden references. The title is "Sitting Pretty," but it says "sviddy-pretty" in the lyrics. When she was a little kid she was making a movie and got, like, abused, and they stopped the whole production. The movie's name was 'Svid'-something. You wouldn't have heard of it." Jenna paused. "Interesting fact," she said in a monotone. I read somewhere that Amabel Hadley auditioned for the Kate Winslett role in *Titanic*. She didn't get it, though, because she was too young."

"She's just celebrity trash now, right? In and out of rehab? We sell her clothing line at the store. Scaredy Cat, right?" The darkness unsettled Stuckey, and he needed something to smoke or drink. A weed buzz would be best, but the beer was easier to fetch. Rolling a joint took too much concentration and manual skill. He wasn't like the cowboys in Westerns who could fashion a cigarette with one hand. Then Stuckey remembered a creepy old movie he'd seen one late night before he'd met Jenna. The actors were genuine circus freaks—dwarfs and pinheads, and one African-American guy with no arms and legs they called the "Human Worm." Using his mouth, the "Worm" lay on the ground and rolled himself a cigarette from scratch, then lit it. The movie, Stuckey recalled with a shiver, had a scene near the end that took place outside on a stormy night like the one that had knocked out their lights. In the scene a mob of freaks chased someone through muck and mire. There was a shot of the human worm rocking himself forward through the slop with a knife clamped between his teeth. Shadows danced frenziedly outside the windows of Stuckey's bungalow, and he chose not to get up for his beer. He pressed his shoulder against Jenna's.

"Let's listen to the wind," she said.

The lights flickered on. Things jumped back to life—the refrigerator hummed, the television crackled. Stuckey wasn't ready. Everything was too bright. Jenna's white head frightened him. She snatched her wig from between them and pulled it back on. When the lights went out again, Stuckey blinked like he was staring at an x-ray of his girlfriend.   "Shit," he muttered. He felt like the two of them were on a seesaw they couldn't balance—as if Jenna sat on the ground, and he floated over her, his feet wiggling in the air. "When the electricity goes off and on, that means they're close to having it fixed," he said. He needed to hear his own voice, and he searched his mind for a topic. He could tell Jenna about the conversation he'd had over the weekend with Dora, the elderly widow who lived in the cottage next door. Stuckey had been at their mailbox when Dora waved him over to her porch. He worried that she was going to ask him to rake her lawn or move some furniture around inside her house.

"Did you know that this whole block was an amusement park?" the old woman had begun. Stuckey listened to himself share Dora's story with Jenna.

"Dora says that this whole block used to be set up like a permanent carnival— it was an old-fashioned amusement park. She said there were rides— a Ferris wheel and a midway with a merry-go-round and a stage where they did shows and booths with games and food. There was a trolley bridge across the river that brought people from downtown. It was a really big deal. She said she'd seen pictures of it at night, and you could see the lights from the Ferris wheel reflected in the river. It must have been pretty."

After a few seconds Jenna asked, "Dora saw this herself?"

"No. She said this was way before her time. Her folks told her about it and showed her the pictures." Stuckey had a crazy thought. "You know what I think all the blowing out there is tonight? I think it's the ghosts left over from the amusement park days: people from a hundred years ago partying it up and having all that fun right here, and the ground got soaked up with all the good feelings, and now it's coming out of the trees— like ghosts of happiness." He let the idea run: "I bet some people wanted to keep partying and hid until the place shut down for the night. They were probably drunk—then, in the dark, maybe they fell off the bluff, right in our backyard, and they drowned. And their ghosts have climbed out of the river and are grabbing for the happiness they lost."

The lights burst back on. Jenna was close and bright and real. She didn't comment on Stuckey's ghosts. Squinting out from under her wig, she announced, "Stuckey, I've been thinking, and what I want to do is have a baby."

Stuckey sat back. He wished he'd gotten up for the beer. A baby? Maybe she'd never actually had one after all—maybe she had some kind of deep longing that gave off a confusing aura. Maybe this was the moment she'd chosen to share some actual details. But the fact that she wanted to take their relationship to the next level overwhelmed him with joy and dread. Jenna's declaration required him to make a confession he'd always known had to come, unless he became a priest or a hermit.

"Okay," he said. His eyes hadn't adjusted to the light, and he focused on the TV screen's soothing blue. "But I've got a problem." He wanted to explain an important fact about himself to Jenna in a way he'd be proud of when he thought about it years down the road, but the details of his history raced ahead like phantom sprinters. "My folks bought a cheap house in a new development when I was just a baby— we lived there until I was almost a teenager. Then it turned out the whole neighborhood was built on a waste site—some kind of nuclear dump. They did tests, and the radiation levels were off the charts, and people—my family and all—had to move out. People I didn't know supposedly got sick, and there were lawsuits. Nobody in our family had any symptoms except our husky dog. He got big lumps all over after a few years, and he wasn't that old when we had to put him down."

Stuckey stared straight ahead, but he felt Jenna's bugged eyes sticking to him. The digital clock on the cable box blinked "12:00-12:00-12:00." "A couple of years ago," Stuckey continued, "I got a letter from a lawyer saying there was some kind of class action lawsuit I could sign up to join. But I chose not to participate. There was going to be a thorough physical examination, and I was smoking a lot of weed at the time, and the word was that they'd test your piss and send the results to your employers. But afterwards I got to thinking about living over that waste dump and Wolfy's lumps—one under his neck was as big as a softball. I asked my doctor what kinds of tests I should have, and he said for my blood and my sperm count. So, my blood came back okay. But my sperm count did not." Stuckey turned toward Jenna, but kept his eyes lowered—he'd reached the main point. "The doctor told me I had the lowest sperm count he'd ever seen. Just like that, as if he was congratulating me for setting a record. 'You have the lowest sperm count I've ever seen,' he said. 'I'm afraid it's unrealistic for you to expect to produce a child.'" Stuckey's tongue felt like it was coated with paste. He took Jenna's hand. The sweat from his armpits smelled like vinegar.

Jenna smiled. "Don't worry, honey," she said. "I don't want *your* baby. I want to have somebody else's. Not another guy's—I mean I want to have one planted in me. What I'd like is to be an incubator. For the money. Other than that, the baby wouldn't have anything to do with either of us."

As Jenna explained it, she'd had plenty of money to start with when they'd met, but with the cost of rent and groceries, her reserves had dwindled. "I had money I was supposed to use for college," she said, "but now I'm completely cut off from my parents," she said. She snapped her fingers in Stuckey's face as if she was waking him from a trance. "Completely. Unsalvageably. With what I can get being a surrogate—that's what you call it, a 'surrogate'— I can have a real life. It's not such a big deal having a baby."

Stuckey was speechless. Jenna closed her eyes, and he saw her stars. Their outlines pulsed red, as if there was a fire inside her head. They reminded Stuckey of the radioactive waste that had simmered secretly beneath his house while he was approaching puberty. Shouldn't Jenna at least have expressed sympathy over the news of his sterility—not just for what it meant for him, but for what it meant for their future? "I don't want *your* baby," she'd said. There was no comfort in that.

New mysteries invaded life in the bungalow. Jenna left the house for "appointments." There were phone calls and messages from doctors and agencies. Stuckey waited for her to share the details of whatever she was getting herself deeper and deeper into, but she didn't, and he felt himself falling behind. One evening when he came in from work, she was lounging on the couch. As usual, he heard the theme music from *Titanic*. Jenna lifted the remote from her stomach and paused the movie. As she pointed the device, Stuckey thought she was going to try to shut *him* off, and he almost held up his hands. But she laid the remote back on her belly. "That's it," she said. "I'm pregnant. About a month, so far. Early first trimester, they call it. I probably shouldn't have told you, because it's bad luck to say anything this early."

An electric buzz passed through Stuckey that felt good until he remembered how little the pregnancy had to do with him. "Congratulations," he said. "Should we celebrate?"

"I've got a list of *dos* and *don'ts's* from the agency and the doctor," Jenna said. "There's a contract I've signed where I agree to all kinds of things the parents want. I don't know who they are, or their circumstances. They don't want me to know. But they're giving me an allowance, and somebody from the agency will be coming to check things out at home—on a regular schedule, but some surprise visits, too. Number one on the 'don't' list is 'no drugs or alcohol.' I'll be provided with what they want me to eat and drink. Oh—and you're going to have to move out. I told them I live alone. I guess we should have discussed that beforehand, but I didn't know all the ins and outs of until this morning." The eyebrows Jenna had drawn on her forehead were unusually thick and black, and as flat as hyphens.

Stuckey thought he hadn't heard right. He sat down on the edge of the recliner. "Move out?"

"And no sex, the parents say. It's in the contract. They're afraid that'll mess things up inside, even though my doctor says that's not true. But they're renting my womb, right? I guess I can understand their not wanting someone screwing around with it. And no more pot smoking around me—no exposure to secondhand smoke, cigarette or otherwise. They're giving me an allowance. Enough so I'll help you pay the rent on a cheap studio in town. For a while. I'll visit you. But if the agency thinks I'm screwing up any details, it'll jeopardize the whole deal."

Stuckey felt like his stomach was filling with ice water. Was Jenna telling him he was homeless? She hadn't used those words, but that seemed the gist of it.

"You have a day or so to vacate, I guess, since I just signed things today," Jenna said. She propped up the remote on her stomach and let it fall like a domino, over and over. The pause on the TV must have been released, because the music resumed. Jenna's eyes jerked to the screen. She thumbed the movie back to silence. She patted the sofa, inviting Stuckey to join her, which made him feel a little better. But he didn't move right away. "The parents were a little hesitant at first about me—because of the alopecia, I think," she said. "But I've got a special doctor friend who convinced them that my condition wouldn't be a problem. It doesn't affect my general health, and it's not hereditary or contagious. That's no secret to us, right? Come on, sit by me, Stuckey."

Stuckey still didn't feel enough strength in his legs to take a step. "And how much will you get?"

"Enough, like I said. I'm not at liberty to disclose the exact amount."

Chapter 11— His Pictures

"Call me 'Dr. Mo,'" Seamus Morrison told the young woman waiting for him in his office. She was pretty, with big eyes and long black hair. He took a seat quickly—most of the extra weight he carried was in his belly, and he habitually sought to hide it behind his desk. "'Mo' is for 'momentum'—it's my job to get the ball rolling. So why do you need a reproductive endocrinologist?"

The woman, not much more than a girl, looked confused. "You're a fertility specialist, right?"

Seamus had learned how to chuckle paternally, though he'd never been a father. "Of course. 'Reproductive endocrinologist' is a fancy name for it." He wasn't naturally jolly, but being plump, and suspecting himself of being slightly wall-eyed—a defect he could never quite catch in the mirror— he cultivated a pleasant manner. No handsome white knight surgeon of romance novels, he was accustomed to the disappointed faces his computer service dates were unable to disguise when they met him in the flesh.

"Well. I'm interested in surrogacy—" A dimple emerged with the young woman's half-smile. "—'surrogation.' Is that a word?"

Seamus blinked. Was she bright? Women who were both pretty and smart made him uncomfortable. "We use 'surrogate birth.' What about your spouse? You have a partner?" She was his first appointment of the morning, a new patient, and, with the whole day stretching before him, he'd yet to hit his stride. Most of his consultations were with brand-new brides— panicked would-be mothers who'd expected to get pregnant on their first try.

"There's just me," he heard her say as he scanned her information.

"'Jenna Klein,'" he read aloud. Twenty. Unmarried.

"I wasn't sure if I should bring a resume," Jenna Klein said, as if she might be joking.

Seamus set his features into a professional smile-frown. "You're having difficulty conceiving?"

"What? Not that I know of—" She leaned forward, elbows on thighs, and seemed to study Seamus's face, which made him uncomfortable. Suddenly, the young woman's expression brightened, and she sat up straight. "Oh—I understand—you get a lot of patients with something wrong with them. I don't think that's me—what I want to do is be a surrogate—'a bearer of good news,' right?"

Seamus found himself staring at Jenna Klein's eyebrows. They were drawn on and cupped her eyes like parentheses, which made her look vulnerable in spite of her boldness. He flipped to the second page of data. "No" was checked for each item on the long list of medical conditions until he got to "other" at the bottom of the page, where Jenna Klein had printed "*alopecia totalis.*" He closed his eyes for a beat before refocusing on her smiling face.

"*Alopecia totalis,*" she nodded before Seamus could speak. Her eyelids fluttered—she had no lashes. So the black hair flowing over her shoulders was a wig—obvious when you knew. "I'm smooth. I have to shave little patches of hair that grow here and there because '*totalis*' doesn't mean total. Not many people are perfectly bald. One in a hundred thousand. But you would know that, being a doctor. Is alopecia a problem for my surrogation?"

"I don't believe so," Seamus muttered. *Smooth.* He held Jenna Klein's parenthetical gaze while absorbing the lashless lids and false brows, the borrowed bangs that curtained her forehead. What did he remember about alopecia from medical school? Not much. "Do you treat your condition—do you use anything topically?" he asked, trying to sound analytical. "Do you take any medications?"

"I'm clean, Dr. Mo—" She lifted her hands as if he'd just arrested her. "—I don't medicate, legally or illegally. I'm clean all over."

Beneath daubs of brown shadow, Jenna Klein's eyelids were faintly scarred. Stars of David? How long had she had the tattoos before she regretted them? Seamus laid his palms on the glass covering his desk. His fingers looked stubby; he pulled back his hands, leaving moist prints, and clasped his knees.

"You'll need an examination," he heard himself say. "I can take care of that." Seamus hadn't given a patient a physical in years. Generally, he consulted and offered recommendations. What he should have done before bringing up an examination was confirm that alopecia wouldn't impede a surrogacy. Then he should have provided a list of the agencies that handled young women willing to bear the children of others. Instead, Seamus directed Jenna Klein to his examining room. He pointed through the closed door. "Down the hall, second room on the right. There should be a gown on the table. Put it on. I'll be there shortly."

In a matter of minutes, Seamus determined with a computer search that nothing about alopecia should disqualify Jenna Klein from surrogate motherhood. The disease was neither infectious nor hereditary—it couldn't be transferred to an embryo. But before attending to her in the waiting room, he pulled a large book from his shelf— *Balthasar Klossowski de Rola: Balthus, 1908-2001.* A book of paintings.

As an undergraduate, Seamus had minored in art history to boost his GPA and appear "well-rounded" for medical school applications. He could name periods, schools, movements, and the artists and paintings that defined them. He knew enough about realism and abstract expressionism to hold his own in conversation. But the only artist whose work viscerally affected him was Balthus.

He'd discovered the painter his senior year as he dug through art books in the college library in search of a subject for his final exam paper—the assignment was to compare a work of art with a work of literature. He'd been flipping through the pages of *Modern Painting of the Twentieth Century* when his first Balthus appeared: *The Guitar Lesson.* In the painting a seated woman cradled a prepubescent girl on her lap as if the child were a guitar. The girl-instrument's skirt was hiked up over her waist, revealing her smooth pubic area, and the woman holding her strummed a naked thigh. The child tugged at the musician's blouse, exposing the woman's breast. The painting cut Seamus open like a blow from an ax. He'd never before been so moved by a work of art—was that what it meant to be transported? He found a book of Balthus's paintings, then hid in a study carrel, falling deeper and deeper into the plates of naked and nearly naked girls until the library closed.

Exhilarated, he'd had an idea for his project on his way back to his dorm room: he'd heard of *Lolita*—a novel considered great literature about an old man's lust for an underage girl. He could read the book— or at least the notes—and compare it to Balthus's paintings. But later, as he tossed and turned in his dorm bed, he'd had misgivings. Weren't the pictures just pornography? Child pornography? Had he been transported or just aroused? What an ugly thing to suspect of oneself. In the end, Seamus abandoned Balthus as a topic and wrote his final paper on one of the recommended topics: he compared Winslow Homer's violent seascapes to the language with which Melville rendered Ahab's final battles with Moby Dick, and he got his A. But inscribed forever in Seamus's memory was Balthus's self-description for a museum retrospective: *"Balthus is a painter of whom nothing is known. Now let us look at his pictures."* Privacy—if the artist himself was entitled to it, wouldn't that extend to the admirers of his work. That kind of secrecy should have nothing to do with guilt.

On the survey for his online match-making service, Seamus didn't include his obsession with Balthus's work under "Interests and Passions." How could he explain that he was moved by paintings he wouldn't dare hang in his office? "My work is my passion," he'd typed instead. On most of his dates, conversation lagged. Was it that his paunchy belly and possibly off-kilter eye repulsed the women he met? Once, a thoughtful woman asked Seamus if, as a doctor, he was able to appreciate the beauty of the human form, or if he could only look at the body as the object of scientific study. "How," she'd continued, "do you numb yourself to the erotic possibilities of a body you're examining?"

If the woman had had access to Seamus's inner eye while he mumbled, "The first thing they teach in med school is how to compartmentalize," she would have seen he was visualizing *The Guitar Player*. If he suspected any date of seeing through to his core, he grew silent. He found he had little interest in thinking about women outside the frame of a Balthus painting.

Jenna Klein was waiting, and Seamus shut the book of paintings lying before him. He stared at its cover as if it was the surface of a lake into which he was about to dive.

She sat on the examining table, the white gown loose about her shoulders. As Seamus entered the room she shifted, and the paper under her crinkled. He'd forgotten his stethoscope, and for a moment imagined placing an ear against her chest to listen to her heart.

"I know something about you, Doc Mo," Jenna Klein said. She wagged a finger at him, and he leaned against the door he'd shut behind him. "You're a smoker, aren't you?" She cocked her head. "Nic-o-tine stains on the fingers, doc." She pronounced nicotine like *nick o' time*. "And you smell like smoke."

None of his patients—or dates— had ever made that observation. He was fat and maybe walleyed, but he thought he'd hidden his smoking—only occasionally did he buy a single pack on his way home from work at a convenience store. He'd smoke two or three in his recliner while he watched television. How had such casual smoking, hardly a habit, left stains? But when he glanced at his fingers, there they were, as yellow as old bruises.

"When you walked in, the air changed," Jenna Klein grinned. "Like a house around the corner was on fire." The girl's legs were alabaster pale. She'd painted her toenails bright red.

Seamus ignored her allegation. "Would you lie back, please?" he asked. "And lift your gown."

"Your hands aren't cold, I hope," Jenna Klein giggled. He started with her feet and legs. She was as smooth as he'd imagined. She hummed a tune he didn't recognize as he ran his hands over her. She got patchy, she'd said. He wondered where she shaved. His eyes and fingers found no stubble. Her wig had ridden up on her forehead. Pulling her T-shirt off must have unsettled it. Under the examining room's fluorescent lights the penciled eyebrows looked clownish. The scars on her eyelids stood out. Seamus touched his new patient.

When Seamus allowed himself to look at the baby-smooth folds of her pudenda, Jenna Klein added words to the riff she'd been humming: *"Mother-mother-mother-fuck-her, some day-always-makes-me-wanna-cry—"*

"And you are currently sexually active?" Seamus interrupted. His hands had slid back to Jenna Klein's knees and shins, as if he found something noteworthy on them. When Jenna Klein's eyes popped open, it was as shocking as a slap.

"Until very recently, Dr. Mo. I've been saving myself—for this. For the surrogation. The last day I had sex was June seventeenth. I remember the date because June seventeenth is Amabel Hadley's birthday. It's her song I'm humming—how about that? You heard of Amabel Hadley, right?"

"It's 'surrogacy,' not 'surrogation,'" he said, adopting a professional tone as he squeezed his patient's ankles. Though he tried to keep his focus on what his hands were doing, her smooth thighs tugged his attention up her legs. He cleared his throat and pulled back his hands. "Yes, I've heard of Amabel Hadley, the actress. Could you lift your gown to the neck, please? Just rest your head on the examining table."

Jenna Klein gathered the cotton fabric over her ribcage and closed her eyes again. "She only recorded two CDs. Only a couple of the songs were any good."

Seamus felt the girl's small breasts. Three teardrops descended from her left nipple—tattoos she hadn't had removed, like those on her eyelids: wouldn't it be interesting to learn the history of this young woman's choices? He lifted his fingers and wiggled them—

he'd forgotten what he was searching for. His new patient lay still, humming. The melody buzzed in his head, an earworm now, and he shut his eyes. This examination was a necessary medical procedure, he reminded himself. Jenna Klein wanted to be a surrogate, and it was important to ascertain that she was in perfect health.

Jenna-Jenna-Jenna-Jenna-Jenna-Jenna-jenn-uh-tail-ee-yuh.

Good God, had he actually sung that aloud? Seamus opened his eyes. His hands clasped Jenna Klein's hips. They slipped under her knees, down her calves, and for a third time, gripped her ankles. Her red toenails were the only spots of color in the room. His hands jerked away from her when she kicked.

"My ankles are ticklish, sorry, Dr. Mo," she laughed. "I've behaved up 'til now."

"Pull your gown down," Seamus turned his back on the young woman and picked up the folder with her information from the desk beside the examining table. He pretended to make notations. Had he actually sung about her genitalia? While he was touching her? He coughed and tasted stale tobacco, even though he hadn't smoked in days. "You can sit up now," he said. The paper cover crackled. When he faced her, Jenna Klein seemed much too close, her head huge. Her eyes bugged. Her brows seemed clumsily drawn—one was too thick, the other too long. Her wig exposed too much forehead. Her lips were chapped.

"So, do I pass?" she asked.

"You seem to be in perfect health," Seamus said. "When you're dressed, we'll meet in my office, and I'll give you a list of agencies that arrange for surrogacy." Had he shelved his Balthus book, or was it on his desk? The painting on the cover depicted a naked girl on a chair behind a robed man. Before she came in, of course he'd hide it. Then Jenna Klein would sit across from him and he would give her the promised list and send her on her way, and all would be as if she'd never been there.

"Agencies? I thought *you* would arrange something for me," she said. "Seeing that you found me 'perfect.' You remember what you said."

Seamus coughed. His mouth was dry. Did she mean what he *said* or what he *sang*? A cigarette would have composed him, but those were at home. Jenna Klein swung her feet off the table like a toddler wanting out of a high chair, and her red toenails flashed. "Agency staffs are prepared for these kinds of things," he said. "They'll have a list of prospective—clients. They'll arrange for proper representation and appropriate remuneration."

The girl shook her head. "But I want *you* to do all that. I don't want to deal with all the choices. I'm an *incubator*, Dr. Mo. Some need motherhood. Not me. I'm just the oven. Come on—you said I'm the picture of health. There's nothing wrong with me except that I'm smooth. And I've got excellent hearing."

Seamus turned away again, back to Jenna Klein's folder. "Get dressed, and we'll discuss things." His forehead burned, as if the word "GENITALIA" had been seared over his brow.

"You *have* to help. I'm not going to let you say no. And you shouldn't smoke. You should suppress the desire. Smokers leave a bad impression. If you quit, you won't feel like you have something to hide."

"My office," Seamus said over his shoulder, "after you dress."

"People can change, Dr. Mo. It's easier than you think—" Jenna Klein said, and Seamus stopped, his hand on the doorknob. "—I used to worship Amabel Hadley when I was a kid. But I grew up. She's trashy, and I don't let her rule my life anymore. Now it's Kate Winslet. Have you ever seen *Titanic*? I read someplace that they offered the role of Rose to Amabel Hadley, but that couldn't be true. Amabel would have been just a kid. But Kate Winslet? *She's* beautiful!"

Chapter 12—Puddles

For a while after Stuckey moved out, Jenna visited his downtown studio apartment nearly every night. But as her pregnancy progressed, she showed up less and less. His futon was uncomfortable to sit on, she said. And she wouldn't dare spend the night for fear that she'd be caught violating her surrogacy agreement.

"You really think somebody is spying on you?" Stuckey asked.

"Who knows," Jenna said. "The clients have a lot invested, and so do I. It's too cramped in here. Can't we just talk on the phone for the next few months? We'll meet for coffee someplace not too public. I'll drink juice, I guess. I'm not supposed to have coffee. Let me do the calling."

Stuckey's shoulders slumped. He was sure Jenna was impatient to get back to the bungalow he used to share so she could watch *Titanic*. She stooped to kiss his forehead on her way out, and he hugged her around the thighs from his seat on the futon, ducking under the belly swollen with a rental baby. The second she stepped out the door, Stuckey lit up a fatty and opened his first beer. The truth was, he'd been okay with his time alone—Jenna had grown too pesky about his indulging. He got why she didn't want to expose herself to second hand smoke, but there was no such thing as second-hand fetal alcohol syndrome. Was he supposed to give up everything? Her surrogacy had thrown things out of whack. Just a few months, though, and life would be back to normal—better than normal, because Jenna would get the money for the kid she carried. On the library computer he'd found out that a surrogate could earn as much as thirty thousand for a healthy baby.

But when Jenna didn't visit or even communicate for two weeks, Stuckey began to worry. It wasn't pride exactly that kept him from calling her. It was a fear that he'd find out something he didn't want to know—something he could keep suspended if they didn't talk. And what would he say if he did call? What if he got tongue-tied or sounded wasted? The best he could do was to force her into his dreams, but her smoothness, her big eyes, her lid-scars merged in frightening combinations, and he had nightmares about snakes and aliens.

One evening Stuckey was looking for a pen to sign his rent check when he came across a tote bag of Jenna's in the closet. For a moment, he thought she might have paid a visit while he was at work. Then he realized he must have taken the bag by accident when he'd left the bungalow. Jenna probably didn't know she was missing it—if she did, she certainly would have called. The Scaredy Cat logo winked at Stuckey from the tote, and he dumped the bag's contents on his futon.

It wasn't quite as exciting as discovering a diary, but these were Jenna's things, and it had been a long time since he'd touched or even seen his girl. Piled beside him were video cassettes and DVDs of Amabel Hadley movies—old ones he'd heard of, like *Switcheroo* and *Penny Starlight: Girl Astronaut*, and some unfamiliar direct to video releases. There were a pair of CDs, *Wicked Wench* and *Mine is Tasty*— Stuckey looked for the song title Jenna had sung, but none jogged his memory. He considered the collection—if Jenna asked about it, he'd return it. Until she did, he'd hold it hostage.

Stuckey watched the Amabel Hadley videos—all of them. The oldest, the ones on VHS cassettes, were full of giggling tween girls playing pranks on each other and prattling about boys and the hapless adults in their lives. Amabel was always at the center of the high jinks, talking and laughing loudest and coming up with the plans that lent the movies their thin plots. The first few, the familiar ones, were set in exotic locations like Hawaii and outer space. The later ones seemed like excuses for Amabel to model Scaredy Cat merchandise and toss her auburn hair and looked like they'd been filmed in someone's living room. Stuckey thought of Jenna watching these videos and felt a stab of longing.

After a few nights, Stuckey had established a favorite Amabel Hadley movie, and he watched it over and over—*First Time*, definitely a direct to video. This film showed an older Amabel—she looked to be at least twenty—playing seventeen. Her breasts filled the tight Scaredy Cat T-shirts, halter tops, and bikinis she wore, though there wasn't a single beach scene. The movie was about Amabel's character's "first time." It featured muscled "college boys" who must have been in their thirties. Amabel wore a lot of makeup and a sly look throughout the picture, as if the idea of a "first time" was a joke. Her voice had a husky slur, and most of her movements ended in a weary slouch.

It became a nightly habit for Stuckey to get home from work, heat up something in his microwave, get high, and jerk off to *First Time*.

At Walmart, he found excuses to pass through the girls' clothing section, where the winking cat –eyes of Amabel's merchandise aroused him so much that he often had to retreat to the stockroom to hide his hard-on. It wasn't long before he realized he was thinking more about Amabel Hadley than he was about Jenna. And why not, he rationalized. Jenna may have been someone else's surrogate, but Amabel Hadley was his surrogate for Jenna.

The evening Jenna surprised him with a visit, Stuckey was on his back on the futon with his pants down to his knees, engrossed deeply in *First Time*. Maybe this would be the night he'd see it through to the end. The knock at the door threw off his rhythm. It was Jenna's coded rap—three, pause, three more. He shut off the television, wiped himself off with a crusty dish towel, and shoved the DVD cover with Amabel's picture under the futon. He didn't have time to eject the disc. What if Jenna asked to watch TV? Would she want to know what he'd been watching? He'd have to confess that he'd taken possession of her Amabel Hadley collection.

It had been weeks since he'd seen her. She'd become more like an idea of a girlfriend than an actual person. And when he swung the door open, he was surprised at how tall she was—nearly his height. Amabel Hadley was much shorter. Jenna's platinum wig reminded him of a space helmet. His gaze slipped from her frog eyes to the belly that seemed impossibly huge.

"Hey," Jenna said. "Busy?" She moved forward, and Stuckey, his attention fixed on her stomach, stepped back.

"Nope," he said. Uncertain that he'd zipped up, he brushed his wrist over his groin to be sure. He waved Jenna Klein toward the futon. "What can I get you?"

His girlfriend, if that was what she was, waddled past him and plopped down in front of the television. She wrapped her arms around her belly as if it were a treasure chest. "Nothing," she said. She patted the spot next to her on the futon. "Come sit down. We need to talk."

Stuckey sat. As Jenna spoke, he tried to listen. She was telling him that she was breaking up with him, that she'd be moving soon, any time now, from the bungalow, and when she was out he could move back there.

"We've already been broken up for a while, right?" she said. "This is just to make it official. To be fair to you."

Stuckey's eyes were on the blank TV screen. He'd picked up the remote, absently, and he caught himself almost turning it on. What would Jenna think if suddenly, right in front of them, Amabel Hadley posed in her bikini, maybe with her hip cocked, maybe with her arms folded under her breasts, hoisting up her cleavage, maybe her mouth twisted into a smirk while her glazed eyes urged Stuckey to get rid of the fat girl next to him so they could pick up where they'd left off.

"Stuckey—you understand?"

He felt Jenna's hand on top of his. What had she been talking about? Was she confronting him about drinking and smoking too much weed? Was this about jerking off? "I could stop," he said. He felt a sudden need to remind her that he was sterile, but he only stared into the empty screen. If she were back in the bungalow, Jenna would be watching *Titanic*. He felt like something alive was crawling around his stomach and thought of Leonard DiCaprio sinking down into the black sea until he disappeared.

"Stop what? Stuckey, you'll be okay. You're a good guy. You'll meet somebody nice." Jenna Klein shifted, preparing to get up. She braced herself on the edge of the futon.

Then Stuckey remembered that Jenna loved Amabel, and he wanted to tell her that he loved the actress, too. They could love her together. He wanted to tell Jenna that he'd found her Scaredy Cat tote bag full of treasures. If she stayed, they could watch *First Time* as a couple. The Amabel Hadley song that Jenna Klein sang about "sitting pretty," that played through the opening credits, didn't it? Stuckey felt Jenna's lips on his cheek. It didn't have to be too late.

"Good-bye, Stuckey." With a grunt, she shoved herself to her feet.

***

Amabel Hadley was at Walmart—how had Stuckey missed the approach of such an event? He was in the stockroom when he heard over the intercom that shoppers interested in meeting the Hollywood star should make their way to the front of the store where Ms. Hadley would be giving away signed photos as well as discount coupons for Scaredy Cat merchandise. There would be a drawing, and Ms. Hadley would pick one lucky shopper for a Scaredy Cat wardrobe "valued at nearly a hundred dollars."

It was late on a Thursday morning, and the store was pretty empty. Why had there been so little publicity? Stuckey loaded his hand truck with paper he could stock in the Stationery and School Supplies aisle, close enough to Women's Clothing for him to check out the

129

proceedings. His heart pumped. His hands trembled. When he reached his hiding place, he saw that maybe a dozen curious shoppers had gathered, mostly moms hoping for some discounts. The store manager, Harold, was dressed up in a suit.

There she was! Stuckey must have been staring, because Harold frowned in his direction. He ducked and began unloading reams of copy paper, stacking them on the metal shelves with exaggerated energy. The announcement about Ms. Hadley's presence was repeated, and a few more shoppers hurried past Stuckey's aisle. He slowed his pace, moving one ream of paper at a time, peeking every few seconds for a glimpse of Amabel. Her hair was shorter than in the videos, and she looked thicker than the starlet he'd been sharing his time with every night. What was it about TV and weight—did the camera add or subtract pounds?

The celebrity sat in a folding chair. Stuckey heard Harold chattering into a microphone, but he couldn't make out his words. There was laughter, and Harold looked down at Amabel, a smile creasing his face—she must have made a joke. Stuckey felt warm inside, as if someone had just given him a compliment. He shelved more paper, then peeked again. Amabel was on her feet for the drawing. Stuckey left the boxes of copy paper and took a few steps down the main aisle. Harold the manager was flanked by Amabel and a life-sized cardboard display of the actress—the cut-out figure had flowing auburn hair and sported a tight Scaredy Cat T-shirt on an hourglass figure. The real Amabel wore a baggy, short sweater that revealed a muffin softness above the belt of her jeans. Her face was a blur of red lipstick and blue eye shadow. Stuckey's chest swelled. The crowd laughed again, then quieted abruptly. Amabel was speaking— white teeth flashed between the red lips. Was Harold glaring at him? Stuckey backed into the paper aisle and resumed stacking. The next time he looked up, the crowd was dispersing. The event was over. Amabel was gone.

After the request for "Cleanup in Young Misses," Stuckey was the first on the scene with mop, bucket, Formula 409, and paper towels. He hoped that the cardboard figure of Amabel had been left behind—Jenna would flip out over a souvenir like that. But the cutout was nowhere to be seen. If he'd found it, he'd have brought it along with the Scaredy Cat tote bag full of videos to the bungalow Jenna was about to vacate. He tried to picture his ex-opening the door, but all he could conjure up was her giant belly.

The only thing left of Amabel Hadley's in Young Misses was the folding chair she'd occupied. Stuckey figured he'd balance it on the cleanup cart and wheel it back to the stockroom, and that would be that. He flattened his palm on the metal seat, imagining he felt the star's residual warmth. He didn't need the cutout—he'd return Jenna's videos anyway, and he'd describe the event she missed. She'd be so thrilled she'd probably sing him one of Amabel's songs.

Then Stuckey saw the puddle on the floor next to the seat. It was about a foot wide and two feet long, with a kind of tail—the shape reminded him of one of those talk-balloons in cartoon strips, except it was greenish-yellow and didn't have any words in it. It might have been Mountain Dew, but it was thicker—there were filaments of what looked like mucous strung through it. The puddle had to be Amabel's— something she spilled or maybe coughed up. He stared at it—it was almost a guarantee that the puddle had once been inside Amabel Hadley. Stuckey tore off a half dozen paper towels from his roll and laid them gently on the puddle. He watched the fluid soak into them. He layered on additional towels. Then, using both hands, he swiped the mess together. It was lukewarm. He stuffed the folded towels into a plastic bag that he hung on his clean up cart and mopped up the spot where the puddle had been. A glance about the store assured him that no one was watching him perform what felt like an enormously intimate act.

As he pushed the cart back to the stockroom, his eyes riveted to the bag swaying in front of him, Stuckey had an idea: why not bring Amabel's puddle to Jenna? It would be a better gift than the cutout, which really hadn't looked much like the actress he'd just seen. Everything would be all right—Jenna, Stuckey, and the puddle all together in the bungalow on the bluff over the river.

✳✳✳

It seemed like years since Stuckey had seen the little place he'd once considered the foundation of a comfortable and fulfilling domestic future. He parked, and, casting his eyes up and down the street, half-expected to see evidence of the amusement park that had been gone for over a century. A tree stump on a neighboring lawn looked like the rotting head of a buried carrousel horse, but that was it. His feet mechanically followed the path to the front door that he'd been forbidden to pass through. He looked through the window into the living room. Jenna, her head bare, sat propped on the couch with her feet up, her entire body frosted a silvery-blue by the light from the TV. A wig lay on her belly like a sleeping tabby cat. Stuckey rang the doorbell and knocked. He watched Jenna press the wig against her stomach with one hand and push herself to her feet with the other. By the time she opened the door, she'd covered her head.

"Stuckey," she said. She opened the door wide, but her voice was wary. "You're lucky you caught me—I'm leaving tomorrow. I've packed up the stuff I need. Just a couple of suitcases I can take on a bus or train. I thought you might be the agency checking up on me—I'm not telling them where I'm going. I need a little privacy. I'm tired of being watched. And they really shouldn't see you here, just in case they show up. That could ruin everything." She bugged her eyes over Stuckey's shoulder, and he turned, too, but there was nothing to see.

"I'm just a guest," Stuckey said. "You're allowed to have guests for short visits, aren't you? You're not like a nun in a convent." He held Amabel Hadley's plastic-wrapped puddle under his arm in a Walmart bag that also contained the Scaredy Cat tote full of videos. The idea of his surprise gift for Jenna excited him so much he couldn't focus on what she was saying. He couldn't just hand everything over to her—not without explaining. *I figured out from the videos how much you must be into Amabel Hadley*, he'd say. He wouldn't mention that he'd been watching them. Then he'd tell her about the puddle. "I brought you a little something," he started.

"Oh—" Jenna blinked, and Stuckey examined her face closely for the first time that evening. It looked like a stepped-on doll's face. She hadn't drawn on any eyebrows. A false eyelash hung like a spider from a purple lid. Had he ever thought about the fact that she only sometimes wore false eyelashes? "Okay," she frowned. "You can come in, but just for a second." Jenna waddled from the door back to the sofa, where she sat with a huff, and Stuckey followed her, but continued to stand.

"They're so damned fussy about everything I do," she said. "I mean, I've got their baby inside of me. They're not going to abandon it just because I don't follow all of their rules. Whoever they are—the parents." Her eyes suddenly popped open even wider than usual—something on the muted TV had grabbed her attention. Stuckey craned his neck but couldn't see the screen. He turned and backed toward the sofa for a better look, but still didn't sit.

"This shit's been on the local news all night," Jenna grumbled. "It'll make TMZ tomorrow, that's for sure."

Stuckey caught his breath—on the screen was a picture of Amabel Hadley in a low-cut sparkly dress, her long hair windblown—a clip from an unspecified red carpet event. Then came a snippet from one of the actress's kid movies—*Switcheroo*, wasn't it? Stuckey didn't get it. He'd forgotten where he was and felt like he'd just been nabbed with his pants down jerking off to *First Time*. But there was Jenna on the sofa, lying back as if an elephant sat on her lap. On the TV a grainy video played, something captured by a handheld camera, maybe a phone. There was Amabel Hadley, ducking down, a stocky police officer next to her with a considerate hand on her head as she bowed and half-stumbled into the backseat of a police cruiser. Her face turned back for a second before the door closed: her eyes glittered from the swirling light atop the car, and she smirked, just like she did in *First Time*. Stuckey squirmed.

"Isn't that—"

"Amabel Hadley, that slut." Jenna blew her nose, examined the tissue, and blew again. "This happened right here. At the Kwiky Mart downtown. She was in town today making some kind of public appearance, I didn't hear where." A suited reporter stood in front of a set of gas pumps, talking into a microphone. "Probably a slut convention," Jenna said. In the shot was a red sports car. The camera shifted between the reporter and a Kwiky Mart employee, lingered on the sports car, then tracked to another Kwiky Mart worker who swabbed with a mop at a huge, sudsy puddle spreading from under the car all the way to the store. The clip of Amabel ducking into the police car—the hand on her head, the glittering eyes, the smirk—played again and again. Stuckey watched Jenna, her eyes slitted, peering at Amabel.

"She was pumping her own gas," Jenna hissed, "and she called out to a little kid in front of the store to go in and buy her some cigarettes. The kid was way too young for that, and when one of the workers came out to see what was going on, Amabel started yelling, and then she let the gas overflow from her car—that's the puddle they're cleaning up. The Kwiky Mart guy said she was slurring her words and smelled like alcohol. He said she kept screaming that she wanted her cigarettes, and she pulled out her lighter and flicked it on and started waving it around and threatening to drop it into the gas. A police car showed up—somebody inside the store had called."

"That Kwiky Mart is just down the street from my apartment," Stuckey whispered, marveling that Amabel Hadley had been so close to where he lived.

"I guess the police got her calmed down before they took her into custody." The loop of Amabel squatting into the cruiser continued to play. "That's what happens when you're out of control, Stuckey. Take my word for it, tomorrow they'll have found video of her screaming and waving that lighter around. It'll go viral."

Stuckey took a deep breath. He imagined Amabel Hadley standing in the middle of a blazing fire, grinning triumphantly. "You're right," he said. "You're so very right."

"God, I hate her," Jenna spat suddenly, with a venom Stuckey didn't recognize. She jabbed the remote at the TV, and the screen darkened. "I spent every second thinking about her when I was a kid. I let her take over my childhood."

"Well, you did okay," Stuckey muttered. "You'll do okay." Was Jenna complaining about him? That he'd been the best she'd been able to do? And she was blaming that fact on Amabel Hadley? Stuckey nodded at the blank screen. "There's no telling where that's going to end." He moved to Jenna and bent down to kiss her, closing his eyes as his lips touched her cold forehead.

"Time for you to go," she said. "And don't bother to look for me. The less you know the better." The icy look she gave Stuckey dipped to the Walmart bag he still held under his arm. "What's that?" she asked. "You said you had something for me."

Stuckey clamped his arm down on the bag. "Bread," he said, just as a ringtone sounded a bugle call. Jenna fished her cell phone out from under the sofa cushion, checked the number, and frowned up at Stuckey—at least he thought it was a frown—frowns needed eyebrows, and Jenna wasn't wearing any.

"Just a second," she barked into the phone, and covered it. "I've got to take this," she said to Stuckey. "What did you say?"

"It's bread in the bag. Just bread. I brought it here by mistake. I took the wrong bag from home. Maybe I'll have time to drop the thing I meant to bring in the morning. I'll hang it on the door."

"I'll be gone," Jenna said. She tried a farewell smile, another expression that didn't work well without eyebrows. "Good luck to you Stuckey." She glanced at the phone she pressed between her hands.

"And to you," Stuckey said, and he was out the door. It was dark, and the air was still. When Jenna Klein vacated, he'd move back into the bungalow. He dropped the Walmart bag in old Dora's garbage can and paused, listening for the laughter of happy ghosts.

Chapter 13—Refugees of the Meximo Invasion

Seamus hadn't seen Jenna Klein in months. After guiding her through her initial connections, the party for which she'd be bearing a child had enlisted the care of a medical practice that had not been revealed to him. But there Jenna sat in the children's section of his public library, listening to him read to an audience of half a dozen children who wriggled beside their tired mothers. As Seamus read and displayed the illustrations from *Mend My Tail, Doc*, one in the series of *Emergency Vet* picture books, his gaze flitted to and from the young woman, who wore a yellow raincoat. It had taken him a moment to recognize her because she hid her baldness under an unfamiliar wig— a massive shrubbery of black curls. He flinched when she made a kiss face and fluttered false eyelashes. Was that a new tattoo on one of her scarred lids—a disconcerting open eye? He became self-conscious of the cast he worried about in his own eye and ducked his head to the book he displayed on his lap. He flipped pages: here was the cat being fitted for a prosthetic leg; here the pig with its snout stuck in a peanut butter jar; here the teacup monkey with its tiny, clawed paw super-glued to its tail.

Jenna waited near the checkout desk as the children's section emptied. Her belly swelled out of her raincoat, stretching her orange maternity blouse as smooth as a pumpkin. She held a large paisley bag by its strap. Her height surprised Seamus—her bushy wig made her taller than he was—had they ever stood next to each other?

"Hi, Doc. You're reading to children now." Jenna smiled. "That's sweet. They told me at your office you'd be here."

Seamus wagged his head and looked at her askance to disguise his cast and to avoid staring at her tattooed eyelid. "Yes," he said. "I volunteer. I'm giving back." The truth was a failed date had told him he needed to "get out in the world and practice communicating." Reading aloud was as close to genuine conversation as he could get.

"'Giving back,'" Jenna echoed. "Noble." Her hands were clasped under her belly as if she were offering him a gift. "We've got a lot of catching up to do. Would you like to get some coffee? You drive us, and I'll treat. It's hard for me to squeeze behind a steering wheel these days. I had to take the bus to get here"

As they settled into Seamus's Escalade in the library parking lot, the sun was setting. Jenna rummaged in her bag and pulled out a pistol. She held it down by her belly so it couldn't be seen through the SUV's windows and angled it at Seamus's face. "I'm afraid I'm going to have to ask you to give me everything in your pockets," she said. "Keep your keys for now. But I want your phone, wallet, everything else." The gun didn't look like a toy. "I'm not joking, Doc Mo."

"You're robbing me?"

"No. You won't lose a thing. This isn't a robbery. It's a kidnapping. Or no, a *doc*-napping." She paused, licking her lips as her attention dipped to her swollen stomach. "Though I guess it *is* a kidnapping, too. That depends on who you think this baby belongs to." Her eyes flashed at Seamus. "I've decided to call it mine. I've got a promise of fifty thousand for it in Mexico City. It was so nice of you to arrange things here, but fifty thousand? That's almost twice what I'm supposed to get here." She extended her palm. "So the wallet and the phone—and whatever else you've got that identifies you. Keep the keys in the ignition. Start up and get us out of here—take the Interstate south." Without lowering the pistol she took in the SUV's interior. "Nice car. How's it on fuel? Once we get to the border, it's still twenty hours to Mexico City."

Seamus couldn't think of the questions he knew he should ask. He tugged his wallet out of his back pocket and his phone out of his front and placed both in the hand of his former patient. He started the Escalade.

"So—you want me to be your chauffeur?"

"Oh, you'll be that and maybe much more, Doc Mo. Listen, I could have picked anybody to drive. But I chose you. We clicked right from the start, remember? I owe this baby to you. And now you're my insurance policy." She glanced around the parking lot, clutching the gun like it was a small animal needing restraint. "Just get us out of here. We'll get food and gas on the road. There's a long way to go, and I've got to stop a lot to pee."

An hour later, Jenna Klein pinned her gun between her knees while she peeled the plastic wrap from the sandwiches she'd bought with Seamus's cash. It had gotten dark. The only light in the SUV was the luminescence of the dashboard and the occasional swimming beams of northbound cars and trucks.

"Do you ever use your four-wheel drive?" she asked with a full mouth.

"No," Seamus said. "I'm not even sure how it works."

Jenna swallowed, then rested her sandwich on her belly. "You got what I meant by 'insurance policy,' right? You understand your purpose?"

Long-legged Jenna had pushed her seat back to its limit, and, because of his weak eye, he had to screw his head like an owl to see her face. He hadn't much of an appetite for his sandwich and chewed half-heartedly.

"I'm your driver—chauffeur. So you can get to Mexico."

"Go on—*and*—"

"'And'?"

Jenna laughed. "And you're a *doc*, Doc! I'm due any second—what if my time comes before Mexico City?"

"I haven't delivered a baby since med school."

"A delivery's a delivery. I've got towels and alcohol and scissors and a threaded needle in my bag here, just in case."

"You could just take some of my money and buy yourself a plane ticket," Seamus said.

Jenna patted his shoulder—he felt the thrum of each long finger. "That's a nice offer, Doc. Really. But why would I pass up an opportunity to get to know you better than I already do? It's a long ride—we'll be road buddies by the end. And the thing is, I've got passport issues. As in, maybe I've misplaced mine. Or I never got one, I guess. Besides, air travel's unsafe this late in a pregnancy."

"You'll need a passport card to drive into Mexico. There's one in my wallet."

"We'll cross that bridge when we come to it—so to speak. It's funny—we're sneaking a little somebody into Mexico when everybody else is sneaking out. But keep both eyes on the road, Doc!"

Seamus had edged onto the shoulder and eased the SUV back into the center of their lane. "I've got a bad eye," he apologized.

"Yeah," Jenna purred. "I remember. And I'm smooth—nobody's perfect. For a minute there I thought you were getting a little crush on me, sneaking peeks—getting a little Stockholm-ish. You know—Stockholm Syndrome? Everybody falls in love with their captor, right? How do you like *my* new eye—this extra one on my eyelid? I used to have stars when I was fifteen, but I had those removed. You can still see the scars when the light is a certain way. You probably noticed. This new eye is better. It's supposed to be spiritual. Hey—" She touched Seamus's shoulder again. "—we could get matching eye-patches. Like a couple of pirates. Ouch!" She wrenched herself back in the seat, and her huge stomach rose beside him. The gun was still between her knees. "Christ, it's hard to get comfortable. And your car smells like stale smoke. What did I tell you about that nasty habit?" Seamus saw her pale hands float like lily pads on her belly as she settled herself.

They drove in silence into the white tunnel the Escalade's headlights cut through the darkness. The tattooed lid made it impossible for Seamus to know if Jenna slept. An excess of stars swam through the sky. He craved a smoke. Jenna's voice startled him. "This little monkey inside me is a blondie, isn't he?"

"Excuse me?" Seamus shivered himself alert. He'd need to rest soon.

"This baby I'm carrying— you know more about where he comes from then I do. But I've got a feeling that he's golden—like I'm the goose with a golden egg, right? And I heard the nurses talking about 'Hollywood royalty.' This is some movie star's kid. Maybe a movie star couple. You don't have to tell me." Seamus felt Jenna's eyes on his face. "But if I could prove this was supposed to be, say, Kate Winslet's kid—do you know how much it'd be worth?"

Seamus shrugged. "I wish I could confirm something, but, like I said when we began making arrangements, I don't know any more than you do. Probably less." His contact had been a third party, a law firm representing a client "insisting on anonymity."

Jenna Klein sighed audibly. "Doc, here's what's going to happen next—" She hoisted herself up as if she were pinned under a boulder, and when he glanced over, he saw that she again aimed the pistol at his head. Her hands might have been cupping a kitten. "The next cheap motel we come to, we're going to get a room. Both of us need to sleep. I'm going to handcuff you to the bathroom sink. Underneath. Don't worry, I'll give you a pillow and some blankets. It'll probably be a little uncomfortable—sorry in advance. I'll be stepping around you to pee in the middle of the night. Or maybe I'll need you to deliver the Hollywood royalty. That'd be a riot. Think I can keep the gun on you while that's going on?"

The sudden illumination of a carcass on the side of the road stopped her short. "Ugh—what do you think that used to be?"

Seamus blinked at the body as they flashed by—only a long torso, really, its head long gone, its legs crushed to a ruby froth. "I don't know," he said. His joints ached— the bathroom floor? Would he be too wide to fit under the sink? But escape was out of the question—he was too weary. "A coyote, maybe. An antelope?"

"That's a life no emergency vet is going to save, right Doc?

***

The Blue Daisy Motel had one room left with a private bathroom. In it, Jenna Klein offered suggestions for Seamus's comfort: "You'll have to lie on your back, and we'll cuff your right wrist to the drainpipe. Wedge your pillow in the corner there. See—you can stretch your legs around the toilet. Don't worry. I'll step over you." The cuff she pulled from her bag and snapped around his wrist pinched slightly. She grunted as she kneeled to fasten the other end to the pipe. "My stomach's in the way," she puffed. "You do it." After Seamus locked himself up securely, Jenna lurched to her feet. A meaty odor wafted from under her skirt, tainting the cool air. Seamus stared up at the sink's filthy, rust-stained underside and closed his eyes. There would probably be at least one more bathroom imprisonment before Mexico City.

"I'm leaving the light on and the door open. When I have to pee, I'll tiptoe," Jenna announced. Seamus could only see her legs. Her blue running shoes looked new, and her ankles were swollen and chafed. A quarter-sized bruise yellowed on her shin. She left the bathroom, and he heard the bed springs creak under her weight. Was she on top of the covers or under them? Had she removed her clothes? She'd be smooth, of course—but hadn't she mentioned patches that needed shaving? Would she do that in the morning while he watched? Maybe she would need his help. For a moment, as he struggled to picture Jenna Klein on the bed, Seamus felt a kinship with Balthus—this must be what it was like being inspired to create a work of art. He tried to envision new versions of some of the paintings in his art book, but he was too tired and uncomfortable to create a coherent composition and could only recall the yellow bruise marking the young woman's shin.

"Oh—" Jenna called, "if you need to go yourself, just give a shout. I'm a pretty heavy sleeper, though. You might have to hold it."

***

Seamus woke, stiff, unsure of where he was. His wrist touched something cold and metal, and he jerked back, thinking *gun*—and he remembered that he was chained up and why. He strained for sounds of Jenna's breathing, but heard only the faucet dripping above him. He imagined that she'd been unable sleep and had called to him:

Tell me a story, he pretended she'd asked.

About what?

Tell me about a time you wanted to save something but couldn't—or you didn't want to save something, but had to.

Seamus thought hard and remembered an incident from the summer he'd spent during college as an unpaid intern for a veterinarian. There'd been an emergency at a dairy farm—Seamus pictured the distressed cow with Madonna eyes that was suffering through a breech delivery. The cow trembled. Twig-legs protruded from a leaking opening beneath her tail. The vet grasped a slick leg and yanked and the calf slid out. The raw smell of blood dizzied Seamus. Then the vet swore—there was a second calf, a twin, still in the womb. The vet plumbed with his arm while Seamus barely clung to consciousness. "Dead," the vet said of the second calf. "Stillborn." Seamus watched the vet extract the dead calf while its sibling shivered on the barn's dirt floor, waiting for its mother to lick it to its feet.

***

Jenna's voice jarred Seamus awake. Her smooth legs gleamed.

"Morning, Doc. You sleep okay? You were dead out when I came in to pee. Both times. I'm going to wash up, then I'll give you the key so you can free yourself for a minute and take care of business." She straddled his hips to get to the sink. Water hummed through the pipes and echoed over Seamus's head. He watched Jenna's hand descend with a wet washcloth, which she ran over her legs. Her skirt rose and fell with each stroke. He glimpsed her pale underbelly and closed his eyes until he heard the jingle of the handcuff key.

"Okay, Doc Mo, free yourself up."

By the time Seamus released himself, Jenna sat on the edge of the bed, watching him. He resisted a long, groaning stretch, thinking himself brave for hiding his discomfort.

"Hurry up and do what you've got to do," his captor said. She clasped her paisley bag under one arm. "Leave the door open, please. Any funny business and you'll be sorry for it. I'll squint—that's the best I can do for privacy. She shot him a look, "What're you staring at?"

The eye tattoo had disappeared—there was only a dark smudge on Jenna's lid. "Your third eye—it's gone."

She snorted. "Oh—yeah—that was washable marker. You don't think I'd make that mistake again, do you? It hurt like hell when they removed the stars." She picked up her gun and flicked a glance at its muzzle. "This is all the 'third eye' I need, right, Doc?"

Seamus didn't answer. He washed his face and rinsed his mouth, then used the toilet, peeking now and then at Jenna Klein, who had squeezed her eyes nearly shut. A smudge instead of a tattoo on her lid was a disappointment—no twin patches; no pirate gang.

* * *

Back in the Escalade, Seamus behind the wheel, they breakfasted on Twinkies, corn chips and Mountain Dew from the machines in the tiny lobby of the Blue Daisy Motel. The morning sunlight sharpened the borders of the black highway that knifed through the parched land. The broken white line leapt at them like bursts from an assault rifle as they made their way south, and the blue sky spread over them like the roof of a limitless tent. Jenna's thumbs pattered over Seamus's phone.

"I'm going to crack your access code," she said. She bent over her beachball belly, her synthetic curls hiding her face. "What's your date of birth?"

"Why don't I just tell you the code?"

"No—I want to figure it out. I'm good at it."

"My birthday's May 28, 1975."

"5-28-75— no—no—" she grunted as she tested permutations. Seamus peeked at the gun in the folds of her skirt. "Hey—that's tomorrow! Happy birthday, Doc. This kid's birthday will be just about the same as yours. We should sing. Not 'Happy Birthday'—that makes me sad. How about the theme from *Titanic*?" I'll make like Celene Dione. This desert is kind of like an ocean. It's flat, and it goes on and on forever, and you could sink in it, and nobody would ever find you." Seamus felt Jenna's eyes on him. "But *'you're here in my heart*,' she sang flatly, "*'and my heart will go on and on!'*"

A blush crept up Seamus's neck into his cheeks. Was Jenna trying to remind him of the time he'd hummed *Jenna Genitalia* in his examining room?

142

"Too bad we don't have a cake. Hey—I'm in!" Jenna Klein laughed. "Wow— '528doc.' I'll check your messages. Then I'll send some. I'll tell all your contacts that you're on your way to Alaska. Okay, good, the GPS works—I see where we are and—there's Mexico! I love the GPS! It's like a big eye in heaven that's picked us out of nowhere. Mmm—looks like there's no text or voicemail messages for you, Doc."

"Thank God for air conditioning," Jenna sighed. "It cuts the cigarette smell." Even with open vents blasting at full power, she was flushed and sweating.

"I'm trying to quit," Seamus murmured. The last highway signs they'd seen placed them near the Mexican border, a fact the GPS corroborated. The blue had drained from the morning sky, leaving a pale midday haze. Seamus suspected Jenna was planning their attack on the border, and his heart beat faster. She'd been texting non-stop for an hour—his phone buzzed like a jar of bees. Now and then she mumbled or laughed at something she read without telling him why, and he wished she trusted him enough to share. It had been years since he'd been in the company of another person for so long.

"I have an idea," Jenna said. "Let's pretend we're refugees. Let's make believe we're on the run—"

Aren't we? Seamus wondered.

"—There's a joke I heard on TV—somebody on a late-night talk show. Whoever it was said that Mexico and Canada were planning to attack the United States together. There'd be Eskimos attacking from the north, pulled by sled dogs and waving harpoons. Riding up on horseback from the south would be Mexicans with big floppy hats and rifles and those bullet belts crossed on their chests."

"Bandoliers."

"Right, okay. The invaders were going to squeeze in on us from the top and bottom. They'd call themselves the 'Meximo Army'— Mexicans and Eskimos, get it? So let's pretend you and I are running away from them. We're refugees of the Meximo invasion!"

"We don't use 'Eskimos' anymore," Seamus said. "It's 'Inuit.'"

"But that spoils it. It's so easy to ruin a joke." Jenna paused. "What if—" she began again and broke off. She restarted, speaking softly, as if she were talking to herself. "—What if my mother had died giving birth to me?" Jenna sat still for several seconds, then suddenly patted her belly and huffed. "Woof—I forgot for a second what we're doing here—but listen—if I *had* grown up without a mom, that would explain why I lack a nurturing impulse—no maternal role model. Not that I *didn't* have a mother. I did. Very controlling. Maybe she meant well. I'm just saying, if I did lack a mother and a nurturing instinct, that would make me the perfect surrogate, right? And if I didn't have a mom, I wouldn't ever have to feel guilty about her, right? Except maybe if she *had* died giving birth to me, I would have been the one who killed her." She paused. "Did you ever 'use-ta' something, Doc? As in 'use-ta believe'? And then you stopped believing it? So you had to try to start believing in something else because, well, it's not like anyone can believe in *nothing*, right?"

Seamus didn't answer. He'd only been half-listening. If he had a cigarette between his lips, it might have lent him some composure. He pictured himself parking his car in front of his regular convenient store late at night. He saw his reflection—like a photo negative in the glass door—his bulky outline, his features impossible to distinguish. Like a ghost. The door opened, and his image slid off the glass and disappeared as an exiting young couple passed through him as if he wasn't there. And the realization struck Seamus like a punch in the gut that he was attached to nobody in the world.

When Jenna next spoke, startled Seamus bumped the side of his head against the window.

"I guess you don't feel like talking, Doc. Would you please pull off here at this exit? Hey—Doc—dream boy— take me off the Interstate. I've got to pee before our next move."

***

Off the highway, they headed due west along a narrow tar road. Weeds grew in its cracks. The dry land, the sparse brush, the gullies and arroyos, the distant hills and cattle fences looked the same as they had from the Interstate, but Seamus felt different, as if he and his passenger had been swallowed by the scene, and they were seeing things from the inside. He wondered how difficult it would be to engage the four-wheel drive. The Escalade's owner's manual was in the glove compartment. Was she really going to have him attempt an illegal border crossing? Would they have to ford a river? Would there be a border patrol that shot first and asked questions later? He sneaked a look at Jenna. Maybe he wasn't so terribly alone. She had picked him, something no woman had ever done before. Though they weren't pirates, they shared something. They were pioneers of modern survival.

Jenna Klein had given him a new purpose: she was an incubator in need—an *entrepreneurial* incubator— and he was her deliverer.

"Here is good," Jenna said when the road cut through a sandy stretch along a dry creek bed. Seamus slid the SUV to a stop, little stones popping beneath the tires. Jenna still toted the gun, but Seamus doubted she'd force him to follow her while she went off to squat behind a bush or boulder. She probably wouldn't even ask for the keys. After she did her business, they'd plan the crossing—from north to south, right through territory under the sway of the Meximo Army.

But Jenna didn't budge. "I think I just saw an animal in distress," she said, staring straight at Seamus, her face as cold and flat as a China plate. "I did. Definitely. Down that empty creek bed. It was limping." Seamus peered past her, to the right and left. There wasn't a sign of movement, and he could see for miles. "It was a burro, I think," she added. "Probably escaped from a ranch. Poor thing. A burro or a mule. What's the difference?"

Seamus focused on the gun, which seemed to have woken up and taken an interest in his chest. Jenna braced it on her belly next to the phone. He choked the wheel. "A mule is the offspring of a horse and a donkey," he said. "Mules are sterile."

Jenna Klein shook her head. "I meant what's the difference *what* it is? You've got to investigate, right? Aren't you sworn to help those in distress?"

"I'm not a veterinarian."

"No, but aren't animals as important as human beings these days? Some people believe that, right? You were reading about animal emergencies to those children. You're a healer, Doc Mo." She started a deep breath and cut it short. "Okay, so, the thing is, we're practically at the border—less than an hour away now, and my contacts will meet me when I cross."

"What about Mexico City?"

"Oh—" Jenna wrinkled her nose. "I guess that was just something I made up. All I need to do is get over the border. I'll flash your passport card. Believe me, nobody will give it a second glance. Anyway, we kind of look alike, don't you think?"

Seamus's thoughts unspooled. No Mexico City? And Jenna thought they resembled each other?

"No contractions yet," she said. "I don't really need you as my insurance policy anymore. But it's been nice talking to you. What I would like now is for you to get out and walk down the creek bed—off the road a ways, please. Leave the keys. Just right there in the ignition, thank you. This is a beautiful vehicle. Real value." Jenna peered up and down the road. Seamus noticed for the first time that her eyes were the color of lilacs. Maybe not. Maybe they were brown. Or even gold.

"Let's go, Doc. Think of that suffering creature out there. Who's going to investigate if you don't?" The phone buzzed, but Jenna Klein ignored it. She gestured with the gun. "Go on— open the door and step out. Maybe now would be a good time for a cigarette, if you've got one."

Seamus lost his balance as he swung the door open, staggering as he set his shaking legs down. Fresh tar oozed from the cracks in the road. The air above its surface shimmered with heat. His cheeks tightened, and he held his hands out to his sides as if he'd dropped something. His gaze swept the terrain to the horizon. There was no injured animal.

"Which way did you see it go—the hurt animal?" His voice sounded thick in his ears, like they were stuffed with cotton.

"It doesn't matter," the young woman said. "Just start walking. And don't look back. That way, I guess, off the road. Hurry up." As he shuffled around the Escalade, Seamus heard the passenger window whine open. He kicked up dust on his way to the creek bed and glared at his feet: his brown moccasins looked new—when had he bought them? Where? He passed rocks and pebbles striped with glitter. When he was a kid, he'd collected similar stones, pretending they'd make him rich. Maybe it had been a hundred years since anyone had looked closely at any of the rocks scattered around him. Maybe they'd never been noticed by another soul.

"Keep going!" Jenna seemed only a few feet behind him, but he'd walked at least thirty paces. He shivered a breath. His shadow leaned away from him, and he watched it pass over larger rocks and the withered bushes that would become tumbleweeds when they broke off in the wind. A half-hope rose in his throat—maybe she didn't mean to shoot him. She wouldn't have to—she was going to Mexico. Should he remind her of that? His elbows brushed his hips; he regretted his fatness and his poor posture, and he tried to stand straight. But he didn't want to look like he was marching. He waited for an instinct to tell him to run. It had been so long since he'd done it, he couldn't remember what running felt like. The Escalade started, and the drone of its engine rolled out to him. This would end up no worse than a desertion, he reasoned. He'd need water.

What if Jenna Klein's water broke? What if, as she lowered her dirty lid to take aim and tightened her finger on the trigger, she suddenly exploded? The water would gush between her legs and flood the upholstery. Her dress would be soaked. Contractions would begin. Driving would be impossible, and she'd need to redeem her insurance—she'd call Seamus back to the Escalade. But he would plant his feet in the dust, fold his arms over his chest, and wait. Until she begged. Time would crawl by. He'd outlast her. Where are your associates now, he might chide. Seamus would have to deliver the baby.

There might be complications. The newborn, a fine boy, would slip into Seamus's steady hands, but Jenna, lying back on the reclined passenger seat of the Escalade, might hemorrhage uncontrollably. He'd drag her bloody and unresponsive body from the car while the infant squalled. Her wig would fall off, and he'd kick it behind a cactus. Jenna's bare head would look like a huge egg. Seamus would cover the young woman—she'd either be dead or the next worst thing— with brush and rocks and sand. Then, while he drove south overland, his phone would buzz with orphaned messages. Behind him, all of nature would be drawing toward Jenna's body. Scavengers, sun, and wind would pick her clean until her bones merged with the country.

The baby would belong as much to Seamus as to anyone. Years in the future, Seamus would share with the handsome child the true story of how they came to live in their villa. The Meximo invasion would be over—all borders would be dissolved, but Seamus would faithfully describe the world as it had been. He saw himself flipping through a picture book, lingering over each illustration, pointing out details.

But each turn of a page was a scuffed step into the dessert, and, as Seamus edged further from the SUV, a question rose like a monument—would he hear the shot before he felt it?

Chapter 14—Ahab

Moving day. Dana's new husband Laser-Russ still slept. She stood in the doorway of her daughter's bedroom, grimacing against the blades of sun slicing through the blinds. Dana hadn't seen or heard from Jenna in years—finishing three, beginning four. But she'd boxed the girl's—the young woman's— clothes, which would accompany Dana and Laser-Russ to a new, down-sized home in the gate-less community in which her husband the sex offender had already registered himself. Neighbors, she assumed, had been notified. *Laser. Russ.* She only said the last syllable aloud. The first half was bad luck, though it was the name that sang through her fingers when she ran her hands over his body and read his tattoos as if they were Braille.

All Dana had left of Jenna was in these boxes stacked about the otherwise bare room. The walls were as totally smooth as her alopecia-afflicted daughter after a fresh shaving. Dana closed her eyes and shook her head, disgusted with herself. She was moving kids' clothes. How many sets of Scaredy Cat eyes had mocked her from the T-shirts, skirts, and underthings she'd smothered in boxes? The light in those feline eyes had left Dana restless during her last night in the house she was glad to be leaving. In the dark she'd rubbed her husband's shoulder where she knew he had a tattoo of a whale crushing a ship in its jaws.

"Tell me something else about *Moby Dick*," she'd whispered, and Laser-Russ, who Dana knew didn't expect her to read the novel herself, told her about Ahab: how he looked like a man burned at the stake and had a scar like a lightning streak.

"Ahab had 'a crucifixion in his face,'" Laser-Russ said. "The crew of the Pequod would have followed him to the end of the earth."

Dana hadn't slept after that. She'd been raised Jewish, and she was uneasy visualizing a crucifixion in anybody's face. Before Laser-Russ's description, she'd pictured Ahab as a kind of nautical Abraham Lincoln, with a tall hat and black beard to go with his whalebone peg leg. Now Honest Abe had a scarred cheek and crosses in his eyes. The crosses spun a quarter turn and became X's, like the eyes of dead people in cartoons. And Dana knew that what really haunted her were the remnants of Jewish stars on her daughter's eyelids. Perhaps the scars had finally faded.

The morning light struck the boxes—in the new house these would be pushed into a basement corner. Dana's gaze dropped to a red and white boot box on top of the nearest pile, and she sniffed. "AHAB" was printed across its lid. Just when she was thinking about him? She bent to look closer, her hand on her chest, eager to turn coincidence into a miracle. But there wasn't any miracle. Jenna had written "AMABEL" atop the box, and the "EL" had disappeared into the red half of the cover. "AMAB," not "AHAB." You see what you want to see, Dana thought. She opened the box and lifted out a black scrapbook-diary with gold glitter initials on its cover—"A H". For Amabel Hadley, of course, but also the beginning of "AHAB." Amabel. Jenna had idolized the teen celebrity.

Dana sat on the bare mattress of Jenna's bed and opened the scrapbook. Pasted or taped onto the first few dozen pages were pictures of the young film star cut from magazines. Each photograph had been dated with a glitter pen. Amabel Hadley posed on red carpets, waved at paparazzi, stood before huge posters displaying her Scaredy Cat logo. Amabel smiled in most and seemed as aware of her luxuriant auburn hair as she was of the logo. It might have been a wild animal perched on her head. There was a face-on-the-milk-carton melancholy to these pictures, probably because they were old—some older than a decade, and Dana flipped to the next section of the scrapbook.

There she found dozens of Valentines, birthday cards, and "Thinking of You" note cards. All were from Amabel to Jenna. The celebrity had corresponded with her daughter? But the handwriting was Jenna's—Dana recognized the open loops and the tiny hearts dotting the i's. Jenna had written to herself in the guise of Amabel. There was a birthday card with a happy hippopotamus holding up a placard with the number thirteen—the card itself was practically that old. Maybe not quite. Inside was a note: "Dearest Jenna —I think of you like a daughter and a sister all rolled up into one—Happiest of Birthdays, Love, Amabel."

And inside a Valentine's Day card was a picture of an older Amabel, mini-skirted and splay-legged on a lounge chair at a Hollywood nightclub. The celebrity's hair had been bobbed and dyed pink—a perfect match for the wig teenage Jenna had used to cover her baldness. The Valentine's message: "When you're free, my starry-eyed love, we'll live together in total bliss, and nobody will ever, ever guess the SECRET we share!" Beneath the Valentine, Jenna had replied to her Amabel-self in glitter ink: "Witch-woman doesn't touch us now—I shave myself and stay pure."

Dana's cheeks burned. "Witch-woman"? Tears welled but didn't spill. Dana had hated shaving the nasty patches that sprouted over her otherwise smooth daughter, it was true, but the gesture had proven her love, hadn't it? The nightly ritual had bound her to Jenna—and she'd been despised for it? Dana breathed slowly to calm herself. Nothing she was finding in this scrapbook was anything beyond normal teen rebellion. As a principal, every day she counseled parents whose children acted out publicly with greater vitriol than this. Still, what was to be made of "starry-eyed"? Those tattoos had been a turning point, hadn't they—probably they'd cost Dana her daughter. But hadn't the same stars led her to a husband? Was love a zero-sum game? Dana flipped bravely to the scrapbook's final pages.

There she found a list of Amabel Hadley's movies and the dates Jenna had seen them. Dana had accompanied her daughter to several of the early ones and remembered Jenna's near-feverish excitement— how she'd sit, mouth agape, watching the larger-than-life silliness on the screen, how the girl's wet eyes would sparkle when she'd glance at Dana. Some of the last titles on the film list were unfamiliar, except for one, marked by an asterisk—*Svidrigaylov's Dream*. Her daughter left a note beside it— "unfinished"—and had drawn an arrow suggesting the film should be at the top of the list—it was a beginning, the start of things. Dana winced. Somewhere along the line she'd connected that name back to the horrible Raymond Walchuk, who she'd barely prevented from ruining her production of *Alice in Shizzel-land*. But his boy had been so sweet. It had always made her uneasy that Laser-Russ had that same unpronounceable Russian name tattooed over his stomach. From *Crime and Punishment*, her lover explained. Another novel Dana would never read, framing her indifference as a protest.

On the scrapbook's very last page was a list of dates of Amabel Hadley's concerts and public appearances. Most of the latter were at Walmart stores where she'd have been promoting her line of Scaredy Cat products. A tearful frowny-face followed an entry for a summer concert that had been scheduled on the day of Jenna's fifteenth birthday. When the event was canceled due to lackluster ticket sales, Jenna had been inconsolable, spending three days in bed. She'd refused to shave for a week, and darkening spots had mottled her wigless scalp. How many months after that had the stars appeared?

Dana shut the scrapbook, placed it back in the boot box, and left the room.

There were more boxes in the kitchen. Movers were due to arrive soon to clear out everything. Dana and Laser-Russ finished their breakfast sharing sections of the final newspaper Dana would read at the only address she'd known for almost twenty years. Since Jenna was a toddler. Since before her divorce from the girl's father.

An item in the local section under "Community Notes" confused her: "Hardly to Appear at Local Walmarts." Were words playing tricks on her today? Was language falling apart? Why—or how— could something "hardly appear"? A misprint, she assumed with a frown—she might not have been as well read as Laser-Russ, but she was confident in her knowledge of grammar and usage—that fluency, she believed, had contributed to her reputation as an exemplary Language Arts teacher. She read the brief note: "Celebrity Amabel Hadley will be appearing at the Fort Garcia Walmart this Thursday at 10 AM. Drawings will be held for discounts on Scaredy Cat merchandise."

Dana slapped the table. "Russ—" she nearly shouted, "Amabel Hadley—at Walmart!" It was beyond coincidence: last night she'd learned from Laser-Russ about Ahab and his dedication to his quest, and this morning she'd seen AHAB on the box containing Jenna Klein's scrapbook. And the scrapbook had concluded with a list of Amabel Hadley's Walmart appearances. The last appearance listed in the scrapbook was six years old—but Amabel was coming back tomorrow. An intuitive certainty tightened around Dana like a boa constrictor, and she couldn't catch her breath: Jenna would come to the Fort Garcia Walmart to see her idol. And Fort Garcia was less than an hour away from Dana and Laser's new house.

***

"Russ, I'll be in 'Misses' until they announce that she's here. You'll be in 'Home Electronics'?"

"Until they announce Amabel." Russ had slipped without a second thought into the last third of his first name, La-za-rus, though he'd gone by Laser since grade school. Dana had been using Russ for the four years they'd been sleeping together, and now that they were finally married, the name fit as comfortably as the khaki pants and button-down shirt he sported these days instead of denim and leather. His official sex offender name was still Lazarus.

On his way to "Home Electronics," he paused at the full-length mirror on a post beside a rack of golfing jackets, slid a blue one from the L section, and shrugged into it. Who was he looking at? Where were the nose ring and ponytail? He could identify the bits of tattooing that leaked out of his cuffs and collar only because he was aware of their existence. Ahab and Amabel and Walmart. Dana's quest was to find her daughter. Somehow, his Moby Dick tattoo had launched this endeavor. He wouldn't tell his wife that Ahab found his whale but lost everything else. Russ studied himself in the Walmart mirror. He hadn't gotten a tattoo in years. The only new stories to be found on him were fresh interpretations of old ink. Twice, a few years before they were married, Dana had asked him to tattoo "Jenna" over her collarbone, but he'd sold all of his equipment and ink before he could get around to it. He'd forgiven Dana's daughter for falsely accusing him in court. He'd known he was playing with fire when he'd offered the freshly inked, clearly underage girl a ride home. But it would be bad luck, maybe sinful, to tattoo her name anywhere, even on her mother.

"SVIDRIGAYLOV"—the name he'd marked across his stomach in prison— threatened to burn through his shirt and the jacket, and he turned from the mirror to avoid seeing the letters glowing through charred fabric. Dana's search might be fruitless, but the fact that she towed Russ along kept him from sinking. There was movement over in "Misses." A public address system clicked and hummed.

***

Dana had a plan. She and Laser-Russ would lurk at the periphery of the crowd and scan faces. She hadn't seen Jenna in so long she worried she might not recognize her. Of course her daughter would be wearing a wig. What if she had gained or lost weight? Disguised herself with cosmetics? *But a mother will know her child,* Dana thought. And what if Jenna's star-blemished eyes suddenly blinked at her from behind a mirrored post? Would her daughter rush to her or turn and run? Would Dana chase her? Of course she would.

Honey, it's Mom, she'd shout. And what if Jenna cried to Amabel Hadley to rescue her?

***

When Amabel arrived, Russ and Dana were studying faces in the waiting crowd. The celebrity simmered in the Walmart fluorescence. She patted the store manager's arm and whipped her shorter-than-expected hair over her shoulders as she posed next to a cardboard cutout of herself.

"Don't be shy," Amabel rasped at the smallish group. "Take all the pictures you want. I'm the real thing." Then she bowed. She staggered a step when she stood upright. "Oops." She winked at the store manager and plopped into a waiting folding chair. "Everyone will think you got me drunk, Hal." The blushing store manager grinned, cleared his throat, and described the drawing and the discounts on Scaredy Cat apparel.

"Hal—don't forget the accessories," Amabel barked with her eyes closed. "We're featuring lovely jewelry. Jewelry to die for. That's how the guy at the last store put it. Wherever we were." Her eyes opened and she fluttered painted lids like fluttering bats as she struggled to bring the store into focus. "And belts," she said. "We've got lovely belts. Amabel's got belts. Am-a-belt. You're a belt! Get it?" The celebrity made a kiss-face at the store manager. "*I'm-a-belt*. We're all belts!" Amabel guffawed until she choked and bent forward, sinking for a moment out of Russ's sight. The store manager stared down at her with a frozen smile, his microphone tucked under his chin. Amabel rose, coughing and wheezing something that sounded like, "Oh, shit." Those standing closest to her, including the store manager, backed away.

"You going to suck that mike, Hal?" she asked. "Hand it over— have lips, will suck, that's what I say. That's why I'm here, right? To suck?" The store manager moved in front of Amabel, and Russ remembered that he was supposed to be looking for Jenna. He caught sight of his wife—her eyes, narrowed with concentration, glided over face after face.

A drawing was conducted, merchandise and discount coupons were distributed, and Amabel Hadley and the display disappeared from "Misses." Russ and Dana met up next to the celebrity's empty folding chair. Russ shook his head. "That lady has a few problems."

"Yes. You didn't see Jenna?"

Russ shrugged a negative. He stepped aside for a young man in a Walmart smock who'd arrived with a clean up cart. The former tattoo artist was thinking about the night school class he was taking in computer graphics. He still liked creating designs, but the tap of his fingers on a keyboard could never replace the buzz of his tattoo machine in his palm, the smell of ink and antiseptic, and the feel of flesh shuddering beneath his touch. He wondered what kind of tattoos Amabel Hadley might have and where they might be.

The Walmart worker with the cleanup cart stooped over a yellowish puddle beside Amabel's seat. Russ examined the soles of his shoes to see if he'd stepped in it, but they were clean. The worker dropped paper towels over the puddle, then scooped up the mess like it was a clutch of golden eggs and stuffed it in a garbage bag that hung from his cart. Then he mopped the floor.

* * *

"I think we're close," Dana said as the couple exited Walmart through the sliding doors. Dana had taken Russ's hand and led him toward the row she thought they'd parked in. Wrong direction, Russ thought, but said nothing and followed his wife.

"Amabel will be going to more Walmarts," his wife said. "I can find her schedule online. We're definitely on the right track"

"There are Walmarts all the way to Mexico," Russ said.

Chapter 15—X

I

The man who finds her stands with the moon over his shoulder, his slim silhouette a hole in the desert night-sky; he's darker than the greater darkness surrounding them because he blocks the stars.

"Why are you in my yard?" he asks. "Can I help you?" He crouches as he speaks, still two dimensional. Her bald head is cold, her throat dry.

"Sick," she says, which is a kind of truth. "Cancer," she whispers, which is a lie to explain her baldness. "Attacked," she says, a second lie, this to explain the dried blood on her thighs that streaks to her bare feet.

A pair of hands emerges from the silhouette and slides under her. Only after she's hoisted—as easily as if she's the husk of something—does she feel the shape of the rocks she's been lying on. She's swung away from the moon, wants to see it, but hasn't the strength to turn her head.

***

She wakes swathed in cool sheets on a bed in a lit room. Poster-sized artwork covers stucco walls. Her abdomen aches. She touches herself, peers under the sheets that are so white they seem fluorescent. Crusts of blood edge her wounds, but most has been washed off. Red spots startle her—just the polish on her toenails; she's not hemorrhaging. But when she hears a male voice, pain wracks her. The speaker stands in the door-less entry to the room. He is tan, with hair like straw. The voice and thin body match those of her rescuer. He won't allow his gaze to shift from her eyes. His are blue.

"I washed and cleaned your wounds. You stopped bleeding. I haven't called an ambulance or notified the authorities. Do you want me to?"

She remembers—before she'd become too dizzy with pain and exhaustion to think straight, she'd created the beginning of a story: she was sick, the narrative went—cancer; she'd been on her way to Mexico City on the promise of an alternative treatment when she'd gotten lost on a side road, and her car broke down; a gang of young men in a beat-up car stopped to help; though she was suspicious, the day was so hot and the road so empty that she had no choice but to accept. What rescuer, seeing the blood, wouldn't believe that she'd been assaulted? Who wouldn't marvel at the will to survive demonstrated by her courageous escape? And she *had* run—that much was true—but she'd lost consciousness before coming up with a reason why the police should not be summoned.

The man in the doorway purses his lips—he isn't young—age spots mark his hairline, and his weathered face is deeply creased. His beard is so white it makes his teeth look stained.

"You've been on television. We're less than a hundred miles over the border, and I get American TV. They know who you are. The child you gave birth to is healthy. A boy. Did you know that? Did you see? Before you ran? If you're hungry, I've got soup, Jenna—your name is Jenna something, right?"

"Water, please," Jenna whispers, admitting nothing. Screaming has left her painfully hoarse.

"Beside you." The man nods to the glass on a night table, and when Jenna reaches for it, her ribs ache and her thighs cramp. What's the right play here? Should she hide her pain or exaggerate it? But when she tries to lift the water, her palm stings, and she sets the cup back down with a short cry. She looks at the heel of her hand, the heels of both hands—tiny puncture wounds—her nails had done that when she clenched her fists? She picks up the glass in her fingertips and drinks. The water sears her throat like cool fire.

"You said 'Cancer,'" the man says. His voice echoes—the floor is tiled, the ceiling high with track lights to illuminate the pictures. Jenna reaches for her bald head. How much does this man know? Does he know there's no chemo, that she's hairless because of alopecia? Does he know that she's not perfectly smooth? Patches surface: one on her thigh, another under her arm, and an inch wide strip that runs front to back on her head like an off-center bird's crest. *Almost perfect*—being absolutely hairless would be divine, but her patches are an insult. Shaving herself smooth has been a lifelong chore. Her fingers ease over her scalp until—bristles. When she groans, her empty uterus spasms.

"The reporter on the news said, 'Look for a young woman in a yellow raincoat. An orange dress. They might be blood-stained. She could be wearing a wig, because she doesn't grow hair.' Did you lose the wig?" The man shakes his head and lowers his voice. "Cancer is something you shouldn't fake," he says, as if that pretense is the worst of her crimes.

Jenna feels her nostrils dilate. An instinct tells her to escape, but she knows her body wouldn't obey if she tried to run. Where would she go? Her eyes glide around the room, over the pictures—searching for an exit. Large windows, three on the wall to her left, one on the wall in front of her, are set above the pictures, too high to reach and black because it's night. To her right is a small bathroom—she sees a shower stall, a sink, and toilet— no window or door. The only way into or out of the room is through the doorway that frames her host.

"Don't call the police," she says. "I just need rest. Where am I?"

"You're where you fled to. No one expected you to run. You confused the border patrol. They underestimated your strength. But they found your bag and ID, Jenna, and your gun. They're looking for the man whose vehicle got you to the border. They know he was your doctor. They assume he was your accomplice. He must not be a very brave man to leave you alone."

He's dead, Jenna remembers. *I kidnapped him back home—to drive, and in case I started labor early—and I shot him in an arroyo when we got close to the border. No one will ever find him.* But she'd miscalculated her needs— her first contraction came just moments after she pulled the trigger—the gunshot had been so loud she had nothing in her experience to compare it to. She thought she could still make it over the border to her Mexican connections. And they did find her, too late, somehow recognizing her yellow raincoat as she dodged through traffic. When they swept her into their black-windowed car, she was empty-armed and exhausted.

"Where is the baby?" they'd demanded as she gasped and bled over a creamy leather seat. The man in back with her offered her his handkerchief. She thought they'd shoot her, but instead they drove and drove, on shrinking, rutted roads, until the red sun dropped behind scorched hills, and they pushed her out of the car.

"Call us when you got something, *puta*," she heard, before the car spun off, spitting pebbles.

"Hungry," she says. When her host—captor?— cleaned her, he'd have wiped away her drawn-on eyebrows. What had he thought as he erased her rakish expression? What else had he noticed? Certainly the drops of mother's milk tattooed beneath her nipple that some of her lovers mistook for tears or blood. And the whole world now knows she's smooth. Did her bristly patches confuse him? She would rather shave than eat, but she won't ask for a razor—he might think her desperate and dangerous. Where are the mirrors? None visible even over the bathroom sink. Just pictures, everywhere.

"Soup," the man says," but—" Before he can finish, something bursts between his legs, streaks across the floor, and leaps onto Jenna's bed—a speckled, piglet-sized dog with radar-dish ears and frighteningly pale eyes. Its sudden weight rocks her and wakes her pain.

"*Mee-go!*" Jenna hears as she covers her face and lifts her knees, her last sight a lolling tongue between grinning jaws. The snorting creature digs with eager paws at the sheet between her legs and tries to tug it away, and Jenna screams as if she's giving birth again.

II

"I find that I'm a different person in different rooms of my house," Claude says without looking up from the wooden tablet he cuts into with one of his knives. Every morning he brings a tablet, a portable worktable, a folding chair, and a leather case of carving tools into Jenna's sunlit bedroom. While he works, Jenna often gazes up at the windows, waiting for a bird, an airplane, even a cloud to pass. When something does float by—or when it rains, and the glass seems to melt—Jenna's heart beats faster, as if she's about to learn a secret. Then the windows return to rectangles of skim milk blue or white or gray. At night they're always black. Beneath the windows the pictures— prints made from woodblocks, she's been informed— are bright with colors, but Jenna focuses on the figures in them only when Claude points them out.

This morning she's staring at the carving tool in Claude's hand. When he lifts it, her eyes trace its path as if it's a magic wand. The blade reminds her that she hasn't shaved her excess hair for over thirty days—since she woke up in this room. She's marked the passing of time by notching the bedpost with her thumbnail. Claude pares her nails, but not too short to make her marks.
Migo curls against Jenna's thighs, his snout against his hindquarters, as if he's one of those snakes that swallow themselves.

"I only have this room, so that's all I am." Jenna says. She has no idea how many rooms are in this house.

"But you had a life back in the States. You lived somewhere. Who were you then? Always the same, no matter which room?" Claude peers up from his work, his forehead grooved like his tablet. *Each woodblock I cut is for a different color of a print*, he's told her. *After all are inked and printed onto the paper, the picture is complete.* She imagines that Claude is cutting her face and figure into his tablets, and when he inks the print, she'll be able to see herself. But before too long she discovers that what he's actually fashioning are poster-sized versions of the small woodblock prints produced by Yoshitoshi, a 19th century Japanese master. Claude's "expansions" hang on Jenna's walls. *You'd be surprised what they sell for*, Claude said. *Only the most foolish tourists mistake them for originals. But they are original, in a sense. It's like making a book into a movie—a different version of the same thing, just bigger. I contribute size.*

Rooms? Who was she in the tiny custom's booth where she disgorged someone else's child? There was space only for herself and the sweating official between her legs. A roll of unfurling paper towels flew over her, struck one of the windows filled with faces and white and blue uniforms. Pain— a Milky Way of exploding stars—then a wail, and then the blinding sunlight, confused shouts, and car horns.

History: the night before the customs booth, a room at the Blue Daisy Motel with fat Doctor Morrison—Doc Mo. He spent the night chained to the drainpipe under the sink in the bathroom he'd never have guessed would be *his* final room. Who was Jenna as she dry-shaved her bristling head-strip—for the last time—on the Blue Daisy Motel's sagging mattress? She'd been someone who thought that the fifty thousand dollars promised her in Mexico was nearly double the fee she'd contracted for in the States.

III

Migo is blind and deaf, Claude has said. "He knows you by your scent." Jenna runs her hand along the dog's rash of spots. His blind eyes glow white—sometimes she strains to see herself in them.

"His name is 'Amigo,' but without the 'a'," Jenna says as she watches Claude cut into a fresh woodblock with a thin blade. Purple ink from a print run stains his fingers. "Does that mean he is or isn't a friend?"

Claude's glance lasts a blink. It's morning, and Jenna spoons oatmeal sweetened with brown sugar from the bowl on her breakfast tray. Claude prints a few hundred copies of each of his enlargements. The prints he hangs in Jenna's bedroom are first runs, their colors especially vibrant.

"Friend," Claude mutters, as if it's an idea he hasn't considered. Jenna still doesn't know if she's a guest or a prisoner. Since Claude has established no restrictions, if she asks for nothing, then nothing is denied. This is freedom. She's brought three meals a day, and the bathroom is stocked with shampoo, soap, toothpaste, fresh towels, and the terrycloth robes that are her only clothing. Before Jenna settled in, she wondered if anyone else lived in the house—maybe it's honey-combed with dozens of chambers just like hers, like a hive. But Claude couldn't care for so many guests and still spend most of his day in her room, working. She's free to explore, as far as she knows, and free to inquire, but the curiosity that might prove her freedom a false idea has shriveled. She's quit counting days—there's no more room for fresh grooves on her bedposts and headboard, and no point in deepening old ones.

IV

Jenna recognizes two universes—her room and her body. Bored with the windows, she now studies the prints that surround her and leaves her bed to study them. Claude has told her that the Asian men and women featured in the prints represent figures from Chinese and Japanese history, literature, and legend. Today, while Claude works, she lingers before a new print, hoping that Claude will explain it.

"That's Wu Gang," he says, putting down his knife. "Because he abused the practice of Taoist magic, he's doomed to chop down the golden-blossomed cassia trees which give the moon its brightness—every time he cuts down a tree, a new one grows in its place. The print shows Wu Gang resting over his ax. The moon hangs over him, his perpetual burden."

"That's like the myth of what's-his-name," Jenna says, "the guy who pushed the rock up the hill, and it kept rolling down."

"Sisyphus," Claude says. "Same idea."

Later, alone, Jenna returns to the print of Wu Gang and the moon made of golden flowers. It's the magician's ax, not the blossoms, that attracts her. With a blade like his, she could shave off the lengthening hair on her head and the patches on her thigh and under her arm. And if she polished the ax, it could serve as a mirror. She runs her hand over her naked scalp until her fingertips bump against her lop-sided crest. Jenna remembers seeing horses with braided manes, and winds a finger around a lock of crest-hair, thinking of ribbons. It's a wonder that Claude never mentions her unusual feature, or the two other fuzzy places that mar her smoothness. His only involvement with her appearance is the trimming of her nails.

When Claude slices off Jenna's fingernails with one of his cutting tools, he works delicately and quickly with the same intense concentration he gives to his woodblocks. Jenna holds out each hand like the brides she's seen in wedding ceremonies on TV shows— palm down, fingers spread, in anticipation of the ring. When he's finished with her nails, Claude shifts back to his worktable, while Jenna eats, examines the prints on her wall, or showers.

***

Jenna often sings while she showers: she runs a bar of soap over her smooth flesh and kinked patches as if she's shaving and hears in her own voice the sing-song rhythm her mother used when she scraped away her little girl's unsightly bristles—*Sooo-smooth, sooo-smooth*. Or Jenna mimics hip-hop performers and sways her hips and slaps her wet ass—*mothah-fuckah* this and *mothah-fucka* that— memories and tunes that are rootless and carry only sound. Jenna's crest-hair has grown long enough to shampoo, and massaging it to a soapy froth delights her. *Mine*, she thinks, as she squeezes her fists through the foam, *all mine*.

Often, after showering, when she returns to her bed in a clean, white terrycloth robe, Jenna discovers that Claude has hung new prints. This morning, as she lies back on her pillow, water leaking from her crest down her neck, she notices two.

"Prostitutes," Claude says with a swipe of his tool in the direction of the prints. "Yoshitoshi called the first 'Moon of the Pleasure Garden' and the second 'Streetwalker at Night.'"

Jenna listens to the titles and tugs her robe to cover her cleavage. Migo, already comfortable against her hip, lifts his head and stares toward her like a blind sphinx. Her first day in this room, the dog had crawled onto her legs, stretched himself along her aching abdomen, and tucked his muzzle under her ripe breasts. *He wants my milk*, she remembers thinking.

Then, as now, she'd thought of the tattooed droplets and clamped her arms over her chest.

"Migo is ugly," she says.

"Migo is a beautiful and perfectly bred truth," Claude says, returning a blade to the tool case and selecting another.

"His head comes to a point, like a sharpened pencil. And his spots look like some kind of filthy disease."

"Both result from generations of street-breeding— the pointy head so he can stick it in tight spaces for trash to eat, the spots for camouflage in garbage dumps."

"He has fishy breath. How did he get here?" It's the new prints that vex her, not the dog, Jenna knows.

"I found him in my yard with a broken leg. Probably hit by a car. A street dog like him isn't likely to wander this far away from a populated area, so he's something of a mystery."

"Was he blind when you found him?"

"No, but his vision was probably failing, which may be why he got hit. And drivers here often aim for small animals."

"They hit things on purpose?"

"Dogs, armadillos, tortoises, anything that isn't likely to damage their vehicle. Not much regard for life."

Claude finishes for the afternoon, leaving Jenna alone until dinnertime. The sky in the high windows is the washed-out blue of the streetwalker's scarf in one of the new prints. The depiction of this prostitute includes a verse in Japanese, which Claude had translated for Jenna: "Like reflections in the rice paddies—the faces of streetwalkers in the darkness are exposed by the autumn moonlight." This woman in the print is of the lowest class of prostitutes, and she carries her rolled straw mat along a riverbank. For what purpose will she next roll out the mat, Jenna wonders—to sleep or to ply her trade? Jenna turns from the white-faced streetwalker to the woodcut with the elaborately robed courtesan—lucky enough to reside in "pleasure quarters." This woman's face is hidden as she watches cherry blossoms sift from tall trees like moonlit snow. An attending child watches the falling blossoms with her mistress.

What's to become of this little girl? She's sure to follow her mistress's trade, but will she inherit the "pleasure quarters" or will she be dismissed to the streets with a rolled mat? Jenna presses her hand against her stomach, anticipating a pain that doesn't come.

V

"Can you bring me ribbon?" Jenna asks Claude. It's the first request she's made since she's occupied the room. If she pulls the hair from her crest over her ear, it reaches her jaw. The hair is honey-colored, much lighter than the patches in her armpit and on her thigh. At night she lies on her back and tickles her nose with strands of it. She hopes Claude will bring a pair of sheers made of polished metal with the ribbon—she imagines admiring herself in the blades after she's cut off decorations for her crest. A fragment of a nursery rhyme floats to Jenna like a moth: about Johnny who went to a fair, and, in trade for a kiss, "He promised to buy me a bunch of blue ribbons, to tie up my bonny brown hair." Jenna blushes at the sudden idea that Claude might think of kissing her. She peeks at his crimped face as he works. He's so old. Is he frowning because he's mulling her request for a ribbon? In what ways does she inhabit his thoughts? The eyes of many men she's known have run over her like thirsty fingers after they've learned of her smoothness. To kiss Claude—Jenna watches him bite his lower lip with his stained teeth while he works, and her mouth clogs as if she's stuffed it with the yolks of hardboiled eggs.

"What color ribbon?" Claude asks, flashing his eyes.

"Blue." Jenna clears her mouth with her tongue and blinks from Claude's face to the sky in her windows. She gasps— bisecting the view from the middle window on the long wall to the left of her bed is a thinly branched tree.

"There's a tree!" she exclaims, shrugging herself up on her elbows, turning back and forth from the tree to Claude. Her flesh goosebumps— her underarm and thigh tingle under their growths.

"That's Migo's tree. I planted it last night. It's a Mexican Sycamore."

"Migo's?" Jenna's excitement contracts into a knot deep in her chest. It's been days since she's seen the dog. "Where's Migo?" she whispers.

"Migo's dead," Claude says. Does his gaze slip from her eyes to her crest? "He didn't wake up the other morning. I mixed his ashes in with the roots when I planted the tree last night." An arched eyebrow: "You had feelings for him?"

Jenna sinks back into her pillow and stares at the tree—its trunk and branches remind her of a fish skeleton hanging from the lip of a trashcan. She remembers the feel of Migo's mottled coat under her hand, his weight against her side. Claude had said Migo was "beautiful."

"I got used to him," Jenna murmurs. "He was familiar."

A groove between Claude's eyes deepens. "He was a killer. Did you know that? Before I took him in, my house was full of life. I had a parrot and a cat. And another dog—an old husky. The parrot talked. '*Buenos noces*,' he could say, and '*hermosa luna*': 'good-night,' and 'beautiful moon.' One day Migo brought me the parrot's body—he jumped on the couch next to me with the bird in his jaws as if he was carrying a rolled newspaper— and dropped it on my lap. The perch was too high for him to reach. I don't know how he lured Rodrigo down. The cat, which I admit I never liked much, I found murdered in the yard. And Migo tortured my old friend the husky for months, biting him on his back and belly and ears when I wasn't around. I'd find Mukluk bleeding. I tried to separate them, but the husky whined to be with his tormenter—Mukluk understood that murdering was part of Migo's nature, part of his perfect breeding, and he longed for the company, even if it was killing him. Eventually, his big heart burst. So, for a long time— until you came—it was just Migo and me."

Jenna shivers and pulls her sheet up to her neck. She runs a palm over her bare scalp, finds her crest, and pats it. Claude nods toward the window with the tree, the creases on his face lengthening with his smile.

"Keep your eyes on those leaves," he says. "See if they don't grow bloody teeth."

VI

Jenna's eyes spring open. She's safe in her room. It's morning. Migo's tree, its branches now thick with leaves, blots out most of the ashy sky in the middle window. Lately, Claude has been replacing the prints on her walls while she sleeps instead of when she showers, and she glances about for any changes. She half-expects to see a Yoshitoshi print he described the previous afternoon, though he'd told her its lack of color would make it unprofitable to reproduce:

"In the print the ghost of a maid rises from the well she's haunting," he'd said. "She committed suicide because she broke a dish, part of an extremely valuable ten place table setting. The ghost counts to nine, over and over again."

"She killed herself because of a broken dish?"

"Why not? It was her duty to maintain a complete set of ten. But people needed the well she lingers in. How do you think her ghost was exorcised?"

Jenna had tried to picture the obsessively counting ghost, but instead saw her mother— emerging from a fog, waving the pink Lady Schick razor she'd used to shave Jenna clean. "Oh," Jenna sobbed. Claude's head had snapped up from his work, and she found herself staring at him.

"'A broken dish'," she repeated. "Oh—your hand—"

"Ah—" And Claude had lowered his gaze—he'd sliced open his index finger. Blood ran along it and dripped onto his woodblock. He'd grinned wryly before wrapping his finger in a white handkerchief – a red stain bloomed. He'd gathered his things—awkwardly, because of his wound—and left without a word.

VII

Jenna's dream and the memory of Claude's blood spreading on the handkerchief have left her restless. Now he's late with her breakfast. Should she take her shower before eating? She reaches for her crest. It's festooned with blue ribbons that dangle past her shoulders. Each shower soaks the ribbons, which stiffen after drying and rustle like wind-blown branches when Jenna tosses her long crest-hair. She looks at Migo's tree, as she does a hundred times a day, and remembers the feel of the dog's body against hers. She shakes her head a second time, glimpsing bits of blue. Claude had brought her the roll of blue ribbon, but not the shears with mirroring blades she'd hoped for—he'd sliced the ribbon into pieces himself with one of his knives. As Jenna cranes her neck, enjoying the weight of her hair, she discovers two new prints, side by side over her headboard. Hung while she dreamed. Turning, she looks up at them from her knees.

The first print depicts a nobleman squatting on a mat. In a nearby dish of water he sees the reflection of a female demon about to attack him from behind, and his hand tightens around the hilt of his sword. Jenna sucks in a breath—the puddles on the floor of her shower—had she ever tried to see herself in them? She hops off her bed, sheds her robe, and hurries to her bathroom. But when she steps into the shower and turns the faucets, nothing happens. She twists the faucets until her palms hurt, but no water. She tries the sink—again, nothing. The toilet, if she'd thought of looking, might have provided the most reflective surface of all, is dry. Jenna licks her lips. Her mouth and tongue are pasty. Where is Claude? Disappointed, thirsty, and hungry, she returns to her bed. Glancing once again at the "demon in the water dish," she heaves a sigh, slumps onto her side, and frowns at the second new print. Its central figure is a lovely young woman.

This woman contemplates a broken wooden bucket lying at her feet. Like many of the prints on Jenna's walls, this one features a Japanese inscription. Examining the calligraphy, Jenna feels her lips move, as if she's uttering a prayer, and a translation emerges: "The bottom of the bucket has fallen out—the moon has no home in the water." *But I don't understand Japanese*, she thinks, bewildered. *What can this mean?* And she hears herself whisper an answer: "No reflections."

Jenna's face drops onto her pillow. Lying on her stomach, she scratches the itchy patch on her thigh, then picks at the hair under her arm and sniffs her fingers. She worries that her crest is really nothing more than an off-center Mohawk. Its dry ribbons irritate her neck. She imagines quenching her thirst from the nobleman's water-dish, in spite of the demon in it.

VIII

She waits. Darkness comes, then light, then darkness again. Maybe it's the same day with rare dark clouds; maybe many days pass. When it's light, the leaves on Migo's tree glisten, sharp and dangerous. From her bed she calls, or thinks she might call, Claude, but she doesn't hear her voice or feel it in her throat. "I'm hungry—" she whimpers with closed eyes, as if she's a baby. It's hard to fill her lungs. When she lifts her lids the pictures on the walls spin around her like a color wheel. The wheel slows and stops. Directly across from her, right where it's always been, is the print of Daruma, the founder of Zen Buddhism. Daruma sits in his red robe, his legs folded under him. *It took Daruma nine years of meditation to reach enlightenment*, Claude has told her. *So much time that he lost the use of his legs. But you can buy little round figures of him. 'Dharma dolls,' they're called. You can get them anywhere, even in the shops that sell my prints. The little red dolls are self-righting—tip one over, it pops back up. They symbolize optimism.*

Jenna tries to hold the image of the meditating holy man. Red spheres swirl like tiny planets around her head—no, not planets— legless dharma dolls. Jenna hugs herself and draws her knees to her breasts, curling around an emptiness that's the size and shape of one of those dolls.

An acrid odor burns her sinuses. Is that her? Her eyes would tear if they weren't so dry. No water to drink or wash with or see herself in. She reaches for her crest, her arm as weightless as paper mache. The ribbons, stuck in clumps of waxy hair, crumble at her touch. Has Claude been allowing her ugliness to ferment? She thought he was protecting and nurturing her, but maybe he's been trying to protect the rest of the world. From her. Had he been saving the world from Migo, too? At the expense of his other pets?

Jenna pictures Doc Mo collapsing in the arroyo, *feels* the volume of the gunshot that started her labor. How long would it have taken for the doctor's fat body to decompose in the desert heat? Bacteria first, insects next, crawling inside his clothes, then winged and four-footed carrion eaters—gathered like guests at the Mad Hatter's tea party, Jenna imagines. But now she sees herself perched on the dinner table, and the figures surrounding her are the legendary subjects of Claude's Yoshitoshi prints—warriors and poets, buddhas and courtesans, demons and ghosts. Circling the table is the mad young woman from a print Jenna had forgotten— this woman wanders the streets at midnight, her letter to a dead lover unspooling all the way to a silver moon.

Who would be looking for Jenna? Authorities couldn't be bothered—the parents of the baby she'd unsuccessfully stolen have the child and the money they would have paid her. Her Mexican associates have perhaps found other willing thieves. Would she recognize the child she bore? He's no kin to her, though her blood fed him *in utero*. She winces at Dharma, meditating on the wall across from her. How long until her legs become useless like his? She lifts herself to her hands and knees in the center of her mattress. Her robe hangs open, and her breasts dangle like forgotten fruit, the tattooed drops of milk crawling like ants from her nipple. The strip of exposed stucco between her headboard and the newly hung prints is daubed with red— Claude's blood? She looks at the doorway he left through, and it seems no more penetrable than any of the prints covering her walls.

IX

The doorway—Jenna's fingers spread like the petals of a white flower on its dark frame. The wall outside it is close enough to touch.

She feels the weight of the stone tiles under her feet. She closes her eyes and tries to remember the exhilaration of her rush to freedom after giving birth— too numb for pain, the blinding sun thrown at her from the metal and glass of a thousand cars, the baby she'd hoped to barter abandoned behind her.

To her left— the hallway ends abruptly. To the right—she blinks, startled: on an easel stands a print, more colorful than any in her room—yellow, green, blue, red, purple, orange—a print like this would have required a dozen woodblocks. She leans on the doorframe, one foot hovering over the threshold. The print is less than ten feet away, its colors spin, and Jenna understands—it isn't a print at all, it's a *mirror*. The mirror is angled so it reflects not her, but something incredibly beautiful—a garden? —at the end of a connecting corridor. A few paces, and she'll see herself, then run to paradise. But she hesitates— at the base of the easel there's a little red globe—a dharma doll. Stuck in its head like a pick in a 'fro is a gleaming blade. An invitation to shave? Jenna grabs her crest, and ribbon-dust falls into her eyes. There's a mark on the dharma doll's belly.

"X," Jenna reads. *A dead-eye X?* Not a Japanese character, but still a message. Her heart hammers harder and faster until the beats don't separate. She envisions Claude, the blood leaking from his hand like a silk rose from a magician's sleeve, his last words to her a question left hanging . . . about the ghost of the maid who broke the dish and endlessly counted to nine. *How was the young woman's spirit exorcised?*

Jenna comprehends: "Not 'X'," she cries. "Ten!" And as she hears her own voice, like ripping paper, the colors in the mirror whirl into a blinding, saturating brilliance that fills her core. Her limbs dissolve, and she is absorbed by her completion.

***

Part III
No More to Rise Forever

T'ings

Chapter 16—"No more to rise forever

"Thousands of mortal men, fixed in ocean reveries," Raymond thought he heard through the intercom on the ferry to Santa Catalina Island. He was barely winning his struggle against seasickness. What about those "mortal men"? And who was delivering Ishmael's speech from the opening of *Moby Dick* over the intercom? Raymond listened intently to the rest of the line he'd noted down himself not too long ago: *"they must get just as nigh the water as they possibly can without falling in."* He huddled among the other passengers in the rows of seats in the ferry's cabin. He felt the sympathy of the small woman beside him as palpably as if she'd laid a comforting hand on his shoulder, though the casual observer might think she paid him no attention at all. Did he look bereft, or had the radiance of his thoughts created an aura around him she couldn't ignore? Could it be that she recognized him from his past successes? That hadn't happened in a while. He'd aged: he was balder, grayer, heavier. And the successes were long gone.

The boat ride to Santa Catalina seemed to defy time. How long did an hour actually feel? Keeping hold of an abstraction like time had been an important consideration when making a film. How long is the movie to be? How long will it take to make? How much time to devote to individual scenes, to close ups? It had taken five hours in a single engine plane flight across vast expanses of endless and empty Pacific Ocean to reach Kiriwina Island from Port Moresby, Papua New Guinea on Raymond's most consequential scouting trip. He visualized a sweeping view of the cave atop the mountain shaped like a skull—but that was from *Kong's Daughter*, wasn't it? The only mountain on Kiriwina was the one he created for his film—just as his father had laid down an airfield during the second World War. It was difficult to keep fiction and reality straight.

The woman beside him stood, turned her back on Raymond, and shuffled past the feet of nearly a dozen passengers on her way out of the row. He watched her nod apologies all the way down. But his was an end seat—why hadn't she simply stepped by him and been on her way? Could it be that his aura was even more imposing than he'd thought? If she'd begun a conversation, he would have told her that he'd abandoned his plans for a remake of *Moby Dick*. No, it wasn't the sea he needed to return to—it was an island. Find an island, survive its isolation, escape it, find another. Each project, each film, each life was an island unto itself, wasn't it? Hadn't it been? Kiriwina, Skull Island, *Teddy, Svidrigaylov's Dream*. Raymond shivered. He observed the woman as she took the long way around the deck on her way to the restroom. There was a line out the door of women and girls waiting with bowed heads and crossed arms. Some leaned on the wall. Were they all seasick? Each was on her own island. He thought of his next project, his reason for this trip to Catalina—not so remote as Kiriwina and better suited for his non-existent budget: with a bit of luck, Raymond could transform Catalina into the island originally captured by H. G. Wells in his haunting novel—the horrifying *Island of Dr. Moreau*.

What better vehicle for a comeback? What better metaphor for the solitary nature of the creative impulse than the scalpel-wielding doctor who attempts to transform beasts into humans by cutting and slashing on his operating table? Raymond had visions for his film that were so painfully vivid he only dared cling to them for a moment at a time: a malformed dog-man servant; a moonlit vivisection; piercing shrieks. He settled into his seat, stared between his shoes at the polished deck boards, where other images appeared: his own knife-wielding reflection in a toothpaste-flecked bathroom mirror, beside child-Carl, who was made up as Salinger's Teddy. Mice bits bled on the sink. And in a straw-strewn pit where the bathtub should have been nested the feather covered chicken-woman from *Freaks*, clucking absurdly from her human mouth.

Raymond heard a child's giggle and lifted his head. Three rows ahead of him a little girl with brown pigtails and rosy cheeks stood on her seat, one hand on her father's shoulder, the other on her mother's head. The child stared back at Raymond, blinking seashell eyes. She wore a T-shirt featuring Mickey and Minnie Mouse. The cartoon rodents were dancing—musical notes floated around them. Minnie swished a grass skirt and wore a crown of daisies. Red flowers bloomed like wounds on Mickey's Hawaiian shirt. The little girl smiled at Raymond, and he felt himself grin back. Then he ducked—had he seen a Scaredy Cat logo on the sleeve of the little girl's T-shirt? Had Amabel Hadley's clothing line expanded to include toddlers? He never went long without thinking of Amabel, whose child-prostitute face hung in his mind's eye like an accusing moon. Amabel and Disney? When had that partnership been struck?

He peeked at the little girl, avoiding eye contact, focusing instead on the cartoon couple dancing on her shirt. They were neither animal nor human. Their pipe cleaner arms and legs were twisted and misshapen. White gloves hid fingers that were certainly clawed. Their squeaks parodied human speech. Only their giddiness distinguished them from the miserable beast-humans Dr. Moreau created on his island of terror, a fact that implied Walt Disney was the superior insane vivisectionist: he gifted his pseudo-humans with happiness. Raymond pressed his palms together, mimicking prayer. With any luck he'd soon be back to work making monsters of his own.

The ferry pounded on. Soon the hump of Catalina Island would appear. Something brushed against Raymond's ankles, but when he looked down he saw only the shiny floor, his worn shoes, and his neighbors' feet. Sobbing—the little girl a few rows up was in her father's arms, her pretty face crumpled in distress. Of course—her shirt was blank: her dancing mice had run away. They'd come Raymond's way, he was certain—*I felt them*, Raymond almost shouted, but held his tongue.

A sudden wind—someone had opened the cabin's rear hatch. Raymond turned and squinted at a familiar figure in the doorway, a middle-aged man in a robe, a figure he recognized from a Balthus painting, a motif from *Svidrigaylov's Dream*. In the painting, a half-dressed girl sat on a chair behind the robed man. Raymond never finished his film. Circumstances. He had a quirky thought—what if Carl decided to complete the quiet but disquieting masterpiece Raymond had intended? A father-son project like no other. Such an interesting inheritance to leave his boy—a puzzle that needed to be solved. A better legacy than a house full of Kika dolls. Something like hope beat in Raymond's chest. What had his own father left him? A story of luck and magic on Kiriwina Island? The hope in Raymond's heart gathered weight, felt as heavy as a promise, or a curse. The moment he realized he'd been staring into the eyes of the robed figure standing at the exit to the deck, the man briskly turned and stepped out, letting the door swing shut behind him.

A tinny voice sang through the intercom: "*Twenty-six miles across the sea, Santa Catalina is waiting for me, Santa Catalina, the island of romance.*"

***

Raymond stood on the deck, alone except for a few gulls chasing the ferry. Pennants snapped violently from thick poles. His legs felt like marble. His shirt fluttered in the chill breeze that kept the other passengers inside.

"But my core is warm," he said aloud, feeling his voice in his chest. He'd followed the robed figure—the mice, too, he assumed—through the cabin door, leaving the little girl, who was still clinging to her father, inside. He looked at the sea, at the foamy wake fanning behind it. How long had it been since Jerry Convenience—the notorious Unfinity—had sought to drown him? Thirty years? Forty? King Minus.

Raymond leaned over the side rail. It dug into his ribs. He gripped it so hard his knuckles turned white. He looked down—the tips of his shoes stuck out an inch from the deck. Like a surfer, he thought, picturing the purple board sticking out of the back of Jerry Convenience's station wagon. His gaze tumbled to the water beneath him. It churned from blue to green as the hull of the ferry slid through it. Further out the sea rolled gently like a sheet flapped over a bed perpetually remaking itself. A wax paper sky spread to the horizon. Raymond smelled the coconut odor of suntan lotion and wiped his palms on his billowing shirt.

* * *

Raymond on the deck's edge, fondled by the wind. If he'd made *Moby Dick*, Ishmael would have narrated solemnly while the camera lingered on a lone sailor high in the Pequod's masts, silhouetted against a pale sky:

"There is no life in thee, now , except that rocking life imparted by a gently rolling ship . . . but while this sleep, this dream is on ye, move your foot or hand an inch; slip your hold at all; and your identity comes back in horror. And perhaps at mid-day, in the fairest weather, with one half-throttled shriek you drop through that transparent air into the summer sea, no more to rise forever."

* * *

Raymond glanced at his chafed knuckles. Below, the ferry's hull sliced ceaselessly through the sea. But—when had he climbed *over* the rail? Why was his back toward the ocean and horizon, why did he hang at arm's length over the water, his feet tucked under the ferry's bottom rail on the last bit of deck as if he were counterbalancing a

174

sailboat? When he realized he hadn't the strength to haul himself back over the rail and that his grip was failing, Raymond grunted a resigned chuckle. His hands slipped off, and he dropped into the sea. He heard a splash, then his ears filled with a dull rumble as he spun down and around through darkening water. He rose slowly, weightless, and broke the surface, gasping and coughing, suspended with arms and legs spread wide as if he were skydiving. The ferry's wake caught him, lifted, lowered, and passed him. He waited to feel cold. Eye level with the sea, he watched the ferry continue toward the horizon.

Raymond rocked in the swells he'd observed from the deck just minutes earlier. He thought of Carl floundering off the shore of Kiriwina Island after escaping P. P. Frederico's overly amorous little girls. Here came half-Grandpa, stretching out from the mysteriously carved canoe full of village elders. When Raymond had been unable to move. And what about Kika, holding the orphans aloft to the rescue helicopter as Kong's Island collapsed into the sea around her?

The ferry shrank. Bubbles rose around Raymond, and he waited for the tremendous surge of a great body—Kika? Or Moby Dick? Bubbles continued to surface—hundreds, thousands swarmed around him. Each was a grinning and winking plastic-wrapped Kika doll. What if, way back when, he'd devoted his energies to a sequel to *Kong's Daughter* instead of to *Svidrigaylov's Dream*? Imagine if Kika, after saving the children and sinking under the surface, had dove deep, and, with a powerful undersea stroke, headed for a safer shore, another island, maybe America.

Give me any film, any film, Raymond prayed. *Moby Dick, The Island of Dr. Moreau, The Return of Kong's Daughter*—he'd put into it all that he knew, all he believed himself to have learned.

In the sky directly overhead, across a thin layer of cloud, Raymond pictured a scene he'd intended for his Dr. Moreau film: an unidentifiable creature belted to an operating table under the mad eyes of the doctor; a glint from a silver scalpel.

A lifting swell, a mouthful of brackish water, the ferry a dot. Long ago, the bluest surf Raymond had ever seen exploded into white spray against the cliffs below the Pebble Beach Golf and Country Club on the Monterey Peninsula. As a show business celebrity, he'd been invited to the pro-am tournament. He was no golfer, but he'd brought Carl along to enjoy the festivities. Green grass, acres of it, solid under foot. Then ... the invitations stopped.

Chapter 17—T'ings

"We are not men—we are T'ings; we are not beasts—we are T'ings. You made us T'ings!"—Bela Lugosi as Beast-Man to Dr. Moreau, vivisectionist, *The Island of Lost Souls*, (1932)

"God's shark and hummingbird are perfect, but His platypus is an example of clumsy editing." Raymond Walchuk, filmmaker (1954-201?)

Summoned back to the U.S. after two years spent in the Brazilian rainforest pretending to make a documentary, Carl had been informed by the director of the Andrea Spears Benton House, an upscale hospice facility, that his 56-year-old mother was terminally ill. And expecting a baby.

"Breast cancer caught very late. Your mother declined aggressive treatments," the pudding-faced administrator said. "She hasn't very much time left. She could have received hospice care at home, but she has chosen to stay with us. Some of our guests find home a burden. Too full of expectations and memories—feelings of responsibility. Christine wishes to tell you about the pregnancy herself."

Carl's mother, reclining on the sofa in the living room, exuded the temporary air of a wounded bird. Her voice shook. "Why are you wearing that purple feather? And what are you going to do about the baby?"

Dark curls tumbled to his shoulders, but Carl wasn't wearing any feathers. His mother's morphine hallucination? During his time in the rainforest he'd been asked few questions, and he'd lost the habit of formulating answers.

"Hi, Mom." He didn't ask his mother how she felt and gave her a hard look—to assess her condition—and leaned over to kiss her cheek. Through her puff of grey hair, her scalp looked like the surface of the moon. Her eyes, wet and small, stuck to his.

"There's a surrogate, of course," she said. "But I'm the mother and you're the brother. What did you think?"

Carl didn't reply. He sat, careful not to disturb Christine's slippered feet. With no information, how would he have known what to expect? The diet foisted on a transcontinental traveler had little overlap with the Pirahan fare of roasted monkey and root porridge, and he hadn't eaten a full meal in days. His mother and he were alone in a replica of a suburban living room, familiar, yet foreign to someone who'd been sleeping in a hut: two sofas, a coffee table, a patterned carpet, heavy drapes, a large landscape painting—valley, mountains, glimpse of a river, a village. Carl remembered sitting naked on his sleeping mat of woven grass, young *Click*, his Pirahan lover, her name unpronounceable, spooned in his lap. His chin had rested on her shoulder, his journal had been spread open over her knees, his arms had reached under hers as he'd scribbled a February date. Up in the U.S. it would have been Presidents' Week, which meant sales at the big box stores. He'd tried to picture *Click* in tight jeans, a leather jacket, and pointy-toed heels, her long hair sliced above her ears. He imagined them standing, her arm looped through his, before washer-dryers, espresso machines, racks of dresses, a wall of flat screen televisions— things she'd never seen and never would. Things she couldn't possibly have imagined. Carl had lost that journal. Its shredded pages probably lined an exotic bird's nest high up in the rainforest's canopy.

A husky attendant dressed in khaki trousers and a plaid flannel shirt entered, greeted Christine with a nod, and raised an eyebrow at Carl. Was he tiring his mother? Should he have been doing or saying something he wasn't? The attendant left. Carl caught a whiff of an odor like that left by an electrical fire. His heart felt small.

"Don't be squeamish," Christine said. "I'm not the pigeon—the one that showed you'd never be a scientist. Remember?"

Of course he remembered. One summer afternoon when he was little, right around the time his parents had separated, he'd been playing in the yard with a prosthetic limb—a severed leg, bloodied at the knee. It wore a sneaker. The leg was a souvenir from the set of one of his father's films. Carl created scenarios around the limb: the rest of the body had been devoured by cannibals, sharks or Godzilla; it protruded from the mouths of pretend caves, from under the garage door, from underneath the tractor mower. Maybe from the jaws of a gigantic version of his pet cornsnake, Elvis, like in his father's movie *Swallow*, which Carl knew all about, though he'd not yet been allowed to see it. When he came in for a drink, Christine had also been taking a break—she conducted much of the business for her gaming publication, *MindGames*, from her home office. *MindGames* would become a small empire. She'd sell it for millions. But at the time Carl knew it only as the thing that kept Mom too busy to play.

His mother had been waiting for Carl in the kitchen. "Here," she said, handing him a lunch bag from the freezer. Something hard was in the bag, a bottle, he'd thought, a drink that would stay iced for hours while he played outside. But what slid out instead of a Coke was a dead pigeon, blue-gray, sealed in plastic wrap. Its eyes were frosted pearls. "You could look at it under your microscope," Christine had said. "Bit by bit. I thought maybe familiarity with a real bird would cure you of that chicken-woman fear." The frozen bird had chilled his fingers. What did "bit by bit" mean? He should break off parts like from a chocolate Easter rabbit? He'd trembled as he envisioned his bedroom desk strewn with chunks of downy feathers and strings of muscle and tendon, bones like broken soda straws, pink clawed feet. Of course the frozen bird-in-the-hand had revived his dread memory of the final scene from *Freaks*, the one movie his father should have protected him from, though he'd begged to see it: the lovely but wicked bareback rider transformed into a helpless chicken-woman. The night after he'd seen the movie, he'd lain in bed, feverish, feeling feathers sprouting on his shoulders and the backs of his hands. His lips and nose merged into a beak. When he opened it to call for help, he squawked.

His mother had blamed her ex-husband for the episode. But what kind of mother gives a kid a frozen bird? And why bring it up now, when she's dying? Guilt? A confessional didn't suit his mother. Was she trying one last time to prove she'd been right, that a dead pigeon was just what he'd needed? *I self-therapized*, Carl wanted to tell her. *I let myself be transformed into the White Rabbit—in the middle school play you missed*, Alice in Shizzel-land. *I was swallowed up in a bunny costume for days and days, and I came to terms with the fact that costumes are just costumes. I wish I'd known that when I played young Jesus.*

"You dropped the pigeon in the trash," Christine reminisced. "You were pale as a ghost. Not a budding scientist."

Carl's thoughts slipped back to the rainforest: *Click* snuggled beside him in the cabin of Andrew, the anthropologist, purported subject of Carl's documentary. The researcher held court, sipping the drink he'd plucked from his generator-powered refrigerator. "Sexual relations with outsiders keep the bloodlines fresh, negating the theory that the Pirahan's linguistic peculiarities result from inbreeding." *Click* had hooted and whistled, waving at Andrew's soda bottle. "They hate Coke," Andrew said. "One sip, they spit it out. The carbonation hurts and it's too sweet. But they love the cold. I give them bottles to hold, straight from the fridge, as a reward for testing—when the cold leaves, they forget about them. I collect full Coke bottles from wherever they're dropped around the village and put them back in the refrigerator. Powerful magic." Andrew had handed *Click* his soda bottle, and her face so close it was a blur, she touched Carl's chin with its cool neck.

"Creativity isn't what your father thought it was." Christine wore a trickster's smile as Carl measured his mother's withered figure. "It's not infinity. It's 'yes' or 'no.' You can't have everything. I was not a comfortable mother, but I was competent," she said. Maybe hers was what all dying faces looked like. Her eyes glittered. "*MindGames* was my baby. Then I sold it." Carl didn't doubt that his mother had always loved him, but she'd done so without tenderness. And the compressed history she shared overlooked his infancy, childhood, and adolescence. She had reduced him to the pigeon story she'd offered with too confident a degree of self-congratulation.

"A year ago—before my cancer was diagnosed and they started chemo— I was still menstruating—extremely unusual at my age," Christine said. "I was fertile. Your father froze his sperm, way back, when we were still married and you were just a toddler. He had a theory that the world would run out of artistic geniuses. He talked about a creative black hole in the universe. He called his sperm 'the emergency reserve.' I'd forgotten all about it. Then we had our separate lives— sharing you, of course—and then he disappeared from the deck of that ferry. And the sperm lab contacted me because I was still listed as the beneficiary." Christine touched Carl's hand, startling him. "I had eggs, sperm and money. Actuarial tables projected I would live for another thirty years. And Klaus's dementia . . . I would have been alone."

Carl felt a twinge of guilt—his step-father's early onset Alzheimer's had progressively worsened during Carl's first year in film school, and as a last resort Christine had arranged for her second husband's transfer to a facility in Germany—near an uncle Carl had never met— where the former chess champion would receive "special treatment." His mother had discouraged a good-bye visit. "He wouldn't know the difference between you and one of his chess pieces," she said. Carl had assumed he'd see the kind man again, but Klaus had died before a year passed. His mother hadn't told Carl about his stepfather's death until well after a funeral that she herself had failed to attend. "You were taking finals," she'd said.

Christine's pink velour track jacket shifted. It's possible she had shrugged. Carl winced at the thought of her ravaged breasts and forced himself to picture instead the robust, casual nakedness of the Pirahan women, for whom chastity was not on the radar. Always nursing babies. Carl reached toward one of his mother's pink pants legs, but he was afraid he'd find it empty. According to Andrew, the Piraha had no words for colors. They could only compare. *Click* might have expressed that the pink of Christine's tracksuit resembled "the flesh of a skinned monkey" if there'd been a skinned monkey nearby to point at. He should have brought his mother flowers: "These roses are the color of the blood that binds us," he might have said. Except he didn't see or feel the blood.

"Eggs and sperm—opportunity was knocking." Christine had closed her eyes. "Motherhood no longer seemed like such an imposition."

An imposition? The word bruised Carl: his mother thought of him as a failed experiment? "I wish I'd been better at science," he apologized. "But I was a good actor—remember? Until I grew out of it. I lost my cuteness." After middle school and the White Rabbit he'd quit performing for good. "I've had quite a time in the rainforest," he said, but his mother wasn't listening.

"It's not necessary that you meet the surrogate," Christine said. "I've only met her myself through proxy—on paper. She's in excellent health, and doesn't drink or smoke. There was some question about a dermatological condition but the doctors determined it was irrelevant. I've seen the ultrasound photographs. Your little brother is thriving. There—now you know the sex." Christine's head dipped at an awkward angle. "Due in one month, and I won't be here." Minutes seemed to pass. Had she fallen asleep? "My love child." Her eyes popped open. "Where were you?"

Carl was lost. Love child? She couldn't have meant him. She and his father had always seemed like two incompatible species, his conception the result of a freak accident.

"I was in the rainforest making a documentary," he said. But in South America Carl had lost his recording equipment almost immediately. It had simply disappeared, swallowed by the forest. Who would have taken it? The Pirahans had shown no interest in the cameras, the lights, or batteries. Andrew still believed the documentary was being made. Embarrassed, Carl didn't acknowledge the loss. Instead, he'd followed the anthropologist, asking questions, taking notes in his journal. Weeks grew into months; Andrew, either absorbed by his work or simply befuddled, refused to notice that Carl hadn't the means to record him. Then Carl had lost the journal, too. On a whim he tried charades—he wound an invisible camera whenever Andrew spoke. The anthropologist had seemed satisfied. *Click*, ever present, had mimicked Carl's pantomime, cranking away at nothing. on faith alone.

"They're managing my pain," Christine sighed. Carl didn't understand hospice care. His mother seemed exhausted. Would someone attend to her, or were they waiting for her to shrivel and drop from the vine of her own accord? By comparison, his father's end played like only one of many regrettable anecdotes Carl might have overheard at a showbiz party.

***

In the weeks before the sea had swallowed him, Raymond, a pariah in the film community after a string of catastrophic misjudgments, had hatched a new scheme. "I'm going to remake *The Island of Lost Souls*—the old movie from the H.G. Wells story about Dr. Moreau. It's got to be a period thing—set back in the 1920s, black and white—spooky, like the original. Moreau plays god on his island, operating on animals over and over, trying to transform them into humans. *Carving* animals into human beings. Releasing the human being trapped in the beast. None of this cloning crap. Vivisections— that's what your God-dreamer does. Tear up the old to make the new. I'm going to set up meetings." Where, Carl wondered, had the inspiration for a Moreau project come from? He thought of the chunks of mouse, the swirl of blood as tiny body parts defrosted in a cup of water. And the chicken-woman.

There would be no meetings. There'd been no one left to call. A generation's worth of ape doll sales from his father's only mainstream hit, *Kong's Daughter*, had for years paid for his father's food, clothing, and shelter.

No one had witnessed Raymond slip or jump from the deck of the express ferry to Santa Catalina Island, "the island of romance," according to the old song. Raymond had been seen on board, but never on the island. It had taken a month—Carl waiting across the country in film school for confirmation—before authorities officially accounted for Raymond's disappearance by declaring him drowned.

Unlike Klaus, who'd faded in Carl's memory until all he remembered were his own impersonations of the man, Raymond seemed ever-present to his son. It was like Papa Kong stood behind him, helping him find the right path by suggesting the wrong one.

"There are no such things as epiphanies in life," Raymond told Carl the last time they'd been together. "But we put them in our narratives anyway, even when we're telling our own histories. We lie to ourselves. We're all complicit. We're all a bunch of epi-phonies. Especially us artists. We're epi-*faux*-nies. With an f-a-u-x."

"That's pretty epi-funny," Carl had said. "Why tell me unless you think I should be watching out for one?"

"Watching out—?"

"For an epiphany."

And, after a second, Raymond had laughed and laughed. "I guess we're just guileless creatures of faith, right? We insist on believing." There'd been tears in his father's eyes, and, in spite of himself, Carl had been proud to have put them there. His father was waiting for him to say something else, but Carl kept quiet. After a minute Raymond had nodded. "That's right," he said. "Silence is perfect."

Christine might have been dozing. Her head drooped like a wilting carnation.

"There are no epiphanies," Carl said, and her lids lifted.

"That's your father," she said. "'No epiphanies.' Of course there aren't any. But there's always a sum. Things always add up."

"The Piraha can't count," Carl said. "Not past two. After two it's 'many'. If they were counting a pile of beans, they'd say, 'One, two, many,' and they'd be done." It was dawning on Carl that he would never see *Click* again—could he feel his heart breaking? He remembered: *Click*'s head just beneath his shoulder when he embraced her from behind; cupping her breasts in his palms; the feel of her nipples between his fingers; her fresh vegetable smell; her steady gaze; and her earnest winding of the invisible movie camera. After a year of unprotected intimacy, *Click* had shown no signs of pregnancy. But it was possible that in his absence she would bear him a child.

There was a terrible stench. Carl refused to believe it emanated from his mother. He looked around the room, at the doors, hoping for help. He touched her leg, finally, and found a rod of bone no thicker than a stick of chalk; the slightest pressure would crush it into powder.

"You're alone," Christine said, stating the thought Carl had been shaping about her.

Things add up, she'd said. "One, two, many," Carl counted.

"One too many?" Christine whispered.

"I'm alone." *And so are you.*

"There will be papers to sign," Christine said, as if a signature were a passport to parenthood. "Custody issues. Arrangements have been made. For childcare. For accommodations. A trust has been set up for you and the child. Everything's taken care of."

A paper baby—documents and ultrasound photos—in a month. Why wasn't Carl feeling the enormity of the moment? He pictured a string of paper cut-out children, holding hands. His mother had seen a non-existent purple feather, but Carl saw her shrunken body, a reality impossible to doubt.

"Daddy," Christine murmured. Carl frowned. She was right— he'd be more of a father than a brother. She'd beaten him to the act of re-creating himself. Fatherhood would be a weighty role, and after a deep breath Carl assumed it like a crown—an emergency coronation at a time of crisis. But really, was he different from a teenager whose girlfriend, her eyes swollen from crying, had just told him she'd missed her period?

"To the Piraha, the people I've been living with, when someone goes around a bend in the river, they say he's 'gone out of experience.'" Carl said. "He doesn't exist anymore. Not until he comes back, and he's there to touch." Try as he might, he'd never been able to pronounce *Click*'s full name: the dexterities of his lips, tongue, and throat had been forged for a different language. The sounds were fading: *Click. Tweet. Flap.* If she missed him, if her thoughts followed him around the bend in the river, she would be ruined, no longer Pirahan. "Their women use one less phoneme than the men," Carl told his mother, summarizing one of Andrew's unrecorded lectures. "The language of Pirahan women lacks a sound. I don't know which one—I never learned to speak Pirahan. Imagine if American women didn't have one of our sounds. Like 'g,' say. Women wouldn't be able to say 'goodbye.' Or 'God' would be just 'Odd.'"

One early morning after several months in the rainforest, Carl followed the hunters out of the village. They disappeared down a path— "out of experience." He was lost. He'd wandered through trees and creepers, inventing trails where none existed—following flowers, insect buzzes, mossy patches at certain heights on the trunks of trees, all of them false clues. He'd flinched at the cries of birds. There'd been a rustling in the brush, and a thick, panting dog appeared, one he'd seen in the village. Its eyes and smooth hide matched the eyes and skin of the Piraha—it was one of them, just a different incarnation. Its gaze had drifted over him as it hunched to shit, and Carl recognized the village's latrine area. Through the trees he saw huts and Andrew's cabin. Partly from nerves, partly from suggestion, like a yawn, Carl had squatted and relieved himself. He was just another version of the dog. A White Rabbit. A chicken woman.

The husky attendant returned, this time pausing beside Christine, his hands at his waist. "Nap time," he said. Carl rose, wondering when the next domino would fall, from where, with what weight and speed. Support, his mother had said. He was on his way to thirty. He was out of one jungle, but maybe thrust into another. Was she giving him a life or taking one away? He tried to visualize a baby, and he saw himself cradling something—an ape doll wrapped in plastic. Its button eyes and broad mouth were surprised and mocking. It squirmed, and he pressed it tight to his chest.

Like a magician spinning in his cape, the attendant whisked Christine from the sofa as if she were a hollow prop and carried her out of the room. Carl's last sight of his mother was her dangling feet and her raised arm, her index finger pointing at the ceiling.

Chapter 18—Dr. Moreau's Pet Shop

Is there such a thing as being 'fresh out of rehab' when it's your sixth time?" Amabel asked as she settled into the bucket seat of her red convertible, coaching the B-list reporters who followed her after she'd signed herself out of the facility. "Maybe say 'rotten out of rehab' or 'spoiled.' Or 'stale'. . . 'Stale out of rehab Amabel Hadley.'"

In her condo, an odor of something neglected in the refrigerator lingered, and was exactly how she felt: stale, detached from the thickened figure facing her in her bedroom mirror. She wouldn't even try to lose the rehab donut weight this time. There seemed no point in whittling herself down to a self so easily condemnable. With less effort she could crop her hair, maybe brutally short; the new look would match the voice that countless cigarettes had scrubbed into a growl.

Amabel's harsh and court-ordered abstinence from outside communication was over, and her agent had left word about a job on her voice mail: "P. P. Frederico is remaking *The Island of Dr. Moreau* as a full-length animated feature. He wants you to voice a character named 'M'ling.' I told him you'd be thrilled."

Amabel hadn't been so sure. She'd seen enough has-been actresses lose themselves in the world of animation: usually they'd be animals—gloriously feathered and distinctively beaked birds, sinuously-waisted minks, cobras hooded like Cleopatra—that were all sad memorials to faded careers. She'd be turned into a cat, Amabel guessed, with huge green eyes, a whiskey purr, and a slender body. For a cartoon no one needed to trim down, either by exercise or diet pills or a finger down the throat.

A *Moreau* script was delivered, but Amabel didn't bother to read it. She knew the story—a crazy doctor on a remote island operates on animals, trying to turn them into human beings. Her character's name, M'ling, hinted at a wickedly seductive antagonist, maybe with a vaguely threatening Middle Eastern allure. Too late in the arc of her reputation to give her voice to a heroine.

It wasn't until the telephone interview arranged by the studio a week before recording was to start that Amabel discovered what she'd gotten herself into. The interview began with the usual questions about her rehab stint and her legal trouble. Did she think she'd stay sober this time? Would she think twice before threatening to light a pool of gas at a fuel pump? Would she consider an apology to PETA and the vegan coalition she had enraged with her observation that "only stupid people don't eat meat—meat, including brains, is brain food. Even zombies know that." Curled up on her bed in sweatpants and a too-snug T-shirt from her own "Scaredy Cat" line for tweens, she watched herself yawn and smoke in her dresser mirror as she asserted her "every confidence and hope" that her new sobriety would lead to better future decisions. Amabel considered herself adept at deflecting awkward questions provocatively yet insubstantially; when asked what she thought PETA's take on her involvement with P. P. Frederico's *Moreau* project would be, she saw the languorous drag she took from her cigarette and the careful way she patted the bed around her hips for the Snickers bar she'd half unwrapped before the call. She could still mesmerize herself with her own eyes, though at the moment they were no more bewitching than frozen peas. And when had her chin begun to melt into her neck?

"It's just a cartoon," she said. "No animals, I can assure you, will be harmed during filming."

The reviewer chuckled. "Right. But since P. P. Frederico has already commented on his intentions of releasing this as the first graphically violent cartoon in the history of cinema—"shocking," I think was the word he used, do you get the feeling you were cast *because* of your comments on meat?"

Amabel watched her brow furrow, thought "worry," and deepened the frown. Cigarette ash dropped onto her chest into the open green eye of her T-shirt's winking "Scaredy Cat" logo. The identical logo was tattooed in color on the small of her back.

"You mean do I think it's unusual for a filmmaker to inspire interest in his film by introducing a note of controversy?"

"Animals surgically altered—torn apart by Dr. Moreau and reconstructed as humanoids—deformed, suffering creatures treated first as experiments, than as slaves by the evil doctor." The reporter seemed to be reading this from a press release.

"What cartoon doesn't tear apart animals and make them half human? Mickey Mouse and Goofy and Bugs—they're *freaks*, right? Talking biped animals. Bipedophiles—is that a word?"

"No—but the film's theme seems to glorify suffering—"

"It's a *horror* cartoon. And I like meat."

"Hmm. Well, are you put off by the absence of a female presence in the film?"

"I'm M'ling."

"Right." The interviewer waited. Amabel traced a circle around her reflected face with her cigarette butt. She imagined herself with a snout and protruding yellow teeth, shivered, and looked away.

"Well, I'm sure that some suppressed sexual tension will bubble to the surface—isn't that what horror films are all about these days—red-lipped vampires burying their fangs into the necks of— "

"Of course, but how do you feel about the fact that M'ling is a male?"

"Excuse me?"

"How do you feel about the fact that for your first role in almost four years, you've been cast as a male?"

Amabel pictured her script, still in its Fedex envelope in the center of her black granite kitchen island. "Um—" She wouldn't surrender the truth—that her career was in the toilet and this was the only job she'd been offered. "—I'm sure it's integral to the film. Mr. Frederico is an artist, and a certain liberation from convention should be—expected. Are we almost over? My publicist is pointing at her watch. I think I have an appearance at a charity event scheduled." Amabel watched the figure in her mirror tap her wrist.

"Just one thing more. What's your reaction to Carl Walchuk's involvement with the screenplay? You know the *Moreau* project originated with his father, right? The production is something like a memorial to Raymond Walchuk. He gave P. P. Frederico his start, after all. Do you know Carl?"

"Not really. Maybe we met at some child star thing years ago, before he quit acting. I don't remember if he was on the set of *Svidrigaylov's Dream*, if that's what you're getting at. That whole mess with his father got settled, and everybody involved moved on. Raymond Walchuk is dead, right? I've really got no comment beyond that."

After the interview, Amabel shrugged back on her pillows and shut her eyes. Raymond Walchuk, the filmmaker responsible for *Svidrigaylov's Dream.* Who would try to make such a movie? Who would cast a child as the object of a perverted Russian nobleman's nightmare, choosing a little girl whose features were most precociously adult? It hadn't been difficult to transform her into a dream-whore. But what responsible director would emphasize to the child that the goat-bearded character imagining her was "thinking fucky-fucky"? All done for the sake of art, Raymond Walchuk argued when her parents brought a civil suit against him for moral turpitude. The settlement and publicity had ruined him, but, paradoxically, had launched her own career. She had been the winner. There were long stretches, months at a time, when she didn't think about being the little girl in *Svidrigaylov's Dream*, the movie that was never finished; but, when she *was* conscious of *being*, she was never anyone else.

The chicken or the egg? The life that followed—a few family movies and teen romps, G and PG, then a love affair with drugs, with older actors, male and female celebrities of similarly tattered reputations, raunchy paparazzi photographs, moments when she glimpsed her own mascara-ringed eyes or caught a whiff of her cigarette breath or the fermented smell of bodily fluids she only half-remembered sharing. It hadn't taken long for the butterfly to revert to a worm that had a love-hate relationship with the spotlight's shriveling heat.

Her parents should have known, Raymond Walchuk maintained. Had they been so eager for their daughter to succeed that they had at first ignored the obvious subject of *Svidrigaylov's Dream*? Hadn't they read the script? Weren't they familiar with *Crime and Punishment?* But Amabel's parents had been old, her mother in her fifties, her father nearly seventy when Amabel was twelve. The world moved too quickly for them. Their only fault was to mistake indulgence for nurturing, and Amabel had eventually retired them to a pleasant condo on the edge of a Palm Springs golf course, where they remained snug and advice-less until they faded into their graves. And now orphan Amabel found herself marooned on *The Island of Doctor Moreau*— trapped again in a Raymond Walchuk fantasy.

✻✻✻✻✻

Amabel finally read the *Moreau* screenplay. There was a note that the description of her character M'ling had been transcribed directly from H. G. Wells's novel: "*a misshapen man, short, broad, and clumsy, with a crooked back, a hairy neck, and a head sunk between his shoulders. He . . . had peculiarly thick, coarse, black hair . . . the black face was a singularly deformed one. The facial part projected, forming something dimly suggestive of a muzzle, and the huge half-open mouth showed . . . big white teeth.*"

The story seemed pointlessly grim and violent—live animals torn apart by Moreau and reconfigured as gruesome humanoids. It was a story of degeneration and madness; there wasn't a shred of redemption or hope in it. As a cartoon, maybe it would develop a cult following among the morbid, but it was nothing but a grim, gratuitously violent slaughterhouse of a project. When Amabel called her agent to tell him she wanted out, he pooh-poohed her.

"Classic author, classic story, classy connections. You need a touch of class. It's P. P. Frederico! And now is not the time to quit smoking, if you're thinking about it. Your voice is your signature now. There's a fortune in cartoons and commercials."

* * *

Amabel's dangling legs ached, and her ass had cramped from sitting for almost two hours on a rung-less stool. Her headphones pinched her ears, and her scalp was sweating under her new buzz cut. On the screen in front of her, a human-ish blob haunted a glimmering vacancy. Her voice would aid its transformation into M'ling. She wouldn't see the completely realized character until the film's premiere.

She had just delivered her sixteenth take of her first line: "They—won't have me forward." M'ling, the only one of Moreau's "transformed" animals to be trusted as a house servant, was being abused by sailors on a ship transporting fresh animals to the mad doctor's island.

"Ms. Hadley—" P. P. Frederico's words buzzed like hornets in her headphones— "according to Mr. Walchuk's faithful transcription from the original text, M'ling should deliver this line 'slowly, with a queer, hoarse quality in his voice.' You've captured the 'hoarse'—but that's just your natural rasp. Where's the 'queer'? Once again, please."

Amabel craved a cigarette, but no break seemed imminent. "They—won't have me forward," she said for the seventeenth time.

"Ms. Hadley. Amabel. What does 'queer' mean to you?"

"'Queer'? Amabel had made a dozen films and had never repeated a line more than twice. And this was just a god-damned cartoon. "For H. G. Wells it would have meant 'strange,' right? 'Weird.' But there's a lot of 'weirds.' I think you need to tell me a little more of what you're after."

"'*To you, to you, to you. To you. To. You*—' I said. M'ling's words don't belong to H. G. Wells any longer. They're ours, and we're in the 21st century. What does 'queer' mean *to you*?"

"Hunh," Amabel sighed. *To-yoo-to-yoo-to-yoo.* Frederico, the birdman. If she turned she'd see him through the glass wall of the control booth, his face surrounded by feather-petals, pecking at his microphone with a tiny beak. On the screen in front of her the gingerbread man blob standing in for her character floated impassively, waiting for her voice. Queer? A Youtube video gone viral flashed through her mind: a kiss—less kiss, really, than glottal assault—she'd shared with a one hit pop nymphette. Amabel remembered the video clip, but not the actual kiss. She looked at the M'ling-blob waiting for her answer. "'Queer' means 'gay' to me," she growled into her microphone.

"Exactly! Could you lend something of your new understanding to your characterization, please? Oh—wait a minute—visitors. Take five. Hello, Carl—and how's our little man?" Amabel heard a click and dead air. She plucked off her headphones and slid from the stool. She stamped the pins and needles out of her numb legs before hurrying out for a cigarette.

* * *

They won't have me forward. Amabel sat on the hood of her lipstick red convertible in the parking lot of the sound studio, trying to enjoy a second cigarette she'd lit from her first. Her fingers shook from nerves or anger or nicotine hunger. *I'm keeping my voice in shape,* she thought as the smoke burned through her throat and filled her lungs. She'd been out-of-rehab sober for weeks. Two. The truth was, cigarettes were her only craving. She tried to remember what her other urges had felt like. A haze Amabel imagined rising from the united efforts of all the city's smokers obscured the distant hills. *Queer* wasn't one of her words—it didn't measure her liberal attitude toward her own sexual proclivities or history, clips of which swam through the stew of her memory along with the Youtube kiss.

Amabel thought harder, surprising herself with a desire to grasp P. P. Frederico's intent. Her character M'ling had been carved by Moreau into human form from what? A dog? He'd suffered a kind of extractive rape, torn from one body, one species, into another. Forced to fit an idea of "human." Dragged from a natural self into an isolating "otherness." *They won't have me forward.* Amabel felt an unexpectedly sensual swelling behind her eyes—she wasn't far from tears. Poor, queer M'ling. How cruel of Moreau to have thrust him into the human condition.

"P. P. says you're doing great." A young man pushing a blond toddler in a stroller had passed through the glass doors of the sound studio lobby and now stood squinting at Amabel through the milky sunshine. Not eager for company, she pretended that it was the child who had spoken. The toddler was sunk deep into the stroller's seat, and his limp arms and legs hung from his stubby torso like the appendages of a sock monkey. He'd fixed her with a pale-eyed gaze that seemed to insist on an apology. What if, she wondered, what if this little boy was dying, what if his brief life was ebbing away with each heartbeat? She mewed with relief when the child hurled his doll, a naked, flaxen-haired Barbie, toward her. It was a healthy toss. The doll struck the headlight next to Amabel's knee and fell face down onto the blacktop. Amabel caught her breath and choked up a cough that turned into sobs. Two heaves, and a third, before she bowed into her shoulder, smothering her tears. "Sorry," she said. "Wrong pipe."

The young man, who was not robust, rolled the stroller closer, leaning on it as if it were a walker. Though his hair and eyes were dark, the shape of his head and the tilt of his posture were identical to the child's. "Pipes can be ornery," he said. He waited for her to compose herself. "P. P. isn't always able to communicate his needs. He wants me to tell you to give M'ling a little lisp. He thinks it'll get audiences to think about a dog's inner life."

Amabel's nose was full. Without a tissue, she snorted back her salty mucus and swallowed demurely. "A dog's life?"

The young man's dark curls receded like an eroding coastline. Amabel shielded her eyes with her cigarette hand as if his forehead gleamed. With sudden dexterity he bent, caught the child under the arms, and swung him out of the stroller. The clean, white rubber bottoms of the toddler's tiny sneakers flew past Amabel's head. Set on his feet, the child tottered toward his doll, picked her up by one of her long, flesh-toned legs, and flipped her into the parking space beside Amabel's convertible.

"Careful for cars," the young man warned, though Amabel's was the only vehicle within a hundred yards. "Careful. Yeah—" He kept the corner of his eye on the toddler, while shifting the bulk of his attention to Amabel— "so P. P. sees each species as having a kind of 'hook'—something subtle about them that the change into human form exposes. I can't tell you about the other animals, because he thinks too much information will muddle your performance. But he wants his dog-people kind of fey."

"'*Fey.*'" It was an odd, antique word. Amabel doubted she'd ever spoken it.

"P. P.'s approach to creating a film can be idiosyncratic." The young man's tone and expression begged for patience—or was it with Amabel he was showing patience? "His idea is to keep all the parts separate until they meet in the final cut. Like a recipe where the ingredients don't mix until they reach your palate. Or a painting where each brush stroke is a distinct entity. When you see the whole, you also feel the impact of each separate part."

"Hmm." Amabel threw her cigarette butt to the pavement on the opposite side of her car from the busy child, who had squatted and was marching Barbie along the yellow parking line.

"It's like he's arranging flowers," the young man continued. "P. P., I mean."

"Okay, so which is he? A chef, a painter, or a florist?"

The young man smiled; his patience had been for Amabel. "He's a magician. Where he comes from, magic was a thing."

"Fay-Fay-Fay!" The little boy had picked up his doll and was banging it into the door of Amabel's car.

"Hey!" she yelled and slid to her feet. She almost stepped on the child. His shortness surprised her. She wanted to grab his arm but couldn't remember ever touching a toddler and didn't know how to go about it. One of her legs trembled. The child paused in mid-blow, Barbie suspended like a hatchet, and his gaze boiled at Amabel. Two teeth from his thrust jaw bit into his upper lip. His sudden ugliness froze Amabel. When the young man whisked the toddler from the pavement and settled him upon his narrow shoulders, the child's mouth dilated into a cavernous O. He wrapped one arm around the balding head and drummed his heels against the man's concave chest while clenching Barbie around her thighs and whipping her long hair in circles as if she were a pole dancer. The young man eyed the car door.

"I'm sorry. He hasn't had his nap." He held the boy's ankles firmly with one hand while he ran the other over the glossy red finish. "You better take a look. Wray-Wray, say you're sorry to Ms. Hadley. I like your hair short, by the way."

"Thank you." She smoothed a hand over the door. "Nothing here."

The child squeezed his knees against the young man's neck and continued to whip his doll in circles. "Fay-Fay-Fay—"

"Probably has to pee. Do you have to pee, Wray?— You might not get an apology. I'm not sure I ever taught him 'sorry.'—Hey up there—have you got a 'sorry' for the nice lady?"

What did Amabel know about children? Didn't they all have syndromes these days? Aspberger's or ADD or something. What had she heard about babies on the news? Mothers had six or seven or even eight at a time; toddlers tumbled from windows or into tiger pits at the zoo. Sometimes they were found, alive or dead, in dumpsters. Amabel's thoughts spun as if she were the doll that the little boy—Ray-Ray?—continued to whip in circles, and she tried to spot a focal point like a ballet dancer. The child rested his chin on the fringe of the young man's curls, and their heads, one atop the other, reminded her of a totem pole.

"You're Carl Walchuk—" she blurted. She supposed she'd known all along: Carl Walchuk, screenwriter of *Doctor Moreau*, erstwhile child star, and the son of Raymond Walchuk. Why hadn't they met decades ago on the set of *Svidrigaylov's Dream*? Had he seen her wearing all that makeup and been scared off? Would he have known what a monster his father had made of her? "—And this is your little brother." *Not* Carl's son. She'd seen it on E News a couple of years ago: how, after Raymond Walchuk had been dead for years, his ex-wife used his defrosted sperm, over which she still held custody, for the *in vitro* fertilization of her eggs. After the zygote had been implanted in a surrogate's womb, Carl's mother had died before her second child's birth. Which left Carl to inherit the infant—a surprise little brother, a quarter of a century his junior. But—and Amabel's heartbeats accelerated—hadn't the end of the story been even more bizarre? Hadn't the surrogate run off to Mexico with a plan to sell the kid? Something happened at the border—had the surrogate died giving birth to the little blond child now scurrying around this parking lot? Amabel couldn't remember.

Carl Walchuk smiled as if he'd been following the progress of Amabel's thoughts. "This is Wray. The famous 'miracle child.'" He dipped the boy toward Amabel. "We spell his name with a W. He's named after our father, homophonetically. His initials are W. W. People usually use initials to make their names easier to say. Like P. P. Frederico—his real name is impossible to spell. But 'W. W.' is six syllables. Remember veterans referring to 'double-ya-double-ya-two'? That abbreviation takes twice as long to say as 'World War Two.' The initials made the war shorter and longer at the same time—a love-hate relationship for the greatest generation. My grandfather spent that war on a Pacific island—the same one that we met P. P. on— Kiriwina, Papua New Guinea. My dad made *Kong's Daughter* there. Oh—and this doll is Fay. Her *name* is Fay. I don't know how she identifies herself sexually; I don't believe lesbians use 'fey,' but I'm no expert."

"Wray and Fay."

"Embarrassing, I know. Really, on his birth certificate it's Raymond, after our father, like I said. Mom's last wish, God knows why. You and I could have met a long time ago, but we never did, even though I told my friends for years that we were thick as thieves. I even told them you kissed me. On the cheek. Under mistletoe—on the movie set. They say we dig ourselves in deeper when we tell elaborate lies, but I think you can make a lie work if you use the right details." He shifted the child on his shoulders. The boy made a V of Barbie's legs and wedged them around his throat, aiming the figure at Amabel like a divining rod. "He really loves this doll. I tried a GI Joe, but he didn't take to it. He didn't like his stuffed Kika either—remember the golden ape they marketed with *King's Daughter*? We've still got hundreds of them at home filling all the closets. You want one? Mint condition, wrapped in plastic, definitely worth something on eBay. I don't know at what age Wray will identify himself as a particular sex, or if it's happened already. The W will help if he's transgendered, though, don't you think? 'Wray'— that could be male or female." If Carl was joking, his expression didn't show it.

"I had a Kika. The little ape." Amabel hadn't thought of her Kika in years, but suddenly she could almost feel the doll's plush weight in her cradling arms.

"Sure you did. Every kid had one after *Kong's Daughter*. That doll kept my dad out of the poorhouse."

Amabel looked at the toddler perched on his brother's shoulders. "You're raising your little brother."

"My miracle bro'. Mom's dying gift to the elder son she was about to turn into an orphan. The beauty of an indestructible egg, a surrogate's wholesome womb, and Daddy's frozen sperm. Whenever I think of little Wray's origins, I think of the frozen mice my dad and I used to defrost to feed our pet snake, Elvis."

Amabel grimaced. "Yuch." She imagined Raymond Walchuk bending over her with a snake in his hands, preparing to offer her directorial advice.

Carl jostled the little boy. "How's Fay, Wray?"

"Fay-Fay-Fay," the boy muttered, then began to chew Barbie's foot.

"We're quite a novelty act," Carl said. "Little guy's the Ninth Wonder of the World. I pretend I'm the Empire State Building. We're on constant lookout for biplanes. I suppose one day he'll find out all about his Kong legacy. We should all know our personal histories, right?"

"So you'll tell him someday that he was born in a customs booth at the border? While he was being stolen?"

Carl shrugged. "When he's old enough, I guess."

"That'll be when?" Amabel persisted, though she didn't know why. Rudeness felt like a reflex. Her cheeks tightened as Carl held her gaze for a few seconds without speaking. Then he grinned.

"I'll have to check his calendar. He's a busy little guy. He's sure to find out anyway—imagine discovering *that* about yourself on the Internet. You ready to go back to recording? Trust P. P. and fey it up. It may seem simplistic and offensive, but he's got amazing instincts—or incredible luck. Didn't I say magic was a thing back on his island? I told you your hair looks good short, right?"

Usually a man would compliment Amabel's eyes, and then his gaze would settle on her breasts like sculpting hands. She patted her head, felt its contours under the bristles and, when her palm passed over her face, sniffed her breath—tobacco scented, but not foul. "You did," she said. "Thanks again."

* * *

The lilting sibilance Amabel gave M'ling's growl struck the right chord, and after the twentieth take, P. P. Frederico approved her rendering of the character's first line.

"Your breakfast, Sir," she recited next, to P. P.'s immediate satisfaction. Though M'ling was present in most scenes, he spoke rarely. Most of Amabel's contribution consisted not of words, but of background gutturals that the director insisted be precisely matched to a setting that existed only in his own mind. Amabel locked her gaze on her character's featureless blob as if it were her reflection and listened to P. P.'s directions ("try a long 'grrr,' almost a whimper, here") while her thoughts wandered. She fancied a pair of lips on the blank face whispering "Kika." She'd loved *Kong's Daughter*. She'd made her parents take her to see it in the theatre three times, and the video and doll had been gifts for her ninth birthday. The giant baby ape was so cute, and heroic, too. A role model: a strong woman.

Of course, by the time she was twelve she'd outgrown the attachment to the doll, which was understandable for any self-respecting near-tween. But she would have fun, she'd thought or been told, working with the man who'd made her favorite movie. And Raymond Walchuk had been so kind when she first met him, smiling and smiling, and offering her compliments and confections. And Amabel had brought her Kika along to *Svidrigaylov's Dream*'s first day of filming, coddling the doll like a nursing infant and waiting for Mr. Raymond Walchuk himself to confer a blessing on the little ape. But Kika had been snatched away by an assistant and left with her mother seated behind the lights, while Amabel's child-face had disappeared beneath the brush strokes of the director's makeup experts.

"He's thinking fucky-fucky," Raymond Walchuk explained to Amabel, who was waiting beneath her transformed features. She hadn't understood. "You're the dream Svidrigaylov can't help from happening." Amabel had huddled before the cameras in the bed Raymond Walchuk laid her in. She'd smiled with her made up face the way the filmmaker told her to, hummed a laugh, and licked her lips as directed—she had never forgotten their sweet, slick taste, remembered it with each of ten thousand adult applications of gloss. From time to time she heard rumors that rough cuts of her scene from the unfinished *Svidrigaylov's Dream* survived, but Amabel knew the nightmare belonged only to her.

* * *

Amabel wondered how much of *Svidrigaylov's Dream* lay between them during her first night in bed with Carl. He'd been an attentive, even fastidious lover. She couldn't recall fucking on cleaner sheets.

At the end of her week as the voice of M'ling, Carl had invited her to share a meal with "les frères Walchuk," and she'd accepted, although she might have begged off if she'd known how trying the last recording session would be. The script finished, P. P. Frederico requested "a treasury of utterances" so calling back Amabel wouldn't be necessary if a particular effect were required. For half a day she fulfilled his demands for snarls, snorts, barks, whimpers, and an array of howls in different pitches. Most harrowing was the last vocalization P. P. solicited: a long wail broken by a string of sobs and ending with a strangled cough.

She left the studio drained, responding with a grim smile to the director's observation, "Now that was cathartic, wasn't it?"

But a meal with the Walchuk boys had been salubrious. The three of them had shared a spaghetti dinner around the kitchen table of Carl's Studio City home. The toddler ate with his fingers the strands his big brother had cut into bite sized pieces, and soon his cheeks, T-shirt, and overalls were sauce-stained. "Submersion-emersion!" Carl announced, which Amabel discovered meant a raucous, splash-filled, pre-bedtime bath that included a vigorous scrubbing not only of Wray, but also his ubiquitous Barbie. "Pity," Wray-Wray said about the plastic figurine at one point, quieting down amid his bubbles and inserting Barbie's head into his mouth. "He means 'Pretty.' I think." Carl said. The doll's wet hair must have been soapy, because Wray-Wray jerked her out and spat, then held her at arm's length and gazed at her. "Fay," he'd sighed with such exaggerated rue that he might have been acting.

Carl's baby, Amabel thought as she held the wriggling child out for him to towel dry. Then Wray, freshly pajama-ed, had curled between them on his over-sized bed. He lay facing Carl, who read *The Cat in the Hat* with excessive passion, both brothers lost in the destructive high jinks of Thing One and Thing Two. Wray had drawn up his knees fetally and planted the soles of his small feet on Amabel's breasts as if he were preparing to spring off them toward his brother. But he wasn't exactly Carl's baby, was he? Had Carl been such a disappointment to his mother that she'd felt the need to try again with a test-tube pregnancy? Was the idea of creating a new life so irresistible? Is that why she'd chosen to duplicate her first child's genetic code with Raymond Walchuk's dangerous sperm?

With a formality Amabel found charming, Carl granted her permission to smoke in his bed. It was a sentiment she'd never before applied to a sex-partner.

"So what the hell are Thing One and Thing Two?" he asked. "They remind me of the nasty French kids in the last movie I made. Sometimes, when I'm in the right kind of mood, I blame those French boys for the end of my acting career. The truth is, puberty robbed me of my cuteness. I quit before you even started. I Google around for those guys from *Les Garcons Seche* every so often, but they don't seem to have amounted to much. Is it wrong for me to be happy about that? They were kind of monsters. What's your take on forgiveness?"

Amabel lay with a wineglass- ashtray perched on her belly; its stem sticky with diet Coke. She'd spilled her cigarettes over the sheets, and Carl played with them as if they were Leggos he'd just discovered at the bottom of a toy chest. He sighted her down the line of one of them.

"They *are* monsters," Amabel said, ignoring the question about forgiveness. "Thing One and Thing Two are monsters." She tried to remember how the creatures looked when they popped out of the box the Cat kept them in. Was there anything French about them? A look in their eye? A foreign gesture?

"Well—where'd the Cat get them from?" Carl asked. "Who are their parents and why didn't they give their children better names? Maybe they came from Doctor Moreau's pet shop." He raised his eyebrows. "Do you think I'm screwing up my brother?"

Amabel hesitated. He'd baited the nature vs. nurture trap, and it was a discussion she wasn't eager to have with the son of Raymond Walchuk. "I don't think so," she said, "But I don't know anything about kids."

"Who does?" Carl put a cigarette between his lips, then a second and a third. "We're all novices," he murmured.

"I'm not a novice," Amabel said. "I'm just not in the game. I don't qualify at all."

Carl spit out the cigarettes. One clung to his lower lip, and he left it there. Amabel watched it bounce on his chin while he spoke until it finally dropped to the bed: "How do I know if there's something wrong with the kid? What if he's got Asperger's? Or maybe infantile Tourette syndrome. Is there such a thing? Obsessive-compulsive disorder? Ecolalia? You see him with that doll. How do I even know if he's a boy or a girl inside—or something else entirely. You have to admit, he lacks coherence."

"He's a baby, Carl. It seems to me you're doing a wonderful job."

"But you've declared yourself unqualified. And I will brook no platitudes." Carl scratched his head, as if he himself was questioning the origin of his last statement.

"He seems happy. I think he's happy—at least not unhappy."

"I'm remarkable, I know. Heroic. Maybe I'll get nominated for bro-dad of the year. I like to make it awkward for people not to compliment me. You know, we didn't even know he'd been stolen until the authorities contacted us. The surrogate hadn't missed a single checkup. She just took off at the last minute—been planning the whole thing for a while, as best as they could piece things together. They never found her or the fertility doctor whose SUV she drove."

"I thought she died. Didn't she die in childbirth?"

Carl snorted. "Nothing so dramatic. She got away. Left the baby and split. She must have been strong as a horse. It was a little crazy about that doctor, though. It never seemed to make sense that he'd abandon his practice to traffic in infant smuggling. The rumor is the two of them are still on the lam in Mexico."

"Maybe they're in love." A blush singed Amabel's neck and shoulders. Suddenly chilly, she tugged at the sheet, but couldn't gather enough fabric to cover her breasts. She twisted away, looking at Carl over her shoulder.

"Who's in love?" he asked.

"The doctor and the surrogate. Maybe they fell in love and tried to run away with Wray and start their own family in Mexico."

"'The little dog laughed to see such sport, and the dish ran away with the spoon.'"

"Like that," Amabel nodded. "A fairy tale."

"Not quite a fairy tale. A nursery rhyme." Carl said. "Less potency. But I've got a question for you—a big one."

Carl was playing with the cigarettes again. He threw one after the other like darts at Amabel's hip—no, at her ass, and she imagined him impossibly lodging one between her cheeks and grinning over his achievement. Or was he trying to poke the eye out of her Scaredy Cat tattoo? Given the indulgences she'd allowed her flesh in the past, Amabel surprised herself with her modesty. She shifted the target out of Carl's range, careful not to slop the soggy ashes from her wineglass. The idea of a "big question" from Carl made her nervous. Everything was going to boil down to Raymond Walchuk, wasn't it? Amabel was startled by her sudden certainty that while she and Carl had been fucking, he'd been envisioning her as that leering child-whore his father had turned her into so long ago. Sex under the shadow of Papa Ray's tombstone. He was the pimp of her history. Maybe she had screwed the son to make his father's ghost jealous. Demanding the Bic lighter, lost somewhere in the sheets, Amabel ran the hand holding a fresh cigarette through her brush cut, tapping her skull with her fingertips. After her career was well underway, during a month of public middle school she'd tried before retreating permanently to on-set tutors, someone had slipped an envelope with her name on it into her locker. She'd torn it open excitedly—was it a secret admirer's note, like the one her character received in *Penny Starlight: Girl Astronaut*? Instead, Amabel had found a photocopied picture captioned "Parisian prostitutes shaved bald for associating with Nazi officers." *WHORE!!* was printed across the picture, in red marker, over the women's faces.

"I haven't seen the lighter. Never touched it, M'ling—M'ling One." Carl said. Carl was studying her, and Amabel saw his father's eyes in his; Raymond Walchuk was in Wray-Wray's eyes, too, and she heard the three Walchuk men whispering in chorus, "He's thinking fucky-fucky." Carl stretched his leg beneath the sheet and his foot found Amabel's thigh. She remembered the feel of his baby brother's soles on her breasts.

"My question is," he said, "which one was afraid of women, Moreau or H. G. Wells? The character or the author? There are barely any women in the novel. It's a story about creation, and there aren't any women. For the first movie, the one from the 1930s, they invented Lota, the Panther Woman. Jesus—she might have been my first love! I remember getting dizzy when they showed she had claw-hands, and you figured out she wasn't human. I think Panther Woman might have been the whole point for my father." Carl paused reflectively. "It would have been interesting to see what kind of film Dad would have made. But P. P. insisted I strip the screenplay down to the original story's male-fest. He's making the movie as a sort of tribute to my dad. I guess that's pretty obvious"

Amabel sucked on her unlit cigarette, and her eyes watered. Carl made a show of checking his arms and shoulders and craned his neck to get a look at his back.

"You didn't leave scratches, did you, Lota?" he asked. Am I bleeding? It's okay if I am. I don't mind. I knew another set of twins—P. P.'s daughters, if you can believe it. I used to play with them on the island where my father made *Kong's Daughter*—now *that's* a story I imagine we'll get to sooner or later, me and those girls. Talk about leaving scratches! P. P. brought them with him to the States, where my dad helped him launch his career. They went to Stanford, I believe. Don't know what they're up to these days. You'd have to ask P. P."

I don't want to be Lola—I want to be Kika, Amabel wanted to say, but the name of Kong's daughter stuck in her throat. She released a smokeless breath, wondering if Carl would dare to embrace her again. "You're 'M'ling Two,'" she said.

* * *

Amabel was on her way back from New York, where she'd flown to discuss a theatrical role, Boo Boo Tannenbaum, a young mother, for an adaptation of J. D. Salinger's short story, "Down at the Dinghy."

"Really, the play's about the entire Glass family: Seymour, Franny, Zooey, Buddy—Buddy Glass narrates like the Stage Manager in *Our Town*," she'd told Carl over the phone before leaving her hotel for the airport and her return to the West Coast. She read the script this time, and had accepted the part after a single meeting with the director. "They didn't even ask me to read. P. P. apparently said some pretty nice things about my worth ethic." Carl had congratulated her and told her Wray-Wray would be sorry that he missed her call. "Tell him, '*It wasn't the planes—it was Beauty killed the Beast*,'" Amabel said. Maybe, she fantasized, the Walchuk boys could relocate to New York City for the run of *Dinghy*, and she could show Wray the real Empire State Building.

At JFK, conscious of heads turning toward her, Amabel waited for her return flight and thumbed a message to Carl on her phone: "I love you." She'd hardly the time to marvel at the words she'd texted before a young woman in military fatigues asked for an autograph and echoed them. "I loved you!" she gushed. A small fever sore cracked over the woman's upper lip. "Back when you played those triplets in *Switcheroo*. For years I thought there were really three of you."

"Just me," Amabel said, as she signed what looked like the back of an official military communication.

Minutes later, settled into her seat on the plane, Amabel caught her breath when her phone revealed a new voicemail from Carl. She cupped it to her ear, anticipating anything but what she heard.

Carl's voice, raw and electric: "You must be in the air. I'm at the hospital. Don't worry, everything is going to be okay. Wray choked—he bit the head off Barbie. I called 911, but he turned blue, and his eyes rolled back. I Googled 'tracheotomy.' I stabbed him in the throat with a shishkebab skewer, where the picture showed, between his—I forget what they're called. Oh, God—blood spurted out, not much, and bubbles. I stuck a soda straw in the hole like it said to do, and I held him on the kitchen counter with a dish towel under his head and my hand on his chest, and he looked at me, like, 'What the hell are you doing?' but he didn't move, and the paramedics showed up and took over and said I saved his life. But it's okay. I did okay. Wray's going to be okay—I—we're—at the hospital, Cedars-Sinai, I—"

The call ended abruptly, as if Carl had dropped the phone or it had been snatched from him. Breathless, clenching her teeth to hear because of a ringing in her ears, Amabel listened to Carl's message again and again. Finally, unable to wave off the flight attendant bowing over her—the time for silencing electronics had long passed— Amabel gave up. She shut off the phone, tucked it in her bag, and showed her empty hands to the attendant, who smiled and moved down the aisle.

Amabel shrank back in her seat. How could news be delivered this way? It was as if an old-fashioned postcard, one with a picture of a monument or tropical sunset, had blown onto her lap through an open window. As if the message on the postcard were addressed to a different party, and by reading it Amabel had invaded their privacy. Carl had sounded exhilarated, triumphant—tragedy had been averted. How had he found the strength to do what he'd done? Little Wray's limp body in his arms—skewering the baby's throat—a *soda straw*! When, Amabel wondered, had she entered Carl's thoughts? Had he cleared her out as he dedicated himself to saving his baby brother? How long before she reappeared?

Maybe the accident had been her fault—maybe Carl had been distracted by her text— *I love you*—maybe he'd lingered over it a moment too long while Wray chewed off the head off his doll. What had Carl been about to say when his message was cut off? Amabel felt like a victim and was angry at herself for it, but that anger was inside a greater anger she couldn't name. But—Wray was fine. Thank God.

With horror she remembered an early date with Carl at a restaurant where he'd been certain they'd be safe from prying eyes. That night she'd fantasized about choking, because she *had* choked, just for a moment, on a clot of the melted cheese blanketing her French onion soup. She'd strained for air with a rush of panic before clearing her throat, then wondered how the man across from her, his eyes on his own plate, would react if she really were choking—would he rescue her? Would he wrap his arms around her and try to squeeze the death out? Why hadn't she been the one he'd saved?

The flight attendant offered a beverage, and Amabel asked for a scotch out of habit, and when it was brought, immediately ordered a second. Responding to Carl's message was impossible—they'd ascended into turbulent skies, and the signs prohibiting electronics remained lit. Carl was a hero. There would be publicity. Layers of privacy would peel away like old wallpaper. Carl would be the toast of Hollywood. Carl Walchuk: son of Raymond Walchuk; savior of his test-tube brother; lover of Amabel Hadley, rehab slut—it was too soon for her to be redeemed. No one would believe she'd earned it.

She hated jets, but on her flight to New York Amabel had been so busy reviewing the *Dinghy* script that she hadn't bothered with the Xanax prescribed for her. Now she gagged down a double dose with her second drink. The cabin seemed to shrink. The jet struggled against the storm, and Amabel imagined the fuselage gripped by a huge hand, which shook her into a tormented sleep. She dreamed she saw Carl's back as he hunched over a granite counter. The perspective shifted— she watched from directly overhead, just as Carl raised what looked like a silver spike and drove it downward into the small figure sprawled across the granite. It was Wray, she knew, but it was also a little golden ape, and its limbs jerked when the spike pierced its throat. There was no blood, just a gust of warm air against Amabel's face. Carl yanked the spike out, and Amabel saw only the bloodless wound, like a rosebud mouth, flesh glistening pink and red against the golden fur.

Then it was dark. Amabel knew somehow that she stood behind a curtain on the stage of a theatre. She heard a distinctive voice she couldn't place—but there was no doubt that it issued from the lips cut into the pale throat. She heard "Moreau" and "M'ling One" and "Walchuk." Then she heard her name—she was about to be introduced! Amabel reached reflexively for her face, but her fingers couldn't find her features. Instead, she smeared makeup, like a child finger-painting. She heard the rosebud lips on the other side of the curtain whispering into a microphone: "and Amabel has come a long way from the little girl of Svidrigaylov's dream . . ." There was applause, thunderous with expectation. A finger on those lips would hush the voice. She could feel the suction on her own fingertip as she plugged the end of an invisible straw.

Amabel woke an hour later, according to the time on the buzzing phone she fished out of her bag. She blinked away cobwebs and shadows, felt the weight of something she couldn't quite remember. There was a text from P. P. Frederico: "*With Carl at hospital. We've lost Wray.*"

Chapter 19—Lactophilia

Bronwyn was in New York, sitting in a theater hard at work evaluating new talent. The play, *Dinghy*, was an adaptation of a Salinger short story about one shard of the author's famous Glass family. Central to the narrative were a young mother and her hypersensitive pre-school son. Playing the mother was Amabel Hadley, an early discovery of Bronwyn's. Bronwyn had low expectations, in spite of rave reviews, but so far had been surprised. Amabel's performance was touching, even memorable. How had this childless woman, notable in the last decade and a half only for her bad behavior, learned to play a mother? Was nurturing taught in rehab?

Bronwyn watched the young woman squat and smile bravely at her pretend son. The world threatened to overwhelm him, and, afraid she was losing the child to his fears, she tousled his blond curls. A simple gesture. Pretense. Was that all you needed to be a good mother? Critics who'd noted the remarkable empathy Amabel lent to her character, Boo Boo Tannenbaum, nee Glass, were right. This play, this performance, would resurrect Amabel's career. As if motherhood were all she needed after surviving the turmoil of young adulthood. The first act ended. Applause fell like tin confetti as the last scene froze, presenting a tableau of the mother standing at a kitchen island behind a mixing bowl, her son at her feet, stacking boxes of instant pudding.

The intermission would be brief—ten minutes. Bronwyn scanned faces in the audience and recognized no one, which was unusual. The seats on either side of her were empty, paid for by her agency in case she'd asked clients along. She smiled at the cloud-haired woman two seats over who squinted in her direction. But the woman was gazing past her at someone else. No one who looked at slender Bronwyn would have guessed that she'd be having a baby herself in less than two months. June 25th was the official due date— "Demi-Christmas." The name had been her friend Kirkland's idea: "My birthday's the day after Christmas," he complained. "It's always an afterthought. Second rate presents—leftover junk that didn't fit in the stocking. Birthday presents wrapped in paper covered with Santa Clauses, as if it's my fault I was born so close to Jesus. June 25th is the perfect birthday—exactly halfway around the calendar from Christmas.

You've got to tell everybody that Henry's arriving on Demi-Christmas. There can never be too many holidays."

Papers had been signed, and, on or about that date, the nineteen-year-old carrying Henry would give birth and immediately surrender her newborn to Bronwyn. And Bronwyn would become a real mother, not pretend like Amabel Hadley. Had it really been twenty years since the actress had showed up as a little girl at Kidz, Limited, eager to audition for the film-turned-fiasco that had been *Svidrigaylov's Dream*? The agency had barely escaped the lawsuits and scandals accompanying that mess and had washed their hands of Amabel, who had manipulated the notoriety to land a few Disney roles. And of course *everybody* had washed their hands of Raymond Walchuk. Clean hands, that's what show business was all about.

Who had Bronwyn been thinking she might see in the theatre? Certainly not Raymond Walchuk, who'd been dead for years. Fallen off a ferry, though a body had never been found. And Christine, Raymond's ex-wife who Bronwyn knew in passing from Pilates— Christine was dead, too. Who of the Walchuk clan remained, besides Carl, who'd lost not only both parents, but also the little brother, more like a son, his mother had left him. Bronwyn couldn't remember the little boy's name. The "Miracle Baby," the media had christened him after his Mexican border birth. Had they ever found the thieving surrogate? But poor Carl—he'd failed to keep the Miracle Child safe. Did he blame himself for that awful accident? It seemed like a curse was following those Walchuks. Bronwyn shivered. Bad luck to even think about them. But Carl and Amabel were an item—either married or about to be—so it wasn't so absurd to think that he might be attending this play. Except its theme was parenthood — wouldn't it force him to relive his own tragedy?

Bronwyn unrolled the Playbill she'd been clutching. Amabel was on the cover. She'd lost weight from the tabloid shots Bronwyn remembered, looked good, fit—but, on second look, maybe not. Gaunt, cheekbones too prominent, her eyes burning fiercely like fires in the back of twin caves. Acting skill, make up, or eating disorder? Those eyes, a blazing green, had many years ago led Bronwyn to pull the child's glossy from an agency slush pile—Bronwyn's guess at what Raymond Walchuk wanted for his dream-child-hooker. *I'm a bell, you're a bell*—isn't that what the kid had said when they'd met for the first time.

Bronwyn's thoughts drifted to another interview, so many years—literal lifetimes—later: young Sandra, the unmarried teen who was carrying Henry. She wasn't an actor—but she was playing a role. Bronwyn considered Sandra her "birth agent."

I will be Henry's mother, Bronwyn thought, so distinctly she wondered if she'd spoken aloud. But nobody's head turned toward her. She looked at the program again. Amabel. How hard had she taken the death of the littlest Walchuk? Did the tragedy inform her *Dinghy* performance? What role was she playing for Carl now? Perhaps her recovery had given her the strength to reach outside herself and be supportive of someone else. Carl had been such a sensitive little boy. Awkwardly so—Bronwyn had known from the start he'd never last as a performer. He lacked the grit and the ambition—and had no stage parent: Raymond's ambition had been for himself, not his boy.

Bronwyn flipped through the program, half-thinking Carl's *Teddy* poster would materialize among the pages. Instead, she turned to a photograph of the little blond boy playing Lionel in *Dinghy*. It was this child she'd come to see, since her agency specialized in children, and his performance had received accolades echoing Amabel's. But Bronwyn had found the boy disappointing, an insipidly unexceptional dandelion fluff of a nothing: the worst kind of an imitation of a child. When Amabel hugged him on stage, whispering playful gibberish into his ear, she might as well have been cuddling a stuffed monkey doll.

Bronwyn fished a compact from her bag and opened it. She watched her reflected lips purse. Her eyes retained the surprised look they'd never lost after her most recent botoxing. She put the mirror away and tried to think—in a twisted way, might it have been the story of the Walchuks that had stimulated Bronwyn's own desire for motherhood? How could Christine Walchuk, as old as she'd been, have eggs fresh enough to freeze when Bronwyn's much younger womb had been a failure? Bronwyn frowned, wished she hadn't put away the mirror so she could see if the expression produced any new lines. The last time she'd spoken to Christine—offering a word of condolence and a shoulder pat outside the Pilates studio after Raymond's drowning was announced—Bronwyn had been surprised by the response: "Someone in your business should have stuck by him, don't you think?"

What could Bronwyn have said? *Your ex sank himself over his warped devotion to "art"*? *You left when you had the chance.* But then Christine might have answered, "I'm going to give him one more child." Which she'd done. Mercifully, Christine would never learn the final outcome of her gift. Long ago, Bronwyn had sat with Raymond and Carl in the darkness of another theatre, watching the premiere of his blockbuster film, and she'd wondered about the risks, the cost-benefit, of connecting herself romantically to the father. But now, unlike then, her taut skin was unblushable. Whether she'd subliminally found them inspirational or not, she'd positioned herself firmly outside the cycle of Walchuk tragedies.

Bronwyn had seen enough—of the little boy and of the play. Of Amabel Hadley. It was ironic, considering her profession, how bored Bronwyn was by movies and plays. They were too long. Commercials seemed to her the perfect length. But the house lights blinked and the theatre darkened. The audience had returned to their seats, and Bronwyn had missed the moment for an inconspicuous escape. She sighed, and the sigh became a yawn. Just as well that she was stuck— she owed Amabel a backstage visit after the show, didn't she? She imagined the reunion: there would be expressions of wonder, maybe a forced laugh or two about the passage of time, the vicissitudes of fate. Should she mention Carl? No—enough to congratulate the rehabilitated star on her performance. And if she crossed paths with the child actor, she'd grant him a platitude and hand his parent her card. No telling when a need might arise for an insipid fluff.

Bronwyn settled back into her seat in the darkness, burrowing into the audience as if it was a giant, gently purring cat. It would be easy, maybe optimal, to lose herself in thought and doze with her eyes open for the duration of the play. There were lighting effects that had bothered Bronwyn's vision during the first part of the play, strange wisps and streaks of blue that she realized very late in the act were turning into words she probably should have tried to decipher. But when she'd squinted at the blue lights, they'd seemed to disintegrate into ash, swirling frighteningly into black dots that reminded her of bats swarming from a cave. When she'd refocused on the stage, on Amabel and the boy, the black ash remained for a few seconds, obscuring Bronwyn's view.

Now, as the second act began, Bronwyn listened to the patter of dialogue on stage without distinguishing the words, and, rested her gaze on the back of the chair in front of her, where, for a fraction of a second, she thought she saw the black ash again. It wasn't the first time she'd seen the specks—she made a note to visit her eye doctor. Disengaging herself entirely from the play, she allowed herself to contemplate her own impending parenthood. What had the teen—

Henry's birth agent—said about Henry's father? The girl, Sarah, had a clipping showing the photograph of a handsome young man who'd lost his life in Afghanistan. "Our relationship was a secret," she said, her big blue eyes brimming with tears. "He never knew I was pregnant." Attractive genes on both sides, if the photograph was accurate. And there was no reason not to trust the girl. When and if Henry asked, Bronwyn would tell him that his male birth agent had been a war hero. She was certain her baby would be gorgeous and deep-souled and took her confidence as proof that her mother's intuition still functioned, despite her obstructed birth canal and eggless uterus.

Although Bronwyn was more than twice Sarah's age, weren't the two like Siamese twins, connected not physically, but through Henry? It was a strange kind of tug of war: Bronwyn needed to possess the baby, and the girl was determined—*contracted*—to let him go. On the day after Demi-Christmas, or thereabouts, the partnership would be dissolved the moment Henry passed into his true mother's arms.

Bronwyn yawned again and let her lids droop. With empty seats on either side, she could fade into a practiced light slumber without discovery. On stage a phone rang with a harsh, old-fashioned *brrrrr*— Bronwyn snuggled even deeper into her seat. She tilted her head away from her nearest neighbor, the cloud-headed woman.

She melted into a suspended darkness and silence, a peace interrupted by a different phone, a buzzing cell phone in her hand. Of course she'd turned her phone off and secured it in her purse. Of course she was dreaming, and her awareness of the fact amused her. She watched herself lift the phone to her ear, as if she was in a play herself.

This is the hospital," a voice whispered. "*Your baby is here early. Come immediately*." And before she could draw a startled breath, Bronwyn was there, in the hospital, in, she *knew*, the neonatal ward, surrounded by dim figures robed and masked in white. She wore a gown and gloves herself and felt the fabric of a mask over her nose and mouth—her breath was moist and warm. Bronwyn stared down into a plastic box, an incubator, empty except for a tangle of hoses and wires. *Where is*— But she couldn't think of her baby's name. A voice responded: *Ask the mother*.

But where *was* the mother? Bronwyn, now totally alone, backed through a steel door into a white hallway. She pivoted and hurried forward, passing several closed doors before stopping in front of one labeled "WOMEN." The knob was cold through her latex glove, but she stepped inside the bright room and shut the door behind her. Reflexively, she flipped off the light switch, glimpsing before all went black a white sink, a toilet, and her own reflection in the mirror over the sink. Bronwyn pulled off her mask, felt cool air on the face she couldn't see. *Where was—the baby*? Maybe, on the mirror's other side, through the wall, Sarah the birth agent lay beside the dead war hero-father. Maybe Bronwyn's child was nestled between them. Staring into nothing until her eyes ached, Bronwyn, dizzy, gripped the cold sink. *Where*?

Sudden brightness. Bronwyn blinked up at the gray face of the cloud-haired woman from her row. The woman pulled her hand from Bronwyn's shoulder as if touching the agent had given her a shock. The play was over, the house lights were on, and Bronwyn was blocking the aisle.

* * *

A month and a half later, back home on the west coast, Bronwyn attended an art exhibit, "The Scandalous Family," because Kirkland had contributed an installation that he claimed celebrated her imminent motherhood. Demi-Christmas was only days away— Henry could arrive at any time. Half of Kirkland's installation was a black and white film displayed on one gallery wall: a pair of silhouettes set on railroad tracks in a desert. The first shadow figure crouched on all fours like a dog. The second figure—long-legged and spike heeled, Barbie-breasted and obviously pregnant—towered over the first and brandished a whip. Chains linked both figures to the rails.

The scene was projected onto the wall from the headlamp of a perambulator-sized locomotive standing on steel tracks that ran across the gallery's hardwood floor and joined the rails in the film. A small cradle hung from the locomotive's projector-headlamp, and in it a baby doll, hooded in black and swaddled in a leather diaper, rocked. The silhouettes on the tracks ignored the locomotive bearing down on them. Occasionally, the pregnant dominatrix dipped forward, threatening her partner with her whip, breasts, and belly.

Bronwyn sloshed the remnants of her white wine around its plastic cup, while Kirkland warned patrons passing between the locomotive and the projection to "Mind the tracks."

"I can't decide," he said. "Am I part of the installation? I could punch tickets like a conductor."

Kirkland called his work "Madonna of the Whip," and he stood back and gave the display a lingering look of admiration before turning to Bronwyn. "The drama of the American family. Look in the mirror." Bronwyn flinched at the comment, carried for a moment back to her dream in the Broadway theatre—the empty incubator, the dark bathroom. She brushed off her unease but couldn't help sneaking a glance at her phone. She was safe—no messages, especially none from the hospital.

"Careful—" Kirkland touched the upper arm of a young woman wearing glasses who stumbled over his installation's tracks. He held out his palm. "Ticket, please."

The woman paused to take in the artist, the installation, and Bronwyn. Her shadow blotted the figures on the wall into a Rorschach until Kirkland guided her out of the locomotive's beam. After frowning at the silhouettes, she stabbed a finger at the wall on the opposite side of the gallery. "Those are mine."

"Lovely," Kirkland said, squinting. Bronwyn followed her friend's gaze, imitating his wince as if narrowed lids were the secret to understanding art, and saw a set of four paintings. All featured flesh-pink, brown-nippled globes. Dozens of pink melons were arrayed in a leafy field in one. Nippled balls dangled amid tinsel and Christmas lights in another. In a third the pink blobs lined a subway bench like plump, nude commuters. In the last and largest, a fleshy globe had been stretched flat into a map of the world, the oceans a darker pink than the land. The world map's nipple rose like a huge chocolate kiss in the center of North America's Continental Divide.

Kirkland nodded. "I get it. 'Motherhood.' Same as mine. But not as subtle."

The young woman shook her head so hard her glasses shifted and her large breasts swung. Two spots darkened the white fabric of her T-shirt. Were these spots—they looked damp— part of her exhibit?

"Subtlety is dead and buried," she said. "We've cycled back to sincerity." She caught Bronwyn staring at her shirt. "I forgot my pads. Must have been subliminal. Did you know most primates can lactate without pregnancy? Also lemurs and dwarf mongooses."

After the exhibition, Bronwyn and Kirkwood took their new acquaintance, Lizzie, for coffee. Returning from a trip to the restroom, Lizzie opened her backpack and showed Bronwyn a plastic breast pump and a Tupperware container of freshly expressed milk.

"I donate to the milk bank," she said, sipping her latte. Lizzie explained that she'd just ended a long relationship. "When things started, it was all about sex. All about my breasts, mostly—he'd have squeezed, licked, and sucked for twenty-four hours a day, if he hadn't had to go to work. And I'd have let him. But then they swelled. My nipples enlarged. One night, he drew milk, and it shocked the hell out of us. He smacked his lips and wanted to nurse. I cried. I thought sure I was pregnant. But tests said no. According to the doctors, I have super excitable hormones. Pretty unusual, but not unheard of. For a while—for just a very little while—my boyfriend and I both got into it. Lactophilia. It's a fetish thing—there are chat rooms. People have 'adult nursing relationships.' But I got sick of it—I'd wake up in the middle of the night short of breath from the weight of his head on my chest and the sound of him slurping. He wanted to get married. But who wants to marry a giant infant? He'd have fought our babies for his fix. Anyway, I cut him off, weaned him cold turkey, and now he's gone."

Lizzie paused and stretched, thrusting her chest with the half-dollar stains toward Bronwyn. "I haven't let myself dry up," she said. "It's not sexual anymore, but I *like* lactating."

"It's a mothering instinct," Kirkland said.

"Maybe. But I'm not longing for a baby. What I feel is a kind of overwhelming *generosity*. That's why I donate. It's too bad milk banks don't pay, like the blood places used to. I can't make my rent by myself."

"So you need a way to keep yourself in brushes and paint . . ." Kirkland tugged at his smooth chin, then turned to Bronwyn with raised eyebrows. "She's ripe and ready, kiddo," he said, nodding toward their new acquaintance. He leaned back and considered both tablemates. "Do either of you believe in God? Or fate. Or how about just plain old good luck?

"No," Lizzie barked, then paused. "Well, maybe all three. I've heard people only have opinions if they get asked a question in a poll. I'd have to think about it. God, fate, or luck. You can't really believe in luck, though, right? If you believe in it then you're actually calling it fate."

Bronwyn sat quietly. She stared at the stains covering Lizzie's nipples. Kirkland shook his head like a dog drying itself. "Don't you see it's a fairytale?" He extended his left hand, palm up, toward Bronwyn, who looked at it blankly. "*You* are about to have a baby—" He stuck his other hand across the table, grabbing for Lizzie's. She took it, and Kirkland held fast, as if he was about to drag her through their coffee mugs. "And *you* are overflowing with mother's milk and need a place to live." He took a deep breath, skimmed a look back and forth at the two women, and lifted his gaze to the ceiling. "I now pronounce you Mom and wet nurse," he declared.

Bronwyn may not have understood art, but casting was her business, and Kirkland was right. She and Lizzie locked eyes across the table. Bronwyn shrugged, and Lizzie, glasses glinting, smiled. It took less than ten minutes to outline the terms of a contract satisfactory to both. Kirkland raised his coffee mug to toast the new relationship.

Three days later, on Demi-Christmas Eve, Henry was born, a healthy, happy boy. With little fuss, he was handed over to Bronwyn's care, and his new mommy brought her son home, where she introduced him to his designer nursery, his wardrobe of colorful onesies, and his endless supply of fresh mother's milk.

* * *

At precisely 11:00 AM, Bronwyn's phone sounded the notes of "Brahm's Lullaby," just as it had every day for three months since she'd returned to work after Henry's birth. It would be Lizzie calling, with a report on the baby's morning. Bronwyn always picked up, unless occupied with a casting obligation—a meeting with a producer, a director, a hopeful performer, or a stage parent. Over the years her agency, Kidz, Limited., had refined its niche stable of performers to focus on children, with primary emphasis on "specials"—those boasting particular "challenges," eccentricities, or in-vogue ethnicities. Of course Bronwyn kept herself open to any child—even the demographically "normal"— who possessed a certain something that called out to her instincts and experience.

She let the ringtone lullaby play through a second time and studied the background photo on the phone: fuzz-headed Henry in his red PJ's, a milky bubble on his lips, snuggling in a pair of white arms against a bosom that belonged to Lizzie. But Bronwyn didn't pick up— lately she'd been re-thinking the rigid AM arrangement. Routine sapped the joy out of things, and restraint could teach valuable lessons. Best mothering practice might argue that it was time for Bronwyn to wean herself—and Henry and Lizzie—from constant availability.

The ringtone cut out after the third *Lul-la-byyyy*, and the final note hung over Bronwyn's desk. She bowed back to the pile of portfolios culled from her lists: brave, beautiful little boys and girls in wheelchairs, on crutches, or angelically bald-headed, each indispensible in his or her own way for background scenes in commercials demanding diversity. The moms and dads of these children, long steeped in advocacy, were especially involved stage parents.

Bronwyn's assistant buzzed in word of a surprise early arrival— Shawn Anderson, the new client Bronwyn was scheduled to meet for lunch to present her shortlist of "specials." Before she knew it, a thickset, unshaven stranger had pushed into her office and dropped into a chair he humped up to Bronwyn's desk. He ignored her offered hand.

"Can't do lunch," her guest said. His leather jacket was draped over his shoulder— purple fingertips emerged from the ace bandage inside the sling supporting his arm. "Racquetball. I just got out of the emergency room. I've got to see an osteopath—my shoulder's probably dislocated." The portfolios scattered across Bronwyn's desk caught his eye, and he tilted his head for a better view. "I need one of your babies." Then he saw Bronwyn's phone, frowned, and hunched forward. "There," he said, jabbing the index finger of his uninjured hand at the photo of Henry. "That one's perfect."

It shouldn't have taken Bronwyn as long as it did to explain that the baby on her phone wasn't available, wasn't a "child of difference," was, in fact, Bronwyn's own perfectly normal, non-show business little boy." She shivered a little—was it pride? —as she held the phone under her client's chin and scrolled through a dozen photos.

"Here's Henry nursing," Bronwyn said. "That's not me, that's Lizzie. She's Henry's wet nurse. That's him in his crib. He's looking at his mobile. I think he's smiling. Here he is on Lizzie's lap. She's reading to him. It's a book about rainbows or something. But see—there's nothing 'special' about him. He's a darling—my little angel, but I'd have to cast him as a 'normal'—if this was that kind of agency and I was that kind of mother. For diaper ads and baby food commercials."

Shawn Anderson's snort startled Bronwyn. He sat back. "Whatever you say. You're the expert. So what else have you got?"

Bronwyn pulled the portfolio of a lovely five-year-old girl with soft platinum ringlets, porcelain skin, and rosebud lips. Prominent in the child's photos were her thick glasses and hearing aid. "She's got experience," Bronwyn said, and enumerated the child's sitcom and commercial appearances.

"Not exactly what I had in mind." Shawn Anderson frowned, adjusting his aching shoulder. "I want a *baby*. I've got plenty of little girls—too many."

Bronwyn shook her head. "Babies of the kind you're looking for are in short supply. The 'distinguishing characteristics' you want often aren't apparent in infancy."

"But you don't get what I'm envisioning. It's supposed to be an extended family. It's for *life insurance*. I need a baby of a certain kind, I don't know, hooked up to something, maybe in a special stroller; the others—sisters, brothers, parents, grandparents' group around him— then the camera shows them from above, and we see that the baby is the bull's eye of a gigantic target."

As Shawn Anderson described his needs, Bronwyn's concentration lapsed. Her office seemed to darken—had she hydrated enough after her exercise class? Her gaze fell upon Henry's photo, and she blinked hard—where was he? Home, right? She picked up the phone. What was she looking at? An empty incubator? Like the one she'd had in that awful dream back in the New York theatre? Her cheeks throbbed in places she'd thought bloodless. She closed her eyes and breathed deeply. When she opened them and stared again at her phone, thank God, Henry was back in Lizzie's arms. And Shawn Anderson's head bowed over the picture of the deaf girl. His hair was a mess. She could see mottled patches of his scalp. Bronwyn set her phone back on her desk just as he glanced up, his brow clouded.

"I guess this one will do," he grumbled.

"I can recommend another agency if you'd like," Bronwyn said tersely. If Kidz, Limited can't satisfy your needs, we try to accommodate—"

But Bronwyn's new client waved her off. He looked around the room at the posters featuring successful agency placements familiar from commercials, TV shows, and movies. But when Bronwyn followed the sweep of her guest's gaze, she saw, hanging between an advertisement for diapers and a promo for a popular family sitcom, a poster that didn't belong—the young Carl Walchuk, moon faced and solemn, staring straight at her from the deck of an ocean liner. It was her old *Teddy* poster—she hadn't seen it in years. Where had it been? When had her assistant—it must have been her assistant— hung it up? And what was the poster beside it? Bronwyn's nape hair rose. The young Amabel Hadley, smiling provocatively from a chair, with those eyes, those incredible eyes—this was one of the photos she'd taken of the girl to send to Raymond Walchuk for his Dostoevsky production—the one that ruined him. Bronwyn remembered posing the girl to look like one of the children in some disturbing paintings. Why was this on her wall? There'd never been a *Svidrigaylov's Dream*, let alone a poster to advertise it.

"Ms. O'Savage?" Shawn Anderson was clearing his throat. Had he said her name more than once?

"Sorry—" Bronwyn pinched her lips, dropped her gaze to see that Henry was still safe on her phone, peeked over her guest's shoulder at the wall—Carl and Amabel were gone and her regular posters were back where they belonged. "I was just struck by an inspiration for—I just remembered—"

Frowning, Shawn Anderson tapped the glossy in front of him. "I'll take this one," he repeated.

Without further apology, Bronwyn called the girl's mother. She muffled the woman's exclamations with her hand as she passed her new client the phone, which he held several inches from his ear. After a moment, he confirmed the offer, clarified a few details, and ended the connection.

"Sorry about lunch," he said to Bronwyn. "Another time." His attention dropped to the photo of Henry glowing on the phone still in his palm.

"Good luck with your shoulder." Bronwyn reached for her phone, which Shawn Anderson surrendered as he stood.

"They'll probably do an MRI. Wet nurse, you said? That's really a thing?"

"Good fortune threw Lizzie in my path. She also happens to be a talented artist. And my baby adores her." This time Shawn Anderson took the hand Bronwyn extended, stooped slightly as if he meant to kiss it, then squinted at her in confusion as she tugged it away. His focus fell one last time to the phone lying on Bronwyn's desk.

"He looks cold," he said as he left.

Bronwyn sat in her office, dabbing yogurt between lips she barely parted. She studied the phone picture of Henry. She peeked up suddenly at her walls, as if she was trying to catch some secret shifting by surprise, but her posters had returned to where they belonged. Low sugar, she thought. Wasn't that a thing? But what had Shawn Anderson seen in the photo of her son? Her baby looked cold, he'd said. *Cold*? Was Henry noticeably uncomfortable? Or had Shawn Anderson meant the baby looked cold to the *touch*? Was *Lizzie* cold from holding him in her arms? Did Henry chill his wet nurse's breasts?

What *did* Henry feel like? Bronwyn pursed her lips, mimicking the kiss she placed on her son's forehead each night when Lizzie offered him up. Bronwyn remembered the "Nighty-night" she called as the wet nurse toted him to her bed. But was he hot or cold? This evening, Bronwyn would take the baby's temperature. After the gym and a quick bite downtown with Kirkland, she'd go home and paste the external thermometer across Henry's forehead. She was sure it was in the bathroom cabinet. 98.6 was the target. Possibly Kirkland had noticed something peculiar about her baby boy. If the conversation turned that way, she might ask.

But at Pilates, Bronwyn couldn't concentrate on her core. On all fours, as she followed the bends and stretches of her instructor, she thought of the shadow couple chained to the tracks in Kirkland's installation, "Madonna of the Whip." Then her brow contracted, and she felt her features meld somehow with Shawn Anderson's. With a shared face they frowned at the little picture of Henry on her phone. Bronwyn jerked her head with a snap that hurt her neck. She concentrated on her reflection in the mirrored wall behind the instructor. *The core, the core*, she thought, coordinating her twists and stretches with the poses of the dozen other slim figures in her class. For a shocking moment she saw her body laden with the breasts she'd had surgically reduced long ago, when she was still a teen. Bronwyn had insisted, and her mother had given permission. She'd so wanted to dance professionally. But at her new arts school she'd faced a stark truth—the career for which she'd reshaped herself demanded talents she'd never have.

Bronwyn blinked sweat from her eyes and, relieved, found herself again as sleek as her Pilates-mates. But her abdomen felt hollow. She dug her fingers into the mat and focused on her knuckles as she stiffened into a plank. Shawn Anderson's fingertips had been swollen like purple vegetable tubers. Once, when she was very little, Bronwyn had ridden a city bus with her grandmother. The fumes had nauseated her, and Nana had smoothed back her hair and told her to "focus on something." The dark-skinned man sitting across the aisle from her curled a hand with shrunken fingers against his chest as if he held a dying bird. Bronwyn stared, and when Nana noticed, she'd leaned over, her large bosom warm and stale-smelling against her granddaughter's cheek.

"Thank you for your service," Nana had said to the man, who ignored the senseless remark.

* * *

At dinner with Kirkland, Bronwyn began the story of Shawn Anderson.

"He wanted a baby with a difference for an insurance commercial—"

"Your 'babies with differences.'" Kirkland made a face. "And you say you don't understand art. You're as creative as God. You can make a fake person out of anyone."

Bronwyn swallowed her tasteless Merlot, waiting for Kirkland to finish his banter. She had a headache. What did she know about Shawn Anderson? Why had he fixated on Henry's picture on her phone? She thought of his injury. *Thank you for your service.* And then she envisioned another photograph: the one accompanying the obituary of the young soldier that Bronwyn had accepted on faith had been the father of her child. What if that story had been false? The teenage birth agent had insisted that their relationship had been a secret and that the soldier had died ignorant of her pregnancy. Maybe Shawn Anderson knew something about Henry's true father. Who did Henry look like? She'd never asked herself that question before. Not the soldier. And the young woman who bore and surrendered him? Faces were Bronwyn's business—the "art" Kirkland credited her for— but she couldn't conjure up a clear enough image of the young birth agent to compare her face to Henry's.

A rattle of cubes, and a startled Bronwyn upset the glass the busboy was filling. Water and ice collected in her lap, while Kirkwood and the busboy pushed at the spill with napkins. A minute later, Bronwyn stood in a locked restroom stall, rubbing the damp spot on her skirt with a paper towel. Her head ached, and she couldn't think clearly. Photos and posters swirled around her. When she returned to the table she excused herself, pleading a dehydration headache from her workout, and told Kirkland she was going home to rest.

* * *

Bronwyn had taken only a few steps into her front hall when she shrieked so loud in fright that her ears rang and her teeth ached

217

even after she'd collapsed on her sofa. Lizzie, framed by the kitchen doorway, clutched frantic Henry to her side.

"I thought—" Bronwyn gasped. But she couldn't put what she'd thought into words—it was too horrible: she'd parked the car in the driveway, stepped into her house, and called for Lizzie, who'd materialized suddenly, her T-shirt and arms blood-soaked, her hair clotted—and the baby, smeared with red, splayed in her arms.

Sacrifice—the idea had struck Bronwyn like a fist to her sternum. Her arms flailed against imagined knives as she fell back—*Helter Skelter*! Was Lizzie a victim or a perpetrator? Were curses scrawled on the walls with her baby's blood? Who was calling her name?

"Bronwyn—*Bronwyn!* No! Henry and I were *painting*. We were just painting." Lizzie patted her drenched chest, lifted her stained hair from her forehead. "You were supposed to be at dinner with Kirkland. We were just starting to clean up. I'm so sorry—this must look—" Was Lizzie half-smiling her apology? Naked Henry, quieting down, burrowed between his wet nurse's breasts, then pulled back, his face a red mask. Lizzie's glasses were speckled with the paint that Bronwyn had mistaken for gore. Lizzie *was* smiling, her teeth white and sharp.

"You okay now? Okay? We were, like, *finger*-painting. Except I was using Henry instead of a finger." Lizzie bleated a laugh. "Like he's a big stamp pad. 'Baby Parts,' I call it. Red paint on brown paper—I've got it rolled out on the bathroom floor. Don't worry—everything's washable and non-toxic. We'd have cleaned it all up before you got here if you hadn't been early." Lizzie jostled the smeared baby, who reached for her chin and caught her lower lip. "Isn't that right, little man? Really, Bronwyn, I'm *so* sorry. Can I get you something from the kitchen? Water? A glass of wine? I want to keep off the carpet in case we drip."

Bronwyn hoisted herself up and slumped forward, elbows on knees, hands supporting her head. "No thank you. Nothing. Sorry," she wheezed, short of breath. "It's been a difficult day—casting a horror film," she lied. "—My imagination got the best of me." She waved a limp hand. "I want to help with the bath. Give me a minute."

"You change, and I'll feed Henry first. It'll sooth him." Lizzie and the baby disappeared into the kitchen. Bronwyn heard a chair scrape across the tiles. She pictured the wet nurse lifting her shirt. Had the paint soaked through to the skin? Would she wash her nipples so her milk wouldn't mix with the blood— the paint?

"It's all non-toxic, right?" Bronwyn called.

A ten-count passed before Lizzie answered in a low voice. "Um-hmm. Oh—I almost forgot—you had a visitor. A Mr. Anderson? I thought he was the cable guy. He said he was in the neighborhood, and I should tell you he'd thought it over, and he decided against the arrangement you made today. He said to tell you he wanted to go back to his original idea. You'd know what he was talking about, he said."

"Oh—yes." Shawn Anderson in her house? Bronwyn searched the room's dark corners, but they were empty.

"He was kind of weird. He made me nervous, the way he wouldn't leave. He asked to hold Henry. He called him 'My special little man.'" Lizzie's words were muffled, like moths fluttering in a jar. "I told him Henry didn't like to be held by strangers. One of his arms was in a sling. It looked dirty. Stained. He said you knew how to get in touch with him, and he left."

* * *

In her bedroom, Bronwyn stripped in a methodical burlesque, observing her movements in the mirror on her closet door as if she was gathering evidence. Should she place blouse, pants, jacket, and underthings in labeled plastic bags? Her clothes appeared clean, but you could never be certain. If she'd embraced the child, she definitely would have ruined her outfit. She tugged on a sweatshirt and sweatpants. The tub was filling in the bathroom: Lizzie hummed an old song over the gushing water—Beatles or Rolling Stones?

Why hadn't Shawn Anderson just left his message at her office? Why had he invaded the peace of her home? *Special little man*? Bronwyn closed her eyes and shook her head violently, as if she could force an explanation into view. Had he a claim on the child? Did he know of one? *He looks cold*. She remembered that she'd wanted to take Henry's temperature, as if the information might prove something. But what?

"I'm putting him in—hurry up Bronwyn," Lizzie called. Sitting on the edge of her bed, Bronwyn shuddered. She pulled up a sleeve. Goose bumps covered her arm. "Hey—" she heard from the bathroom, "I should call my painting 'Rubber Baby Buggy Bumpers.' You'll see it when you come in. Hurry."

Too late for a thermometer—a bath would affect the child's temperature, wouldn't it? That was the sort of thing mothers knew. Bronwyn slipped her hands underneath her sweatshirt and touched her breasts, but she couldn't feel them. Was it her flesh or her fingers that were numb?

"Bronwyn?" Lizzie must have been on her knees, bent over the tub, the infant naked and slippery in one hand while she scrubbed off the red paint with a washcloth. Rosy swirls must be blooming in the bathwater. Splashes. "We're shampooing now!" Was that a giggle? Had she ever heard her son laugh?

What were little boys made of? A teen whose face you can't remember and her story about a dead soldier?

But Bronwyn had Lizzie. Had it really only been three months? Three months equaled just a single season. But which one? The seasons never seemed to change.

"I don't know you," Bronwyn whispered toward the bathroom.

"What? Do you want to towel him off? This is murder on my back—"

"You're not even my friend," Bronwyn whispered. There was so much more to come—nursery school, grade school, high school, college. Friends. Lovers. Her boy was too small for any of it. Shouldn't he have been bigger by now? Hadn't Shawn Anderson noted that, too? Bronwyn jerked herself upright and pressed her hands against her cheeks. Her mouth opened, but she couldn't speak. Why had it taken her so long to admit the truth: Henry was tiny! He wasn't growing larger, he was shrinking. Now, in the warm bathwater, he'd be melting in Lizzie's hands. And he'd get smaller with every bath—first his little arms would disappear, then his legs—like a frog reverting to a tadpole. He'd soon be a torso with a featureless head—a lozenge— with Lizzie wiping and wiping at him as he shrank away.

"Bronwyn—" Lizzie called, "at least help me get him into his pj's. He can start in bed with you tonight, if you like, for a treat. You can cuddle. I'll take him back when you're done, cause he'll be hungry."

Bronwyn shuddered, but her features relaxed. Her mouth closed. Couldn't she loan the baby to Shawn Anderson? For his commercial or whatever. Life insurance. Wouldn't temporary possession satisfy the man's claim? If she rescued her baby from the tub now before it was too late, before she had nothing left to offer. Certainly arrangements could be made.

"Wait," Bronwyn said. Her tightening chest forced the words from her mouth. "Mommy's coming."

Chapter 20—"a stunning and final girl"

As narrator Buddy Glass spoke, key phrases curled from his mouth in neon blue script and rose with the smoke he puffed from his cigarette. Quotations collected along the top of the stage's backdrop. The words, produced by a technological marvel of stagecraft, hovered straight over Amabel's head; if she broke character and looked up, they'd be unreadable from her angle. This was the last performance of *Dinghy*, the last night Amabel would star as young Boo Boo Tannenbaum, mother of four-year-old Lionel and sister of Buddy. Boo Boo was also sister to five other adult Glasses, who, in one form or another, passed through this adaptation of Salinger's short story.

This was the last night for Amabel, but the first night for Carl, her fiancé, whose presence she felt in the audience. Carl had yet to see *Dinghy*, even though he'd moved to New York to be with Amabel shortly after the show's premiere. The show debuted two months after the death of Carl's little brother Wray, the miracle child he'd parented for over two years.

"*A stunning and final girl,*" Buddy narrated from his pulpit stage-left as the curtain rose on Amabel. She stood motionless in her kitchen, her back to the audience, silhouetted with her hands on her hips in the frosty glow of an open refrigerator. She heard the audience buzz at the trick of Buddy's words sifting into the air with his exhalations, then levitating. Everyone in Salinger stories smoked, and Amabel had smoked for years. She owed her husky voice to the habit. And just that afternoon she'd learned the results of a series of tests she had undergone in secret—not even Carl knew about them. Amabel was dying.

"Now is not the time to quit smoking," her manager told her what seemed like a lifetime ago when she'd lent her voice to M'ling the vivisected dog-man in P. P. Frederico's animated take on *The Island of Doctor Moreau*. At the time, just released from her court-ordered stint in rehab, Amabel had no other job offers. She'd needed her cigarette-ripped voice to yip and growl, and, eventually, howl with blood-curdling urgency. Something in that shredded voice had attracted the attention of *Dinghy*'s director, and eventually led to Amabel's role as Boo Boo. And her Tony nomination.

It had to be the voice, because she didn't look like Salinger's Boo Boo: *"small, almost hipless, style-less, colorless, brittle hair,"* Buddy described, night after night. *"Her joke of a name aside, her general unprettiness aside, she was—in terms of permanently memorable, immoderately perceptive, small-area faces—a stunning and final girl."*

Amabel had read that description in the original story before meeting with the play's director and shook her head with confusion when they met. "Why do you want me? Boo-Boo's twenty-five. I can't play that young anymore. And 'hipless'? 'small-area face'? I may be short, but I'm a curvy girl with a face as broad as the moon."

"What counts is that you're also 'stunning and final,'" the director had said. "Do you think you can stay sober for a long run?"

Acute myelogenous leukemia. Amabel had steeled herself for bad news, but she'd been staggered by the doctor's nakedly pessimistic assessment of her prospects. And the substance of her death sentence now hung over the stage for all to read: *"stunning and final."* Carl, wherever he sat, saw the words. What did they mean to him? What would they mean in a few hours when she'd tell him about her condition?

In a moment the little actor playing Lionel, Boo Boo's little boy, would rush onto the stage. Buddy's narration would cease, and Amabel would unfreeze and pivot from the refrigerator. She would say her lines, and the play would ride along on its own momentum. Performing would keep her safe; it would forbid her peering into the audience for Carl. But by dawn tomorrow, there would be no secrets.

Amabel had thought at first that she was only tired, and who wouldn't have been, after so many shows. The paparazzi had photographed her at her most exhausted, and there had been hints that she'd fallen off the wagon. When the truth came out, she'd expect no apologies. The tabloids had treated Carl cruelly during his own tragedy, then forgotten him. He hadn't actually killed his baby brother— the emergency tracheotomy he'd performed had saved the choking child. The nip of the jugular his skewer took should have been noticed by the real surgeons who treated him at the hospital—but they sealed up the little boy too soon, before the fatal hemorrhaging began.

And here came Lionel on stage, Amabel's pretend child, dashing into the kitchen. This young actor, the latest of the three boys to play the role, was, in fact, a short seven-year-old. Moseying onto the stage behind little Lionel was a silent, translucent hologram of the child's uncle, the suicide Seymour Glass. Seymour would follow the boy until the play's climax, when the hologram would dissolve, signifying Lionel's salvation. What, Amabel wondered during almost every performance, would Salinger have thought of floating neon quotations and a hologram Seymour?

Yes, she was delivering her lines: "Ahoy," she said to Lionel. "Friend. Pirate. Dirty dog. I'm back." Amabel paused while narrator Buddy paraphrased Salinger: *"Boo Boo not only listened to Lionel's voice, she seemed to watch it."* The sentiment had inspired the floating quotations.

"You aren't an admiral," Lionel said. "You're a lady all the time."

"You told me you were all through running away. You promised me." Usually, Amabel ignored the shadow-hologram and focused on Lionel's face while she spoke. But tonight, it was Seymour's ghost she watched. His eyes were dark holes. Had he attached himself to Lionel out of love or hunger?

Carl hadn't needed to explain to Amabel why he'd stayed away from *Dinghy* until this last performance. How could it not be painful for him to see her as the mother of a sensitive little boy? The play parodied the life they'd already begun before Wray's death. But that life had been a sham: she was no mother and Carl wasn't really a father. Little Wray had been cultured in a petri dish and then delivered in a custom's booth on the Mexican border. But Carl's heart had yet to heal. Plans for a wedding, for a family, had been put on hold. For the duration of the play. And now? *Acute myolegenous leukemia.* Beyond tragic: an insult.

Soon the world would know, and why wouldn't she be condemned again for her past? *Slut,* they'd say, *addict*— of course she was diseased. *Unwholesome.* But she'd been sober since the landing of the transcontinental flight on which she'd learned of Wray's death.

Lionel squeaked a few words that didn't sound like his lines, and Amabel—Boo Boo—hesitated. She was watching the ghost's mouth. He was trying to speak to her—to Amabel, not her character Boo Boo—but she didn't understand. Lionel squeaked again, with urgency. But what was ghostly Seymour trying to tell her? *You are the little girl of Svidrigaylov's dream*? Amabel covered her ears with her hands

***

Carl had been approached about hosting a retrospective of his father's films for the Metropolitan Museum of Art. "I told them I needed time to think about it," he'd said to Amabel. "They'll show *Teddy*, of course—the last thing Dad finished. It was my only real acting job, except for the silly French thing. They should get P. P. to do the museum gig. He owes his career to Dad." She and Carl never discussed *Svidrigaylov's Dream*, and Amabel wondered whether Carl was protecting her or the memory of his father. He'd hinted that instead of the retrospective, he might pursue a project that would take him back to the rain forest of South America—where he'd traveled to film a documentary about the Pirahan indigenous people a few years before they met. Where he'd had a native lover—a woman with an unpronounceable name. "Who have *you* loved?" Amabel had asked their first night together, her own notorious sexual history suddenly feeling like a burden. Carl had tried to reproduce his Pirahan lover's name, but they'd wept with laughter at his gurgles and spits. "I sound like you, M'ling," he sighed.

"You must have called her something, Amabel insisted, wiping her eyes.

"*Click*," Carl said. "I called her *Click*."

"'*Clit*'?" Amabel had teased.

"Yes," Carl answered, mis-hearing. "I'm sure she doesn't think of me," he said. "The Pirahans live only in the present. When somebody or something's out of sight, they don't exist anymore."

Carl had started in show business as a Salinger character, and Amabel would end as one. They were fairytale orphans, wandering through a midnight forest with clasped hands. Her parents had melted away in Palm Springs, one right after the other. Carl's mother had died after sticking little Wray in a surrogate's womb, her last-chance egg fertilized with the defrosted sperm of a drowned ex-husband: Raymond Walchuk, father of both Carl and a temporary little boy he could never have anticipated. Raymond Walchuk, who had trailed Amabel all her life like the hologram of Seymour Glass. *"You're thinking fucky-fucky,"* he'd directed.

* * *

The theatre was silent. What had Seymour's apparition been trying to tell her? That Raymond Walchuk's blood was infectious? It poisoned those it pulsed through and everyone they touched. Was Seymour trying to tell her that the Pirahans were wrong— the fact that someone is out of sight doesn't mean he's gone.

224

Amabel felt something stir deep in her throat—a growl—the voice of M'ling, Moreau's dog-man. The world was full of nothing but sad creatures hacked apart and sewn back together in the name of art or science. Amabel searched Seymour's empty eye sockets, then looked again at his moving lips—praying or cursing. She sensed the audience behind her, as solid as a wall of ice. If she turned, she knew she'd see Carl's figure embedded within it. Did he want to return to the rainforest so he could forget little Wray? To try for a child of his own with his Pirahan lover? Amabel hadn't been invited to the rain forest. Carl hadn't said "Come with me." Would he and his *Click* mock Amabel's name? Maybe he'd call her Boo Boo. Maybe they'd never mention her. She would be something that didn't exist—had never existed. Tears blurred Amabel's vision. It was all her fault—how could Carl not resent her for resurrecting a false child over and over, every night for the run of the play?

Lionel tugged at Amabel's sleeve. New blocking? The child's blue eyes were rounded with distress—how excellent an actor he was— yes, they'd saved the best Lionel for last. Deep in the wings, invisible to the audience but not Amabel, waited the other Glass siblings— Franny and Zooey, Walker and Walter. They edged forward, just out of view, anticipating their entrances though they weren't due on stage until the second act, near the play's end, when everything material on the set dissolved and the actors stood before a sparkling crystal lake— an effect so breathtaking that Amabel often heard sobs from the audience.

Buddy's voice—Amabel twitched a glance toward his pulpit. *"The better to look at him,"* he said, *"Boo Boo pushed her son slowly away from her."* But Buddy's emphasis was strange, he spoke too loud. It sounded like code. His words rose in blue cursive wisps, and she followed their ascent. She spun slowly, opening her arms. Buddy's last sentence joined the thin blue cloud that had floated there since the play's beginning—the cloud that had begun with the announcement of her stunning finality. And then, from the cloud, blue snow fell, just a few flakes at first. Then more and more, cascading, swirling, glittering. She opened her mouth and stuck out her tongue, but the flakes didn't reach it. Why not? This snow was new—maybe something special created for the show's final performance. Or was something broken? Amabel held out her arms and spun. When the light failed, she lost her balance, and as she dropped she wondered whose face would greet her if she woke.

Chapter 21—Tornado Baby

"Really," Patricia Johnson, the baby's mother, said, "her grandfather, my dad, should have brought her here. He takes care of Sophette during the week. When Pops is around, she's full of giggles."

"Um-hmm," Bronwyn said, half-listening. The casting agent rocked the plump toddler, holding her tight to her chest.

"So she might not be so shy if Pops was here," Ms. Johnson said, a hint of Jamaican in her accent.

Bronwyn gazed at the reflection of herself and the auditioning baby in the hotel suite mirror. Did all stage mothers suffer from terminal anxiety, she wondered. "A little shy is good," she offered. "Hyperactive toddlers don't perform well." She glanced from the reflection to the flesh and blood baby in her arms and suppressed a shiver—electric blue eyes, golden curls, skin the color of lightly creamed coffee—Bronwyn concluded that little Sophette's father was white. Sophette Johnson was without a doubt the most beautiful potential "special" for her agency that Bronwyn had ever auditioned. Not even her own son fit as comfortably in her arms. Bronwyn's Henry certainly had no future in front of a camera.

The baby cooed, and Ms. Johnson reached for her daughter. Bronwyn swayed like a bullfighter to avoid her.

"She's probably hungry," Ms. Johnson said, clasping her hands under her chin.

"Then it's a plus that she's not fussing." Bronwyn heard the excited edge to her own voice—P. P. Frederico and the team behind *Tornado Baby* would die for this child. "Is she nursing?"

"I had to stop at six months when I went back to work. There's formula in her diaper bag."

"Weaned. That's good. Nursing babies can be too demanding. My Henry is Sophette's age, and he doesn't give his wet nurse a second's rest." In the mirror, Bronwyn caught Ms. Johnson's eyebrows rise at the mention of "wet nurse." "My Henry is adopted," Bronwyn explained breezily. "Anatomical complications prevented me from carrying my own child." She didn't add that she hadn't taken a day off from work since her child had been surrendered to her care. Ms. Johnson was silent, probably uncertain whether to offer sympathy or congratulations. Bronwyn rocked Sophette vigorously, keeping the child's mother at bay. "Can I feed her?"

It's a question Bronwyn had never asked before about a baby—wet nurse Lizzie took care of Henry's nourishment, even now that he'd added solids. Sophette smiled at Bronwyn, and the casting agent drew a breath that tickled her lungs. She didn't want to give up the child, but Ms. Johnson loomed like a sudden shadow, except her lips were too red and her teeth too white. She plucked her baby away, and Bronwyn's arms felt stiff as empty plaster casts.

"Maybe this audition isn't such a good idea," Ms. Johnson said. Her baby coughed prettily and, curls gleaming, plunged her face into her mother's sweater.

"Don't be silly. After I fly all the way up to Springfield, then drive here to Chicopee just to test her? You wouldn't have sent her picture to us if you didn't think she'd be perfect for *Tornado Baby*." Bronwyn folded her arms over her flat chest. "I saw a hundred babies in New York yesterday, and not one of them had her appeal." Bronwyn pointed to the bed behind her. "All I need to do is take these shots and forward them to the studio. To P. P. Frederico himself. He'll see what I see in a second. In fact, I'll probably get the go-ahead to cancel the Boston auditions. Then you and I will hash out some figures."

"Figures?" Ms. Johnson asked, her eyes narrowing.

"For negotiatiating a contract. Money. Your little Sophette is going to be a wealthy young lady."

"This was her father's idea," Bronwyn heard as she turned to the queen-sized bed, ripped back the quilt, mussed the sheets, and pounded the pillows into a nest, which she patted before facing mother and child.

"We'll imagine this is the wheat field where they find the Tornado Baby. Can you believe this really happened? A tornado destroys half a town, snatches a baby out of her mother's arms—sucks her right out the window, for God's sake—and half a day later they find the kid unharmed in a wheat field a mile away— miracle! People love miracles. Major studios love miracles." Bronwyn patted the pillows again. "Put Sophette here. If she crawls around, that's okay. We'll get pictures and a short video—my phone has extremely high resolution—and I'll forward them to P. P. and all the principals. They'll create mock-ups of her surrounded by wheat, smudged with dirt, twigs and leaves in her curls, debris all around. Maybe just a tiny bruise on her cheek, a spot of blood. Whatever their vision calls for. I just cast, I don't tell stories. But I promise you Sophette will bowl them over—she's the perfect baby for a disaster."

* * *

Fifteen minutes later, Bronwyn huddled in her rented car in the parking lot of the Chicopee Holiday Inn. Forgetting that across the country in California the sun was just rising, she shouted into her phone at her son's wet nurse.

"She got cold feet. She said to forget the whole thing, grabbed her kid, and ran out. By the time I got to the parking lot, they were driving off in their SUV." Bronwyn's hand and voice shook. "I changed my whole schedule just to accommodate her. I'm supposed to be in Boston this afternoon." She pulled the phone away from her ear while Lizzie spoke; and gazed at the parking lot's exit, hoping to see a gray SUV re-enter. She took a cleansing breath. "What? The parents sent their baby's pictures to the office and Bridgette forwarded them to me last night in New York. They couldn't get the kid to New York or Boston, so here I am in Chicopee, Massachusetts. But you've got to see this child—she's perfect. She's the Tornado Baby. And I let her get away. She and the mom are on their way to vacation in Cape Cod where the dad is waiting. I guess off-season rates are cheaper. Doesn't she know how much the kid is worth?" Bronwyn squinted. Her eyes had been bothering her, and the East Coast sun carved the world—buildings, cars, traffic lights— into images so sharp they hurt to look. "Listen: I'm going to try to chase Ms. Johnson down. On the road. I'm sure I can talk some sense into her."

* * *

Bronwyn's GPS directed her east—five miles until she hit the Mass Pike, from which a spur would eventually branch off and take her south to Cape Cod. She estimated that she was twenty minutes behind Sophette and her mother. Eleven of those minutes she'd spent rushing in and out of a Walmart where she bought the toddler carseat she belted insecurely into the back of her rental car. And, at the last second, looking for something plush for the baby, she'd grabbed a Kika ape doll from a bin of stuffed animals. She hadn't seen one in years— were there even Walmarts back when those dolls had been marketed with the release of *Kong's Daughter*? There must have been. But didn't they keep better track of their inventory?

228

Along the business route leading to the Mass Pike, Chicopee's business district gave way quickly to pastureland and wooded hills. Bronwyn passed cows and trailer homes with TV radar dishes on their roofs. The new toddler seat wobbled behind her, jostling grinning Kika. Why had she wasted time stopping for the seat? What had she had in mind? She saw the Pilgrim hat sign, marking the junction with the Mass Pike, and stomped on the gas pedal.

But suddenly it seemed like an avalanche of white boulders was bounding across the road. One struck her right front bumper—a surprisingly soft concussion— and Bronwyn skidded to a stop. In the field to her left a dozen or so fat white geese flapped to clumsy landings. She winced into her rearview mirror—feathers drifted through the air like snowflakes. There was a single goose collapsed on the road behind her—obviously the thing her car had hit. But the goose stretched its long neck, lifted and resettled its wings, and struggled to its feet. For a second it stood still. It wove its head and neck in the air like a charmed cobra, then limped after its companions, across the road and into the field where the flock was rooting for something in the soil. Another car pulled up behind her, and, after a few seconds, the driver beeped his horn. Bronwyn eased off the brake and continued on toward the turnpike.

Bronwyn passed through the toll entrance and merged onto the highway, wondering why the geese had chosen her car to assault. Or had she simply been invisible to them—nonexistent, except for the one she happened to share time and space with for an unfortunate instant. Tractor-trailers clogged the turnpike, and Bronwyn waited impatiently to slide into the fast lane. A sudden movement startled her—more geese? No—the problem was with her eyes—the "floaters" that had crept into her vision. Her ophthalmologist told her not to worry about them unless she also saw bright flashes. "If you do see flashes," he said, "contact us immediately." That might mean a torn retina. "You'd see bursts of light, then it might look like a dark screen is lowering. But the floaters you see now are just thickened vitriolic fluid. Most of the time, you don't even notice them, right? Eventually, they'll dissipate."

Bronwyn peered through the floaters, set her sights on a distant bus, and accelerated. She thought of dark screens, of falling theatre curtains, and regrouped: she was chasing Sophette Johnson, the perfect baby. She checked her phone and found Ms. Johnson's contact number. *"Behind you on the Pike,"* she texted while steering with her wrists. *"Let's talk more. About $."*

The floaters were back—like a shifting cloud of blackbirds between her and the road. A childhood trauma: once, driving in the family station wagon with her mother, there'd been a thud on the windshield. The car had veered and slowed. A little brown sparrow had flown into them, and its smashed body caught under the wiper blade. One of its wings fluttered. "Don't look," her mother warned, and Bronwyn covered her face. But then she heard the squeal of the windshield wipers on dry glass—her mother had turned them on in hopes of dislodging the bird, but it hadn't worked, and when Bronwyn peered between her fingers, she screamed. And so did her mother, who pulled over to the side of the road. Both of them jumped out of the car, mortified. The wipers ticked on like a metronome, dragging the sparrow's body back and forth in a semicircle. How the episode ended, Bronwyn couldn't remember

***

Bronwyn sped east along the Mass Pike at eighty-five, passing cars, trucks and buses as she sent texts and made calls. Sophette Johnson's face now glowed on her phone screen, replacing her son's photo. She hummed to herself, thinking of Shawn Anderson and her baseless fears about the man's interest in Henry. Hadn't he eventually relented and hired the older deaf girl for his life insurance commercial? Subsequently, he'd become a regular client, hiring more of Bronwyn's "specials" for other commercials, and never again did he mention her son. His fervor had come and gone—maybe he'd been buzzing on something he'd taken to relieve the pain in his injured shoulder when he'd become obsessed with Henry's photo. But why wouldn't Ms. Johnson respond to Bronwyn's contact attempts?

"She's got a face you fall into, doesn't she?" she told the assistant of P. P. Frederico she'd sent the girl's picture to. "It's a face meant for movies. And she's biracial. Gorgeous skin. I know it sounds silly, but, even now, when she's not even here, I feel like she's looking at me. Like I'm touching her and she's touching me. Tornado Baby dolls will be the hottest thing. Everyone will feel an urge to take her in their arms. Who wouldn't want to hold a miracle baby?"

Bronwyn's head was on a swivel—she scanned in front and behind her for troopers as she sped up, ignoring the floaters that impeded her vision like black snow. But no flashes, no lowering curtains. In her mirror she caught another glimpse of grinning Kika and thought the doll might have winked at her. Again and again her

230

attention returned to her phone and the photo of Sophette. The Tornado Baby's blue eyes stood out like twin pools reflecting heaven. Bronwyn imagined the child in the middle of the field she'd been carried into by the storm. Surrounding her was the flock of geese. With a single call Bronwyn had canceled the Boston auditions—that meant at least a hundred mothers were now headed home with dashed hopes. But when the movie was released in a year or so, each would measure her child against Sophette Johnson and would understand.

Lizzie's ringtone—a double blast on a Viking horn— sounded just as Bronwyn swerved around a truck that was slowing down because the highway grade had gotten steeper. Lizzie's name on the phone screen marred Sophette's beautiful face, and Bronwyn scowled, wishing the call had been from the child's mother. The Viking horn ringtone blared again, but Bronwyn ignored it. Lizzie didn't expect Bronwyn to pick her up when she was working. Bronwyn knew people wondered about her relationship with Lizzie. Some thought they were lovers, but the truth was, Bronwyn didn't think they were particularly close. Circumstances had led to co-dependence—Bronwyn, her own body unfit for mothering, was lucky to have found the lactating, childless artist. But though the three might resemble a family when they gathered on the sofa for late night television, it was the nipple of an employee Bronwyn watched her son suckle as he drifted off to sleep. Soon he'd be weaned, and what that would mean for the relationship between the two adults in his life had yet to be broached.

Propping her phone on the steering wheel, Bronwyn set her jaw and finger-swept Sophette's photo from the display screen. Up popped Henry again—her boy, she admitted, was not cute. His nearly bald head was triangular, like a YIELD sign—his forehead too broad, his tiny chin too pointy. His lash-less eyes squinted like a pig's. She flicked her son off the phone and restored the image of baby Sophette, and at the sight of her Tornado Baby, a blush surged up from her chest and warmed her face. She examined her mottled complexion in the rearview. She saw Kika, and thought of the goose she'd hit—had it suffered internal injuries? Would it die there in the field, surrounded by its feeding companions as if it was no more than a lump of dirty snow? Did geese mourn their dead? If they didn't, who would? Geese weren't pets, like cats or dogs. Geese only mattered when they were sucked into jet engines and caused crashes that killed hundreds. Bronwyn pictured a field not with geese or a beautiful baby, but with the burning hulk of an airliner. If that goose had damaged her rental car, she would have had to call the police and fill out an accident report, and she'd have lost all hope of catching Sophette and her mother.

Viking horn ringtone again. Startled by flashing lights, worried she'd been caught speeding, Bronwyn fumbled her phone and dropped it between her feet. A police cruiser zipped by and shifted to the shoulder to pass the traffic ahead of her—which was slowing to a stop. The brake lights winked. Bronwyn ducked down, holding her breath as if she'd plunged into deep water, and pawed around her feet for her phone, which she found under the gas pedal. Rising with it, she stomped on her brake to avoid the car stopped dead in front of her. The only movement ahead was the crawl of the flashing cruiser and the hypnotic circling of her floaters. The trooper was well up the turnpike now, about to disappear around a curve. Bronwyn groaned—the Johnsons, probably well ahead of this tie-up, were escaping.

***

Bronwyn studied a map of Cape Cod on her phone. Traffic hadn't budged for half an hour, and though she and everyone around her had shut off their engines, the odor of burnt rubber and exhaust lingered. She took deep, nasal breaths to stay calm as she formulated a new plan. The constant Viking horn ringtones make concentration difficult, but Bronwyn wouldn't respond to Lizzie until she heard from the Tornado Baby's mother. Business first. Was it possible Ms. Johnson's phone was broken?

Bronwyn studied the Cape—its shape reminded her of the upturned claw of a dead bird. Getting her bearings was difficult—everything on the East Coast seemed upside down and backwards. When traffic finally started to move again, Bronwyn would hurry to the nearest rest area and conduct a full web search. She would call every hotel, motel, and bungalow colony on the Cape, beginning with the towns closest to the mainland, and, if need be, make her way, locale by locale, all the way to Provincetown on the tip. "Are the Johnsons staying with you," she'd ask, "an interracial couple with the most beautiful baby you've ever seen?" Who could fail to notice such a remarkable family? And if Bronwyn couldn't find the Johnson's lodging, she would call restaurants. If she had to, she would scour every beach and sift through every town, investigating souvenir shops, ice cream parlors, and miniature golf courses.

***

232

Lizzie's ringtone was relentless. The nursemaid's name rose over the Cape Cod map, and Bronwyn closed her hand around her phone and held it away as if it emitted an intolerable odor. She sighed, rolled her shoulders, and reclined against the seat and headrest. What if she were to walk into a Cape Cod surf-and-turf restaurant and find the Johnsons there: mother and father facing one another over opposite ends of a checked tablecloth, their Tornado Baby in a highchair displayed between them like a trophy? Blond-haired Mr. Johnson—the man with the idea for Sophette's audition—would smile and stand and welcome her with eyes as bright as his daughter's. Ms. Johnson would smile, too—husband and wife would have discussed their daughter's opportunity and would be prepared to welcome Bronwyn wholeheartedly. Sophette beamed, and Bronwyn melted. Ms. Johnson rose and motioned for the casting agent to take her vacated seat, and Bronwyn couldn't refuse. Curiously, in Bronwyn's mind's eye, Ms. Johnson wore a waitress's outfit; she pulled a pad from the apron over her short skirt and bent forward as if to take Bronwyn's order. The mom had long, dark legs, lovely and smooth. Baby Sophette chortled, and Mr. Johnson murmured something to Bronwyn across the table, and she focused on his spectacular mouth, until a sudden swarm of flies obscured her vision—her floaters! And then Bronwyn was back in her car, staring at her phone, from which a harsh sound screeched—an industrial grinding like twisting metal or a braking train.

"TRAFFIC ALERT," flashed across the screen, and a highway map appeared. *"Mass Pike accident,"* scrolled across the display screen. *"Multiple fatalities in eastbound lanes. Traffic snarled both directions—hours to clear."*

Bronwyn's fingers fumbled over the keys on her phone, which defaulted to "Messages" and the string of contacts from Lizzie popped up. She saw her son's name in almost every entry: *Henry, Henry, Henry*—she's never seen it printed so many times. But among these was another message: "P. P. Frederico. Re: Tornado Baby Project." With a thundering heart, she punched at the keypad for the text: *"Tornado Baby project off—sorry. Insurmountable production issues. Possible new reality TV show in the works—involves the late Amabel Hadley and Carl Walchuk. Could require lots of children. Interested?"*

Bronwyn had never been deep sea fishing, but she felt the sudden and immense emptiness of a snapped line—it was if she was falling backward through her seat. She shuddered. *Tornado Baby project off?* And a show about Amabel Hadley? The late Amabel

Hadley? Bronwyn remembered shaking Amabel's hand at the door of the star's dressing room the night she'd seen *Dinghy*. Just skin and bones. She was dead half a year later. Was P. P. thinking of some kind of documentary involving Carl Walchuk? But why might there be the need for children, Bronwyn's specials?

The floaters swirled around her like stars around the head of a KO'd cartoon villain. Everything else was still, cars and trucks frozen to the road as if the world was encased in glass. It almost felt like a miracle could be happening. Is that what tragedy was—you get to the wheat field, far from the home the tornado destroyed, and you find maybe your front door, maybe a broken kitchen chair—but no trace of your baby? It was absurd that you'd even allowed yourself to hope. What did it matter on which side of the accident the Johnsons were on? What did it matter if they were among the fatalities?

In front of Bronwyn, taillights blinked to life— the flashes of red joined her floaters in a spinning galaxy. She remembered a table covered with flower blossoms: it was the last day of kindergarten. Her teacher, who was retiring, gave each child a small potted geranium to take home. A symbol, the teacher said. Bronwyn brought her flower home, left it on her dresser, and forgot about it. After a week, the stems of the plant turned brown and the leaves fell off. The dried blossom was still bright red when Bronwyn finally remembered it, but after four cups of water, its soggy petals lost their color and dissolved into the cup of black mud.

The driver behind Bronwyn hit his horn, once, twice, but she wasn't prepared to move. She was thinking about how much she still resented the old teacher who burdened her with feelings she never asked for. Her phone was still in her hand. Why, she wondered suddenly, had there been so many messages about Henry?

Chapter 22—Monkey Meat

The "Buy Now" price Carl set for a genuine vintage "Kika the Ape" doll on Ebay was seventy-five dollars, and, over the last three months, he'd sold nearly two hundred. Now he was packing the last of the grinning, golden, plastic-wrapped gorillas that for twenty-five years had haunted every corner, closet, and surface of the small Studio City bungalow that had been his father's and now belonged to him. The cold, hard fact was that he needed the cash: marrying Amabel just days after she'd revealed her diagnosis of terminal cancer was a noble gesture but had meant incurring the medical expenses inadequate insurance hadn't covered. The money his mother Christine had left in trust for his little brother Wray disappeared the moment the child passed away—redirected to a number of different organizations that funded scientific research, as was the case with the rest of his mother's estate. His recent losses had left Carl in a funk, and he had little interest or motivation in creative projects that might net him an income. In fact, what offers of support did he have? Although he wasn't quite the pariah his father had been, hadn't he come close? Guilty of fratricide, wasn't he? How could he be regarded as anything but poison, a friendless charity case, someone whose cumulative failures, losses, and disappointments were only mildly interesting because of their uniqueness.

His phone sounded the insultingly jaunty ringtone he hadn't the energy to change—another call from P. P. Frederico, which Carl let go to voice mail, though he knew there was no room for any more messages. He made a promise to himself he knew he wouldn't keep to listen to them later this evening—right after he took care of that larger unkept promise he'd been deferring, which was to plan some kind of sustainable future.

He looked down at the Kika he'd stuffed into the mailing carton. The last Kika. Cleansing their house of them had seemed like a purging at first, and for a while he understood the satisfaction exterminators must feel upon ridding a home of the very last vermin. But as the supply of ape dolls dwindled, as closets and counters and corners emptied, Carl had been gradually absorbed by a seeping, debilitating nostalgia. *I should stop*, he told himself, when there were thirty, twenty, ten, a handful of little apes left. *I should save a few—just a couple—for myself.* But the orders kept coming, and, until he'd found himself with just this one last Kika, he'd allowed processing and packaging to give his life the only order he'd known since Amabel's death. Because as he ticked off the final ape dolls, one by one, Carl dwelled on the absences he endured: his father, his mother, his little brother, his wife; even one of P. P. Frederico's twin daughters had passed, an HIV victim after an outbreak of AIDs had swept Kiriwina, the "Island of Love." He had an ominous feeling that P. P. had been calling with some bad news about the other twin, who'd gone back to the island with her sister after graduating Stanford "to do what she could" about "preserving culture" and "fighting social and economic inequities." Carl wondered if "preserving culture" had anything to do with the sex games of children or convincing the elders to surrender their "magic." Was Grandpa, the half-man, Carl's rescuer, still alive? He'd be impossibly old. Carl wouldn't inquire—the list of his dead was too long already. If he asked and found out Grandpa had passed, wouldn't he be responsible for making his death a fact?

But not all of Carl's losses were deaths. There was *Click*, the lover with the unpronounceable name he'd left deep in the Amazon rainforest. To *Click*'s way of thinking, Carl had ceased to exist the moment he'd disappeared around the bend in the river that had taken him back to civilization. It wouldn't even occur to her to have a list of losses. At his worst moments, Carl could *feel* himself "not existing."

He stared down at the grinning ape doll, nestled among Styrofoam peanuts in the mailing carton. Like she was in a little coffin. Little Wray would have been buried in something not much bigger than this if he hadn't been cremated. Each time Carl packed up a doll and shipped it off, it was if he was trying to escape his guilt over his brother's death. But when the last ape was gone, there'd be no more pretense. All that would remain was guilt. There was no Walchuk family cemetery plot, nowhere to gather the bodies, which had been surrendered to flames, to science, and to the sea. Carl picked up the mailing tape dispenser to seal down the box's flaps, but hesitated, remembering a story he'd read years ago, maybe in high school, maybe college. In the story, a pair of Civil War soldiers had been ordered to bury a fallen comrade. They'd dug the grave and lowered the body into it, without coffin or shroud. Then they hesitated—neither was able to dump the first shovelful of dirt on the soldier's face. How the story ended, Carl couldn't recall, but somehow the dead soldier must have gotten buried. He thought of Amabel's final moments— she'd lain unconscious in her hospital bed, sunk amid coils of tubes running fluids into and out of her skeletal body. A blue cap covered her bald head, and a ventilator mask hid her face. He caught the glint of the new wedding band on her chalk white finger and had laid his own hand with the matching ring beside hers. He reminded himself, on advice from hospital staff, that when Amabel breathed her last he mustn't fail to remove the ring and take it home with him.

They'd been married in her private room in the IC unit. At the brief ceremony, P. P. Frederico had bent over Amabel.

"An animated sequel to *Kong's Daughter* is in the works, maybe two years down the road," he whispered. "Kika will speak. Her voice is yours, if you want it."

Carl couldn't bring himself to watch Amabel's response, but he wondered now if she'd smiled around the tubes down her throat that made speech impossible. Or had she taken the offer as a final insult from the Walchuk family tragedy she'd been trapped in since *Svidrigaylov's Dream*?

The golden ape in the carton grinned joylessly. Its black button eyes offered nothing. Carl struggled to keep submerged the image of his wife that rose before his inner eye: of the child, made up like a prostitute, leering from the bed of a perverted Russian aristocrat. His father had taken him to the set. He'd listened to him tell the little girl to "think fucky-fucky." And Carl had snapped her picture with the old Polaroid he'd brought with him.

That this image lived inside him was a secret he'd kept from Amabel. At various times he'd blamed his father for its existence, then Dostoevsky's character, then the author himself, then the whole host of Dead White Male writers and artists who shaped the way men thought, not just about women, but about everything.

If imagination's mold is configured in a certain way, what else can it see? Even the supposedly objective anthropologist Frederico used his Kiriwina research to describe and define the "sex games of children." Couldn't there have been another way to understand those rituals that wouldn't have left Carl squirming with guilt and confusion? Why had the innocently amorous advances of children driven him so far out to sea that he'd nearly drowned? And why, whenever he thought of P. P.'s twins, did images of those nasty French "Dry Boys" arise? Thing One and Thing Two. What, after all, was the natural order of things: cartoon vivisections? ravaged naked mice? baby brothers launched in test tubes and borne by thieves? Svidrigaylov's dream?

What had his father once said about God's creation of the platypus? That it was an example of "clumsy editing"?

But there she'd posed lasciviously, the child Amabel, on Svidrigaylov's sheets. The Polaroid photograph was in black and white, but if it pulsed with color in Carl's memory, with what ravaging energy must it have spun within Amabel's, always and forever, up to the very end. Dead White Males had conceived of and applied the paint that had stolen her innocence. The imaginations of Dead White Males framed the mirror in which she saw herself—in which everyone saw each other.

"Did you meet Amabel Hadley?" he'd been asked in middle school, over and over, even by his *Alice in Shizzel-land* co-star, Andrea Convenience. (And if her father had truly been the Convenience that Raymond Walchuk had offended, if King Minus had successfully murdered the elder Walchuk, there might not have been either Carl or Wray, but Svidrigaylov would have gone on dreaming his dream.)

"Of course I met Amabel," Carl had insisted, always with the Polaroid image in front of his mind's eye. In later years, in college, he'd gone so far as to suggest that he might have stolen an on-set kiss. No one he told did the math, no one calculated that he and Amabel would have been just children. All they knew was the celebrity's reputation, which had long been branded by "fucky-fucky."

Carl placed the packing tape back on the kitchen table and took a seat. He looked around the house, first his father's, now his, and was once again struck by its emptiness. Clean of ape dolls. What had become of that Polaroid of young Amabel? It had sprung up on the internet intermittently over the years, but the route it had taken to get there was a mystery to Carl. It would have to have been stolen from him and posted by someone he knew, but he couldn't guess who that might have been.

The doorbell rang, followed by insistent knocking. Carl stood so abruptly from the table that he banged his thighs on its underside. A face peered through the door's small window: P. P. Frederico. Too late to duck into a corner—the director saw him and gave a wave and a nod. Carl, his heart fluttering as if he'd just been caught red-handed at who knows what, limped to the door, ransacking his mind for excuses against indefinite but inescapable accusations.

***

"You haven't been picking up," P. P. said matter-of-factly, "and I was in the neighborhood, so I thought I'd check in to see how you're doing."

"Been having trouble setting my ringtone," Carl lied. He'd walked the director back into the kitchen, where they stood awkwardly next to the table where Carl had been packing the Kika doll. "Can I get you something? A glass of water?"

"Not a thing." P. P. had been grinning since his entry. He didn't remove his sunglasses, but he turned his head like a spotlight, taking in the room. He'd lost most of his hair, but the fringe and comb-over strands that were left were jet black, probably dyed. His gaze dropped to the Kika doll. "Still with these," he said. "Antiques." He plucked the doll from the box, and a few packing peanuts spilled out onto the table and floor. "Oops—" he smirked, "sorry. These were my idea, you know. Quarter of a century ago. What are you getting for them?"

Carl waved off the apology. "Seventy-five," he said, trying a chuckle that didn't quite catch. "This is the last one. End of an era."

P. P. perched the doll on his forearm as if it were a ventriloquist's dummy. The plastic wrap crackled like the unwrapping of a candy bar in a theatre. "I wonder if their value will increase or decrease when the second generation comes out. Looks like the sequel will be released Christmas after next. The new Kikas are going to look different--more like the animation—bigger eyes and wider smile. More pliant arms." P. P. finger-flicked the button eye of the doll through the plastic wrap. "*Ouch!*" he said for the little ape. He resettled his dark glasses as he turned toward Carl. The light over the kitchen table made little suns in their lenses. "Nowadays these button eyes are considered 'choking hazards.' The new ones won't have that problem." P. P.'s smile flattened into a horizontal—was he recalling the cause of little Wray's death? "Remember I offered Amabel the voice for the sequel?" he murmured. He placed the Kika doll back in the carton. "That was the day she died, wasn't it?"

"A few days before. The day we were married. I know she appreciated it."

"Yes, well—" P. P. hesitated. Was he congratulating himself, Carl wondered, or about to ask for a favor? The director bent back down to the doll, paused, then snatched it up. "You're selling it like this? With a rip in it?" He pushed the Kika toward Carl. "The stuffing's coming out of her. You better sew her back up."

Carl took the doll. Sure enough, a seam in the doll's chest had split, and it was leaking red stuffing. "Shit," Carl muttered. He stared at the tear to keep himself from looking at Frederico. "I can't send it out like this."

"You can just stitch it back up, can't you?"

Carl shook his head. "Once it's out of the plastic it loses its value to collectors." He poked through the plastic over the rip, which opened wider, exposing more stuffing. "I'll have to contact the purchaser and see what he wants to do. I'll probably have to give him a discount."

"Complicated." P. P. shook his head, waited a few seconds, clearly getting ready for the conversation he'd intended since his arrival.

Carl couldn't pull his attention from the red stuffing. *Monkey meat*, he thought. His legs felt suddenly lighter, as if a burden had been lifted. But it had been so long since he'd felt good about anything, physically or otherwise, that he mistrusted the feeling. Maybe his thighs were only now reacting to the whack he'd given them on the table.

"Listen," P. P. began, tilting his head back slightly. The suns in his lenses disappeared. "I'm putting together a new project. Something completely different. Something we've never done. You don't have anything else lined up right now, do you?"

Why was Carl obsessing over the stuffing? He forced himself to pay attention to P. P. What did the filmmaker mean by "we"? Was he going to offer something to Carl by way of charity? Of course P. P. knew that he'd nothing "lined up." Carl hunched a shoulder. "I don't know. I've been thinking maybe I'll try a documentary. Maybe head back to the Amazon. I never really finished the one about the Pirahans—my mother got sick, and then there was Wray—"

Monkey meat! The Pirahans didn't have color names. If they wanted to convey the idea of red, they'd compare it to something of the same color. If they needed to point out that a certain flower was red in color, they might say, "That flower is the color of monkey meat."

P. P. shook his head. "You've survived some difficult times. But, well—there's an opportunity that we can make something special out of your troubles."

"Something special?" Carl was only half listening. He was picturing a journey down the Maici River, clambering onto a muddy shore in the rainforest after, what, five years? He'd ceased to exist to *Click*, but could he be reborn? Would he be resurrected the second she laid her eyes on him? How did memory work when something has disappeared from your reality?

"Carl, you froze Amabel's eggs, didn't you?"

"Eggs?" Carl was confused. He pictured *Click*, her eyes lighting up with an excitement which was more like the thrill of a fresh discovery than remembered happiness. *New* for her, *renewal* for him. But "frozen egg"? A different memory—something ancient—a ball of ice, compacted bodies of naked mice, their hacked limbs defrosting in cups of warm water. Dismemberments gleaming at their ends—*monkey meat*—red. And then, of course, there was little Wray, his own flesh and blood, who'd been conceived in a cup himself.

"Didn't you—or somebody—say that Amabel froze her eggs when she got sick—in case the chemo and radiation destroyed her uterus—"

Monkey meat. Carl was seeing red. "We froze zygotes," he said flatly. "Her eggs were fertilized *in vitro* with my sperm. Around a dozen." Wasn't this procedure a family legacy?

"Yes." P. P. nodded enthusiastically. "And they still exist—and they belong to you, right?"

Ownership? Carl hadn't thought of those eggs since well before his wife's death. Both he and Amabel had known the false hope they'd represented. "I guess they do," he said. "I guess that all I own is the last of these ape dolls and a handful of zygotes."

"So—" P. P. hesitated. "So there's an idea out there. A pretty big one. It's about what we can do with those eggs. About creating a legacy. Something historic. Something to be proud of."

Carl wasn't following. His eyes were on the red stuffing spilling from the Kika doll. *Monkey meat*. A delicacy among the Pirahans. He blinked at a vision—*Click* standing naked beside an equally naked child, big-eyed, paler than his mother, dark-haired, looking like Carl's old Teddy poster. Wasn't it possible—hadn't he always wondered if *Click* might have been pregnant when he left her, that he'd been a father for years without knowing it? He lowered himself slowly into his seat, his inner gaze riveted to the future.

P. P. pulled out the chair on his side of the kitchen table and sat down. "I've started preliminary discussions," he said. "We've already got a working title: 'Amabel's Children.' Let me explain what we've got in mind."

Chapter 23—Amabel's Children

From up here on the ceiling, I see three scalps and one full head of hair beneath me. The fluorescent lights illuminate a shaved and gleaming head. It has an indentation in the center that looks like a sunken grave. One of the scalps has a hairline that recedes into dark curls, and the third has a black fringe and a comb-over that fails to cover skin the color and texture of butterscotch pudding. This head and the head with curls belong to men I knew when I was alive. The full head of blond hair belongs to a woman I also knew.

I've been dead for days and days, and this is the first time I've recognized anyone. I don't know if my presence in this room is by coincidence or design. Being dead has been a completely passive experience. Every morning I wake up attached to something that's living, something different each day, no repeats, at least not so far. Yesterday I was with a Goldendoodle, the day before a Starbucks barista. Today, it's this spider on the ceiling of this office. I've got no will of my own, no physical essence. Where my host goes, I go. And though I share my partner's space, I'm neither seen nor felt. So far I've had no appetites at all. I recognize emotions, but I don't seem to feel them. Like when you fall out of love. I have fallen out of love with everyone. I have fallen out of fear of anyone. And out of hate. I have extraordinary and immeasurable patience. Have you ever spent a day connected to a clam?

This morning the men and the woman down at the conference table are talking about me and the eggs harvested from my ovaries before I lost my battle with acute myelogenous leukemia. Carl, the one with the curls, was my husband, if only for a short while. The comb-over guy is P. P. Frederico, the filmmaker who gave me my big break after my last stint in rehab, years before my death. The shaved scalp belongs to a stranger. The blond-haired woman, Bronwyn O'Savage, is, or at least was once, a casting agent. I can see dark roots along her center part. The four are discussing an idea for a reality TV show—*Amabel's Children*, one of them called it.

"You say you've got full legal rights to Amabel's eggs?" asks the man with the shaved head.

Carl clears his throat. "Zygotes," he says, "not eggs. Amabel and I were told that fertilized eggs would survive the freezing better. I supplied the sperm. The zygotes are legally mine."

Carl's right. My eggs were harvested because aggressive chemotherapy and radiation were going to sterilize me. His sperm fertilized the salvaged eggs *in vitro*, and the zygotes were frozen so we could have our own biological children when I recovered. But I didn't recover.

Light reflects off the stranger's polished head. He must be a network executive. His fingers drum the table. "I don't know. Isn't the point of this show that each couple—each husband of the couple—will fertilize one of Amabel's eggs himself? The way I understood it is you have the competitive stuff first—the sports and the trivia contests and whatever—singing, if you want—with the usual up-close-and-personals, followed by the audience vote. Then the winning dads would fertilize the eggs, which get implanted in their wives."

"We plan at least one show on the science of it all," P. P. says. "Doctors, test tubes, petri dishes. Footage of sperm penetrating eggs. We stagger the implantations so we get about eight weeks' worth of births at the end of the season. Twelve couples is the target."

"Hunh," says Larry, the network guy, "But Amabel is the attraction. People want to be connected to *her*! No offense, but what's the appeal of kids that are half Carl's?"

"Didn't you read the market research we sent?" P. P. asks. "Focus groups couldn't differentiate between "egg" and "zygote." We just de-emphasize Carl. We lose him in the scientific mumbo-jumbo, as far as the TV audience is concerned. For potential competitor-parents—ninety-five percent of those polled deemed the father's biological involvement 'unimportant.' This *is* about Amabel and nothing else, Larry."

"If we include episodes on the impact of environment on child development, it'll be better scientifically if all the kids had the same biological mother and father," says Carl quietly.

"But," P. P. says, "what we're selling is Amabel and her children."

Carl's head has flushed pink. Is he angry? An *in vitro* conception and surrogate delivery are part of his family history—his little brother Wray is somewhere among the dead. The men with him know this, of course. P. P. was with Carl when Wray died. It seems this bargaining with my eggs would have disturbed me once. Was it Carl or

P. P. or Bronwyn who cooked up this reality show idea? They'd collaborated on the cartoon-horror remake of *The Island of Doctor Moreau* that resurrected the career I'd done my best to trash, an idea that originated with Carl's dead father Raymond.

I am no longer afraid of Raymond, wherever he is. The animated *Moreau* tanked at the box office, but the voice I gave to the wretched dog-man, M'ling, found empathetic ears among the lonely and miserable, and my performance was praised. With P. P. to vouch for my rejuvenated work ethic, offers poured in. Broadway called, and I won a Tony playing a young mother. Even illness couldn't keep me down—when work became impossible, I became a role model, a leading advocate for cancer research. Those *Thrive* awareness anklets, the magenta ones you see everywhere? Inspired by my suffering.

"Amabel Hadley is a classic American story of redemption, Larry." P. P. slaps the table. *"Amabel's Children* will immortalize her!" He pauses. "From porn star to angel."

"I don't know about 'porn star'," Carl murmurs.

I don't deny the porn career could have happened. Prior to my final visit to rehab, while promoting my Scaredy Cat line of clothing in a Walmart, I'd made lewd gestures with my microphone before propositioning the store manager. Then I spit up.

"We wouldn't go there," Larry says, "But I'll admit, she had a hell of a life." And I know he's sold on my show.

"Right," P. P. says. "We start with a documentary. Two hours, Carl?"

"Two parts, one hour each."

"M-hmm. Two hours on Amabel's roller coaster life. We'll show the couples who'll be competing for the zygotes watching it and weeping over the highs and lows, the final tragedy. But the winners will have the chance to bear Amabel's children!"

"The couples' demographics?" Larry asks.

"Like any other reality show: rich, poor, minorities—hey, Carl, gay men would need their own surrogate wouldn't they?"

My husband shakes his head. "Too complicated. It would be easier to go with a lesbian couple."

There's silence, and P. P. looks up toward the fluorescent lights. His dark glasses are impenetrable. The other men follow his gaze. Carl's brown eyes look sad. I think Larry might see my spider, but he doesn't say anything.

"She was beautiful, wasn't she?" P. P. says. Carl and Larry mutter assent.

"A beautiful child," Bronwyn adds her first contribution to the discussion. Is her comment intended to remind the others that she "discovered" me? Why is she at this meeting? If the show is to be as described, she shouldn't be needed to provide child performers. Is it possible she hopes to sign up my children—get them under contract, straight from their borrowed wombs? *Sit like this—lift your skirt,* Bronwyn said to me, camera in hand, the day we met. *Hike it up! Smile—wider—try smiling with just one side of your mouth. Flutter your eyelids,* she insisted as she snapped the photographs that would win me my role in *Svidrigaylov's Dream.*

Near the end of *Dinghy*'s run—at the beginning of the end of my life—Bronwyn O'Savage visited me backstage after my performance. As she took my hand, I saw the certainty of my death in her eyes.

Larry's skull indentation reminds me of an infant's soft spot—I could swear something's pulsing in it. Maybe Carl should have been the one to bring up my beauty. Being dead, I don't dwell on it, but somewhere between party-girl bloat and dying-woman desiccation there *was* beauty. And in the beginning, too, when I was an innocent child with Hollywood dreams.

"Reunion shows," Larry says dreamily.

"And guaranteed spin-offs." P. P. adds. "Maybe decades of programming. Amabel's children will be the biggest entertainment phenomenon we've ever seen. Think of the merchandising opportunities. It's like we're breeding our own celebrities."

"You *will* be breeding celebrities," Bronwyn says. I can't see her eyes, but I follow the sweep of her hair as she turns her head from male to male. She is showing signs of appetite—of hunger—signs I recognize, but no longer feel. She directs her attention to Carl, whose head doesn't move. I remember that Wray is dead and wonder if he is somewhere near me.

A cell-phone chimes, and all three men reach for a pocket. Bronwyn lifts the phone she's been holding all meeting. It's lit with a photo I can't make out from way up here. My host spider dashes into a gap in the dropped ceiling. It's dark. Today is about to end. If death holds form, tomorrow I'll wake up with a new partner. I've got forever to find out what happens to my children. As far as I know.

***

245

I'm attached to a pet ferret. Its nose and eyes are tiny and black, and it wears a blue collar as thin as a rubber band. We curl around a pink bunny slipper and peek out from beneath a sofa. Running shoes flank our sides like the walls of a fortress. Two adults and two children sit above us. From time to time a popcorn kernel drops, and the ferret darts forward and nips it up, then retreats. Sounds of nibbling accompany the TV voices like static. The television's flickering light paints every surface.

The children in this home are young—a boy and a girl. Nothing has been familiar since Carl, Bronwyn, and P. P.'s meeting. Unless there's a plan bigger than any I can imagine, I suppose my presence above that table was just a coincidence. I can only guess that my experience is the same as everyone who's dead—we're all attached to a living thing. Wouldn't it be something if the entire universe of the dead travels together without knowing it? If we were all attached to the same body—my ferret, for instance? We're a weightless and volume-less population, we overlap, and, in our perpetually increasing numbers, maybe we all switch to a new body together every night. Who can say? Or maybe we're all alone in death, too, separate and playing a perpetual game of musical chairs.

My ferret's family is watching a documentary about me, the prelude to *Amabel's Children*. There are clips from some of my earliest movies. When I was a child, my eyes were wide and green and impish. My hair fell over my shoulders in auburn waves.

"She looks like Cindy; doesn't she look like Cindy?" the mother on the sofa says. No one answers. On screen my child-self makes a sassy quip, and above me the children and mother giggle. Another popcorn kernel falls and my ferret grabs it. A solemn voice narrates over photographs of me. I'm not so cute here—makeup distorts my features, and I wear short skirts and low-cut blouses that show my developing breasts. When I smile my mouth is open and my tongue shows. Pose after pose in gown after gown on miles of red carpet. How many packs a day was I smoking? When did I develop a taste for Jack Daniels? I'm in a courtroom. My hair is tied back, and I'm struggling to look sorry. A judge speaks without making eye contact. Police officers usher me away, their hands floating beside my elbows without touching them. Then I'm dancing wildly, my eyes raking across space as I twirl. There's my little red Porsche—and there it is again with its front crumpled. The dad sitting above me on the sofa laughs, low and guttural.

"*Rehab*" punctuates every other sentence.

Things were to get much worse before they got better.

There's a grainy video on the screen— a security tape. That's me in sweatpants and a hoody. I'm at a gas pump next to the Porsche, which has either been repaired or has yet to be damaged. Gasoline gushes from a hose dangling from the car—a puddle expands on the pavement. I've wrapped an arm around the pump, and I'm waving a cigarette lighter and howling. Next, an officer protects my head as I'm plugged into the back of a police cruiser: I grin as if I'm listening to a private joke.

There's M'ling—the vivisected cartoon dog-man from *The Island of Doctor Moreau* who led me back to a righteous path.

"Did we see that cartoon? Can we see it?" asks one of the children.

"It's a horror movie. Its R rated," the mother says. My dog-man cowers in the midnight shadows of tropical trees. The narrator mentions P. P. and Carl. I stand between them in a photograph. All three of us are smiling. I'd forgotten that I'd buzzed off all my hair while recording *Moreau*. I knew what baldness was like before chemotherapy.

A *PLAYBILL* cover—I'm wearing an apron. My hair is shoulder length. I'm playing a mother. Then I'm standing at a podium, displaying an award.

Part two tomorrow! Recovery and triumph.

I don't know where I'll be tomorrow. My host may not be near the television, and I'll miss seeing my final chapter among the living. They'll say I "*battled bravely.*" This documentary won't show Carl, though he surely helped make it. He held my skeletal hand as I shuffled in loose pajamas to the rooms of doomed children. In my last days I bowed to them, my head as hairless as theirs, and offered what I could. There'd soon be nothing left for Carl. Maybe I owed him *Amabel's Children*.

* * *

Try to imagine an existence without expectations. Without surprise. Without impatience.

Season One of *Amabel's Children* is about to conclude: the twelve couples who have won my fertilized eggs will be named. Implantations are to take place during the summer hiatus, and Season

Two's opening episode will reveal the successful pregnancies. Viewers are teased by the prospect of a dozen mothers swelling to term with babies due in the spring.

I gather this information while in the company of a speckled catfish. We're suctioned to the glass of an aquarium. Algae and dust obscure the television across the small, dim room. It's a struggle to hear over the pump's hum and filter's bubbling. Other fish waft above, beneath, and behind us. A young man, alone, slouches on the futon beside the table that supports our tank. He's wearing shorts and a t-shirt. One hand is down his pants, the other is holding a beer. The pillow and blanket on the futon suggest it's his bed. I see a sink, a mini-fridge and a counter full of dirty plates. An open door exposes a toilet.

Also on the table with our aquarium is a framed photograph of a young couple, which I study during commercial breaks. The man in the picture is the person on the couch. The woman is . . . me. I glance away again and again, but each time I look back there's no question that I'm looking at myself. I've been photo-shopped into the picture— I'm almost twice the young man's size. I recognize the silver gown I wore at the Tony Awards. I suspect I'm replacing another woman; someone the young man wants to exclude from his home. He continues watching television, unaware that I've discovered his secret. Does my presence count as "haunting" if he never knows I'm here?

Amabel's Children highlights the months of competition that will earn the winning couples my eggs: a young African-American couple stagger through calf deep mud—the man is heavy, stumbles, and pulls his wife down face first into the muck; another couple, tan and blond, argue over a quiz question I can't hear—the woman offers an answer with a furrowed brow, the couple embraces joyfully, and the number of points displayed in front of them grows by a hundred; a pair of young women struggle across a rope bridge over surging rapids while carrying a life size baby doll.

The couples who have competed fill an auditorium. The camera sweeps over eager, anxious faces as all await the outcome of their trials. My catfish dislodges from the aquarium glass, drops to the blue gravel, and wriggles and sucks its way behind a scummy rock. Fish cruise over us like spaceships. Time passes.

My catfish and I are back on the glass. A dozen smiling couples stand on the stage—the winners. The host introduces profiles of the last few: here is the blond couple. Their ages, jobs, state of residence (Massachusetts), and income are posted over a video of the pair frolicking with a golden retriever in their suburban yard. The next couple, a black man and his Asian wife, sit on the stoop of a modest Indiana home. Their posted income is a tenth of the blond couple's. The last duo, a pair of healthy-looking young women, is doing as well financially as the blonds—one is a financial analyst, the other a photographer. They live in an oceanfront condo in San Diego. I wonder which of the two will carry my baby. I missed the profiles of the other winning couples while the catfish was foraging. The closing credits roll over a cartoon picture of a red-haired woman in an apron holding a basket of eggs aloft. I assume that's supposed to be me. Carl's and P. P.'s names and the names of all others associated with the production slide over cartoon me and disappear.

* * *

"Get to bed!" insists the robed mother to my host, a little girl of about seven who lingers barefooted on the linoleum floor of a narrow hallway. Her mother lounges on the couch. Ashes from the cigarette pinched in the woman's lips threaten the face of the infant she is holding like a loaf of bread.

"But the babies are on. I want to see the babies."

"Then you shouldn't have back-talked about your homework."

"But I don't *have* any homework."

"Your teacher says she gives homework every night. That's what she said."

"But I did it in school. I promise! There was time to do it in school today. Can't I see the babies?"

If my host goes to bed, it will be dark, and tomorrow I'll be elsewhere.

"You got your sister Brittany." The mother stuffs her cigarette into a soda can on the table by her elbow. "Get me another Diet Pepsi, and you can stay up," she says to my partner, and the little girl scampers into the kitchen. There are dishes in the sink and bottles in a pot on the stove. A crayon drawing of a pony with a rainbow mane and tail decorates the refrigerator door, and inside it there are cartons of milk and juice, Tupperware of different sizes, and a dozen or so cans of soda. We return to the living room, and my little girl hops onto the sofa after handing the beverage to her mom. She stretches her heels to the coffee table. Grime rims her toenails. The baby mews and snuggles against her mother's belly.

249

"Will Shana be on this one? I like it when Shana's on."

"Shh. How do I know? Keep quiet or you're going to bed."

Shana is three, as are all nine of my children. Ten of the couples winning my eggs had successful, full-term pregnancies. One of my babies, Harrison, died with his mother in a car crash last season. I missed the special memorial program, though I saw the commercial for it: Harrison was shoveling Spaghetti-o's into his mouth, but most of the pasta was on his cheeks and chin. He had reddish brown hair, like many of my children. His mother laughed in the background as she recorded her son's messy eating. If the deaths of Harrison and his mother are like mine, maybe they've seen themselves on *Amabel's Children*. I doubt Harrison would know what he is watching.

The first segment of tonight's show features little Veronica. Her parents have separated and share custody of their daughter. Veronica's dad is a construction foreman, and he brings her to work, where she wears a miniature hard hat. She has curls like Carl's. According to the show's host, Veronica "*was the first of the children to walk*," but there's no video to document the event. I've seen other of my babies' first words and steps, birthday parties, and Disneyland vacations.

No Shana yet for my little host. Her dirty feet waggle impatiently on the coffee table during the show's second segment, which features some of the "scientific" aspects of *Amabel's Children*. There are statistics and numbers. How many hours are spent in daycare? Who was nursed and who given bottles? Hours of television? Hours read to? Nutritional choices? Doctors in white coats discuss the "likelihoods" of this or that, but no conclusions are reached.

"Shana!" my little host cries when her favorite appears, briefly, stacking blocks while an analyst marks down the child's progress on a clipboard. My host has tied her pigtails in rainbow ribbons that match the bow in Shana's red hair.

I don't know what I am to these children. I understand what yearning is, and I understand that a mother should yearn for her children, but I don't. I'm not their birth mother, but their skin and hair and feet, their faces and their heart, have grown from my cells. I'm their First Cause.

The last segment features Simon. His parents are lawyers. He looks a lot like Shana and seems to have an eye for the camera—he poses in ways that remind me of photographs of myself in fan magazines. There must be former fans of mine among the dead. How do they feel about me now? Do they watch my show with interest? Does it matter which me, at which age, they loved? Tonight, while bouncing Simon on their laps, his mother and father discuss "transgendering."

The *Amabel's Children* theme song plays while the credits roll. It's a version of one of my hits from the two albums I recorded. *"Who's your mother? Where's your mother?"* I'd rasped and ranted punkishly. A children's chorus sings the TV show's rendition, slower, and accompanied by a harp. Unless I missed his name, Carl is no longer listed as a "Creative Consultant." Where might he have gone? Is he here?

Baby Brittany wails, her mother swears under her breath, and my host rises, pats her little sister's head, and we're off to bed. My TV children have no siblings in their families. Did I miss a rule prohibiting them? I've seen no signs of a male in this house. It's hard for a single mother to care for more than her infant. Since I've been dead, I've seen the truth of that again and again.

* * *

I've been hosted by countless dogs, but this is the smallest. It must be some kind of Chihuahua. We're tucked between the knees of an old woman. She wears stretch pants and gray slippers that might once have been as purple as the burst veins mottling her swollen ankles. When the dog whimpers to pee, its owner's sagging face tightens like a fist.

"Jingles, can't you hold it?" she whines in a pitch that matches her dog's. She struggles with the lever to her easy chair, and Jingles and I hop to the floor of their double-wide. When she pushes open the aluminum door, we skip from a cinder block to the hardpan, and Jingles squats. The woman clings to the door handle while she waits and looks back over her shoulder at her small television. I can't see much in the dark, but from neighboring trailers I hear quarreling TV show voices from different programs.

Back between the owner's knees, Jingles gnaws on a huge biscuit. It's been many nights since I've seen *Amabel's Children*. They're calling this special show a "reunion," but none of my kids have ever met. When their parents won my eggs, they'd agreed to keep the children apart, "for the purpose of scientific observation." They must have seen each other on TV—they weren't raised in Skinner boxes. The boys and girls are eight years old now. Everyone is dressed nicely;

251

children and adults sit at separate daises. Between them stands a microphone at which a host wearing a tuxedo and several guests I don't recognize take turns reminiscing and joking mildly about *Amabel's Children*.

"The kids could have their own baseball team," a speaker quips. I anticipate other jokes about "nine," but all I can think of is that cats have nine lives, and "lives" don't seem appropriate to mention because of little Harrison. In all the time I've been dead, I've never been hosted by a cat. The children are awkward in the presence of so many biological brother and sister celebrities they don't know. They ignore the host and peek, mouths agape, at the familiar faces of strangers. No two are identical, yet together they present a spectrum of resemblance that runs from Carl to me—dark curls to red hair, brown eyes to green. Looking at them is like looking into a row of funhouse mirrors, and I suspect they feel the same way. Are they inventing bonds or discovering them? Will they accept or deny their connectedness? The parents squint toward their children with clenched smiles and seem anxious to rush over and claim their own.

The kids, their parents, and the television audience watch a video montage that begins with swollen-bellied mothers, then shows the children as infants and toddlers, interspersed with clips of my childhood movies, then shots of me receiving my Tony. A final video shows me delivering a speech at a children's hospital shortly before I died. I am bald and hollow-eyed, but I say inspiring things about thinking positively and devoting oneself to a cause. Finally, waiters roll out a grand sheet cake. "THANK YOU AMABEL" is printed across it. The host prepares to cut into it with a saber-sized blade and invites the children to gather around with their plates. There has been no mention of Carl.

Tears sparkle like jewels on the cheeks of Jingles' owner. Have I heard or am I guessing that this is the final episode of *Amabel's Children*? P. P. Frederico had predicted more than a single decade. While my anthem "Who's Your Mother?" plays, the camera pans one last time across the cake-smeared faces of my children. The song stops as the credits freeze on two names, little Harrison's and P. P.'s, followed by their birth and death years. Maybe P. P., wherever he is, has witnessed this memorial. Maybe he and Harrison are here. Maybe Wray. And Raymond. Maybe everyone's here.

✳✳✳

If my death follows a pattern, I don't have the distance to interpret it. Frequently, I slide through the dark with nocturnal hosts I may or may not see. I have wheeled with bats and lain between crickets' whittling legs. I've experienced the speed and sudden violence of hunting and being hunted, the cries of power or fear. I have burrowed deep into loamy soil and rotting hearts.

When I am indoors, my hosts often dive into darkness, and I catch only winks of light. Tonight I hear whispered endearments and murmurs of pleasure: there's lovemaking, but I'm with neither partner. Too dark even for shadows—I must be attached to a dust mite between a mattress and box spring. We rock with the sex, and if by some chance Harrison or Wray is with us, maybe they remember that rocking gave them comfort. One of the lovers cries out. Motion stops. Every moment is eternal patience.

* * *

I'm coupled with an infant—I can't recall the last time I was attached to a human. His face presses into his mother's breast. He gasps, exhausted and ecstatic from suckling. His mother watches television, but her embracing arms block the screen.

"Shh," the mother whispers.

Physics means pondering the imponderables, the TV voice says. All television voices sound like the announcer's from *Amabel's Children*. When I ponder time, I picture the lines a prisoner scratches on a cell wall—four lines and a cross hatch, four lines and a cross hatch—five and five and five and on and on, until everything is shaded into darkness.

My host-baby coos, frets, and reconnects to his mother's nipple.

His mother sighs. A familiar stuffed animal is wedged on the couch beside the mother. Kika—but she has different eyes. These are decals, not buttons, and seem intended to be more expressive. The smile of this Kika brims with confidence. There is a tag on it—it's a new toy. It occurs to me that this is a second generation Kika. Many of these appeared in the homes of my children. On an episode of my show I saw one of my children watching a video of P. P. Frederico's cartoon sequel to *Kong's Daughter*. Who did he find to do Kika's voice? Someone famous, I'm sure, but no one I recognize. How many have ascended to fame since my death?

253

On television, the narration continues: *Paul Dirac theorized that whether light is composed of waves or particles depends on whether you ask of it a wave-like or particle-like question.*

* * *

On this endless day I can't tell to what or to whom I'm attached; time no longer seems to be something that moves. There's light, but I don't ask it questions about particles or waves. The light illuminates the bookshelf I face and have been facing for what feels like forever. I focus on a book with a glossy paper cover; it's surrounded by dusty volumes, but this book is dustless. Studying its spine is all I do.

I haven't lost the sense that I'm attached, but either the dynamics of connection have changed— were *due* to change?—or I'm hosted by something my limited understanding doesn't allow me to perceive. What could be so small? A microbe? A hope?

The book I stare at is titled *My Life as Amabel's Child: the End of Reality TV*. The author's name is blocked by the edge of the shelf because of the angle I see it from. What I *can* see is a sweep of auburn hair spreading over the book's spine from a photograph on the front cover. It might be a photo of me and my hair. It could be the hair of one of my children. I've looked at this spine so long I can't imagine not seeing it. But does "End" mean "death," or does "End" mean "goal"? I can't ask both questions simultaneously, and I know if I alternate I'll get different answers.

As far as you know, you've hosted me and some or all of the dead; if not yet, maybe soon. Maybe tomorrow. My dead. Our dead. We'll all be together. We just won't know it. And maybe that's the end.

Acknowledgments

Versions of chapters in *T'ings* have appeared in the following journals: *Underground Voices*, *LITnImage*, *Foliate Oak*, *MadHat Review*, *Gulf Stream*, *Prime Number*, *FRIGG Magazine*, *Chicago Literati*, *EDGE*, *Roanoke Review*, *Zymbol*, *Apple Valley Review*, *PANK*, *Bop Dead City*, *Altered States*.

9 781774 032978